VENOM & VENGEANCE

Tarnished Angels Motorcycle Club Book 5

EMMA SLATE

©2023 by Tabula Rasa Publishing LLC
All rights reserved.

No part of this publication may be reproduced, distributed or transmitted in any form or by any means, including photocopying, recording, or other electronic or mechanical methods, without the prior written permission of the publisher, except in the case of brief quotations embodied in critical reviews and certain other noncommercial uses permitted by copyright law.

This book is a work of fiction. Names, characters, places, and incidents are the product of the author's imagination or are used fictitiously. Any resemblance to actual events, locales, or persons, living or dead, is coincidental.

Venom & Vengeance
(TARNISHED ANGELS MOTORCYCLE CLUB BOOK 5)

He's grumpy. Older. An ex-con.

Did I mention I'm totally hot for him?

After a near fatal run-in with the cartel, I turn to Viper for protection.

He's muscle for his motorcycle club, and the next thing I know I'm living in a biker clubhouse with my own personal bodyguard.

Viper makes me feel safe…and desired.

No wonder I can't keep my clothes on around him.

The club welcomes me as one of their own, but the timing couldn't be worse.

Now I'm caught in a war between the club and a cartel.

This wasn't supposed to be my life.

But the longer I stay with Viper, the more I realize neither of us want to say goodbye.

Viper wants to keep me.

Forever.

Chapter 1

THE CAST-IRON SKILLET hit the side of his head with a resounding thwack, and the eggs I'd been cooking flew across the kitchen and landed on the floor. His skull crunched and he shrieked in rage as he recoiled and dropped the knife he was holding.

My heart jumped in my chest and my vision narrowed, adrenaline coursing through my blood.

A scowl of fury swept across his face as he came after me again.

Instinct took over and my body reacted, even as my mind cowered in fear.

I crouched as he leapt toward me and I swung the skillet at his knee. He faltered and howled in pain like a baying animal as he crashed to the floor and rolled over on his back.

He was down, and I knew it was my only chance. I gripped the skillet with both hands and wielded it with all my might.

I bashed in an occipital bone on the left side of his face and blood spurted from his eye socket.

I lifted my hands again, and then fractured his jaw with another blow.

He went limp on the ground, but I didn't stop.

I hit him again and again, the skillet pulverizing flesh and bone. Deep, gulping breaths signaled his life was at its end.

Eventually, he fell silent.

His caved-in skull oozed brain and blood, staining the linoleum floor of the trailer.

Finally, my fingers loosened, and I dropped the skillet. The heavy thud of cast iron rang in my ears.

I stared down at the carnage. There was a pile of eggs a few feet from me, and cooking oil and blood all over the kitchen cabinets, ornamented by a corpse with brains spilling from the head of a man who had attacked me in the middle of the night.

It was like I'd floated out of my body, and I was witnessing it all from an aerial point of view.

With calm detachment, I stood up and turned off the stove burner. The blue flame disappeared, snuffed out like the life I'd just extinguished.

The scent of egg, cheese, and blood made my stomach lurch, and I leaned over the kitchen sink and vomited, heaving until there was nothing left. I spat out bile and made a move to wipe my mouth, but my hands were covered in blood.

I turned on the faucet and grabbed the bottle of liquid dish soap and squirted it all over my palms and fingers. I used the scrub brush to aggressively wash my skin.

A maniacal giggle escaped my lips.

Lady Macbeth.

I turned off the water and dried my hands on a ragged, faded white dish towel and then walked out the back door of the trailer into the muggy night.

It was just past midnight, and as I passed the other trailers in the park I lived in, I heard country music, a couple fighting, and the blare of TVs. I was grateful for the sounds and wondered if they had aided in concealing what had just transpired.

I made it to Carla's back door and knocked. When she didn't answer right away, I knocked again, this time with more force.

The door cracked and then flew open as a pair of blue eyes raked over me. She reached out and grasped my hand, hauling me inside.

It smelled like vanilla incense.

I took a deep breath and then instantly regretted it. Vanilla mixed with the aroma of death in my nose almost had me running for the sink again.

"Oh my God! What the fuck happened to you? Are you okay?" she demanded, her plump red lips parting in shock. Carla ran a hand through her dyed blonde hair and blew out a puff of air. "There's blood on your face. You gotta tell me what happened so I know what the fuck is going on."

"Body," I blurted out. "There's a dead body in my kitchen. He broke into my... I don't know who he is, but he was going to... I was cooking eggs and I bashed his head in with a cast-iron skillet." I looked down at the floor.

She shook her head in disbelief. "Fuck, Sutton."

"I know." I gazed at her.

Her blue eyes were rimmed with liner and heavy mascara.

"You're the only one I trust."

"You really have no idea who this guy is?"

"No. He's covered in a bunch of tattoos, but I—"

The heavy clomp of boots across linoleum had me

snapping my mouth shut and shooting an angry glare at Carla. "You didn't tell me you weren't alone."

Carla looked over her shoulder at the blond man who'd entered the kitchen. He was tall, muscular, and wore a leather cut. His blue gaze combed over me, and his jaw clenched.

I lifted my chin and refused to cower, even though I had just confessed to murder.

"Which trailer is yours?" he demanded.

I blinked and glanced at Carla, who nodded. "It's okay. You can trust Savage."

Trust a man named Savage? Yeah, right.

"What are you going to do?" I asked.

"Trailer," he commanded without explaining. "Tell me which one it is."

His tone didn't allow for an argument. "The white one at the end of the cul-de-sac. The back door is unlocked."

He nodded and pointed a finger at me. "Do not move from that spot. I'll be back." He glanced at Carla, and through a look I couldn't quite discern, they seemed to have a silent conversation I wasn't privy to.

Savage opened the door near the kitchen and left. As it shut behind him, Carla rushed to the door to lock it.

"Sorry I ruined your night," I mumbled.

"Stop," she said. She reached for a bottle of vodka on top of the fridge. She opened a cupboard and pulled out two glasses and poured a hefty amount of liquor into both. She handed me one of the cups.

I took it but didn't drink.

"Who is he?" I asked.

"A biker."

"Yeah. I figured that part out on my own. I didn't know you'd taken up with bikers."

"I haven't taken up with anyone."

"Are you dating him?"

She smiled slightly. "You don't date Savage. You fuck Savage and then let him go off into the wild. You do not pen a wild stallion."

Despite the situation I sniggered, and then threw back most of the vodka. It was cheap and it burned.

As we waited for Savage to return, we shared another drink. My hands were shaking.

The knob on the back door made a noise, causing me to jump.

"It's just Savage," Carla said, running to unlock the door and let him in.

The big biker stepped into the room. He looked at me and then at Carla. They had another one of those silent conversations, except this time their look made me nervous.

My gaze bounced between them. Carla's mouth pinched into a firm line and Savage appeared grim.

"It's bad, isn't it?" I blurted out.

"A dead body is never good," Savage stated. He reached into his vest pocket and pulled out a cell phone. He pressed the screen and put the phone to his ear. After a moment, he said, "Hey, brother. I need Ghost. Yeah, and bring Viper. I'm at Carla's." He paused and then said, "Thanks. See you."

He hung up and shoved his phone back into his pocket.

"You got anything of value in that trailer?" Savage asked. "Paperwork? Any sentimental shit?"

I frowned. "No. Well, I guess maybe some clothes and my pistol. It's in my nightstand drawer."

"Doesn't do you any good in your nightstand drawer," Savage drawled. "Though you made short work of that guy with a skillet."

"Short work," I repeated. "Yeah, I guess I did."

He nodded. "You got insurance on the trailer?"

"Yeah."

His grin was wild. "Good."

"Good? Why's that good?"

"Because tonight we're burning that fucker to the ground."

Chapter 2

"Get cleaned up. I'll pack some of your clothes and bring them to you, yeah?"

I nodded at Savage.

Carla had been leaning against the counter. She pushed away from it and walked toward the sink. She crouched down, opened the cabinet, and pulled out a garbage bag.

"Bathroom," Carla instructed. "Now."

I took a few steps, but not before I saw Carla move close to Savage. He said something to her and then cupped her cheek before leaning down and kissing her lips.

Carla's bathroom was bigger than mine. Nicer too.

And here I was about to soil it.

As I stood alone, I looked in the mirror. It was a miracle Carla hadn't screamed when she saw me.

My face was spattered with blood and there was a chunk of brain in my hair. I looked like an ancient warrior princess who had just butchered one of her enemies.

Carla knocked on the bathroom door but didn't wait for a reply. She came into the room and closed the door behind her. "Strip," she commanded and then opened the garbage bag.

I pulled my T-shirt over my head and threw it away. I wasn't wearing a bra, but it didn't matter. Neither of us were shy.

I kicked off my flip-flops.

"Those too," she stated. "Everything you're wearing goes in here."

With a sigh, I leaned over and scooped up my shoes and threw them in the bag as well. I did the same with my leggings and underwear.

I turned on the shower and let it begin to steam before stepping in. I slid the curtain closed, tilted my head up, and let the water bathe my face and rinse the blood from my skin.

"You still in here?" I asked as I brushed the water from my eyes.

"Yeah."

"Thanks," I said.

She didn't say anything for a moment and then she replied, "If I'd come to you in the same position, what would you have done?"

I reached for the bar of soap. "Helped you, of course. No questions asked."

"Then you don't need to thank me. Clean towel is on the sink for you."

The door clicked shut and I was alone. I scrubbed my skin as her words penetrated my heart.

Somehow in this fucked-up world, Carla and I had met. We were cut from the same cloth—we were survivors. And no matter what life threw at us, we never let it chop us off at the knees.

I washed my brown hair, scraping my nails along my scalp, checking for things that didn't belong to me. Eventually, the water ran clear instead of pink, and I was clean.

After I'd turned off the shower, I gathered my hair into a rope and squeezed the excess water from it. I grabbed the towel off the sink and hastily wrapped it around me.

I refused to think about what I'd done. Not yet. Not when I was standing naked, vulnerable, relying on my friend's kindness—and the aid of some biker—who was helping me for some unknown reason.

I opened the bathroom door and peered out into the hallway. "Carla?"

"I'm here," she called before suddenly appearing from the direction of the kitchen.

"Clothes?" I asked.

"Savage brought you a bag. It's in my bedroom."

I trailed after her. My duffel bag was on her bed. I quickly unzipped it. Bras, panties, jeans…

"Oh my God," I muttered, feeling my cheeks flame with heat.

"What?" Carla asked.

"He packed my vibrator." I covered my face with my hand and groaned in embarrassment.

Carla let out a raspy laugh. "He must've thought it was a necessity."

"I'll never be able to look him in the eye again," I quipped. "I'm oddly impressed, though. He grabbed all the stuff I actually need to live. Including my favorite boots."

I quickly pulled on a thong and a pair of jeans.

"Your pistol is in my cookie jar and your cell phone and purse are on the counter," she said.

"Thanks."

There was the sound of a door closing, followed by a male voice speaking in low tones.

"Is that Savage?" I asked.

"Yeah."

"Who's he talking to?"

"Don't know. Let's find out."

I followed her from the bedroom. Savage was standing in the kitchen, and he was speaking to the biggest man I'd ever seen. He was a giant. Savage was tall, but this man was even taller. His leather cut sat on his expansive shoulders, and he wore a black T-shirt that revealed heavily muscled and inked arms.

His dark hair fell across his brow and his brown eyes swept over me, cataloguing me from head to toe.

"This is Viper," Savage introduced. "You're going with him."

Viper and I were staring at each other, and it took me a moment to realize that Savage had spoken.

"Say what now?" I asked. "Go with him? I don't even know him. I don't even know *you*."

"You'll go with him," Savage commanded. "While I take care of shit here."

"Why are you helping me?" I demanded.

"That's not important right now. You just need to go with him. Okay?"

I looked at Carla for direction.

She nodded. "You'll be safe with Viper."

Viper's hands hung by his sides and suddenly he clenched them into massive fists.

Safe? Safe with a man who looked like he could crush my skull with his bare hands?

"Did I get everything from your trailer that you can't possibly live without?" Savage asked, a slow smirk appearing on his face.

I glared at him, whirled, and marched to the bedroom, Savage's laugh booming behind me.

Five minutes later, my hair was up in a messy bun, and I was ready to go.

I came back into the kitchen, interrupting Carla and Savage. He had her backed against the counter, his body pressed to hers, his hands on her hips.

"Sorry," I muttered.

"Don't worry about it," Carla said, placing her hand to Savage's chest and pushing him back. She grabbed my purse and cell phone and handed them to me.

"Where's Viper?" I asked.

"Out front," Savage replied.

"Where's he taking me?"

"Ask him," Savage said. "Though, good luck getting an answer out of him. He doesn't talk much."

I headed out the front door. The lights of the porch illuminated Viper as he sat astride his motorcycle. I came down the stairs and put my phone into my purse and zipped it up.

Viper's intense gaze followed me every step of the way.

Somehow, I knew I'd be safe with him.

That didn't mean I didn't find him incredibly intimidating.

He reached behind him and picked up a helmet and held it out to me.

I slung my purse across my chest and removed my hair tie, letting my damp locks fall across my shoulders and back. I took the helmet from him and placed it on my head and then slid the buckle into its mate.

It was too big.

Before I had a chance to cinch the strap tighter, Viper's hands were suddenly underneath my chin to do it for me.

"Thank you," I said.

He grunted.

Actually grunted.

"Seriously?" I demanded.

"Get on," he ordered. His voice was low and growly. It washed over my skin and goose bumps rose all along my arms.

I slid on the back of his bike and fiddled with my purse, so it rested against my tailbone. Viper reached an arm around and gripped my thigh, causing me to jump.

"Scoot closer. Wrap your arms around me. And for fuck's sake, hang on."

"Ah, so you *can* string a sentence together."

"That was three sentences."

A flicker of a smile appeared on my lips. As I moved closer to him, he turned on the engine. The vibration between my legs was a pleasant surprise and I tried not to think about it.

I draped my arms around Viper, enjoying the scent of his leather cut permeating my senses.

He kicked up the stand and then we zoomed out of the trailer park.

I was riding on the back of a motorcycle with a strange biker after having just killed a man.

It was terrifying.

And thrilling.

I'd never felt more alive.

Chapter 3

Viper turned his bike down a street and came to a stop in front of a diner called Boots.

It was in a part of town I never went to, so I wasn't familiar with it. I climbed off his motorcycle and looked through the big front window of the restaurant. There were a few customers sitting in booths and on the stools at the counter, but it wasn't crowded this time of night.

Viper cut the engine and kicked out the stand. And then he climbed off his bike, standing at his full height.

I tilted my head back to stare up at him.

He reached out and unclipped the helmet, removing it for me and placing it on his seat.

I quickly pulled my messy brown hair up into a haphazard ponytail. Viper's eyes never left me.

It was unnerving.

Men had looked at me before. But not like this. Not like every move I made was fascinating.

Without a word, I turned away and marched to the front door of the diner. I pulled it open and stepped inside, Viper not far behind me.

The woman at the counter looked up from pouring a cup of coffee for a customer and her eyes widened.

"Table for two please," I said with a bright smile. "In the corner, if you have it."

"Sure thing," she said, her gaze darting from me to Viper.

I wrapped my arm around Viper's middle and snuggled into his side. "We're on our first date."

Viper tensed from my touch, but I ignored it.

The waitress closed her jaw and pasted on a smile. "Wonderful. Follow me."

I dropped my arm from around Viper and trekked after her. She showed us to a relatively private booth in the corner.

"Menus are there." She pointed to the red laminate menus stuck between the ketchup bottle and the salt and pepper shakers. "I'll be back in a few."

She scampered off, leaving us alone.

I tossed my purse into the corner and took a seat. Viper slid in across from me. Even sitting down, he was huge.

"Flying on planes must be really uncomfortable for you," I stated.

His brown eyes surveyed me. "I don't fly on planes."

"No?"

"No. Is your phone on?"

"Yes."

"Will you hear it if it rings?"

"Yes." I frowned. "Why?"

"Get you something to drink?" the waitress asked, interrupting our exchange.

Viper didn't speak, clearly waiting on me to give my order first. "Coffee, please. What kind of pie do you have tonight?"

"Cherry and peach."

"Peach, please."

She nodded. "You want any ice cream with that?"

"Vanilla bean if you have it. If not then no, I'm good."

"No vanilla bean," she said.

"Then just the pie, thanks."

Viper hadn't taken his eyes off me the entire time I was ordering.

"And for you…sir?" she added.

"Coffee for me, too," he said.

I glared at him.

The corner of his mouth seemed to twitch. "Please."

"I'll be right back with that for you," she said. She sailed away, leaving us alone again.

"So why do I have to leave my phone on ring?" I asked.

"Your order."

I frowned in confusion. "My what?"

"Pie and ice cream."

"What about it?"

"It was particular."

"Should it not have been particular?" I asked.

He shrugged.

"What's that mean? Your shrug?"

"Just never saw anyone be so particular about their pie and ice cream combination."

"Have you *had* vanilla bean ice cream?" I asked.

"Do I look like a man who eats vanilla bean ice cream?"

I couldn't stop the full smile from drifting across my face. "No. Then again, you don't look like you eat ice cream at all. In fact, you don't look like you do anything for the pure sake of enjoyment."

"I fuck for the pure sake of enjoyment."

My eyes widened and my mouth suddenly went dry as

I pictured a naked Viper in the throes of sweaty, heated passion.

"And she's finally quiet," he growled.

My cheeks warmed, and I changed the subject. "You still haven't answered my question about the phone."

The waitress returned, carrying a tray. She set down our coffees and a creamer. She placed the pie in the center of the table with two spoons.

She winked at me. "Thought you might want to share, this being a first date and all."

I grasped the plate and pulled it toward me. "He hasn't earned that right yet. Pie is pie, and I don't share."

The waitress chuckled. "Anything else for you?"

I shook my head.

"You got strawberry?" Viper asked.

"Strawberry what?" the waitress queried.

"Ice cream."

"Yep."

"Can I get a scoop of that?" He looked at me. "Please."

"You got it."

"So, you like strawberry ice cream," I said once the waitress left. "Who'd have thunk it?" I took a bite of the pie and let out a satisfied sigh.

"Your friend is gonna call you in a few minutes," Viper said. "Everything's gotta look a certain way. If you're not there when shit goes down, there won't be any questions."

"Oh. What about the, ah, problem in my kitchen?"

"We got a guy who cleans up these kinds of messes. You don't need to worry about it. The club is going to sort this out. We'll fill you in later, but for now, just act surprised when you get the call."

Reality came crashing back. I'd forgotten for a brief moment why I was at a diner with Viper in the first place.

The sweet peaches were suddenly too sugary, and the pie crust wasn't buttery. I pushed the plate away.

"Something wrong with the pie, honey?" the waitress asked as she set a scoop of ice cream in front of Viper.

I shook my head and forced a smile. "It's rich and delicious. I'm pacing myself."

"Glad to hear it. Enjoy." She patted my shoulder and walked away.

I grabbed the white sugar caddy and heavily sugared my coffee and then added a huge splash of cream. "Why are you guys helping me?"

"Not important right now."

"It's not?" I raised my brows.

He picked up his spoon and dug into the strawberry ice cream.

I snorted out a laugh.

"What?" he demanded with a growl.

"You look like you're eating a kiddie size."

He didn't appear as though he'd heard me and continued to devour his ice cream. It was gone in just a few bites. "You gonna eat that pie?" he asked.

"I don't think so."

He slid the plate closer to him. "You're a strange broad."

"Thank you," I said.

Viper shook his head. "You gonna fall apart on me after what you did tonight?"

"Doubt it."

There hadn't been time to fall apart. I'd been on autopilot since the incident. When I was alone, I might deconstruct what had happened. What I'd done. Then again, I might bury it and never think about it again. Self-preservation and all that.

"You grew up rough, didn't you?" Viper asked once he'd demolished the pie.

"Wait, did this just turn into a real date?" I deflected. "Sounds like you're wanting to get to know me."

"You drive me batshit," he muttered.

"So soon? We've hardly been together long enough for that to be true."

My phone rang, startling me.

"Saved by the motherfucking bell," he snapped.

With a glare, I reached into my purse and pulled out my cell. Carla's name flashed across the screen.

"Remember to act surprised," he stated. "She's gonna tell you what you already know."

I rolled my eyes and answered my phone. "Hello?"

"Sutton," she began. "I have really bad news. Your trailer burned to the ground."

"What?" I yelled. "Are you serious? What the fuck?"

"Fire department is here," she said. "They're putting the fire out, but you need to come back right away. I'm so sorry."

"Could my life get any worse?" I screeched. "I'll be there in a few." I hung up and set my phone aside.

Viper was shaking his head at me.

"What?" I demanded.

"Overacting much?"

"Bite me," I said lightly. "I totally sold it. If anyone was eavesdropping, they'll never question it."

"No one in their right fucking mind would believe that wasn't an act," he said.

The waitress rushed toward our table, worry on her face. "Oh my God, honey, what happened? Are you okay?"

I blinked up at her, crocodile tears filling my eyes. "My best friend just called. My house burned down. We have to go."

"Oh, sugar, I'm so sorry. Your check is on the house," she said.

"Oh, no, I couldn't do that," I blubbered, reaching for a napkin.

"I insist."

I blew my nose. "You're so nice."

"It'll be okay, you'll see." She patted my shoulder. "Come back any time."

"I will." I nodded. "Thank you."

When she left and Viper and I were alone again, I shot him a *told you so* smile. "What were you saying?"

"Un-fucking-believable," he muttered.

"Leave her a big tip," I said. "She's really sweet."

He raised a brow.

"We *are* on a first date. Come on, Viper. Sell it."

Chapter 4

THE SCENT of chemicals and ash was in the air. I climbed off the bike before Viper had even cut the engine.

A fire truck, a couple of police cars, along with firemen and policemen were at the scene. People had come out of their trailers to watch the spectacle.

I didn't wait to see if Viper was behind me. I found Carla and went to her side.

"Hey," I greeted.

She pulled her eyes away from the smoldering rubble. Carla wrapped an arm around me. "I'm so sorry."

"Thank you," I murmured, still not believing that the place I'd called home for the last two years was actually gone.

And *why* it was gone.

I swallowed, suddenly overcome with emotion that wasn't at all manufactured. The tears in my eyes were real.

I was homeless. Without roots. Alone.

Carla held me while my shoulders shook, but I quickly got my emotions under control.

That was the thing about the trailer park. People kept

to themselves most of the time, but they had no problem gossiping when drama was right in front of them.

The air was stifling and smoke from the fire entered my nose. Every time I breathed in I was reminded of what was burning in the ashes…

"Sutton Woods?"

I turned my head and met the gaze of the fire chief. He was a tall, burly man whose face was covered in a light sheen of sweat.

"Yes, I'm Sutton," I said.

"I'm so sorry we couldn't save your home."

I nodded.

"We'll find out in a few days what caused the fire. Do you have anyone you can stay with?" He looked from me to Carla.

Carla opened her mouth to reply, but suddenly a growly voice behind me said, "She'll stay with me."

I looked over my shoulder at Viper. For such a huge man, I hadn't even heard him approach.

I didn't care for his complete domination of the situation, but his expression said not to put up a fuss.

I glanced at the fire chief. "I'll stay with him."

The fire chief surveyed Viper.

"He's my boyfriend," I said with a tight smile. "He's madly in love with me, you know. He's trying to lock my ass down, but I'm a wild stallion. I don't want to be tamed."

"Ah, right." The fire chief appeared uncomfortable. "Your friend gave me your contact number. I'll be in touch." He walked away, leaving me with Viper and Carla.

"Stallions are male," Viper pointed out.

I shrugged. "It got the point across, didn't it? Thanks for the offer, but I'll stay with Carla."

"I wasn't offering," Viper said. "I was telling. Let's go."

I placed my hands on my hips and glared up at him. "You're not the boss of me."

He peered down. "You need a boss."

"Do not."

"Fuck this shit," Viper growled. He picked me up and literally hauled me over his shoulder.

"Hey," I protested as I squirmed. "Put me down, beast. Everyone's watching."

His hand settled on the meaty part of my thigh, just below my ass. "Then I suggest you sell that we're in relationship."

I lifted myself up just enough to look at Carla.

She was grinning. "Have fun, Sutton. You deserve it."

"There will be no having of the fun," I snapped. "Viper. Put me down, or I'll…"

"You'll what?" He squeezed my thigh. "Make a scene?"

"You're already making a scene," I hissed.

"Hush, or I'll spank your ass. Though I think you might like that."

I glared at his back.

When we got to his bike, he set me down and handed me a helmet. "Don't test me."

"I have to get my stuff from Carla's." I took the helmet from him and placed it on my head.

"It's at the clubhouse."

"The clubhouse. Is that where you're taking me?"

"Yeah."

"Is that where you live? Is that where you bring all your *girlfriends?*"

He closed his eyes and took a few deep breaths.

"What are you doing?" I demanded.

"Praying for patience."

"You pray?" I asked in surprise.

"Sutton, get your ass on my bike."

I saluted. "Sir, yes, sir!"

He climbed on his bike and then I slid behind him. I wrapped my arms around his stomach and rocked up against him, pressing my heat against his back.

When he made a noise very much like a growl of frustration, I smiled.

We zoomed off into the night and I wondered who was being taken on the ride of their life.

Me or Viper?

~

The gates of the clubhouse opened, and Viper drove through. He parked on a gravel lot and cut the engine. I swung a leg over his motorcycle and climbed off. With a frown, I unclipped the helmet and removed it from my head.

"You look confused," he said.

My ears vibrated from the rumble of the engine. "It's…big."

"Pretty much what all men want to hear."

I looked at him and blinked. "Was that a joke? Did you just make a dick joke?"

"If I said yes, would that make you faint from shock?"

"I don't faint."

"Hmm."

"Hmm? What's that mean?"

He ran a thumb across his lips and scratched the stubble along his jaw. "Never mind."

"Not never mind," I demanded. "I'm curious by nature, so now you have to tell me what that *hmm* meant."

"Guess you'll just have to go on being curious." Viper

strode past me, toward the porch steps of the well-lit clubhouse.

"Why does this look like a compound?" I demanded.

Viper didn't reply.

I hated when he didn't respond to me. It only made me want to annoy him more.

"Where's Savage?" I asked.

He didn't answer.

"Savage is cute. Like *really* cute."

Viper's shoulders tensed as he pushed the front door of the clubhouse open.

"I feel like I should thank him. You know? He did a lot for me tonight. He packed my bag for me. He's going to help me get rid of this problem. Does he like brownies? Cookies? I want to show him how *grateful* I am."

"You will not bake him brownies or cookies," Viper snapped, finally turning to face me.

I grinned up at Viper's menacing expression. I reached out to pat his chest. "Don't worry. I can't bake worth a damn."

The living room was devoid of people, so luckily, there was no one there to witness our exchange.

As I looked around, I noticed the space was oddly tidy.

"You drive me batshit," he muttered.

"You've said that already," I pointed out. "So, where am I staying?"

"Spare room," he said.

"So, not with you."

"Not with me."

"Oh." I nodded. "Yeah, okay."

"You sound disappointed."

"You're delusional. Lead the way."

I followed Viper up to the second floor of the clubhouse

to the room. He pushed the door open but didn't move out of the way. I sidled past him. My duffel bag was at the foot of a double bed with a blue comforter pulled tightly over the top. The room smelled like lemon-scented cleaner.

"Bathroom is through there," Viper said, pointing to a closed door.

He turned to leave.

"Wait," I called out.

He stopped.

"You're really not going to tell me why you brought me here when I could've just crashed with Carla?"

"You'll talk to Prez in the morning," he said. "For now, try to get some sleep."

"Sleep," I said flatly. "I'm supposed to just get some sleep after I—after I *killed* someone?"

His gaze darkened. "That shit right there—you can't go around saying that. You gotta keep it to yourself. You get me?"

"I get you."

With one last look, Viper closed the door.

I was alone.

Great.

Being alone in a safe place meant that my walls could come down. It meant I could finally think about what had occurred. Then again, if I thought too much about it, I was going to spin myself into a whirlwind of anxiety.

It had all happened so quickly. I hadn't thought—I'd just reacted.

I was alive because of it.

But that meant someone else was dead.

I collapsed on the side of the bed, spread my legs, and stuck my head between them.

"You're okay," I whispered. "You're okay. You'll get

through this. You'll get through this like you've gotten through every other hardship."

Once I'd given myself a pep talk, I forced myself to stand. I grabbed my phone from my purse. It was just past three in the morning and because of adrenaline, caffeine, and sugar, I was jacked up.

I shot off a text to Carla, letting her know I was safe and sound. Her reply was almost immediate. I turned my cell on vibrate and set it down on the nightstand.

I opened my duffel bag and looked around for my toiletries. They hadn't been packed. No matter. I'd be able to do without for a night, though I hoped there was at least toothpaste in the bathroom. Sure enough, there was a travel-sized tube on the counter next to the sink.

As I finger-brushed my teeth, I stared at my reflection. My brown hair fell to the middle of my back, and at the moment it was a tangled mess. My cheeks were pale, and my brown eyes looked far too wide in my face. Without makeup and with freckles splattered across my nose, I looked younger than twenty-two.

I turned on the bedside lamp before flipping out the main light. I stripped down to my underwear and crawled beneath the covers. Eventually, the adrenaline ran its course and my body's exhaustion overpowered the whirlwind of my mind.

And then I slept.

Chapter 5

"Jesus fucking Christ," a low, raspy voice muttered.

My eyes cracked open, but my hair covered my face. I hastily shoved it aside and looked in the direction of the person whose curse had dragged me from a sound sleep.

I glared at Viper as he stood at the edge of the bed. He was scowling and looked like he was about to punch a wall.

"What's got your panties in a twist?" I demanded.

"Speaking of panties…" His gaze dropped.

My brow furrowed in confusion. That's when I realized I'd kicked off the covers while I slept.

And my thong-clad ass was on display, along with a healthy dose of skin.

"Try knocking next time," I snapped, hastily grabbing the covers and yanking them up to my chin.

"I did. You didn't answer."

"Probably because I was asleep," I pointed out. "What time is it, anyway?"

"A little after eight."

I peered at him. His eyes were bloodshot.

"Did you sleep?" I asked.

He clenched his jaw. "Prez is here. Wants to talk to you."

"He can wait," I said. "I need coffee first. And a toothbrush. Savage forgot to pack my toiletries."

Viper's scowl turned into a glower. "Prez doesn't wait. And I'll get you a fucking toothbrush."

When he made no move to leave, I cleared my throat and gestured with my chin to the door. "A little privacy, please?"

"You want privacy now?" he asked. "I've already seen your ass."

"*Out*," I barked.

"I'll be back in ten minutes." He pointed at me. "You better be up, or I'll be taking you to Prez just the way you are."

A slow smile spread across my face. "No you won't."

"I won't? Fucking try me."

And because I was feeling brave—and just a bit stupid—I whipped off the covers and slid out of bed, enjoying the tightening of his jaw and the heating of his gaze. "You won't take me out there like this because you don't want anyone else to see me like this."

Silence descended between us, and it swelled with tension. It felt like it was its own entity, and it was growing, surrounding us in a bubble of sexual heat and need.

Viper clenched his tattooed fists and then marched to the door. He pulled it open so hard I thought for sure it would come off its hinges. He slammed the door shut, the vibration of the wood ringing in my ears.

I swallowed.

Teasing Viper might not be the smartest idea on the planet, but it sure as hell was a lot of fun.

I quickly pulled on my discarded jeans and tank top. Then I went into the bathroom. I did my business and after washing my hands, I twirled up my hair, wishing I'd asked Viper for a brush. I had purple smudges beneath my eyes, attesting to the few hours of sleep I'd gotten. I used my finger to brush my teeth again.

I came out of the bathroom and went to the nightstand. I had a missed call from a number I knew by heart but didn't have saved in my phone. A twinge of guilt went through me when I realized I'd missed his call, but there was nothing that could be done about it now. I'd listen to the voicemail later.

The door opened again, and Viper strode in.

"Knock much?" I demanded.

He didn't reply as he held out a cup of coffee toward me.

I took it and peered into the mug. It was light, almost like there was hardly any coffee in it. I took a sip. Yep. Enough sugar and cream to send me into a coma. Just the way I liked it.

And Viper had made it for me this way.

I looked up at him to find him watching me.

My shoulders sank. "Thank you."

He blinked and then nodded.

I quickly pulled on my boots and then grabbed the mug and followed Viper out of the room. We headed to the first floor, through the hallway, to a small office. A man with dark hair and a fierce frown rose from behind the desk. He reminded me of Viper, in size and temperament, so I wasn't put off in the least.

"Sutton," he greeted. "I'm Colt. President of the Tarnished Angels."

"Nice to meet you," I said politely.

He gestured to the chair in front of the desk. I moved toward it and then spun to look at Viper.

I didn't want him to leave, but I refused to ask him to

stay. Something about my prideful nature prevented me from being needy. But he made the decision for me when he closed the door for privacy. He then went to the wall and leaned against it.

I smiled slightly and he inclined his head.

Turning around, I faced Colt again. His brown gaze was piercing and shrewd.

"Viper told me you've been pestering him with questions about why you're here," Colt began.

"Pester? I didn't pester. I asked and he didn't tell me," I said, affronted.

"You pestered," Viper growled.

I glared at him. "Be nice or leave."

"Tell Prez what happened last night," Viper commanded. "He needs to know everything."

I took a sip of coffee. "I was cooking an omelet when the back door opened. I don't remember if I left it unlocked or what, but he just came in. This guy—this *man*—rushed toward me. Dark hair. Covered in tats. Feral eyes. Like, I live in a trailer park, ya know? I'm used to shit going on. I thought maybe he was tweaking and he was just looking for some easy cash to steal and maybe he didn't know I was home…"

I shook my head, remembering the adrenaline that had taken over my entire body. "He stood there for a minute before he came at me… He said I was a *pretty little piece* and…he wanted to *taste me*. He pulled out a knife and told me to be quiet so no one would hear. Said he'd cut me and leave me for dead if I made any noise. I didn't think—I just grabbed the cast-iron skillet I was cooking with, and when he lunged for me, I bashed the side of his head. It stunned him, but he didn't stop."

I looked at the coffee in my hands. "Eventually I hit him in the knee, and when he collapsed I smashed his skull in. Even when he was doing that heavy, labored breathing and I knew he was going to die, I didn't stop until...until he was silent."

My hands shook as I lifted the coffee mug and placed it on the desk. I clamped my lips shut to stop them from trembling. It was one thing to think about the situation. It was an entire other thing to relive it, give it words, give it legs, and make it real again. To share it.

"Brave," Viper growled. "What you did."

I lifted my chin, my head swiveling to stare at him. His eyes said more than his words. His eyes said he was proud of me. For not being a victim. For not freezing.

"He's right," Colt said. "What you did was fucking brave as shit, and you were lucky that it worked out that way."

"Yeah." I nodded. "I just couldn't—I mean, I knew he was going to rape me. Rape me and then probably kill me, so I had to fight. You know?"

Colt set his hands on the desk and linked his tattooed fingers.

"Thank you for telling me the truth," Colt said.

"Thank you for cleaning up my mess." I wrinkled my nose. "I still don't know why your club did me that favor."

"Do you have any family, Sutton?" Colt asked.

"I'm on my own," I said.

He nodded slowly. "I'm impressed with how you handled yourself in that situation. I don't know you, but I've got a gut instinct about what you're made of. Viper said you didn't break down last night either. After..."

"No," I agreed. "I didn't break down."

"What about when you were alone last night? In the clubhouse room?" Colt asked.

"No," I admitted. "Not even then."

"Grit," Colt said. "You've got grit. Which is why I'm

gonna tell you the truth about last night. The man who broke into your trailer wasn't some random guy looking to rape you. That wasn't his end goal."

I frowned. "How do you know?"

"Because of his tattoos," Colt explained. "You killed a member of the cartel."

I blinked. "Cartel?"

"Yeah."

"There's a cartel in Waco?" I asked in shock.

"Yes," Colt admitted.

"Shit," I muttered.

"The cartel is involved in the skin trade."

"Skin trade? You mean human trafficking?"

Viper's heavy boots tromped across the wood floor and suddenly, I felt his large hand on my shoulder. Colt's gaze darted away from me to Viper. A moment later, his eyes returned to me.

Something about Viper's touch calmed me. I wasn't alone.

"Yeah, human trafficking," Colt finally said. "It's a huge fucking problem in Waco."

"How do you know all this?" I demanded. "Unless…"

Colt's voice dropped low. "Unless?"

"Unless you're involved…somehow?"

"The club's involved," Colt admitted. "We're involved in stopping it. We're currently at war with the cartel. They don't want to stop the skin trade, but we're determined to end it. At least in Waco."

"Oh. Oh, I see." I nodded.

"I don't think you do," Colt said. "You were going to become another statistic. If you'd lost that fight, he would've most definitely raped you. And then he would've taken you across the border where you'd have been sold and never heard from again."

Nausea swam in my belly.

"You're in this shit now, darlin'," Colt said, his tone grim. "You're in it now, whether you want to be or not."

"I prefer not," I said bleakly.

"Don't really have a choice," the president of the club said.

Viper squeezed my shoulder and then let go.

"We just disappeared a body for you. We cleaned up an awfully big mess. You're staying with us until all this shit is sorted. We can protect you if you're here."

"Don't make it sound like an invitation," I said dryly.

"It's not," Colt replied.

"So, am I a prisoner?" I asked. "I might not have a home anymore, but I do have a job. I can't just stop showing up. I have a life."

"Do you want a life? Or do you want to live?" When I didn't reply, he asked, "Where were you working?"

"I was a server at Spurs."

"The cowboy-themed restaurant?" Colt asked, a slow smile drifting across his face.

"The one and only," I stated. "And before you ask, yes, I had to wear cowboy boots and daisy dukes to work."

Colt chuckled. "My wife owns a bar. We can get you a job there. We can keep an eye on you—you can still have a job and stay busy. You'll meet the club and fit right in, I'm sure. Life will be sort of normal for you, all things considered."

I suddenly felt indebted to Colt and his club, and I didn't like it. But if I wanted protection, I'd have to suck it up and deal. "Thanks. I'd appreciate the job."

"You'll be safe here, Sutton."

"Thank you," I said with a sigh. "I mean it, really. Not just for offering me a place to stay, but also for what your club did for me."

"You're welcome. I think it needs to be said, too, that you can't talk about this with anyone except Viper or Savage. No one else can know what happened. Not a peep. Do you understand?"

"I understand."

"I'll talk to my wife about a job for you," Colt said, rising from his chair.

"Thanks."

"Viper, stay a minute," Colt instructed.

I stood up and headed for the door. At the last moment, I looked behind me. Both Colt and Viper were watching me, but it was Viper's gaze that caught my attention.

I quickly averted my eyes and left the office. In my haste to get away, I'd forgotten my coffee, but I wasn't going to go back for it. Instead, I went in the direction of the kitchen.

Savage was at the coffee maker, pressing a button. The machine gurgled to life.

"Morning," I greeted.

He turned. "Morning. You sleep okay? Dumb question maybe."

"Not dumb," I assured him. "I slept hard, actually. I don't know if I got a chance to say it last night, but thanks. For what you did."

"Sorry about your home."

I shrugged. "I have my life. That's worth more."

"Still shitty."

"Yeah. Definitely still shitty. Looks like I'm bunking here for the time being."

"It's not all bad," he teased. "We have great parties. There's always food in the fridge, and we have a cleaning crew twice a week."

"It's like a biker hotel," I quipped.

"Viper treating you all right?"

I blinked. "Yeah. Why?"

He shrugged. "He's a little rough around the edges."

"A little?" I joked. "Luckily, for me, I'm not a wilting rose. I can handle him."

"That, I've got to see," Savage said. "He's one surly fucker."

Was Viper surly, intense, and a bit growly? Yes, but he also knew how I took my coffee, which meant he'd paid attention last night even though we'd only had a few minutes together. And the way he'd placed his hand on my shoulder in a silent show of support…

"Damn it," I muttered.

"What was that?" Savage asked.

"Oh. Nothing. Can I get a cup of that coffee?"

Chapter 6

I sat on the couch, sipping a cup of coffee as I passed the time with Savage. Viper and Colt were still locked away in the office.

"I can see why Carla likes you," I said with a smile.

He flashed a grin. "Yeah, she likes me all right."

"Do not make a dick joke," I pleaded.

"It would've been too easy."

"I was going to say she likes you because of your sense of humor," I said.

"Don't let my lighthearted side fool you. My name is Savage for a reason."

"Noted." I snorted.

"So, you know Carla well then, yeah?"

"Well enough to go to her in the middle of the night with a *really* big problem. What about you? How well do you know her?" I asked.

"We just met, actually. About a week ago." He rubbed his jaw. His blond hair had that artful look of having had fingers run through it recently, and it totally worked for him.

"Don't fuck with her," I said quietly.

Savage frowned. "Fuck with her? In what way would I fuck with her?"

I didn't want to spill anything about Carla's history to Savage, but as her friend, I felt like it was my duty to at least send a warning shot. "She's had a crappy past with men. So don't promise her anything or lie to her about whatever it is you two are."

"Ah." Savage took a sip of his coffee. "I get you. And believe me, you don't have to worry. Carla has made it very clear what she wants from me—and that's nothing serious."

"Okay." I nodded.

It wasn't any of my business, getting involved in Carla's love life. Just like she never got involved in mine. But she was the closest friend I had and the last thing I wanted for her was another broken heart.

We didn't have time for broken hearts. We were too busy trying to wrangle life.

I heard the door to the office open and a moment later Viper and Colt strode across the wooden floor.

"You ready?" Viper asked me.

"Ready?" I frowned. "Ready for what?"

"You need some girlie shit, don't you?"

I raised my brows. "Girlie shit? You mean, like, a hairbrush?"

"Like I said, girlie shit," Viper said and then left the clubhouse.

I looked at Savage, who had a smirk streaking across his face.

"Mia will be at Shelly's around three," Colt said to me. "You can meet her then."

I nodded and stood up. I went to the sink and washed out my mug before putting it in the dishwasher.

"Later," I said to Savage.

"Later. Don't let him intimidate you."

"I won't," I assured him.

I headed outside, breathing in a lungful of humidity. Viper was already at his bike, waiting for me.

He handed me the helmet without a word.

"Are you my designated chauffeur now?" I teased.

Viper grunted.

"I'll take your grunt as a yes. Just as well," I muttered. "I don't have a car."

"No car? How were you getting to work?"

"There's this thing. Maybe you've heard of it. Long, metal contraption. It has an engine, and a bunch of people wait for it every day and it takes them places."

When he didn't reply, I added, "I took the bus. Spurs is close to the trailer park. Wasn't a big deal. I could even take the bus to Shelly's if it's—"

"Fuck that," he growled.

I batted my lashes at him. "So, I really do get my own personal chauffeur? I feel like a lady of luxury."

"Easier to keep an eye on you if I drive," he said.

All levity fled as I was jarred back to reality, and reminded of the true reason I was under the protection of the club.

"Viper?" I asked quietly.

He looked away from his mirrors to stare at me. "What?"

I boldly met his gaze when I stated, "I'm glad I killed him."

His expression hardened. He took the helmet from me and placed it on my head, his hands lingering when he clasped the buckle. "You did good, Sutton. Real good."

After Viper took me to a store to grab some basic necessities, he drove us to Shelly's. He parked his bike and kicked out the stand before climbing off and following me inside the bar.

It was a cool spot. Wood floors, a jukebox, a pool table, and large booths. I liked the atmosphere immediately.

A petite brunette was standing behind the wooden bar, holding a clipboard and pencil. She turned and smiled. "Hi, Viper," she said.

"Mia," he growled in response.

Mia's gaze slid to me. "You must be Sutton." She held out a hand and I shook it. "You want something to drink? Water? Soda?"

"I'm good, thanks," I said. I looked at Viper over my shoulder. "Thanks for driving me."

He smiled slightly. "That sounds like a dismissal."

"It is," I said pointedly.

"I'll be in the corner booth," he replied. With a chin nod at me, he turned and walked away.

When I faced Mia again, I noted the look of surprise on her face.

"Why does everyone have that expression after seeing me interact with Viper?" I demanded.

A grin trembled along her mouth. "Seriously?"

"Seriously."

"It's the fact that he hardly speaks—even to his own brothers in the club—and here you are, without fear, talking to him like he's a regular guy. And he replies back in non-monosyllabic words."

"So, everyone tiptoes around him and handles him with kid gloves?"

"Handles him? More like avoids him."

I leaned closer and stage-whispered, "Can I tell you the truth?"

"Please."

"I refuse to cater to him. He wants to be aloof and grumpy, fine. But I've made it my mission to make him as uncomfortable as possible."

Her brown eyes lit with humor and slid away from me to glance over my shoulder. "He's staring at you."

"Is he?" I smiled. "Good."

"Good? You like him, don't you?"

"Hey, I thought this was a job interview," I protested. "Not an interrogation about me and Viper."

"So, there is a you and Viper?" she pressed.

I shook my head.

With a sigh, she set the clipboard down. "Colt said you needed a job."

"Yes."

"He said you're staying at the clubhouse for the foreseeable future because of some shit."

"Also yes."

"He didn't tell me the details," she said. "And I don't ask. That's kind of Old Lady code. Need to know basis."

"What's an Old Lady?"

"A biker's woman."

"Oh."

"Colt said you also have serving experience."

"I work...*worked* at Spurs."

"The cowboy bar?"

"Yeah." I wrinkled my nose. "I had to wear cowboy boots, a flannel shirt tied up around my middle, and daisy dukes. Made decent money, though. That's the only reason I put up with it."

"Well, there are no uniforms at Shelly's. So dress comfortably."

"Wait, I have the job then?" I asked with a frown.

"Of course, you've got the job." She cocked her head

to the side. "The interview was just a formality. You get that, right?"

"I mean…I guess so?"

"Look, I told you I don't know the details of your situation, and I don't need to. When I needed help, the club was there for me. Now we can be there for you. It's just what we do." She paused. "I can tell by the look on your face that you don't believe me."

"I don't live in that world," I quipped. "I'd prefer to know where I stand at all times. I don't buy into this altruism thing."

"This isn't altruism," Mia assured me. "It's community."

"Huh. That's a novelty for me."

She smiled. "Don't worry. You'll get used to it."

Chapter 7

"Can we make a quick stop before we head back to the clubhouse?" I asked.

Viper handed me the helmet. "Where?"

"Spurs. I have to clean out my locker and tell the manager I'm quitting."

My stomach suddenly rumbled.

"When was the last time you ate?" he demanded.

I frowned in thought.

"If you've got to think about it then it was too long ago," he stated. "You didn't eat this morning."

"You said that like an accusation," I quipped.

"Your belly confirmed it." He climbed onto his bike and started the engine. "We'll go to Spurs. You'll quit, get your shit, then we're getting you food. You gotta eat, Sutton."

I hopped on the back of his bike and wrapped my arms around him. It felt easy, natural. Like I belonged there.

But I didn't belong there.

Viper watching out for me and giving me rides was out

of necessity and protection. I couldn't forget that.

Spurs wasn't a bad place to work. We got a free meal every shift, the mangers usually left us alone, and we didn't have a skeevy boss trying to take advantage of us. I hadn't been there long, but I'd found a rhythm. I evolved quickly and easily though, and leaving Spurs to work at Shelly's wouldn't be a problem.

"Hey, Sutton," Delilah greeted from the host stand. "I didn't think you were working tonight." Her painted smile slipped when she noticed Viper's huge form behind me.

"I'm not. Who's managing tonight. Jim?"

She nodded. "He's in the office doing next week's schedule."

"Great, thanks." I looked at Viper. "I'll meet you at the bar when I'm done."

"I'll stand outside the office," Viper said, his tone not allowing for argument.

The door to the restaurant opened and an elderly couple came in. I pulled Viper off to the side so Delilah could greet them and show them to a table.

"Please, Viper," I said, pitching my voice low. "It's weird if you come back there with me."

"Don't care." He cracked his knuckles.

With a sigh, I marched across the floor. When I arrived at the office door, I turned to Viper. "Wait here."

He nodded.

I knocked on the door and cracked it open. Jim was a balding man in his forties, and he was sitting behind the desk. He looked up when I popped my head in.

"Hey, Sutton," he said with a smile. "It's your day off. What are you doing here?"

"You have a second?" I asked.

"Sure thing."

I opened the door farther and then entered. Jim's gaze

tracked Viper, who stood in the hallway, leaning against the wall. He didn't have to do anything to look menacing because he *was* menacing. I shot Viper a glare and then closed the door.

"New friend of yours?" Jim asked.

"Boyfriend," I lied. "Recent."

"Oh." Jim frowned. "So, what's up?"

"I'm quitting," I said.

"Quitting? Why?" He looked in the direction of the closed door. "This isn't your boyfriend's idea, is it?"

"What? No. I got another job," I said. "One where I don't have to wear daisy dukes and cowboy boots."

He sighed. "Yeah. Okay. You sure this isn't about that guy, though, right? I mean, he's not trying to take you away from all your friends, and change your entire life, is he? That's a classic abuser sign. Take you away from people you know."

"It's not like that," I assured him. "I know how it looks, okay? But he's a good guy."

"He's a biker," Jim said, tone low.

"Don't judge a book by its cover."

He sighed. "Sorry you're leaving the team. You were getting along well."

"Yeah." I nodded. "Thanks, Jim. I appreciate you giving me the job. Sorry to leave you in the lurch."

"Don't worry about it. Delilah's been wanting to take a few waitressing shifts. It'll work out."

With a wave, I left the office. As I closed the door behind me, I looked at Viper, who hadn't moved.

I gestured to myself. "See? No harm. No foul."

"He thinks I'm coercing you into quitting," he said.

"How did—were you *eavesdropping*?"

He exhaled in annoyance. "I don't eavesdrop."

"No?" I crossed my arms over my chest. "If you weren't eavesdropping, what else didn't you hear?"

His mouth flickered and a smile cracked across his face.

It was such a change in his countenance it had me blinking in stupidity for several seconds.

"You called me your boyfriend."

"Easiest way to explain you."

He reached out and dropped his arm over my shoulder, pulling me into his side. "I think that lie rolled off your tongue a bit too easily."

I pushed against his side, which did absolutely nothing except make him laugh.

Like outright laugh. Not a chuckle. Not a chortle. A real laugh.

"Come on," I muttered. "Let's go to the locker room so I can grab my stuff."

~

I was ravenous by the time Viper pulled into the parking lot of the restaurant. It wasn't anything fancy. Just a bar and grill that smelled like fried oil, burgers, and wings.

The hostess sat us in a booth, and I immediately seized the menu.

"Get you something to drink?" the server asked as he approached our table.

"Oh, uh, the lightest beer you have on tap, please," I said.

"Sure. May I see your ID?"

I dug my wallet out of my purse and extracted the ID.

The server stared at it for a moment and then smiled. "Happy belated birthday."

"Thanks."

"For you, sir?" the server asked, looking at Viper.

"The darkest beer on draft," he said, glancing at me.

"Sure. I'll need to see your ID, too."

Viper finally turned his attention to the sever and raised his brows.

"Policy," the server blurted out. "I know you're old enough, but I could lose my job if I don't card everyone."

"Jesus, Viper, just show him your ID," I muttered.

Viper pulled out his wallet and complied.

"Thank you. I'll be right back with your drinks."

I held out my hand across the table, palm side up.

Viper placed his hand on mine.

"Cute," I said. "But not what I was hoping for." I wiggled my fingers. "ID."

"You want to see my ID?"

"Yep."

"Why?"

"Because I want to know your age and legal name."

"Then why don't you just ask me?"

"And you'll tell me?"

"Yeah, I'll tell you."

"Can I have my hand back now?"

"No. I'm not done with it."

"Careful, Viper. You're playing the role of fake boyfriend all too well."

He grunted.

"So, what's your name?"

"Rhett Maxwell."

"Rhett Maxwell," I repeated. "You don't look like a Rhett."

"What do I look like?" he demanded.

"I dunno. Dave, or Sam. Ralph."

"*Ralph*? I look like a Ralph?"

I grinned. "*Gotcha.*"

The server returned with our beers, and I hastily pulled my hand from Viper's and set it in my lap.

"You ready to order?" the server asked.

"I didn't look at the menu yet," I said. "But I'm starving and if I don't eat, I'll become hangry and mean."

"Well, we definitely don't want that," the server said.

"You go first," I said to Viper.

I hastily perused the menu while Viper ordered.

When he was finished, I said, "I'll have the buffalo burger, medium rare, with cheddar, lettuce, tomato, no onions, and a side of sweet potato fries, please. Oh. And a house salad with bleu cheese dressing."

"Very good. I'll get that going for you right away." The server disappeared and I looked at Viper, who was shaking his head and smiling.

"What?" I demanded. "What's that smile for?"

"You ordered a salad. That shit fucking kills me."

"I also order it with bleu cheese dressing, so it negates any and all healthy stuff."

Viper grabbed his pint and took two huge swallows before setting it aside.

"So, Rhett," I began. "Can I call you Rhett?"

"Absolutely not."

"What's your middle name?"

"Haven't got one."

"How old are you?"

"Thirty-six. You want to know my blood type, too?"

"Nah, that feels kind of invasive."

"Now you," he commanded.

"Sutton Eloise Woods. I'm twenty-two."

He ran a hand down his face. "Christ."

"What?"

"Nothing."

"Not nothing."

"You're just…young."

"Yeah, I guess." I frowned.

"I'm too old for you."

"You lost me."

"You and me. We're never going to happen."

I grabbed my pint of beer. "Mkay."

"I mean it, Sutton. I'm too old and jaded for you. And you're…"

"A young damsel in distress, caught in the clutches of an evil fox?" I rolled my eyes. "You know what I love more than presumptuousness? Condescension."

"I just want to be clear," he stated.

"Well, you have nothing to worry about," I assured him. "I have a type, and you most definitely are *not* it."

"You're twenty-two. How the hell do you already have a type?" he demanded.

The server approached our table carrying my salad. He placed it down in front of me and then asked if I needed anything else. He left when I said no.

I grabbed my napkin and set it across my lap.

"Sutton," Viper growled.

"Yes, oh grumpy one?"

"I asked about your type."

"It doesn't really matter, does it?" I asked. "I mean, since you made it clear that we won't be getting together. Which, frankly, is a bit of a relief. You're far too intense for me. And growly. And *moody*. You've got a lot of flaws, Viper. You should work on yourself first, you know?"

"Work on myself? What the fuck does that mean?"

"Drink your beer," I commanded. "Before it gets warm."

Chapter 8

Viper silently fumed while I ate my salad. Manipulation and teasing always did bring out my appetite.

What Viper failed to realize was that I already understood everything about him. Other people might've been scared of him, or even felt rebuffed by his attitude and his desire to remain aloof and distant, but in the short time we'd spent together, I'd come to realize that he was a protector, even if he didn't want to be.

He'd taken me back to the clubhouse after the fire.

He'd stayed with me while Colt spoke to me, and even offered his silent, physical support as the conversation got intense.

Viper said he was too old for me, but his actions proved he didn't believe it.

He wants me.

Big, tall, scary Viper didn't like getting close to people, and he used his nature and his size to keep others away. Most people didn't bother trying to get past his defenses.

But I wasn't most people.

As I finished my salad, our burgers arrived. Finally, Viper had something to focus on instead of glaring at me.

"How's the food?" I asked after I polished off the last of my sweet potato fries.

"Decent," he muttered.

"If it's just decent, then why are you only three bites away from finishing it?" I asked with a cheeky grin.

"Because I'm hungry. Sometimes food isn't about taste—it's about necessity."

"You grew up poor too, huh?"

He paused in his movements, looking up from his plate to stare at me. "Yeah. I grew up poor."

"Your parents still around?" I asked.

Viper didn't reply.

"I know I said you were too broody for me, but I'm totally lying. It works for you, and I find it hot."

"What are you doing?" he demanded.

I widened my eyes in sham innocence. "I'm not doing anything."

"I told you I'm too old for you, and you think it's a good idea to call me hot?"

"Sexy? Would you have preferred the term sexy?"

"Jesus Christ, Sutton."

"Admit it, you find me adorable and charming, and so you're using the age thing as a wall between us."

"Oh, I am, am I? Are you some sort of expert on men or something? At the ripe old age of twenty-two?"

"You're only thirty-six," I shot back. "Not sixty. And would you say your age has made you an expert on women?"

"It'll take you more than a day to figure me out."

"Challenge accepted."

"That wasn't me throwing down a gauntlet." He sighed. "This isn't a game I'm playing. I'm too jaded. Too fucked from this life. I'm a mean bastard who's better off alone. And you're…"

"I'm what?"

"Not."

My phone vibrated in my purse, pulling my attention. It was Carla.

"Hey," I said into the phone. "Give me a second."

I scooted out of the booth, cell to my ear, and made my way to the bathroom.

"Okay, hi, I'm here," I said.

"Hey, I was just calling to check up on you."

"Sweet of you. I'm okay. I think."

"You think?" she asked.

"Well, I'm kind of sleep-deprived and everything has been happening really fast."

"Where are you now?"

"At a restaurant with Viper."

"Viper…how's that?"

"I don't even know." I leaned against the sink counter. "I'm not really sure what's going on there."

"Do you want something to be going on there?"

"It seems like a bad idea."

"Not what I asked," she said with a laugh.

"Your call actually interrupted the conversation."

"The conversation about what?"

"That Viper is too old for me. His words, not mine."

"And what do you think?" she pressed.

"I think he keeps to himself because it's easier for him that way. Not because he actually likes being alone."

"Do any of us like being alone?" Carla asked. "I wouldn't have married my two ex-husbands if I'd learned how to be alone."

"Do you know anything about Viper?" I asked.

"I know he's from Spearfish, South Dakota. Savage

told me there was a club chapter there, but it disbanded after they lost their president. There were a few guys, including Viper, who came down to join the club here."

"Oh," I said quietly.

"Any word from the fire chief?"

"Not yet." I paused. "Is it weird that I'm not that torn up about losing my home?"

"Kind of, yeah."

"My home wasn't like your home," I said.

Carla had bought the trailer after her second divorce. Paid it off, renovated it, made it feel and look like a comfortable, warm haven. My trailer was just what it was. A trailer. One giant plastic and cardboard box that reminded me that I was going nowhere in life.

"You want me to come to the clubhouse tonight?" she asked. "I'll bring a bottle of bourbon and we can talk about it all. If you want."

"Thanks," I said. "But no. I don't want to talk it all out. I don't want to think about it."

"Careful burying that shit. Better if you deal with it now," she warned. "It's the type of shit that comes back to bite you in the ass."

My full belly churned. "You think talking about it will help? I'm not even supposed to talk about it unless it's with Viper or Savage. That's what the president of the club said. But it doesn't matter because I don't *want* to talk about it. I want to forget about it. I want to leave it where it is and move on."

"Okay, I get it. Bad shit happens and there are definitely times you don't want to dwell on it."

"So, Savage?" I asked.

"What about him?"

"It that going to turn into anything?"

"You mean will he become ex-husband number three? I haven't decided yet."

I chuckled. "You deserve happiness. You get that, right?"

"So do you, Sutton. So do you. Keep me posted. I'm intrigued about your relationship with Viper."

"There is no relationship with Viper," I protested.

"Liar."

She hung up before I could respond, and silence drilled into my ear.

With a sigh, I returned to the table. The plates had been cleared and Viper was laying down cash on the check presenter.

"What are you doing?" I demanded.

"Paying the bill."

"I see that. But why?"

"Because that's what you do when you go to a restaurant. You order food, you eat it, you pay for it."

I rolled my eyes and reached for my purse. "I know. I just meant—I wanted to pay."

"Why?"

"Because I'm not a charity case."

He frowned. "Okay."

"You paid for dinner last night."

"No, I paid for coffee and dessert. I don't understand what the hell is going on here."

"Your club is already helping me," I said. "You've given me a place to crash and a job. The least I can do is treat you to a meal."

His tight expression didn't change but he took the bills from the check presenter and then handed it to me.

I blinked as I took it.

"You know this shit really doesn't matter, right?" he

said. "You're not in debt to the club. You don't owe us anything."

I clutched the check presenter tighter and nodded.

I didn't believe that people ever helped one another without asking for something in return. Carla was different, but then again, we both rarely ever asked one another for help. We lived by the same code.

"If it feels like a debt, then it's a debt." I stuck cash in the check presenter and then set it down on the table. "And I always pay my debts."

Chapter 9

THE CLUBHOUSE WAS SWARMING with people when Viper and I arrived. Rock music blared from the speakers inside. The kitchen counters were littered with several bottles of liquor, mixers, and stacks of red cups and shot glasses.

I didn't recognize anyone.

Savage traipsed down the hall and when he saw me and Viper standing near the door, he immediately came forward. A grin spread across his face as he slapped Viper on the back.

"You guys are just in time for the party," he said.

I wasn't in the mood for a party. I wanted to escape to my room with my new toiletries and then take a shower and crash for a bit. I was only running on a few hours of sleep, and my conversation with Viper was still churning over in my brain.

"What do you want to drink?" Savage asked me.

"A beer, I guess," I said, against my better judgement.

"Haven't got any. Just liquor," Savage said. "Bourbon, Scotch, Irish whiskey, or tequila. Mixers and ice if you want them."

Viper muttered something under his breath.

"What was that?" I asked him.

"Nothing," he growled.

"Bourbon," I said to Savage. "With Coke."

"You got it," Savage said and moved toward the kitchen.

I watched as a biker who was standing with a woman in the corner slid his hand up her denim skirt and cupped her ass.

She sent him a flirtatious grin and placed her hand on his chest.

I turned away, feeling like I'd seen something I shouldn't have. Then again, they were getting handsy in public. Maybe they didn't care if people watched. Maybe they *wanted* people to watch.

Savage returned with my drink and a bottle of bourbon which he handed to Viper.

"We'll light the bonfire when the sun sets. Have fun, kids. And remember, no glove, no love." He chucked me under the chin and then sauntered off.

I took a huge swallow of my drink and then glanced at Viper, who was glaring in Savage's direction.

"So, I'm guessing these gatherings get a bit wild?" I asked.

"Wild. That's putting it mildly," he said, his tone bland.

"I'm not in the mood for anything wild," I stated. "I'm tired, so I think I'll head up to my room."

I threaded my way through the people in the living room to the stairs. Viper dogged my heels, though I wasn't sure why.

I took the stairs and pushed open my door. Viper came inside without invitation.

"Oh, are we hanging out?" I asked in amusement,

dropping the plastic bags onto the bed. "And here I thought you were sick of me and wanted to party."

Viper took a drink from the bottle of bourbon. "You won't be able to stay in here the entire night. You'll get hungry at some point."

"Then I'll come out for food." I shrugged. "And maybe after I've had a nap, I'll decide to have a drink or two around the bonfire and meet some new people."

"Why don't I just bring you food?" Viper asked. "Then you don't have to leave your room."

I frowned. "What's wrong with coming down and fixing myself a plate of something to eat? I don't need you to bring me food."

He rubbed the back of his neck. "I just don't think you being at the party is a good idea."

"Why not?" I raised my brows. "Because it gets *wild*?"

"Because it gets…"

"What?" I demanded. "It gets what?"

"Dirty."

"What do you mean, *dirty*?"

"I mean, those guys downstairs are single. There are no Old Ladies or kids here tonight. It means they don't have to be on their best behavior. So they won't be."

"I saw a guy put his hand up someone's skirt," I said as I set my drink on the nightstand.

"That's PG shit. When the sun sets…"

"Yeah?"

"Just stay up here," he growled.

"Ah, I get it. You're talking debauchery, huh? Like full-on debauchery." I crossed my arms over my chest.

"Yeah, that's what I'm talking about. My boys know how to party."

"Maybe *I* want to party. You ever think of that?"

"Sutton…"

"Don't *Sutton* me. So you want me to stay up here—alone—away from the party. Away from orgies and drinking, but are *you* going to be partaking in anything?"

"I didn't say anything about orgies."

"Didn't have to." I smirked. "Usually you're blunt as hell, and for some reason, you couldn't bring yourself to say it."

"Orgy. There, are you happy? Yeah, there's gonna be some group activities and I don't want you involved."

"Not really your choice, is it?" I threw out. "We're not dating. We're not anything. So, I'm a free agent—and so are you."

He shut the door and flicked the lock closed.

My eyes widened when he removed his leather cut.

"What are you doing?" I demanded.

"Making sure you don't go to the party," he said. "You don't belong down there. And the only way to make sure you don't go down there is to keep an eye on you."

"I didn't invite you to stay."

"Too bad. I'm staying."

My gaze narrowed. I picked up my drink from the nightstand and threw half of it back. "I don't get you, Viper. How often do you guys have parties like this?"

"Often."

"Are you going to stay in my room with me every time there's a party just to make sure I don't go down there and get an eyeful?"

"Yep."

I bit my lip. "But don't *you* want to be down there? I mean, partaking in all that stuff?"

"No."

"Why not?" I blurted.

"Because I don't." He shrugged. "Take off your boots."

"Why?"

"Stop asking me questions. Take off your boots and get comfortable."

I plopped down on the edge of the bed and set my drink onto the nightstand again. I leaned over and unlaced a boot.

When I removed one and tossed it aside, I looked up. Viper's gaze wasn't on my eyes, but lower. I looked down, remembering that I hadn't worn a bra underneath my tank.

I pretended not to notice and removed my other boot.

King of mixed signals, this one.

"Is Savage going to be involved in the debauchery?" I asked once I was comfortable. I grabbed my drink and then leaned back against the wall.

"Why are you asking about Savage?" Viper hadn't sat down. Instead, he leaned against the opposite wall, facing me.

"Because he's dating my friend. And if he's sticking his dick in other holes, I think she should know."

"Had no idea liquor made you vulgar."

"The trailer park made me vulgar. Now answer the question."

"He's here, isn't he?" Viper stated. "He's at the clubhouse party and she's not here. So, what do you think?"

"I think that's rotten."

"He didn't make her his Old Lady. She doesn't have a claim on him."

"So if she was his Old Lady, he wouldn't fuck around on her?"

"Didn't say that either."

"Charming," I muttered.

I liked Savage. The idea that he—or any of the bikers

—fucked around on their women made me sad. Not surprised, but sad.

"Are all you guys cheaters?" I asked.

"Bold accusation there," he said. "And Savage and Carla's relationship is their business."

"What about you?"

"What about me?"

"Do you fuck around on your girlfriends?"

"I don't have any girlfriends."

"Past girlfriends," I clarified.

He took a drink of bourbon. "Not all men cheat."

"You didn't answer my question," I snapped.

"Bourbon makes you mean."

"Bourbon makes you not answer questions," I replied.

"No. I don't cheat. No. I don't fuck around on girlfriends. No. I don't lie to women, tell them what they want to hear, and dick them over."

"Well, that's nice, I guess," I muttered.

"I also don't have relationships," he said. "I'm not cut out for them."

"Because of conversations like these? Or because you don't like commitment?"

Viper pushed away from the wall and came toward me. "Cup."

"Huh?"

"Hold out your cup."

I held up my red cup.

He poured a hefty shot into it. "Drink."

"So you think I'm too young to date or have an orgy, but I'm not too young to drink straight bourbon."

"I'm trying to mellow you the fuck out. It's not working."

"I thought we established bourbon makes me feisty."

"Why don't you have a boyfriend?" he asked.

"Oh, hello, left field. Nice to meet you."

"Sutton," he growled.

"I don't have a boyfriend because I don't want one. And even if I was looking for one, my life just got really complicated, and at twenty-two I already have a lot of baggage. I'm no prize."

"No prize? Jesus Christ, Sutton. You don't get how different you are, do you? You've got bigger balls than most grown men I know."

"Why? Because I killed a guy who was determined to rape me and then sell me?"

"That's one reason, yeah. And the fact that your home burned to the ground and it's like it hasn't even fazed you."

I drank some bourbon, wrinkling my nose at the fumes. "You guys did me a favor. I hated that fucking thing."

"Then why were you living there?"

"Because I didn't have a choice."

"We all have choices."

"It was cheap," I said. "It was familiar. Doesn't mean it was right."

"So what were you doing?" he asked.

"About what?"

"Working. Were you just working at Spurs to make barely enough to live the exact same life year after year? Were you saving to go to college? Were you saving to get out of town? What?"

"Can I get some more of that bourbon?" I demanded.

"Pace yourself."

"I have a full stomach—and English blood. I process liquor just fine."

I held out my cup and Viper poured in a splash.

I shot him a glare, but he didn't have a heavy hand.

"Don't make me fight you for it," I quipped.

"I'd like to see you try."

"All I'd have to do is take off my tank. You'd be putty in my hands."

With a sigh, he poured a bit more into my glass.

"Oh wow, you care about my honor. I don't know whether to be offended or pleased."

"Back to our conversation," he rasped.

"None of it," I stated. "I didn't have any plans for the money. I was just going to earn it and have it. Sitting there."

"Doing nothing."

"What did you do when you were my age?" I demanded. "What dreams filled your head? What excitement roared through your veins?"

"I've ridden my bike from coast to coast," he said. "I've seen shit...*done* shit you can't imagine. I didn't stay in my town or settle for the status quo."

"You don't know anything about me," I said. "You have no idea why I am the way I am."

"Why *are* you the way you are?"

"Because I've been on my own for a long time. I don't need anyone. I don't rely on anyone. If I wanted to pick up and leave, I could have. I didn't. But I could have. No ties. No boyfriend. I do what I want when I want. That's why I lived the way I lived."

"And yet you're glad we burned down your home. So clearly it wasn't working for you."

I glared at him. "You sure you don't want to go back to your own room?"

"No. I'm having fun."

"You're having *fun*? You. Rhett Maxwell is having fun and actually carrying on a conversation."

"*Do not* call me Rhett."

"Why not? It reminds me of Rhett Butler."

"That's who I was named after," he said.

"Your mother had a thing for the antiheroes, huh?" I asked.

"The villains."

"Rhett wasn't a villain. He loved Scarlett despite her flaws. He waited for her, hoping she got past her teenage infatuation with a weak man who lived with his head in the clouds."

He tapped the side of the bottle. "I wasn't talking about Rhett being a villain. I meant my dad."

"Oh…what did he do?" I asked softly.

"Knocked her up. Then took her to Vegas to marry her, but on their way to the chapel, stopped at a casino where he proceeded to gamble away the small inheritance my grandma had left her."

"Oh fuck, really?"

He nodded. "She was young and stupidly in love with him—and ended up marrying him anyway."

"Damn," I murmured. "They still together?"

"Nah. She divorced his sorry ass when I was five. Worked two jobs to support me. Scrappy. She was a scrappy woman."

"Was?"

"She died a few years ago."

"I'm sorry."

"It is what it is."

I raised my glass. "I'll drink to that."

Chapter 10

"You've had enough," Viper said.

"You cutting me off, barkeep?" I asked.

The corner of his mouth flickered, but then he smiled. "Yeah. I'm cutting you off. You're a cute drunk, but you're definitely drunk."

"I'm not cute," I stated.

"Yeah, you are."

"No." I turned on the bed to face him. At some point—maybe an hour earlier—Viper had finally sat down on the edge of the bed, and we'd been drinking steadily since.

My pointer finger pressed into the center of his chest. "I'm not *cute*. Women don't want to be cute. It would be like calling you cuddly. Do you really want to be cuddly?"

"But I'm not cuddly."

"You're definitely not," I agreed. My gaze swept over him. "You're…you're…"

"I'm what?" he asked in amusement.

"Terrifyingly hot," I blurted out.

"I'm what?"

"Terrifyingly hot."

"I don't know what that even means."

"It means you're so hot I want to cry. And I must be a masochist because every time you tell me you're too old for me, it just makes me want you more."

A raspy chuckle left his lips. "Yeah, you're definitely drunk. You're going to remember this conversation when you're sober and be really embarrassed."

I shook my head. "I won't be embarrassed. It's not like I'm hiding how I feel about you. Horniness. Full on horniness. Viper, I haven't had sex in months."

He groaned. "Stop. Just stop."

"I can't." I inched closer to him, close enough that I could smell the bourbon on his breath. Close enough that I could run my fingers across the stubble of his jawline and cheeks. Close enough that if I just lifted my leg, I could climb onto his lap and press myself against him.

But I did have some pride.

Sort of.

We were staring at one another and when his gaze dropped to my mouth, I bit my lip.

"You're drunk," he murmured.

"Not that drunk."

"Drunk enough."

"So are you saying if I wasn't drunk you'd kiss me right now?"

"No. I wouldn't kiss you."

I reached out and probed the collar of his T-shirt with my fingertip. "I think you would. I think you'd cradle the back of my head in your big, tatted hand and kiss me so good and so deep I'd feel it all the way to my toes."

He gently grasped my finger and stilled my movements. "You need bread."

I frowned. "Bread?"

"I knew we should've eased up on the bourbon," he

muttered. "Or maybe I should've at least fought you harder when you started drinking right from the bottle." He slid off the bed. "Wait here."

"I'm not going anywhere."

Viper quickly pulled on his boots and left the bedroom, closing the door behind him.

With a sigh and a smile, I fell back against the pillow. I had him just where I wanted him.

～

I cracked an eye open. In my direct sight, I saw a loaf of bread, a bottle of water, and four aspirin.

With a frown, I slowly sat up and ran a hand down my face. My tongue felt like it had swelled to twice its usual size.

I grabbed the bottle of water, unscrewed it, and guzzled half of it.

Had I...*passed out?*

"Damn, really?" I muttered.

I looked at my phone. It was only six p.m. I wasn't sure how long I'd been asleep, but Viper was gone.

I had every intention of tracking him down—even if that meant leaving my room and going to the bonfire.

We had unfinished business, he and I.

But first, a shower.

I found the bag of toiletries and brought them to the bathroom. As I did, I thought about our conversation before I'd fallen asleep. He seemed to think I'd be embarrassed when I recalled our interlude.

But I was awake now, and I didn't have bourbon remorse. In fact, I was grateful for the liquid courage.

I quickly stripped out of my jeans and tank, and then hopped into the steamy shower and shivered from the warmth. I lathered my hair and closed my eyes, thinking about what could've happened between us if I hadn't been inebriated.

I thought about what he looked like naked.

Was he a man who liked complete control? Would he tell me to lay back and then take care of me? Or would he want me on top, letting me have my fill of him?

He was rugged and masculine, and I needed to feel every hard inch of him inside me.

My hand slid down my body, gliding to the seam of my legs. I played with myself, imagining it was Viper, imagining he was in the shower with me.

I wanted him to lift me up and hold me against the wall while he drilled into me.

He was a big man, and I had no doubt he was *big* everywhere.

I whimpered as I pictured him stretching me, filling me, my pleasure bordering on pain.

Viper would know. He'd know *exactly* how to touch me.

"Come for me, Sutton," he'd growl in my ear.

I came now.

Hot water washed away my release as my tremors subsided.

Instead of feeling satisfied, it only lit me on fire.

The fever of want burned hot and desperate.

I finished my shower and went back into the room and changed.

The bread and bottle of water Viper had left was sweet, but it wasn't a full meal. I was ready to leave my room in order to find real food.

But as I slipped into a pair of flip-flops, my gaze landed on the taped note on the door.

"I'll be back. Don't leave the room."

The man was utterly delusional.

I ripped open the door and stuck my head out into the hallway. I heard nothing, not even the music that had been playing earlier in the afternoon.

The clubhouse living room was completely deserted, but I heard laughter and conversation coming from the other end of the hallway. I followed the sound, pushed open the screen door, and went outside. A bonfire had been lit. Bikers were sitting on logs and camp chairs, holding bottles of liquor and cups. Women perched on their laps or sat in front of them.

Some people were getting handsy and kissing, but I saw no orgies.

"Sutton!" Savage called out.

Heads swiveled in my direction, curious gazes sweeping over me.

"Come here," Savage stated, patting the seat on the log next to him.

I hastily looked around but still didn't see Viper.

"Where have you been?" he demanded.

"In my room," I said. "With Viper."

"Oh, really," he drawled.

I rolled my eyes at his suggestive tone. "Get a grip. Nothing happened. Well, not nothing happened. I thought I could go toe to toe with him when it came to drinking bourbon. Even on a full stomach I ended up taking an afternoon nap."

"I still don't understand why you and Viper were in the same room together, locked away, when you both could've been at a party. There's only one reason to ditch out of a party, and if you two weren't playing explorer with your genitals, then I don't get it."

"You're vile," I retorted.

"But I'm not wrong. Why were you guys holed up together if you weren't fucking?"

"That's none of your beeswax."

He handed me the bottle of bourbon he was holding. "You're grouchy. Either you're hungover from your bout of day drinking, or you're mad that you weren't getting up close and personal with Viper's dick. Bourbon will help with either scenario."

With a glare, I took his bottle and drank.

"Have you seen Viper?" I asked.

"Not for a few hours. Though, now I get why he was MIA."

Savage wasn't wrong, and I was more annoyed about it than I should've been. "He left a note on my door that said not to leave my room and he'd be back soon. Clearly, I ignored him."

"Clearly," he agreed.

I handed him back the bottle. "I'm a little bit surprised."

"About what?"

"The party," I explained, pitching my voice lower.

"Why are you surprised about the party?"

"There's no orgy going on," I blurted out.

Savage raised his brows. "I can't tell if you're upset or relieved."

"Confused. That was the reason I was stuck in a room with Viper. He said he didn't want me down here because these parties get wild, and he didn't want me to see…things."

Savage laughed and his shoulders shook. His laugh was so loud, it caused other people to stop speaking and stare at us.

I elbowed him in the ribs. "Stop it, you baboon."

That only made Savage laugh harder.

Suddenly, he stood up. "Come on, half-pint. Let's go for a walk."

"Half-pint? Did you just nickname me?"

"Yup. Come on. Let's walk."

"Why would we go for a walk?" I demanded as I stood.

"Because I think I have an idea about why Viper pitched that line to you."

"So, it was a line," I guessed. "And it's bullshit?"

"Well, not entirely," he recanted, slinging an arm around my shoulder in friendly affection. "But I think we should talk about what's going on between you and Viper."

"Nothing's go on between me and Viper," I groused.

"Bingo. And judging by your tone, you want there to be. So, let's talk. And I'll help you make a game plan."

I sighed. "Am I that obvious?"

"Yes. But if it makes you feel any better, it's obvious Viper is into you, too."

"Not as into me as I'd like," I said before I could stop myself. I hastily covered my mouth as if that would undo what I'd said.

It only made Savage laugh again.

We headed off toward the picnic table, away from most of the partiers and the bonfire.

"Okay. Before we get into the Viper sitch, let me explain to you how the club works."

"Class is in session," I quipped. "I'm all ears." I pointed to the bottle of bourbon, which he relinquished into my care.

"You've heard of Old Ladies?" Savage asked.

"Mia said something about them, but I think there's more to it than she said."

"Right. Old Ladies are wives, steady girlfriends, fiancées of the brothers. But it means more. It means they've been claimed. It means they're off the market. It means you don't touch an Old Lady unless you want your hands removed from your body."

"Wow."

"Yeah." He nodded. "It's an honor, and we take that commitment *very* seriously. Now, not all brothers who have Old Ladies are faithful, but that has nothing to do with being a biker, and more to do with a man who's a cheater." He pointed to a group of bikers with women hanging all over them.

"These women are basically club groupies. No one has any claim to them. They can fuck whoever they want, whenever they want. Stacy can fuck Raze tonight, then leave his bed and fuck Bones an hour later if she wants. Get me?"

"*Take one down, pass it around*…yeah, I get you." I frowned. "So, the groupies sleep with whoever they want, whenever they want. And the bikers don't care?"

"They don't care. If one of the guys starts caring enough about someone to stop them from sleeping around, they make her an Old Lady and then she's off-limits."

"I see." I nodded.

"It's rare, though. That a brother will make a club groupie his Old Lady. Brothers are fine sharing, but an Old Lady is gonna be the mother of your kids one day. Don't really want every other club member having blown his load in one of her holes, you know?"

"Classy." I wrinkled my nose. "So, let me guess. I'm not an Old Lady, so I'm free to do whatever I want with whoever I want."

"Technically, yeah." Savage grabbed the bottle and took it from me. "However, Viper keeping you away from the party kinda proves he doesn't want you fucking around with his brothers. And you're not one of us, so you haven't been with anyone he knows yet."

"Yeah, I get that. That all makes sense. But he—ah fuck, I'll just come out and say it. It's like he's trying to resist mc or something. Saying I'm too young. I'm *not* too young. I'm twenty-two. I can hang with the big boys."

Savage was quiet for a moment as he took a long drink. "He's had a rough go of it the last few years. He's trying to get his head screwed on straight."

"And that's why he pulls back every time something almost happens between us?"

"You'll have to ask him about that."

"I have. He blames my age. Or his age. Says he's too old, too jaded for us to be together."

"He might not be wrong about that. You'd do well to listen to him."

"Yeah, okay, but I'm not asking for anything. I'm not asking to be his Old Lady. Christ, we *just* met. I was hoping for some…I don't know. I could've died last night, you know? I just want to live a little."

"Not a bad attitude to have," he said. "Not at all. But here's the thing about the club. A lot of the brothers have claimed their women fast. It means something to us—the Old Lady thing. And if Viper won't fuck you, then I'm guessing there's something more to it than just the age thing."

"Wait, are you saying…no, no way."

"No way what?"

"There's no way he wants to *claim* me."

"You don't know."

"We barely know each other."

"Sutton," he said gently. "You've already spent more time with Viper than anyone else in this club. And he's been here for weeks."

I blinked. "Weeks? I don't get it. Oh, wait. Carla told me he's from the South Dakota chapter, right?"

Savage nodded. "Bones, Raze, Smoke, Kelp, and Viper are all from South Dakota. They came down recently because they needed a club, and we needed more men. For this cartel shit. The other guys, they already feel like they've been part of club for years. But Viper? Viper keeps to himself. Mia and the other Old Ladies have invited him to their homes for dinner. He rejects any offer of kindness or friendship."

"But why?" I asked, mouth agape.

"Just who he is, I guess." He frowned, looking like he wanted to say more, but he clamped his mouth shut. "The fact that he's choosing to spend time with you over anyone else says a lot."

"He's not choosing me," I protested. "He's my bodyguard because of the shit I've been pulled into."

"He doesn't have to talk to you, does he?" Savage pressed. "I mean, I've seen you guys. I'm flummoxed."

"Talking is a loose term. He's a wall of muscle who prefers grunting to actual words."

I looked past Savage to see Viper standing on the other side of the bonfire, his eyes trained on me.

"Ah, there's the sexy caveman now."

"So, you like that he speaks in grunts, do you?" Savage quipped.

"I just like him," I admitted. "And it's hell on my ego that he rejects me."

Viper began to march toward us, his expression murderous.

"Uh-oh," I said.

"Uh-oh, what?" Savage asked.

"Hi, honey," I said to Viper. "How's the family?"

Without a word, Viper came over to the table, lifted me in his arms, and hoisted me over his shoulder.

"What the fuck?" I demanded.

"Hey, Viper," Savage drawled. "Nice night for a romantic walk, isn't it?"

"Shut up," Viper growled. He grabbed the back of my thigh and gave it a squeeze. "I told you to stay put."

"I'm not so good with the staying-put thing. Nor am I good at following directions," I said. "Is this you proving a point? That if I'm bad, you'll punish me. Oh God, *please* punish me."

Viper cursed under his breath but didn't design to give me a response. He spun on his heel. I lifted myself up so I could see Savage.

He grinned and saluted.

I grinned back.

Maybe the way into Viper's pants was pissing him off so royally he had no choice but to unleash his sexual frustration upon my naked, willing body.

I can dream, right?

Viper strode through the party.

"Girl, you are so lucky!" One of the club groupies called. "I love angry sex!"

A biker near her grinned and said, "Yeah? You want to get into a fight and then make up?"

I didn't hear the rest of the conversation because suddenly we were in the clubhouse and the screen door was slamming shut behind us. Perhaps this was my impending doom.

I couldn't wait.

Chapter 11

"Put me down," I protested.

"No," he snapped. "Why the fuck can't you follow simple directions?"

"I'm not a poodle," I clapped back. "You don't get to tell me to sit and stay. I woke up and you were gone. I'm an adult. I do what I want."

"Not only did you ignore the note," he gritted. "But you were down at the party."

"And there was nothing going on. Everyone still had their clothes on."

"They haven't busted out the moonshine yet. A few more hours and it will be a fucking fertility ritual out there."

"If you're trying to dissuade me, you just made me infinitely more curious."

We took the stairs and a few moments later, he opened his bedroom door and carried me across the threshold.

The wood reverberating in the doorframe was ominous, and trepidation swirled in my belly.

Viper tossed me onto the bed. He loomed over me, staring down.

Annoyance flashed across his face. "You disobeyed me."

Trepidation morphed into anger. I arched a brow. "*Disobeyed* you?"

I flipped my body so that I was on all fours. I peered at him over my shoulder. "So spank me, you brute."

"Sutton," he growled.

"Yeah, didn't think so," I taunted. I stood up on the bed, and for the first time I got to look down on him.

I slung my arms around his neck and jumped onto him, wrapping my legs around his waist.

His hands immediately cradled my ass, giving me a nice little perch.

"Better," I purred.

"What are you doing?" he demanded.

"Seducing you."

"Sutton, don't."

"Don't what?" I leaned forward and brushed my lips along his whiskered jaw.

"Don't do that," he said, though his voice sounded far less sure.

"Savage explained something to me that made a lot of sense." My fingers curled into the dark hair at his nape. "Want to know what he said?"

His voice was suddenly soft, like a caress. "By all means."

In that moment, I could imagine his lips trailing all across my naked skin. The vision caused goose bumps to erupt along every inch of me. "He said if I was down at the party, I was fair game because I'm not an Old Lady."

"That's right," he said.

I moved my lips to the other side of his jaw and

mirrored another kiss. "And it's become clear to me that you don't want me as fair game. But you also don't want me as your Old Lady, because being an Old Lady means something serious. Doesn't it?"

"It does."

I inched closer, pressing the heat of me against his stomach and ever so slowly rubbing against him.

"So you're kind of caught in this place, where you don't want anyone else to claim me, but *you* don't want to claim me, even though I know you want to fuck me. So, here's what we're going to do." I pulled back so I could stare into his heated brown eyes.

His voice was whisper soft, but deep and masculine. "What are we going to do?"

"I'm going to let you off the hook," I said. "For as long as I live in the clubhouse, I'm yours. I'll be off-limits. And when it's safe for me to go back to my life, we're done. No promises. No future. No harm, no foul."

"Bad idea," Viper rasped.

My mouth quirked up into a grin. "Or, it's the best idea ever. We let this thing run its course. No feelings. We don't get involved. It's just *sex*."

When he didn't reply, I wriggled against him.

"Oh, *come on*," I teased. "The big, bad biker isn't really saying no to this, is he? I mean, I'm basically dry-humping you here, telling you to have your way with me for as long as you're my leather shadow. Or are you afraid your dick will fall in love with me and then your heart will follow?"

"Haven't got a heart."

Sadness filled me, but I pasted on a bright smile. "Then you have nothing to worry about." I lowered one of my arms from around his neck and slipped my hand between us to rest on his fly.

"You think you can handle me?" he asked.

77

"I guess we'll find out."

Viper took one step toward the bed and gently removed his hands from beneath me.

I slid down his body, falling onto the bed. I leaned back on my elbows and peered up at him, my heart racing.

"You weren't lying, were you?" he asked.

"About what?"

"That it's been months."

"I wasn't lying," I said quietly.

He peered at me, his gaze slowly taking me in. "Better take my time, then."

Viper crouched in front of the bed, slipped his hands underneath my thighs, and pulled me to him. "Up," he growled.

I lifted myself and he eased my leggings off me, tossing them to the floor. I rested on my elbows and watched him.

He settled the heel of his palm against my mound.

I arched into his touch, my nipples pebbling underneath my sweatshirt.

Viper dragged my thong off, knelt onto the floor, and spread my legs.

He ran his finger through the short curls between my thighs. "I like this. I like this a lot."

He swirled a finger through my folds and my body came alive.

"Tell me what you like," he said gruffly.

"I don't know what I like," I admitted.

He lifted his gaze to mine. "What do you mean?"

"I mean, no one's ever…ya know…"

"Made you come with their mouth?"

I sighed. "Nope."

He closed his eyes and his jaw clenched.

"Viper?"

"Gimme a sec. I'm trying not to blow my load at the thought that I get to be the first one to do this for you."

He dragged my legs even closer and threw them onto his shoulders. He then took my hands that were flat against the bed and settled them on the sides of his head.

"Grip my hair," he commanded. "If you like something I'm doing, you grip it tighter. If you don't, loosen your hold and I'll know."

"Okay," I whispered. I gave his hair a little tug.

"Perfect, baby. Just like that."

I was still wearing my sweatshirt and was only bare from the waist down. But I felt fully naked—completely exposed.

Yet I trusted Viper.

The lights were on, and he could see everything.

His head dipped and he settled between my thighs.

"Relax," he whispered, his warm breath caressing my body. He turned his head and gently kissed the inside of my leg. His whiskers rasped against the sensitive skin of my inner thigh, causing goose bumps to erupt.

He slowly moved to the heat of me and gave me a long, slow lick.

I instantly gripped his hair tighter as shivers coursed through me.

He did it again.

I let out a low moan.

"Yeah, baby. Just lie back and enjoy it."

His tongue slid between my folds and his mouth easily found my clit.

My back bowed as he pressed his face deeper between my legs.

"Oh God, Viper," I moaned.

I was hot all over.

Touching myself in the shower, visualizing it was Viper, had nothing on the real deal.

He was an expert.

And he was determined to make me come.

His hands were underneath my ass, holding my body prisoner to his tongue. He alternated between sucking and licking, quick long strokes and short fast ones.

And when I gripped his hair tighter, he ruthlessly continued his ministrations.

My breaths came erratically. Pleasure swirled in my belly until I could no longer hold it in, and I finally came with a howl.

I closed my eyes as I gulped air into my greedy lungs. My jelly legs slid off Viper's shoulders.

When I heard the heavy thud of a boot hitting the floor, I cracked my eyes open.

Viper was staring at me, his mouth glistening with my release. He slowly removed his leather cut and set it down on the chair in the corner. Next came his T-shirt.

His muscular, broad chest was covered in ink.

He undid his belt buckle and shoved down his jeans and boxers in one movement.

My eyes widened.

I swallowed.

"You okay there?" he asked, his voice rough as he grasped his massive erection and gave it a pump.

"I'm glad," I croaked, and then cleared my throat to try speaking again. "I'm glad to know you weren't compensating for anything. You definitely have the goods to back up your massive attitude."

"You like my attitude. You'll like my dick, too."

"Stop flirting with me and get over here."

A smile stretched across his face. "In a minute. I like the begging."

"I don't beg," I protested.

"Hmm. Sounds like begging."

"No, begging would sound like this, '*Please, Viper. I need your huge, monster cock inside me right now or I'll just die.*'"

"Yeah, I like the begging—*a lot*."

I sat up so I could remove my sweatshirt and toss it aside.

"Christ, woman. Do you ever wear a bra?"

I gently caressed my breast and skimmed my thumb over my nipple. "Why would I do something like that? They just get in the way."

Viper growled—actually growled like an animal—and marched over to the nightstand drawer. He wrenched it open and pulled out a condom.

He tore the edge with his teeth and then quickly sheathed himself before coming over to the bed.

I scooted back and fell against the pillows.

Viper climbed onto the mattress and leaned over, positioning himself at my entrance. He gently pressed the crown of his shaft into me. He lifted one of my legs and wrapped it around his hip and held the back of my thigh as he eased into my body.

I hissed as he stretched and filled me.

He stopped immediately, his brown eyes searching my face.

"More," I gasped. I looked down at our joined bodies, watching in fascination as I took all of him, until he was fully seated inside me.

He didn't move for the longest time, not until I wriggled against him.

Viper gritted his teeth as he rocked against me.

"Oh, fuck," I moaned.

His tongue may have been magical, but it was like his

body had been made for this moment. I felt him everywhere, filling me up, his grip on my leg tight.

And when he began to thrust, my eyes rolled into the back of my head. He went deep and hard. His hand moved from my leg to cradle the back of my neck.

I met him stroke for stroke, clenching tightly around him.

It wasn't long before I was coming, screaming my release to his bedroom ceiling.

Because I'd come already, he rutted faster, his heated skin pressed to mine. Viper buried his face in my neck and slammed into me one final time, coming with a guttural grunt.

With a deep breath, he lifted himself up and slid out of me.

He sat on the edge of the bed, removed the condom, and tied it off.

Viper leaned over and pressed his lips to mine, thrusting his tongue between my lips until I nearly begged him for another round.

He pulled back. "I'm gonna shower."

I nodded.

He got up and tromped to the bathroom.

I turned my face away, suddenly feeling stupidly unsure about what had transpired. The door to the bathroom closed, and I jumped out of bed. I quickly pulled on my clothes, wincing at the tenderness between my legs.

As I popped my head through my sweatshirt, I noticed the damp spot on the comforter.

Cheeks aflame, I slid into my flip-flops and left his bedroom. I peeked into the hallway, glad to see no one was out and about. I made it back to my room without running into anyone.

I went into the bathroom to clean up.

Viper hadn't been at all how I expected him to be. I'd thought he'd be more bull-in-a-china-shop. I expected him to get the job done, but I hadn't expected him to thoroughly care so much about my pleasure.

I'd judged the leather-bound book by its cover, but I couldn't have been more wrong about the story inside. A story I was now fascinated to discover.

The last two days had been insane. I'd killed a man with my bare hands, watched as my home burned to the ground, and then fallen into bed with a biker I hardly knew. My emotions were all over the place and I was beginning to feel like I needed to reel them in. Even though it wasn't yet past ten, I was ready to crawl into bed and go to sleep.

I turned off the light and climbed under the covers. I was drowsy and almost asleep when my door burst open and a huge, hulking shadow loomed in the doorway.

I screamed in surprise.

"What the hell do you think you're doing?" Viper growled, slamming the door shut.

A moment later, the main light turned on. His glare was fierce, his dark hair was wet, his chest was bare, and he was wearing…

"You didn't," I said blandly.

"Didn't what?" he snapped.

"Put on the gray sweatpants. Slung low on your hips to show off that tapering *V*-to-crotch area."

"What the fuck you even talking about?" he demanded.

I raised my brows. "You didn't do it on purpose?"

"Sutton, I'm warning you—"

"You're *warning* me? You burst into my room without even knocking, looking like a living wet dream and you have the audacity to *warn me?*"

He rubbed the back of his neck in frustration. "You left."

"Left where?"

"My bed," he gritted out. "I told you I was showering and then when I got done, you were gone."

I blinked. "We were done."

"Like hell we were."

"Sleepovers are for couples. We're not a couple."

"Was I a bad fuck?" he asked bluntly.

"What? Of course not."

"Then I can't for the fucking life of me figure out why you'd leave my bed."

"I told you—sleepovers are for couples, and we're *not* a couple. We're expiration dating. Plus, I like to sleep alone and you're a big guy and I have a feeling you're a bed hog."

He stared at me for a long moment and then finally, he marched to the exit, turned off the light, and shut the door.

Chapter 12

"You look like hell," Savage said the next morning as he came into the kitchen.

I was standing at the counter, staring into my drink. It was more sugar and cream than coffee.

"Thanks," I said with a glare. "You're up early."

"Never went to bed." He grinned. "I'm still a little buzzed."

"Coffee?" I asked.

"Sure."

I poured him a cup.

"Didn't think you'd be up yet," Savage said when I handed him the mug. "Considering Viper took you to his room last night…"

I rubbed my forehead. "Right. You saw that."

"We *all* saw that. Believe me, we were all fucking surprised as hell. I guess every lid has a pot or whatever. So, you guys together now or what?"

"You're such a gossip," I said dryly.

"Yeah, I definitely am." He took a sip of his coffee. "I have no shame about it."

"I don't understand men," I stated.

"Men? Or Viper?"

"Aren't they the same?" I drawled.

"Are all women the same?"

I sighed. "You're insightful. Fuck. I wasn't expecting that."

"I like to keep people guessing. I'm more than a pretty smile with six-pack abs."

"You have a six pack?" I asked in amusement.

"Nah. It's an eight pack. Come on. Let's go out back and I'll help you sort through whatever's going on in your head."

We took our coffees and walked through the clubhouse. It looked worse for wear, and I surmised the party had been a rager.

I hadn't moved from bed after Viper left my room, and at some point I'd fallen asleep. My sleep wasn't restful, and I'd spent most of the night plagued with nightmares about the man I'd killed. And then when I finally woke up, I'd immediately begun to think about Viper.

The bonfire had been put out, but heat still radiated from the coals. Savage and I sat in two camp chairs as the early morning light streaked across the sky.

"This is weird," I said. "Talking to you about Viper and girl stuff."

"Pretend I'm Carla. What would you say to her?"

"Nothing," I admitted. "We don't really talk about stuff that much."

"You guys are friends though, right?"

"Yeah."

"Don't friends tell each other things? Ask for advice?"

"We keep our own council," I said.

"Ah."

"You don't?"

"Sometimes," he said. "But not usually. You haven't met Duke and Willa yet."

"Who are Duke and Willa?" I asked in confusion.

"Duke's one of the brothers, but the three of us have been friends since we were kids. Duke and Willa just kinda got together, so that's a new dynamic, but I still talk to them when I need to talk to people."

"Oh."

"No man is an island."

"Me. I'm an island. I figure shit out on my own. Always have."

Savage shrugged. "You mind if I smoke?"

"No. I don't mind."

Savage lit up a joint and took a drag. He offered it to me, but I shook my head.

"He got offended," I finally said.

"About what?"

"I left his bed. Went back to my own room after we were…finished. Which doesn't make any sense because we agreed to be together, but only while I'm staying at the clubhouse. By the way, I've never had to throw myself so obviously at a man to get him to have sex with me. I should be offended, yet I'm not."

"I really don't think you had to do that much convincing," Savage said with a wry grin. "If he hadn't been interested, he'd have let you know."

I drank some of my lukewarm coffee. "I don't get it, Savage. First, he uses the excuse I'm too young. But then he does a one-eighty almost immediately and we get together—but only under the parameters that it ends when I move out of the clubhouse. And then he gets offended that I left his room."

"Maybe he likes to spoon."

"Maybe you're not helpful," I groused.

"Maybe you hurt his feelings when you left."

I frowned. "I hurt *his* feelings?"

"It may come as a surprise to you, but men have feelings too."

"I know they have feelings," I snapped. "I just didn't think I'd hurt *his*. He can barely stand me half the time."

"You know the only way to get to the bottom of this, right?" Savage asked.

"What?"

"Talk. To. Him."

"What, like now?"

"Might as well. You guys are going to be around each other quite a bit, what with him being your protector. My advice? Wake him up with a blow job. He'll quickly forget his hurt feelings."

"I need girlfriends," I muttered.

"You're welcome," he said, taking another drag of his joint.

I headed back inside and left my coffee cup in the sink. Then I made my way to Viper's room.

I was suddenly feeling nervous. Should I knock? Or just walk in?

This was stupid. The man had seen me naked. He'd been inside of me not even twelve hours ago.

I wasn't shy, and I didn't like bowing down to anyone.

I quietly turned the knob and poked my head into his room.

Viper was a bed hog, and he slept diagonally. He looked like a naked, hulking beast with a gloriously muscled and tattooed back.

I closed the door behind me as I came into the room and tiptoed to the bed.

Just as I neared the side of the mattress, Viper reached

out and grabbed me. Before I knew it, I was pinned beneath him with a knife to my throat.

His breathing was hard, and it took a moment before he recognized me. He threw his knife across the room and it clattered to the floor.

"*What the fuck*," he growled.

"Morning," I wheezed.

He lifted himself off me. "What the fuck were you doing sneaking up on me like that?"

"Seriously?" I snapped. "You sleep with a knife?"

"Yeah, I do. And a pistol over there." He gestured with his chin.

I glanced at the nightstand. "I sleep with a pistol near me also," I reminded him. "Fuck, what have I gotten myself into?"

He sighed and then inched closer to me. He gently grasped my neck in his hands and skimmed his thumbs along the column of my throat. "Fuck, Sutton. I'm sorry. Didn't mean to scare you."

I blinked at the tender sincerity in his voice, and I nodded. "Maybe sleeping in your own bed last night without me wasn't a mistake after all."

His hands dropped from around my neck. "Why are you here?"

"Did I hurt your feelings?" I blurted out. "When I left your room last night?"

He rubbed a thumb over his lips, but it didn't hide the small smile peeking out. "No, you didn't hurt my feelings."

"Then why were you so mad?"

"Because I wasn't done fucking you."

My cheeks instantly bloomed with color.

"Why did you leave my room?"

"You said, and I quote, '*I'm gonna shower*'. Not, shower

with me, or don't move from that bed, or I'm not done fucking you. You made it sound like you were done. Like you didn't want me there anymore. And since I have pride, I left."

"Guess we didn't iron out all the shit like we thought."

"Guess not." I bit my lip. "I enjoyed myself, you know? Last night."

"Yeah, I know. You enjoyed yourself twice." His smirk was wicked.

I pushed against his warm chest, but he caught my hand and yanked me onto his lap. "I'm not good at this shit. I like being alone. I like doing my own thing. But I like your sass, and I *really* like fucking you."

"You like my sass?" I asked in surprise.

"Surprisingly, yeah, I do." He paused. "Everyone else keeps their distance, but you don't."

"You make it hard for people to talk to you when all you do is bark and grunt."

"And yet, that doesn't deter you."

"What can I say, *Beauty and the Beast* was my favorite fairy tale growing up. You're hotter than the beast, though."

"Thanks."

He leaned against the bed, so I was sprawled on top of him. He gripped the back of my thighs and spread them, gently spearing up toward me.

A zing shot through my core.

"You sore?" he asked.

"Yeah. But not that sore."

His eyes darkened. "Then get naked. You can be on top."

Chapter 13

An hour later, Viper and I finally left his room.

We'd made our peace with one another, come to an understanding of how this was going to go, and then we'd fucked each other's brains out.

For as long as I lived in the clubhouse, we were going to be together, and that meant sharing a bed. Including sleeping. I'd never had a sleepover with a man before, so it was going to be an interesting learning experience.

"Ah, I see my suggestion worked," Savage said when Viper and I came into the messy clubhouse living room.

"What suggestion?" another guy asked.

"Never mind," I muttered. "Who are you?"

"I'm Raze. Who are you?" Raze asked.

"Sutton," I said.

Viper moved and draped his arms around me but didn't say a word.

"Got it," Raze said. "You're with Viper."

"I'm not with—hey!" I glared up at Viper. "Did you just pinch me?"

"You want to get out of here and get breakfast?" Viper asked.

"Sure," I said.

"That was a full sentence," Raze said, shooting a look from Viper to Savage.

"Not just a full sentence. An actual question, not an order," Savage remarked. "I think Sutton just might be the one to tame the beast."

A crack of laughter suddenly escaped Viper's mouth.

I shot him an amused look as we shared a secret joke.

"Whoa. Am I still drunk?" Raze asked. "I'm so confused right now."

"Let's get out of here," Viper said to me.

"Bye, guys. See you later." I waved and then headed outside with Viper.

"What was Savage's suggestion?" Viper asked when we got to his bike.

"He said I should wake you up with a blow job to apologize for leaving your room last night."

Viper handed me the helmet. "How'd he know you left my room last night?"

"I told him. We were having girl talk."

"And his suggestion was a blow job for an apology?"

"Yep. Would it have worked?"

"I'm a dude. Of course, it would've worked."

"I'll remember that for next time." I put the helmet on my head. "Though, for the record, I won't be surprising you with shit, because frankly I don't want another knife at my throat. It would've been nice if Savage had warned me about that."

Viper straddled his bike. "Savage doesn't know."

"Oh." I frowned. "Viper? Why *do* you sleep with knife under your pillow?"

"Why do you own a pistol?"

"Fair enough."

It felt like there was more to the story, but Viper was clearly done with the topic because he cranked the engine of his bike and waited for me to climb on.

A hiss of air escaped my lips when I spread my legs across the seat and scooted up behind him. I was more tender than I realized.

The gates of the clubhouse opened, and we drove through. There was something about being on a motorcycle with Viper. Every feeling and concern I had was shoved out of my head and left behind on the asphalt. It felt like I was escaping all of my troubles.

It was ridiculous, of course. But for the first time in a long time, I didn't feel like I had to handle my problems on my own.

Viper pulled into a parking lot and cut the engine. I gingerly swung my leg over the seat and removed my helmet.

"Where'd you bring me?" I asked.

"French café."

I raised my brows. "You brought me to a French café?"

"Yeah. What's wrong? You don't like French food?"

"A diner would've been fine."

"Some of the Old Ladies love this place." He shrugged. "They've talked about it enough. So I thought, why the fuck not?"

I bit my lip, but it didn't stop my smile.

"What?" he growled.

"Nothing."

Before he could get off his bike, I went to him and wrapped my arms around his neck.

He settled his large hands on my hips and stared into my eyes.

"Thanks," I said quietly before brushing my mouth across his.

Viper stilled for a moment and then he angled his lips and thrust his tongue into my mouth and pulled me closer.

When he lifted his head from mine, his eyes were dark and needy. "Let's get some food," he rasped.

Nodding, I stepped back and waited for him to get off his bike before we went into the restaurant.

A hostess stood at the entrance. She smiled at me. "Welcome to La Creperie." Her gaze flitted to Viper and her smile faltered.

"Two please." I quickly wrapped my arm around his middle, sidling up close to him.

He immediately slung a heavy arm across my shoulder.

"Right this way," the hostess said, grabbing two menus.

I tried to let go of Viper to follow her, but when I attempted to move away, he pulled me back into his side.

He finally let me go when we got to the table. I slid into the booth, and he sat down across from me.

"Didn't take you for the PDA type," I said, reaching for my menu and flipping it open to the first page.

"I'm not the PDA type."

I raised my brows. "No? Throwing your arm around me and not letting me go was you *not* being the PDA type?"

He frowned. "What are you getting?"

"Don't know yet," I said. "And stop trying to change the subject."

"People can't hide how they feel about shit," he said. "You think I don't see women flinch when they look at me?"

"Viper," I murmured.

"It doesn't hurt my feelings," he stated immediately.

"It's not about that. But you saw it too—how the waitress stared at me."

"She's a hostess," I corrected.

"Hostess, waitress, they're all the same. You're not. And you wrapping your arm around me was a giant *fuck you*. Like I said, I like your sass."

I smiled slightly. "You're not that scary."

He raised his brows. "You didn't want to go with me the night we met."

"Because I didn't know you," I said. "Not because I was scared of you."

"Huh." He cracked his knuckles. "I better work on that then."

"Good morning," the server said as she appeared at our table. "Something to drink for you?"

"Coffee, please. With a lot of room for cream and sugar," I said.

"Black coffee for me," Viper responded.

"And have you had time to look things over?" she asked.

I glanced down at the menu and skipped over all the egg dishes and went straight to the crepes. "I'll have the chocolatiest crepe. Whatever that is."

The server smiled. "Got it. And for you…sir?"

"The meat lover's crepe." He handed her the menu, and she took mine before sweeping away.

Viper and I sat in silence while we waited for the coffees to be brought out. His gaze was intense as he stared at me, and I was doing everything possible not to look at him.

"Why are you being weird?" Viper finally asked.

"I'm not being weird."

"Liar."

I rolled my eyes.

"You think too much."

"I *think* too much?"

He nodded. "Yep."

"What makes you think I'm thinking?"

"Aren't you?"

I bit my lip and nodded.

"What are you thinking about?" he asked, his mouth stamped with the faintest trace of amusement.

"Starting my new job tonight," I lied.

"Try again."

"Try again, what?" I demanded.

"You're not worried about the job. So, what is it you're really worried about?"

The server appeared briefly to drop off our coffees. She left, and I dumped sugar and cream into my mug and stirred it.

"Two days ago, I was living alone in a trailer park. Now I'm living in a biker clubhouse, having premarital relations with you. Just strange."

"Any second thoughts?" he asked.

"Hmm. No." My cheeks flushed. "It was really good morning. Knife to the throat notwithstanding."

"I'm starting to think you have no self-preservation."

"I've always had more balls than brains," I quipped. "I'm also an *ask for forgiveness not permission* kind of gal."

"Leading with your emotions can do a lot of damage," he said.

"Leading with my emotions got you into bed," I pointed out. "By the way, you were ridiculously easy to get into bed. Crumbled like a paper napkin the moment I shoved my boobs in your face."

"They're nice boobs." He shrugged.

"Nice?" I raised my brows. "Earmuffs are *nice*."

"You want to talk about crumbling like a paper napkin?" He smirked. "You wanted me the second you met me, which was two days ago."

"Are you—is this you *flirting*?"

"Maybe."

"What will we tell the grandkids?" I jested. "We can't tell them how we met, or that you were really easy. Speaking of easy, is this your MO? Find a woman, pretend you don't want her, and then she throws herself at you?"

"I don't want to talk about me, I want to talk about you. How many men have you been with?"

"Does it matter?" I asked. "Whether I've been with two men or two hundred?"

Viper stared at me a while, his eyes suddenly bright. "You've only been with two men."

"What? Of course not," I lied. "Why would you think that?"

"You've only been with two men," he said again slowly. He leaned back in his seat. "Christ, when you said it had been months since you were with someone else…wait, am I really only the second man you've been with?"

"I don't want to be talking about this," I hissed.

"Well, we're gonna. Jesus, if I'd known…"

I crossed my arms over my chest. "If you'd known what? You wouldn't have jumped into bed with me?"

He shook his head. "I would've been gentler with you."

I blinked a few times. "You were plenty gentle. And, ah, thorough. Both last night and this morning."

Viper's grin was slow.

"Stop looking so pleased with yourself," I muttered. "It's unbecoming."

"You're the one who was pleased," he pointed out.

"Oh my God, stop."

"Who was he?"

I frowned. "Who?"

"The other guy."

"I really don't want to talk about him."

"Was he a shit to you?" he demanded. "Because if he fucking treated you badly—"

"You think I'd stand for that?" I raised my brows. "No. He didn't treat me badly. He just wasn't very good. In the way that you're good. We were together for a little while and then we weren't. I can see the wheels in your head spinning. I'm not answering any more of your questions."

"Just answer one last question, and then I'll drop it."

I waited.

"You barely know me."

"That's not a question," I pointed out.

"You barely know me, and yet you were all backbone and sass and fucking bravado. You put on a good show. But why did you sleep with me?"

"Because I wanted to. Plain and simple."

He frowned.

I rolled my eyes. "For fuck's sake, Viper. You were bitching about our age difference and that solidified it for me. I knew you'd have experience. And look at you. I knew it would be amazing. Stop trying to make this a bigger thing than it is."

"That fucker was shit in bed, wasn't he?" he asked. "Well, of course he was. He never went down on you, did he?"

"Ah," the server said, looking flustered and holding two plates of food. "Here we go."

"Thanks," I said with a sigh.

"Can I get you anything else?" the server asked, her cheeks flaming red.

"Nope. We're good," I said.

"I'd like hot—"

"We're good," I interrupted Viper.
"Right, enjoy." The server scampered away.
"I wanted hot sauce," Viper said.
"That was your penance for embarrassing me."
Viper grinned. "I'll suffer in silence."

Chapter 14

"Your turn," I said after I swallowed a bite of the sugary, chocolate crepe.

"My turn what? I'm not telling you how many women I've slept with."

"Oh, I don't care about that," I assured him.

His fork was halfway to his mouth. "You don't?"

"Your dick doesn't belong to me," I quipped. "I mean, it kind of does for the time being, but who you've stuck it in before me is no concern of mine."

The server slammed down the bottle of hot sauce. "Thought you might want this," she muttered.

"I tip well," I drawled. "I'm in the industry."

The server sighed. "Well, knowing that, I feel sort of bad that I've been telling the kitchen guys about your conversation."

"For fuck's sake," Viper mumbled.

"Let me ask you a question," I said to the server.

"Sutton," Viper warned.

"Hush, you. I want another woman's opinion."

"I'm listening," the server said.

"Would you care about how many partners your boyfriend has slept with before you?"

She shook her head. "No. Though, my last boyfriend had a different idea about what was before versus *during*."

"Shitbag," I stated.

"Big one." She looked at Viper. "But no. I wouldn't care. As long as he doesn't have something contagious, you know?"

"Valid," I said.

"Can I get back to my breakfast now?" Viper demanded.

"Thanks for your thoughts on the matter," I said to the server.

She saluted and walked away.

"You're shameless, you know that?" he asked.

"Says the man who carts me over his shoulder like a caveman every chance he gets."

"You like it."

"Of course, I like it. I wouldn't keep sassing the shit out of you unless I wanted you to take me back to your man cave and let you fuck the attitude right out of me."

He leaned back in the booth and peered at me.

"What?" I demanded.

"I like that you say what you mean and you don't hold back. I like that you don't play any fucking games."

"Haven't got time for games," I said. I dipped my finger into a dollop of chocolate on my plate and coated my lips in it.

"Some games, I'm down for," he growled. "You almost done? I'd like to get back to the clubhouse."

I raised a brow. "Yeah, I can guess why. But no. I'm not almost done. I'm enjoying my crepe and I'm enjoying the flirting. Also, you're not as bad at it as you think you are."

"I never said I was bad at flirting. I just don't have a lot of time for it. Like you, I'm a straight shooter."

I snorted.

"You don't think I'm a straight shooter?"

"I think you sent me a lot of mixed signals."

"Well, it's been like two days. So I guess we sorted that out rather quickly, didn't we?"

I licked my lips and reached for my coffee cup. "What is it you do for the club?"

"What do you mean?"

"I mean, what's your *job*? Carting my ass around and shadowing me isn't your regular job."

"And what a nice ass it is."

"Ah, there's that flirting in practice. And good to know you like my ass. Ass and sass."

A laugh rumbled out of him.

"That's pretty much all I've got going for me."

"You've got more than that," he assured me. "You've got courage, Sutton."

"Your job, Viper," I reminded him. "What's your job?"

"Intimidation."

"Huh?"

"My size," he pointed out. "I'm the muscle. If someone's fucking with the club, I talk to them."

"Talk to them. You mean with your fists?"

He inclined his head. "You don't fuck with my club. The club is family."

"Is this the same job you did for your chapter back in South Dakota?"

"Yeah."

"You're more than muscle and brawn. Just like I'm more than ass and sass."

"You think so?"

"I think you're a secret cinnamon roll."

"I don't know what that means."

"Never mind." I took my fork and cut off a bite of his crepe.

"What are you doing?"

"Eating your food."

"I can see that. You didn't ask."

"Girlfriends don't have to ask their boyfriends."

"They don't?"

"Your food is mine, and my food is mine." I rolled my eyes. "Jesus, Viper. It's like you've never had a girlfriend. Real or otherwise."

"I haven't."

I paused mid-bite. "You haven't?"

"Nope."

"But your experience…"

He raised his brows.

"I just thought, surely…"

"What?"

"That you had a girlfriend at some point. I mean, you're like, thirty-six. How the fuck have you… I guess you could've been a sexual savant."

"Thanks for dining with us today," the server said, setting down the check presenter.

"Seriously." I looked at her. "Your timing is impeccable."

"I aim to please," she said. "And from the sound of it, so does your boyfriend."

Viper choked on his coffee.

I smirked at the server. "I think you just became my new best friend."

∽

"You've really never had a girlfriend?" I asked as we stepped out of the restaurant into the sunshine.

"Do you ever stop asking questions?"

"I'm juiced up with caffeine and sugar. I have loads of questions, and plenty of energy in reserve."

"I told you I never had a girlfriend."

"Why?" I demanded.

He looked at me with annoyance.

"What?"

"You want to know? I'll tell you. When I was eighteen, I bought a motorcycle and went on a road trip. My bike broke down in one of those really small, really shitty towns that don't have a lot going for them. In that town, there was a woman, about six years older than me. A widow. I stayed with her for the summer. I've slept around plenty, but she was as close to a girlfriend as I've ever had, and I like it that way."

"You still keep in touch with her?" I asked.

"No. Why?"

"Just wondering if you had her address. I'd like to write her a thank-you note. She clearly taught you well."

He looped an arm around my shoulder and pulled me into his side. "You're a fucking handful, you know that?"

"I know it. Can I ask you something?"

"More? There's more?" he teased.

"You're different."

"What do you mean?"

"I mean, you're growly and surly and you hardly say two words to your brothers. But with me, you're…talkative."

"Don't read into it."

"Well, I'm gonna. You could just keep your mouth shut and tell me to get on your bike and keep your distance from me, you know? But you didn't. You don't."

"I'm starting to regret that decision."

I elbowed him in the ribs, causing him to grunt and then laugh.

"Just for that, you get to take me to the store. I've got to buy an energy drink or something. No way I'm going to make it through a shift tonight without a huge dose of caffeine."

We got to his bike, and he turned me to him. He gently skimmed his thumbs under my eyes. "You didn't sleep well."

"That noticeable, huh?"

"Little bit." He leaned down and gently bit my ear. "You could always take a nap."

"Yeah." I snorted. "I have an idea of the type of nap you want."

"Mine is more fun. I promise to let you sleep…after. And I'll wake you with more than enough time to eat and get ready for your first shift."

"Look at you, thinking of my needs." I smirked.

He moved his body, his erection pressing against me. "I might be thinking about my needs, too."

Chapter 15

"Well, I think that's everything," Mia said as we moved behind the bar. "Oh. If a customer gets fresh or handsy, you're absolutely allowed to use the water gun and hose him down."

I sniggered. "Seriously?"

The sassy brunette smiled. "Seriously."

"You might be the best boss ever."

"I try," she said with a laugh. "If you have any questions, just ask. But if you're quick on your feet, you'll be fine. And because it's your first night, you get to pick the first song on the brand-new jukebox. Just no country."

"What makes you think I'd choose country?" I asked with sham innocence.

"I dunno. Maybe it's the daisy dukes…"

"Or the cowboy boots?"

"Yeah, those, too." Mia glanced at the corner of the bar where Viper had commandeered a stool an hour earlier when we'd arrived. The bar technically wasn't open yet, but Viper wasn't leaving.

Mia brought her voice to a whisper. "He's glaring daggers at you."

"He's mad at my wardrobe choice. But he knows he has no say in the matter. So he has to glare in silence."

"Why's he mad at your wardrobe choice?" Mia asked in confusion.

"Oh, because we just started sleeping together," I said. "And that's brought out his possessive feelings."

Mia raised her brows at me and then glanced again at Viper.

"You're judging me, aren't you," I said with a sigh. "Since he and I just met."

"On the contrary," Mia said with a slow smile. "I'm stupefied. Viper being somewhat of a loner, I just figured…"

"Figured what? He was dating his hand?"

Mia's peal of laughter echoed throughout the empty bar. "God, you're a breath of fresh air. I love this so much. Will you excuse me a second? I need to call Colt. I'll be back in a few."

"Take your time. If a customer comes in, I can handle it."

She walked off the floor and headed to the back office.

Ignoring Viper, I went to the jukebox. I perused the song selection and fed a dollar into the machine. With a grin, I pressed a button. A moment later, Sting's voice filtered through the bar's speakers and "Roxanne" began to play.

I whirled around and danced up to Viper, who still hadn't moved from his perch atop the stool.

"Stop glaring. It's going to scare off all my customers."

"You don't have any customers."

"Yet," I stated. "I didn't ask you to sit at the bar all night during my shift. You're going to get bored."

"I'm not leaving."

I scowled back at him. "Don't make me use the water hose on you to cool you down."

"You might have to," he snapped. "Your ass is nearly hanging out of your shorts."

"Nearly," I repeated. "Not *actually*."

"It's the cowboy boots. I wasn't prepared."

"Prepared for what?"

"Prepared for wanting to see them thrown over my shoulders while my tongue is between your legs."

My eyes widened. "Aww, Viper. I didn't know you were a poet. A regular Lord Byron. Say something else."

"*The great object of life is Sensation—to feel that we exist—even though in pain.*"

"Beautiful," I murmured. "Who said that?"

He smirked. "Lord Byron."

I frowned. "Wait. You just quoted Lord Byron to me?"

Viper shrugged.

The door to the bar opened and a group of guys strode inside, immediately pulling my attention.

"Howdy!" I called out to them with a megawatt grin as I sauntered behind the bar.

"Howdy," one of the men replied with a dimpled smile.

I tossed a few coasters down onto the bar. "What are you fellas having tonight?"

After I poured three pints of beer and the customers took their drinks to a corner booth, I went to bother Viper.

"Howdy? Really?" Viper asked.

"What? It's a valid greeting, and I'm wearing cowboy boots. Plus, we're in Texas. Seemed appropriate."

He cracked his knuckles.

"Relax, cowboy," I said.

"Do *not* call me cowboy."

"Whatever you want, gov'nor."

He leaned closer and dropped his voice. "You're a brat, you know that?"

"Oh, are you going to spank me?" I taunted. "Please say yes."

I filled a glass of water and set it down in front of him.

"Give me a pen and a piece of paper," he commanded.

"Why?" I asked even as I went to the cash register and took a pen and printed off a section of blank receipt paper.

"I'm keeping a tally," he said. He took the pen and paper from me and made a line. "Every time you sass, I'm making a tally. Every tally is a spank."

"Is this supposed to deter me?" I demanded. "Because I gotta say, I like your version of a punishment system."

"You'll be the death of me, woman," he growled.

I blew him a kiss. "Ah, but what a way to go."

He lifted the pen and made another tally.

～

Three hours later, I was in the zone. The bar was busy. Mia was next to me pulling pints and pouring shots.

"Don't tell anyone this," Mia said. "But I've never seen that tip jar fill up so fast."

"It's the daisy dukes—I'm telling ya," I quipped.

"I'm sure it helps," she said with a laugh. "But no. Customers love you."

"They like my sass."

Viper was still sitting at the corner of the bar. He'd watched for several hours as I flirted and teased, but he had somehow managed to stay calm. It was the name of the game. Anyone who'd ever been in the hospitality industry knew that a little bit of banter went a long way.

"Is it wrong that I'm kind of sad that I haven't been able to use the water gun yet?" I asked Mia.

"It's still early," she drawled.

"Then I'll keep my fingers crossed. You mind if I hit the restroom real fast?"

"Go for it. There's a momentary lull, but another rush is coming. I can feel it."

I stepped out from behind the bar and headed to the restroom. I took a minute to myself and splashed some cool water on my heated cheeks. I'd been running around, and despite the top-notch air conditioning, I was hot.

After I washed and dried my hands, I opened the door and ran face-first into a broad chest.

"Okay, ow," I murmured, my hand going to my nose. I looked up and glared at Viper. "You followed me?"

Without a word, he grasped my hand and hauled me to the end of the hallway near the emergency exit. He pushed me up against a wall and caged me in with his large body.

A delicious thrill shot through me. "Whatchya doin'?" I asked breathlessly.

"I can't wait anymore," he growled.

"Wait for what?"

His hands quickly went to my jean shorts and unbuttoned them.

"*What are you doing?*" I hissed.

He didn't reply. Instead, he slid two of his fingers into my panties.

"Oh, God," I moaned, arching into his touch.

Viper swirled the tips of his fingers across my clit. He was relentless in pursuit of my orgasm.

I was so turned on by how he handled my body and the fact that anyone could walk down the hallway at any moment and see what we were doing.

"Please," I begged.

"Please what?" he growled against my ear.

"Please make me come."

He plunged a finger into me and put pressure on my clit with the palm of his hand.

I shuddered in pleasure.

"You know what I love?"

"What?" I gasped as he somehow went even deeper.

"I love that I barely touched you and you were wet."

I placed my hand on top of his shoulder and ground against his finger. It wasn't enough. I wanted another finger.

Or better yet, his cock.

And I had to get back onto the floor.

"I need more," I begged.

He added another finger. Viper thrust them in and out of me until I was gasping for breath and coming.

As I floated back down to reality, Viper removed his fingers from my panties. And then he stuck them in his mouth, licking my release clean from his skin.

I might've had an orgasm, but I wasn't satisfied in the least. I hastily buttoned my shorts. My thong was damp, and I glared at him.

He had the audacity to grin at me. "Now I can sit by the rest of the night, watching you flirt with customers, knowing I was the one that quite literally got into your pants."

"Heathen," I muttered and brushed past him, quickly getting back to work.

Mia had been right—there was another swarm of customers.

I slid behind the bar.

Mia shot me an amused look with raised eyebrows. I immediately felt my cheeks heat.

Viper's stool had been commandeered, so he stood at the end of the bar.

I looked into the sea of faces, surprised to see some that I recognized.

"Hey there, half-pint," Savage greeted with a grin. "I wanted to come and see how you were doing on your first night."

"Hi," I said. "And I'm doing well."

"Look at that tip jar," Mia said, pointing to the jar next to the register. "Sutton is killing it."

"What can I get you to drink?" I asked.

"Two pilsners and a club soda," he said.

"All that for you?" I teased.

"Nope." He looked over his shoulder as he moved to the side. "I'm with Willa and Duke."

"Willa and Duke," I repeated. "Oh right, the threesome."

"*Not* a threesome," the tall blonde woman protested with a grin.

A man with dark hair and dimples rested an arm around her shoulders.

"You weren't lying, Savage," Willa said. "She's adorable."

"You think I'm adorable?" I batted my eyelashes at Savage.

"Hey, don't look at me that way," Savage said as he reached into his leather cut for his wallet. "Viper is standing at the other end of the bar giving me a death glare. I don't feel like dying tonight."

"You're scared of Viper?" I teased.

"Damn right. The man looks like he can split logs with his bare hands," Savage quipped.

"That would be so hot," I stated.

"Holy shit," Willa said, elbowing Savage. "You so weren't lying."

"Told you," Savage said.

"Told her what?" I demanded.

"Told her that you had the hots for Viper," he said.

I definitely had the hots for Viper—which was the only reason I'd let him finger me in a public hallway less than five minutes earlier.

"I'm so fascinated by this," Willa admitted.

I pushed the three drinks toward them. "Don't listen to anything Savage says—he's a gossip."

"Damn right," Savage agreed.

"I like her," Willa said. "Hey, what are you doing tomorrow night? Are you working?"

"I don't know. Mia hasn't given me a schedule." I glanced at Mia.

"I wanted to see how you handled yourself," Mia admitted. "But I think I can toss you right into the deep end. You good to work Friday and Saturday nights?"

"Fuck yeah," I said.

"Great." Mia nodded.

"That means you're not working tomorrow," Willa said. "So, come to our place for dinner. You and Viper."

"Oh yeah, you have to come," Duke said.

I looked at Savage, and he nodded.

"Uh, okay. Thanks. You want to tell Viper, or should I?"

"I'll tell him," Savage said.

"And I'll wait to get the details until tomorrow." Willa winked. She took the club soda and moved away from the bar, Savage and Duke trailing behind her.

"You've done it now," Mia said. She picked up a bottle of tequila from the well and poured two shots.

"Done what?" I asked in confusion.

She handed me a shot and picked up the other. "Piqued the Old Ladies' interest. They will descend upon thee, offering libations and feasts so they may partake in a time-honored tradition of gossip."

I paused for a moment. "They want the scoop on my not-a-real relationship with Viper?"

She grinned and clinked her glass against mine. "Cheers."

Chapter 16

"I want pizza."

Viper cracked a smile. "You're bouncing."

"It's the B vitamins. Shouldn't have had that third energy drink. I might be awake until dawn."

It was just past two in the morning. Mia had shown me how to calculate the money in the till at the end of the night, tallying receipts, and counting to make sure everything matched sales. I hadn't been responsible for any money at Spurs, so it was new for me.

It wasn't hard, just different.

"We'll order when we get back to the clubhouse."

"Meat lovers with extra cheese."

"My kind of woman."

"And anchovies."

"No way."

I laughed. "Kidding. I'm just kidding."

He shook his head and handed me the helmet. "Menace."

"You're not going to sit at the bar every night I work, are you?" I asked.

"Get on the bike."

"Viper, you cramp my style."

"What style? You still pulled in a solid amount of tips, yeah?"

"It wasn't even about that," I muttered. "It was…"

"What?"

"What you and I did in the hallway."

"Remind me."

I snorted. "Faulty memory in your old age?"

"Watch it," he muttered. "And don't tell me you didn't like what we did in the hallway."

"Didn't say that." I put the helmet on. "But that can't be a regular occurrence if you stay and watch me every shift I work."

"Why can't it be a regular occurrence?"

"Because."

"That's not a reason. Get on the bike. I'm hungry. And I'm not talking about pizza."

"Did I just lose this fight?"

"Not a fight. But yeah, you're losing." He suddenly smiled, and it softened the harsh planes of his face. "Hop on. The sooner we get back, the sooner you get pizza, and the sooner I get what I want."

"I want what you want," I assured him, climbing on behind him. I wrapped my arms around his middle.

As we took off into the night, the humid air bathing my cheeks, I wondered why I was so comfortable with Viper. My first impression of him had been all wrong. Sure, he'd come across as scary, angry, and with a distinct *don't-fuck-with-me* vibe, but when we were sitting at the booth in the diner, I'd felt at ease with him.

A stranger had made me feel not so alone, not so terrified about what I'd done.

And the truth of it was that anytime I thought about

what I'd done, I immediately tried to think about something else. I was already burying it deep down and disassociating from it.

Because to think about it meant I had to analyze it. And to analyze meant I had to feel it. And I was queen of *if I don't think about it, it's not real.*

Healthy? Probably not. But it worked for me, and I'd learned long ago that sometimes all we had to do in life was get by.

Two younger bikers were guarding the gate of the clubhouse and they opened it to let us through. Viper parked in the gravel lot and cut the engine.

I hopped off and removed the helmet.

"Don't like you riding in bare legs," he said. "We gotta get you some new clothes."

"You just want to see me in leather pants," I teased.

"You got me."

"So transparent. I like it." I paused. "Savage talk to you tonight?"

"About what?" he asked.

"Dinner. Tomorrow night."

"Oh, that. Yeah."

We headed toward the clubhouse.

"You're good with it?"

"Sure. Why not. Food is food."

"Not just that," I said, pushing open the front door of the clubhouse. "Oh, wow. It's tidy in here."

"Clean-up crew," Viper said. "What do you mean *not just that?*"

"I mean, we were both invited, you know? Not just me. Not just you. We were invited together."

"And?" He went to the fridge and opened the door. He pulled out two cans of beer and handed me one.

I took it but didn't open it. "*Together.*"

He frowned. "Why do you keep saying that word?"

"Because I know how you feel about togetherness. Aside from our genitals co-mingling, I don't think you're a fan of togetherness or coupley things."

He choked on his sip of beer. "And you say I'm a poet."

"Oh yeah, thanks for reminding me," I said, switching gears. "How is it that you can oh-so-casually quote Lord Byron to me?"

"I'm a man with many interests," he said blandly. "And you know, I *can* read."

"I know you can read. I just didn't realize you could quote one of the greatest poets ever."

"Impressed?"

"Kinda. But don't distract me."

"Why not? You distract me all the time."

"By doing what?"

His gaze traveled down my legs. "What were we talking about?"

"I don't think I care anymore." I grinned. "Shower. Then pizza. Then…"

"Then?"

"You. Me. Cowboy boots."

He pulled out his cell phone. "Say less."

Sniggering, I cracked open the beer and took a sip. I ran up the stairs and headed to my room. I heard sounds of people having sex and throaty moans, but I paid them no mind.

I was living in a frat house. A biker frat house. But oddly enough, I liked it immensely. The trailer was lonely and I kept myself occupied so I didn't have to spend a great deal of time there. But going to sleep at night, pulling the covers up to my chin, without even an animal to curl up next to me…

Murdering a cartel member and falling in with a motorcycle club might've just been the thing to prevent me from becoming a crazy ferret lady.

It was a deranged way of thinking, but there it was.

I bent over and grasped one of my cowboy boots and hopped around on one foot to pull it off. The other came next.

As much fun as I had toying with Viper by donning my daisy dukes, I didn't plan on wearing them again. They weren't that comfortable, but I'd felt like I had to prove a point; that I could wear what I wanted, when I wanted.

And Viper had fallen right into my feminine clutches. He might've thought the hallway interlude was his idea, but I had a sneaking feeling that if I'd been wearing jeans, he wouldn't have felt the primal urge to mark me.

"Mark me." I snorted.

He wasn't a feral, possessive animal, but he definitely reminded me of one. It had only been three days with me, and he was already speaking in full sentences. Maybe it was foolish to think I'd had any sort of effect on him, but I felt like I had.

I turned on the shower and stripped out of the rest of my clothes. What changes had I gone through in the past few days?

Yeah, don't open that door.

I showered quickly, scrubbing the smell of a night working at a bar from my skin. When I changed into my pajamas, suddenly all the adrenaline poured out of me.

I didn't even think I'd make it until the pizza came.

There was a subtle knock on the door and a moment later, Viper opened it.

"You look wrecked," he said.

"I am. I thought I had all this energy. But now I just want to go to bed."

He stripped off his leather cut. "Then we'll go to bed."

"Correction, I want to *sleep*. Not have sex."

"Yeah, I know." He hung up his leather cut on the hook on the back of the door and then proceeded to remove his boots.

"What about the pizza?"

"The guys at the gate will take care of it." After he placed his pistol on the nightstand, he lifted his shirt over his head, folded it, and set it on top of the dresser.

I blinked at the immaculate display of ink and muscle, and it reminded me that I still hadn't had the time to explore his tattoos.

He leaned down to brush his lips against mine.

"You have minty breath," I said.

"I brushed my teeth. I had a feeling you were gonna want to crash."

"Look at you. You don't mind sleeping in here?"

"It's a bed, isn't it?"

I fell back against the pillows, my eyes half-mast. Viper took off his jeans and set them on top of his shirt. He hit the light and a moment later I felt the covers lift, and he slid in next to me.

"You have enough room?" I asked.

"No. I don't have enough room."

When I tried to inch away to give him some more space, he chuckled and then pulled me into his side. "That's not gonna do much."

"Ooh, you're a furnace," I murmured, my eyes closing. "Keep me warm. I run cold."

I was just about to drift off to sleep when he murmured, "Nothing cold about you."

∼

"Viper," I muttered into the pillow. "Viper!"

He came awake with a start. "Wha—"

"Ow!" I yelled.

"Shit," he growled. "What did I do?" The sound of his feet hitting wood echoed in my ears and a light came on.

"You elbowed me," I said, sitting up.

"What? Where?" He marched back over to the bed and took a seat on the edge. He gently cradled my face in his hands.

"My cheek," I said. "It's fine. I'm fine."

"Which cheek?"

I pointed to the right one and he skimmed a thumb across the apple of it. "I'm sorry," he said, his tone gruff. "I'm not used to sleeping next to someone."

I smiled slightly. "Me neither. I was smushed up against the wall."

"This wouldn't have happened in my room," he said. "My bed's bigger."

"You don't have to brag." I gripped his wrist and gave it a squeeze.

He let me go instantly.

I scooted down off the bed. "What time is it?"

Viper picked up his cell phone and glanced at the screen. "Little after four."

I rubbed my third eye as I traipsed to the bathroom. When I came back, Viper had moved toward the wall.

"That's my side," I said.

"We haven't slept together long enough to know the sides of the bed yet," he stated. "So, let's try it this way."

I hit the light and then climbed in next to him.

"Sleeping together, take two," I said. "Good night."

I quickly fell back asleep, but an hour later, I rolled over and fell off the bed. I hit the ground with a thud.

"What the fuck—Sutton?"

"That's it." I gingerly got up and turned on the light. "You're done."

"I'm done, what?" he asked in confusion.

"We can't share a bed. I was on the edge because you sleep diagonally. I rolled over and fell onto the floor."

"Fuck. I'm sorry. You hurt?"

I absently rubbed my elbow. "I'll be fine. I need to get some solid sleep. So you gotta go back to your room. We can try this again tomorrow in your bed."

"Oh, we can, can we?" He got up and slid into his jeans.

"You're not protesting going back to your own room," I pointed out.

"Honestly?"

I nodded.

"Honestly, I could use the uninterrupted sleep too."

"Then we're in agreement."

He finished putting on his boots, threw on his shirt, and grabbed his leather cut. His pistol was in a holster on the nightstand which I handed to him.

He took it from me.

"Er—good night," I said awkwardly before pressing a kiss to the corner of his mouth.

He didn't turn his head to meet my lips. He didn't kiss me good night.

Viper pulled back and headed to the door.

"See you in the morning," I called out to him.

With a nod, he opened the door and then left.

Great, now shit is weird between us.

But what the hell was I supposed to do?

I didn't *want* him to leave, but I needed sleep.

What was he really upset about? He'd left without putting up a fight and had even agreed that going back to his own bed was the right call.

Then why did I feel so shitty about it?

What was I doing? Why did I think that Viper and I could be in a physical relationship without all that other stuff like *feelings*.

I really like him.

"Well, that's new," I muttered.

My brain had turned on, and I needed something to distract me from my revelation.

I went to the dresser and riffled through my underwear drawer. With a frown, I pulled everything out, but my vibrator was definitely not where I'd put it.

Had Viper…

No.

Definitely not.

Well, maybe.

Maybe he'd taken it. But why?

I grabbed my phone off the nightstand and was about to send him a text when I suddenly realized I didn't have his number.

I'd spent three days in his back pocket, and I didn't even have his phone number.

That would have to change.

I settled down into bed, listening to my own breathing and the drumming of my heart.

Was Viper asleep already? Or was he in his bed, thinking of me?

My hand moved and slid into my panties.

I touched myself as I thought of him thinking of me.

I glided a finger between my folds. I imagined we were in the same room, and that we were watching each other as we brought ourselves to our releases.

In my mind, I could picture his clenched jaw, his glittering gaze as he stroked his long, hard shaft.

He was beautifully made. A massive, muscular canvas for the art that marked his skin.

I gasped as the first tremors of pleasure bloomed between my legs. I rubbed harder and then faster until I crested the wave of my orgasm.

My body went slack, and my eyes were closing.

Dreamily, I rolled over and fell asleep.

It felt like I'd only rested a few minutes when I was jarred awake by my vibrating phone.

With a groan, I cracked a lid and reached for my cell on the nightstand. I glanced at the screen and quickly sat up.

I pressed the answer button and put the phone to my ear.

"You have a call from an inmate at Botsworth Prison. Say 'Yes' or press '1' now to accept the call, or hang up the phone to deny," said the automated voice.

"Yes," I replied.

"Please hold."

A moment later, the line connected.

I took a deep breath. "Hi, Dad."

Chapter 17

There was already a fresh pot of coffee made and I wondered who was awake. I poured myself a cup, sugared and creamed it heavily, and then wandered to the backyard.

Viper was sitting on the top of the picnic table, a mug of coffee by his side. He was wearing a pair of jeans and his boots, along with a green T-shirt, but not his leather cut.

He glanced at me as I slowly approached.

"Mind if I join you?" I asked.

He frowned. "I don't mind."

"Then why are you scowling?"

"Why are you being so formal? Normally, you'd just plop your ass next me and not bother asking for permission."

"You're mad," I stated with a sigh.

"Damn right, I'm mad."

"Look, if it makes you feel any better, I slept rotten without you there anyway. Okay?"

He rubbed the back of his neck. "I'm not mad at you. I'm mad at me."

"Why?" I climbed up onto the table and perched next to him.

Viper didn't reply right away. Instead, he took a long drink of his coffee. "I don't spend the night with women."

"Okay," I said. "I don't spend the night with men."

"That's because you've only had one other partner," he said. "I was trying to say that I don't spend the night with women I *fuck*. But I *wanted* to spend the night with you."

"And you're upset with yourself for feeling that way?" I asked.

He inclined his head.

"Is this a good idea?" I blurted out. "I mean, should we stop sleeping together?"

"We're not sleeping together. We're fucking. Last night you made that clear."

"This is a mess," I muttered. "It's been three days, and it's already complicated. Why did I even think sex with you was a good idea?"

"Because it *is* a good idea. A great idea, actually."

I bumped my shoulder against his arm. "You're just saying that so you don't have to give up a sure thing."

"So…you want to stop this?"

"My head says we should stop, but my body says *no fucking way*. Do you want to stop this?"

"No."

"Then, we're good. Right?"

"Yeah. We're good," he said.

Nodding, I took a sip of my coffee. I didn't want to examine the feeling of relief that settled in my chest, so I ignored it.

"My turn to ask a question," I said as I gripped my

mug. I looked at him dead-on and asked, "Did you take my vibrator?"

"Yes."

"I'd like it back."

"No."

"No? What do you mean, *no*?" I demanded.

"You don't need it anymore. You have me."

"Well, I didn't have you last night, and I needed some help falling asleep."

"You could've come to my room and begged me to fuck you."

"There are so many things wrong with that sentence." My gaze narrowed. "You're really not going to give it back?"

"Nope."

"Oh, I see." I nodded. "Got it."

"What is it you've *got*?"

"You're jealous of a battery-operated device."

"I am not."

"Of course you are. Otherwise, you would've left it in my underwear drawer where it belongs. And, by the way, invasion of privacy. What were you doing rooting around in my underwear drawer?"

He didn't reply.

"Viper," I warned.

"You're adorable."

"Thank you. Now answer the question."

"You don't need your vibrator anymore because you have me," he said again.

"Some couples use it as an added bonus," I stated.

"We're not them."

"Jealous of a device. I was thinking of getting one of those robot vacuum cleaners one day. Or will that offend you as well?"

"I'm not offended," he said, his voice lowering. "I just know I can do a better job than your vibrator. Besides, why would you want to settle for a vibrator when you can use the real deal?"

"Okay," I said with a nod. "You can keep the vibrator on one condition."

"What's that?"

"You're not allowed to touch yourself."

"What?" he bellowed.

"You heard me. If I'm not allowed to use something, neither are you. So, if you want it, you get it from me, not your hand. Understand?"

His mouth twitched like he wanted to smile, but if he did he never let it show. "So then…any time I want sex, you're saying all I have to do is come to you?"

"That's right."

"What if it's the middle of the night?" he asked.

"Wake me."

"What if we're in public?"

"We'll find somewhere private for a quickie," I said, my cheeks heating at the thought.

"What if you're working?"

"Then you wait until I'm done working. I don't want to take advantage of Mia's generosity by sneaking off the floor once a shift so you can get your jollies off."

"Twice a shift," he said with a smirk. "Last night, I wanted to pull you off the floor again, but I contained myself."

"Bravo, Viper. So, does the same go for me? What if *I* want it in the middle of the night?"

"Climb on top and have your way with me."

Grinning, I continued our little game. "And if we're in public?"

"Bathroom doors lock."

"I see." I took a sip of my coffee. "I feel like we need to seal this verbal contract with a handshake."

"If you mean your hand shaking my dick, then yeah, I'm good with how we seal the deal."

"Viper, you charmer, you." I chuckled. "Why are you up so early?"

"Never went back to bed."

"You don't sleep regular hours, do you?" I asked.

"I'm lucky if I get a solid six hours of sleep in a row, undisturbed. I'm not a heavy sleeper."

"How are you not exhausted all the time?"

"I am." He smiled slightly. "I've just learned how to deal with it."

I finished off the last of my coffee as I mulled over his words.

The back door opened, and Savage strode outside with a mug. His blond hair was askew. His eyes were bloodshot, and his skin was pale.

"You look like hell," I said in way of greeting.

"Morning to you, too." He glowered.

"How are you hungover?" I asked him. "I poured you like, two beers."

"I met up with Carla," he muttered. "And fuck, that woman can drink me under the table."

"That's my girl." I grinned. "You just come from her place?"

He nodded.

"How did you stay on your motorcycle?" I asked.

"Sheer force of will. Breakfast is on the way."

"Breakfast. I'm so in the mood for breakfast," I said and looked at Viper. "Boots?"

"Yeah, Boots."

"Wait," Savage said. "I just said breakfast is on the way."

"That implied that you ordered food for yourself," I said. "Did it mean something else?"

"I begged Brooklyn," Savage said with a grin.

"Fuck yes," Viper growled. "Well done."

"Brooklyn? Who's Brooklyn?" I asked.

"Brooklyn is Slash's Old Lady," Viper said.

"She owns Pie in the Sky," Savage added.

"Never heard of it," I admitted.

"It's a bakery café and her biscuits are the best thing I've ever had in my mouth. Not including breasts and—"

"You better be talking about chicken breasts," I said lightly.

"Hmm, fried chicken," Savage moaned. "I could eat some fried chicken. I'll beg Willa to make it tonight for dinner."

"Do you just have a roster of women who rotate feeding you like an animal?" I asked in amusement.

"Yes." Savage grinned. "It's the best deal there is. All right, lovebirds. I'll be inside sucking down more coffee. Food should be here soon." He went back inside.

I looked at Viper, who was staring at me with an expression I couldn't decipher.

"What?" I demanded.

"Nothing."

"Not nothing. Tell me."

He rubbed his thumb along his whiskered jaw and said, "You fit in here."

"I guess." I shrugged.

"You talk to Savage like you've known him for years."

"He makes it easy."

"I don't make it easy?"

"We weren't talking about you—we were talking about Savage."

He was quiet for a moment. "Do you tell him things?"

"Things? What things?"

"Personal things."

"No. We just talk and joke."

"What do you talk about?"

"You, mostly."

"Me?" He arched a brow.

"Well, he was concerned that your gruff attitude was going to put me off. He just gave me a heads-up is all."

"What kind of heads-up?" he demanded.

"Nothing particular," I assured him. "He just said you had a rough past and that I shouldn't take your surly nature personally. Which I don't, by the way. I don't get my feelings hurt easily."

He snorted. "You do have certain resiliency."

"You gonna drink the rest of your coffee?"

"It's black. We could just go inside and get you a refill."

"I'm enjoying being out here. With you," I added.

Viper handed over his mug.

"Viper?"

"Hmm?"

"Is your past the reason you sleep with a knife?"

"We addressed the knife situation already."

"No, we didn't. At least not to my satisfaction."

"I take care of your satisfaction just fine."

"Stop being cheeky," I mock-warned.

"Why? Are you afraid you won't be able to keep your hands off me?"

"I think it's been proven that I haven't been able to keep my hands off you. It was a very immediate gratification moment. One I do not regret."

"Good."

"Don't deviate. The knife, Viper."

"I like your sass, Sutton. I like that you're demanding and vocal in bed. But this inquisition shit has got to stop."

"Demanding? Vocal? Say what now?" I asked, feeling my cheeks heat.

"You tell me what you want, and I like that. And you're noisy. I like that very much."

I buried my head in my hands. "Does that mean everyone can hear me?"

"God, I hope so."

"What? Why would you want that?"

"So everyone knows," he said quietly. "Knows that I'm pleasing you."

"That sounds kind of egotistical."

"Damn right it is."

I wasn't sure what to say about that and I didn't want to continue down this line of conversation. "I think I'd like breakfast now," I said, jumping off the table.

"Not so fast," he said.

I turned to look at him over my shoulder.

His grin was slow.

"You're serious?"

"Yup."

"Now?"

"Yup."

"Before I even get breakfast?"

He got up off the table and came close to me. "If you hadn't kicked me out last night, I'd still be in your bed."

"And that means…"

"It means I would've been sliding into you from behind, making you scream my name before you even had your first cup of coffee."

I swallowed, my throat suddenly dry.

He gently grabbed a fistful of my hair and wound it around his knuckles and then tugged me toward him. "Doesn't that sound better than bacon and eggs?"

"I don't eat eggs anymore," I said, my mood suddenly souring. "Not after…"

"Fuck. Right."

I didn't want that reminder to interfere or take up space in my brain, so I forced a smile. "But pancakes… I could delay my desire for pancakes, but I'm going to need you to make it worth it."

Chapter 18

Savage and a few brothers whose names I didn't remember were sitting in the living room, chowing down on food.

"You just missed Brooklyn," Savage said. "She had to get back to the bakery."

"Bummer. I would've liked to thank her for bringing over the food." I went into the kitchen and started opening cabinets, looking for plates.

"You'll meet her soon," Savage said. "She said she understood, though."

"Understood what?" I asked as I avoided the quiche and took only bacon strips and sausage patties.

"Why she didn't get to meet you." Savage picked up a pastry-looking thing and took a bite. "She knew you were having sex with Viper, and she totally didn't blame you."

I blinked, my gaze darting from Savage to the other guys in the room who were sniggering.

Savage winked at me, clearly trying to get my goat and embarrass me.

Well, I liked to play with fire.

"There are very few things in life better than a

morning screw," I said. "You might want to look into it. Anyone need anything while I'm still standing?"

They shook their heads.

"Where's Viper?" Savage asked. "Did he fall asleep after you had your way with him?"

"Okay, enough," I stated.

"Sorry, darlin'," a dark-haired man said. "But if you stay here, your business is *everyone's* business."

"Which one are you?" I asked.

"Bones."

"Bones. I could make things very unpleasant for you."

He leaned back in the recliner. "You gonna sic Viper on me?" he grinned. "He's my boy. We've been brothers for years."

I took a bite of bacon and chewed it before answering. "The next party you guys have where there's some random woman sucking your tongue into her mouth like a vacuum, I'm going to tell her you've got a very contagious, very prominent rash that two rounds of antibiotics couldn't cure."

Bones blinked blue eyes and then grinned. "Well played."

"Thank you." I beamed.

"Come sit over here, darlin'. Right on my lap will be fine," another biker said, patting his knee. "Let's get better acquainted and see if I can convince you to throw Viper over for me."

"And you are?" I asked.

"Smoke."

"Hmm. I don't want to be the cause of any bloodshed, so I think I'll eat over here. And for the record, I'm with Viper, so no funny business from any of ya."

"No woman is ever *with* Viper," Bones said. "He doesn't put up with their shit."

"I'll gladly put up with your shit," Smoke flirted.

"I put up with her shit just fine," Viper announced, the trod of his heavy boots across the floor.

"You do, don't you?" I batted my lashes at him and then handed him an empty plate. "Wasn't sure what you wanted."

"I'll get it." He took the plate and filled it. Then he came to stand behind me, caging me between him and the counter.

"Well, fuck me," Smoke murmured.

"No thanks," Savage drawled.

"Viper seems almost…" Bones trailed off.

"Almost what?" Viper demanded.

"Tame," Smoke said. "Right? Like he's speaking in full sentences."

"She tamed the beast," Bones said in agreement.

"That's what I said!" Savage quipped.

I looked up at Viper. "Eggs and blood don't go well together."

I would know.

"You would deny me the joy of punching them in the face?" Viper asked.

"Postponed gratification," I said.

Viper sighed. "I can wait."

"She didn't just tame the wild beast," Bones said. "She slayed the dragon."

"The grumpy as fuck dragon," Smoke said. "It's amazing what some tail will do to a man."

Viper slammed his plate onto the counter and stormed across the living room to a grinning Smoke. He grabbed Smoke by the shirt collar and effortlessly hauled him up. "She's not tail, fucker. Show a little respect."

Viper released Smoke and then stormed outside, slamming the front door.

The living room was quiet for a moment and then Smoke started to laugh. Savage and Bones followed suit.

"I don't get it," I said.

"You will, half-pint. You will," Savage retorted.

With a frown, I grabbed my plate, filled it again with some more food, and went out to the front porch.

Viper stood at the railing, staring out toward the gate of the clubhouse. I didn't say anything as I went to stand next to him. I set the plate of food in front of him.

"I've never had a man defend my honor. Gotta say, I'm a fan."

The corner of his mouth twitched.

I reached up to touch it. "Come on. Smile. I know you want to."

Viper's lips pulled into a grin.

"Ah, there it is." I dropped my finger and stayed next to him.

He picked up the fork and began to eat.

"Why do you live at the clubhouse if you don't like everyone being in your shit?" I asked.

"Before you got here, I didn't have any shit. Now my shit is front and center, and I'm not used to it. That means you, by the way."

"I *am* wearing very cute jeans." I wiggled my butt like I had tail feathers. "You shouldn't let them get to you. They were just trying to rile you up like friends do."

"I don't want to be riled up," he said. "Though, I guess I can't really blame them. I'm not what you call chatty."

"You're chatty with me."

"No. I talk to you. Big difference."

"Okay." I fell silent.

"Thanks for this," he said after he'd finished the food.

"Sure." I clasped my hands and rested them on the wooden railing. "So, if I'm not tail, what am I?"

"A pain in the ass."

"That's still tail," I pointed out dryly.

"Look, I wasn't thinking. Before I knew it, I was marching over there, ready to punch his face in."

"Nope."

"Nope what?"

"I don't buy it. I don't take you for a guy who just reacts to something someone said like that. You're too collected, too confident for that."

"Believe what you want." He shrugged.

"You didn't like him calling me tail," I said. "It's okay, Viper. The first step is admitting you have a problem."

"And what's my problem?"

I stood up on my toes and kissed his cheek. "You're starting to fall in love with me."

"Fuck no, I'm not."

I couldn't stop the bubble of laughter that escaped my lips at his horrified expression.

"Of course, you are," I said in delight. "If all you cared about was sex, you would have let him talk about me like I was just a piece of ass. But you were ready to flatten him for assuming that's all we were. Ha, get it? Ass—*ass*uming?"

"I'm warning you," Viper said.

"*Big tree fall hard*. Don't worry. It'll be our little secret."

"Falling for you isn't happening," Viper snapped. "This shit is ending as soon as you move out of the clubhouse. Feelings are bullshit." He pushed away from the railing and headed down the front porch steps. "I'm going for a ride."

Without another word, he strode toward his bike. He pulled a pair of sunglasses from his leather cut and perched them on his nose. Viper climbed onto his motorcycle, cranked the engine, and pulled out of the gravel lot, a trail of dust stirring up behind him.

The guys opened the gate, and Viper drove through and disappeared out of sight.

I heard the sound of the door open behind me but didn't turn.

A moment later, Savage sidled up next to me with a fresh cup of coffee in his hands. "Where'd Viper go?"

"A ride," I said, staring off in the direction that Viper had ridden.

"So," Savage began.

"So," I repeated.

"Viper doesn't think you're a piece of tail."

"Apparently," I said with a rueful smile. "I don't think he realized it until he said it. Are you guys gossiping about it in there?"

"Damn right we are."

I grinned. "I love that you have zero shame over it."

"What about you?"

"What about me, what?"

"Is Viper just a piece of tail for you?"

"Viper and I have an understanding," I said. "When I move out of here, our relationship, or whatever this is, is over. Done."

"Hard to be done when there are real feelings involved."

"According to Viper, feelings are bullshit. I'm inclined to agree."

"Ah, another one who's emotionally stunted. Have I seen you at the meetings?"

I sniggered and bumped against him. "Is that why you're so go-with-the-flow when it comes to Carla?"

"We're not talking about me and Carla. We're talking about you and Viper."

"Can I ask you something? I mean, really ask you something, and have you give me an honest answer?"

"Sure."

"It stays between us, okay?"

"Okay."

"I mean it. Your gossipy lips need to be sealed."

"I swear. Now what's on your mind?"

"Do you think it's weird? I mean, Viper and I hardly know each other, but we have this rhythm. It's easy, you know?"

"Easy? With Viper? I don't believe it."

"Okay, not *easy*. But his attitude doesn't scare me. His surliness isn't a turn off. I get the feeling…"

"What?"

"He's lonely," I said softly. "Like, deeply lonely. And even though he's part of this club, it's still easier for him to keep himself separate, so he doesn't have to deal with all the stuff that comes with really being a part of something."

"Hmm. I'm not what you call sensitive, and I know jack all about psychology, but it sounds to me like you're doing this thing called *projecting*."

"Projecting? What the hell does that mean?"

"It means you're putting what you feel all onto Viper. You keep yourself separate so you don't have to deal with the consequences of really letting someone in." He shrugged.

"Huh. Not sure how I feel about your assessment. I'm going to choose to ignore the potential insight and mash down any sort of thoughts on the matter."

"Hey, that's how I live my life. It works pretty well." He smiled.

"You're a good egg, Savage," I said. "Thanks for shooting the shit with me."

"Happy to shoot shit any time," he said.

Chapter 19

The shower curtain slid back, and Viper stepped into the tub behind me. My eyes widened. "Excuse me, have we met?"

Without a word, he wrapped his hand around a fistful of my wet hair and tugged me toward him.

I pressed a hand to his muscled chest to steady myself.

He let go of my hair and then hoisted me up, pinning me between the wall and his body. I felt his erection against me.

His eyes were dark with need and his jaw was clenched. He leaned down and captured my lips with his. His tongue thrust into my mouth, ruthless and dominating.

I ripped my mouth from his. "What are you doing here?"

He bent his head and nipped my neck. "I thought it was obvious."

"The beastly biker needs servicing?" I asked.

Viper reached down and lifted my leg to wrap around his hip and then his hand dove between my thighs.

"Oh," I moaned as he teased me.

He slid a finger into my body, pumping slowly.

I gripped his shoulder and gasped, wanting—needing—more. "Viper."

"What, Sutton? What do you want?" he growled as he continued to thrust his finger inside me.

"More."

He slowly added another large finger, stretching and filling me. He knew exactly how to touch me to make me crazy, to make me want more.

I undulated my hips in rhythm to his thrusting fingers and it wasn't long before I was coming. I gripped his shoulders and screamed out my release.

He pumped his fingers a few more times before slowly sliding them out of me. Viper kept me pinned between him and the wall, and didn't take his eyes off me.

I wiggled against him, and he slowly lowered me to the tub. I backed him toward the shower head, so the hot water streamed down his shoulders and back.

I knelt in the tub and grasped the back of his thighs and then I took him into my mouth.

His hands immediately sank into my hair and gripped my head. He was big and I couldn't take all of him, but I wanted to make him come with me on my knees and him in my mouth.

I let go of his thighs and gently cupped his testicles, with my other hand wrapping around his shaft at the base. I gave it a squeeze while tonguing his crown.

"Yes," he hissed. "Just like that."

I licked him, devoured him, and when I wanted to make him lose all control, I took him as far as I could, nearly choking.

He groaned and fucked my mouth, deep enough that I felt him at the back of my throat.

"I'm close," Viper stated.

He tried to pull out, but I refused to let him go. I squeezed and sucked until he had no choice but to come in my mouth.

I swallowed him down, every last drop of him.

When he was finished, I released him and stood.

Viper had his hand pressed against the wall, as if to keep himself upright. He shuddered. "Fuck, Sutton."

I grinned.

He grasped the back of my neck and pulled me to him.

"Next time, do you think you could knock? Give me a little heads-up?"

Viper paused. "I scared you."

"Scare is too strong a word. But yeah, you gave me a little heart jump."

"Sorry about that," he said, his tone low and soft.

"The orgasm was a good apology. You're forgiven."

He cracked a smile.

"You were gone a few hours. Was it a good ride?" I asked, handing him the soap.

"Hmm."

"Was that a yes or a no?" I demanded.

He began to wash, and I was momentarily entranced by his glistening skin.

"It was…enlightening."

"What was enlightening?"

"Just had some thoughts that needed to be put in their place. And they're now put in their place." He stepped underneath the warm spray and washed off the soap.

"Are you gonna share those thoughts with me?" I asked.

"Nope."

I wrinkled my nose at him. "So, you're not angry with me?"

"Angry? Why would I be angry?"

I reached out and traced a tattoo on his left pectoral. It looked familiar, like I'd seen the design before, but I couldn't quite place it.

"Because I was teasing you," I said. "About feelings."

"I'm not angry."

I knew nagging him wasn't going to do anything, so I let it be.

It was probably better that way. The less both of us discussed deeper things like feelings, the better off we'd be.

I got out of the shower and dried off. I'd laid out the clothes I wanted to wear that night to Willa and Duke's. I slid into a pair of tight, dark jeans and a loose white tank.

Viper came into the bedroom, a towel slung around his waist. How the hell did I want him again after what we'd just done in the shower? He was turning me into a sex maniac. I wasn't sure I minded.

"You can't wear that," Viper said.

"Excuse me?"

"You can't wear that."

"Okay, buddy, let's get something straight. You don't get to tell me what to wear."

"Sutton, you can't wear that because I can see your nipples."

"Women have nipples."

"I can see your areola, and if *I* can see them, so can other people. And I'd prefer not to be at dinner with a bunch of people staring at your tits. So for the love of God—and my sanity—will you please wear something else?"

I blinked. "I'll wear something else."

He grunted.

"For the record, I had no idea you could see my nipples."

"So you didn't do it on purpose to get a rise out of me."

"Rise, or...*rise?*"

He dropped the towel. Sure enough, he had a massive erection.

"Are you always hard?" I asked in surprise. "Like do you just walk around with a boner?"

"You."

"Me what?"

"My boner is all because of you. Your mouth gets me hard. Your nipples get me hard. Jesus, you smile and I get hard."

My smile turned into a full-face grin. "God, you're getting really good at compliments." I dragged my finger down across my tank, over my nipple.

"Don't," he muttered. "You start doing that, then we're going to be late."

"Fine," I said. I reached for the hem of my tank and pulled it over my head.

"Sutton," Viper warned.

"What?" I demanded.

"You're doing it on purpose."

"Doing what on purpose?" I walked to the dresser and placed my hands on the top of it and spread my legs. I looked at him over my shoulder and grinned.

"Evil."

"Can't resist me, can you?"

Viper's expression shifted as he grasped his shaft and gave it a pump. "No. I don't think I can."

"Well? What are you waiting for?" I shook my butt at him.

He released himself. "Nah. I think I'll make you wait."

"Make *me* wait?" I frowned. "Making me wait means making yourself wait."

"Yep. Delayed gratification."

"I thought we had a deal," I said. "Any time I want it or you want it, we do it. That's the opposite of delayed gratification. That's *instant* gratification. I'm a fan of instant gratification."

"Too bad. I'm going to make you suffer for the next few hours."

"That sounds like a challenge."

"It is."

"I just want to make sure I understand this correctly; you'd rather us both be tortured by our own horniness, when instead you could have your way with me right now."

"I'm thinking of hours from now, when you're so horny you can barely contain it, and we get back here and you jump me like you'll die if I'm not inside you."

"Oh." I blinked. "That sounds good too."

Chapter 20

Willa and Duke lived out in horse country. When I climbed off the back of Viper's bike, I breathed a sigh of relief. I hadn't realized how cooped up I'd been in the clubhouse.

Viper cut the engine and then swung his leg over the motorcycle. He grabbed the plastic bag with dessert from his handlebar.

I might've been homeless, accepting the kindness of the club, but that didn't mean I was going to show up to dinner empty-handed.

We walked up the porch steps and I rang the bell.

A moment later, a red-haired teenage girl opened the door. "Hi, Sutton," she greeted.

"Oh, uh, hi."

She grinned. "I'm Willa's sister, Waverly. I know all about you. Hi, Viper!"

He grunted.

I elbowed him in the ribs. "Say hello like a normal person. Sheesh."

"Hello," Viper said flatly.

"Come on in." Waverly stepped back and let us into the foyer.

I glanced at Viper, who immediately winked at me. I couldn't help the smile of amusement.

"Everyone's in the kitchen," Waverly said.

We followed her down the hallway into the large room. Duke and Savage were at the kitchen table. There was a man sitting with them who I didn't recognize. Upon closer inspection, I realized he was a teenager too. Waverly walked over to him and immediately plopped down onto his lap. He looked at her with adoration.

"This is my boyfriend, Dylan," she said. "Dylan, Sutton. Sutton, Dylan."

"Nice to meet you," I said.

"Dylan and Viper have already met," she explained.

"Can I get you guys something to drink?" Duke asked.

"A soda would be great, if you have it," I said.

"We have it," Duke assured me. "Viper?"

"Beer's fine." He set the grocery bag onto the island.

"Where's Willa?" I asked.

Savage sniggered. "Puking her guts up."

I frowned. "And that's something to laugh about?"

"She's pregnant." Waverly rolled her eyes and flicked Savage's ear. "And this asshole thinks it's funny."

Duke went to the fridge and pulled out a bottle of beer and a soda. He handed me the can and then popped off the beer bottle top with the opener on his keychain before handing it to Viper.

The front door opened, and I heard the sounds of arguing. A petite blonde teenager walked into the kitchen carrying a few bags of takeout. A biker trailed behind her, also carrying bags.

"Ah, food is here." Waverly hopped up off Dylan's lap and went to the young woman and helped her.

"Thank God, I'm starving," Willa said as she entered the kitchen. Her face was rosy, but she didn't look any worse for wear from the pregnancy puke.

"Hi, Acid," she greeted the biker who'd come with the girl.

"Hey, Willa." He touched her shoulder.

"Sailor, do you have—" Before Willa could finish her question, Sailor handed her a container. Willa ripped it open, took out a corn bread muffin, and chomped a huge bite.

Duke cracked open a can of ginger ale and handed it to his wife.

"Thank you," she muttered through a mouthful of corn bread.

Duke pulled Willa into his side and settled his hand at the back of her neck.

"For the rest of us who aren't heathens," Savage drawled. "Maybe we should get plates."

"You *are* a heathen," Waverly said to him.

"What are we eating?" I asked.

"Fried chicken," Savage replied. "From Cluckers."

"Not just fried chicken, but biscuits, green beans, Mac and cheese, coleslaw and beans. Wait, I'm missing something," Sailor said.

"Collards," Acid supplied.

Waverly went to the cabinet and pulled out a stack of plates, and the feeding frenzy commenced.

"I'm sorry it wasn't a home-cooked meal," Willa said to me.

I frowned. "What are you even talking about? This is perfect."

Willa took a full plate of food and waved me over to the large kitchen table. "I had plans to do a real dinner, I swear it, but I was on deadline for a client, and I just couldn't make it happen."

"What do you do? For work?"

She beamed. "I'm a web designer. I run my own business."

"That's so cool," I said.

"This is really hitting the spot," Willa said after taking a bite from her drumstick.

Viper sat next to me. He set his hand on my thigh and gave it a squeeze before digging into his massive plate of food.

"You mind if we eat outside?" Waverly asked Willa. "You guys are grown-ups and stuff. Talking about grown-up things."

"Go for it," Willa said.

"Light the bug torches while you're at it, will you?" Duke called out.

"I'll do it," Dylan said.

The three teenagers went out the back door.

"How's the food?" Duke asked me.

"Perfect," I said even though I hadn't yet tasted it.

Savage, Acid, and Duke carried on a conversation, but it was dude-centric. Motorcycles, the garage the club owned, and other things I had no interest in. Viper was quiet, not contributing much to their conversation.

I stole a hand across his back and then picked up my fork.

As I took a bite, I noticed that Willa was staring at me with raised brows.

I couldn't remember the last time I'd sat around a table with a group of people and just felt normal.

But I wasn't normal. I didn't make friends the way a lot of people did. I wouldn't call myself closed off, but I kept things light. Easy. My relationships were very surface level.

I hadn't thought there was anything wrong with that until now.

The way these people interacted with one another was easy, carefree, but it was clear they knew each other well. They joked and teased. There were no boundaries. When Savage got up from the table for a few seconds, he brought Willa another ginger ale without her even asking. And when he sat back down, Duke took one of the cornbread biscuits right off of Savage's plate.

The three of them really were close, almost like they were a single unit.

It was beautiful.

Foreign.

Once I was stuffed, I pushed my empty plate away and sighed in happiness.

"Props," Savage said to me. "I didn't think you'd finish all that food in one sitting."

"It's gremlin energy," I teased.

"You want to leave the guys to their man-talk and get a tour of the house?" Willa asked me.

"Love to," I said.

Viper's hand slid from my thigh before I stood up.

"You finished?" I asked him.

He nodded.

I took our plates and carted them to the dishwasher.

"Leave them in the sink," Willa said. "The kids will do them."

"The kids," I snorted. "They're teenagers, right?"

"Still kids. Still have curfews. Still living under my roof. So they have chores."

"They don't really live under our roof," Duke said as he brought his plate to the sink. "Waverly and Sailor share the guesthouse."

"You must trust your sisters a lot to let them share a guesthouse without any parental supervision."

"It's a unique situation," Willa said. "I'll explain later."

"Fire pit?" Duke asked Willa.

She smiled. "Sounds good. We'll meet you out there once I give Sutton the tour." Willa leaned in and pressed her lips to Duke's. He grasped the back of her neck and gave her a real kiss, and I discreetly turned away.

Viper was looking at me and something inexplicable moved between us. Something I didn't want to explore.

I was all too eager to follow Willa out of the kitchen, down the hallway.

"This is my office," she said as she opened a closed door. There was a large green desk in front of the window that overlooked a pasture of horses.

"Love this space," I said. "And the desk."

"Waverly did it. Well, she didn't make the desk herself, she flipped it."

"Very cool," I said.

"She flips a lot of furniture," she said. "So, if you need anything…you know, after what happened to your home…"

"Ah, yeah, the fire." I nodded slowly. "You know about that?"

"No real secrets in the club. All the Old Ladies know about the fire. Any word about what happened?"

"Not yet," I lied. "Still waiting on the fire chief to call."

"I can't even imagine. I mean, I've lived in some shitty places over the years. Waverly and I both have, but we've never had our house burn down."

"Wasn't a house. It was a trailer."

"Still," Willa said. "It was your haven."

"I guess," I said, suddenly feeling uncomfortable.

"How's staying at the clubhouse?"

"It's okay. Fine. It's…"

"A lot of dudes."

I chuckled. "Yeah. I don't mind that so much. I kind of like the comfort of having a lot of people around."

"And Viper?"

"Oh, I see. I was lured into a house tour under false pretenses." I laughed. "Though, Mia did warn me that if I had dinner with you, I'd get the third degree."

"If it makes you feel any better, I got the third degree about me and Duke constantly. It's just what us Old Ladies do. We scope people out, you know?"

"And whatever I tell you, you'll report to the crowd, huh?"

"Something like that." She smiled. "More like I'll give my opinion on you. The other Old Ladies are kind of chomping at the bit to meet you."

"Why?" I asked. "As soon as I move out of the clubhouse and go about my life, you'll never see me again."

"Right, you're only staying at the clubhouse for a bit." She grinned. "Yet, you and Viper are looking pretty chummy."

"We're chums," I quipped.

"Yeah, right. Let me show you Waverly's shop. It's cooler than the upstairs."

"What do you mean, *yeah right*?"

"Look, I'm not going to pry. I'm not going to ask you about your relationship with Viper, but…"

"But what?"

"These men. They're different."

"Different how? They don't have wings and tails do they?"

"No." She snorted. "But that would be fun. What I meant was, these guys, they kinda…"

"Kinda what?"

"*Know*. I mean, they know when they want a woman to be their Old Lady. They claim fast and don't care for societal norms. It's part of the club culture."

"Viper hasn't claimed me." I rolled my eyes. "We're sleeping together. That's it. Just for as long as I live at the clubhouse. He doesn't want something long term, and neither do I."

"He can't take his eyes off you," she said. "When he thinks you're not looking, it's plain as day he can't stop staring."

"Yeah, because he wants to get into my pants, which isn't hard to do because I want him just as badly."

"He talks to you. I mean, really talks. Like opens his mouth and uses words."

"So what, I'm the Viper whisperer? I'm his *snake* charmer?"

Willa laughed. "You're good, I'll give you that. But what do you know about him? Like, have you talked about your pasts? Your family? Anything?"

"Some things," I admitted. "Not a lot. I don't need to know a lot."

"Need and want are two different things."

I didn't feel comfortable sharing with Willa that Viper slept with a knife under his pillow, or that he'd pulled it on me. It was a major red flag, and if I'd been rational at all, I would've stopped sleeping with him immediately and disappeared from the clubhouse.

But red just so happens to be my favorite color.

I knew there were things Viper wasn't telling me. Just like there were things I wasn't telling him.

I was afraid that if we opened up to each other, I mean *really* opened up to each other, we'd both be traveling down a path neither of us wanted.

Permanence.

Chapter 21

"This is so fucking cool," I said when we walked into Waverly's workshop. There were several pieces of furniture in different states of completion. Tools I had no idea how to use were strewn about.

"Waverly, Dylan, Sailor, and Waverly's best friend Jessica run a furniture flipping business," Willa explained. "They're doing pretty well, too."

"Wow. I'm super impressed. Your sisters are bright, aren't they?"

"Yeah. Only, Sailor isn't my sister."

"No? Is she Duke's sister?"

Willa shook her head. "Sailor… We've kind of unofficially adopted her and she stays with us. We take full responsibility for her."

"It takes special people to do something like that," I said. "Opening your home to a teenager."

"She's a good kid." Willa shrugged. "I'm glad we could help." She absently rubbed a hand across her flat stomach.

"How far along are you?"

"Few weeks," she said with a smile. "You want kids?"

"I'm twenty-two."

"I'm twenty-four."

"Yeah, but you're, like, an *adult*. You've got an adult home, an adult job, a husband, and you take care of two teenagers. I don't even have a fish."

"Age is kind of bullshit," Willa said with a laugh. "I was nine when Waverly came along. I was more a mother to her than our own mother was. But I get ya. Can't really see Viper as the dad type."

"Oh, I don't think that's fair to say," I protested. "I think he'd be a good dad. He's protective, and he's always making sure I have enough to eat and—"

Willa cracked a grin. "Gotcha."

"Gotcha what?"

"You like him."

"Of course, I do. I'm sleeping with him, aren't I?"

"You can sleep with people you hate. You *care* about him. Admit it."

"No." I crossed my arms over my chest. "I'll do no such thing."

"Savage told me Viper almost flattened Smoke for calling you a piece of tail."

"God, can Savage keep a secret about anything?"

"Only when it actually matters," Willa stated. "He holds some of my darkest secrets, and he's never spilled. But when it comes to gossip? That's a different beast altogether."

I chuckled. "That guy."

"I haven't met the woman he's currently sleeping with," Willa said. "She's your friend, isn't she?"

"Carla? Yeah. She's my friend. It's not serious between them though. According to Savage, anyway."

"Nothing with Savage is ever serious—relationship-wise. I don't want your friend to get her heart broken."

"Carla's twice divorced and learned her lesson. She's careful with men now. I doubt she has much of a heart left to break anyway. Besides, Savage told me it was *Carla* who said they weren't anything serious."

"One of these days, I'd like a woman to come along and knock Savage on his ass. I want him to fall in love. I worry sometimes that he's incapable of it."

"Rough past?" I asked gently.

She paused a moment and then nodded. "Viper had a rough past too. Though I'm sure you know all about it."

"I don't actually."

"Oh." Willa nibbled her lip. "We should get back to the guys."

"*Nah-ah*, no way. You can't leave me hanging like that. You *have* to tell me."

"I can't. I'm an ass for even bringing it up. Ask Viper."

"Viper. Close-lipped, has-sex-with-me-as-a-distraction-when-I get-mouthy Viper? *That* Viper?"

"Okay, you don't have to brag." She smirked.

"Sorry. I have very little filter."

"Wait until you spend any sort of time with my sister. She's got zero filter—and curses like a trucker."

"My kind of gal."

"Yeah, I'm sure you'll get along."

We left Waverly's shop and ambled through the backyard toward the fire pit where everyone had congregated.

We were still out of earshot and I felt comfortable asking, "Viper's past. Is it bad?"

"I guess it depends on your definition of the word."

It was clear Willa had loyalty to Viper because she was an Old Lady. They protected their own.

I'm never going to be Viper's Old Lady.

The thought came unbidden, striking like lightning.

Viper and I had amazing sex. Though that was new for

me, even I wasn't naive enough to believe that you could build a foundation on sex alone.

Everyone was sitting around the fire when Willa and I came to join. There was a chair next to Viper, which I immediately took. The fire pit was gas, and looked to be more for ambiance than actual warmth. Not that we needed warmth. It was the beginning of summer in Texas.

Willa perched in the seat next to Duke, who clearly felt she was too far away. He grabbed her chair and pulled her closer, and then rested his hand on her thigh.

Waverly's head was buried in her phone, and she typed something quickly before setting it down in her lap. "So what did you think about my workshop? Pretty snazzy, right?"

"Super snazzy," I said with a grin. "You guys are doing really cool stuff."

"Viper said your house burned down and that's why you're staying at the clubhouse," Sailor said. "Sorry to hear that."

"The house burning down, or staying at the clubhouse?" I asked with a smile.

Sailor's blue eyes twinkled. "Both."

"The clubhouse isn't that bad," Acid said.

"It's a dude haven," Sailor said.

"Have you been to one of their parties yet?" Waverly asked eagerly. "Like, not a family potluck or whatever. I'm talking a *real* party."

"Why do you look so intrigued?" Savage queried her.

She shrugged and feigned nonchalance. "Just curious."

"Oh, I know that look," Duke said with a laugh. "Waverly's about to turn our hair gray."

Waverly straightened her spine and tossed long, red hair over her shoulder. "Just a glimpse of what you're in for when your little moppet comes along."

"Thoughtful of you," Willa said to her sister. "Dylan, you're supposed to be a calming influence on her. Do something."

Dylan looked at Waverly. "I'm supposed to be a calming influence."

"Then limit my caffeine intake," she sassed. "I'm unhinged." Waverly's phone buzzed. She picked it up and scrolled through the text. "It's Jess."

Sailor rose. "Her house?"

Waverly nodded and then asked, "Is it cool if the three of us take off?"

"Yeah," Willa said. "Home before midnight. And please don't come back with any tattoos or piercings."

"Tall order," Waverly quipped. "But okay. It was nice meeting you, Sutton."

"You too," I said.

The three teenagers departed, taking their energy and lightness with them.

"Your sister is a pistol," I said.

"Right?" Willa grinned. "How's the job at Shelly's? Do you like it?"

"I've only worked one shift so far, but yeah. I think I like it. Mia's a good boss."

"The late hours aren't killing you?" Duke asked.

I shrugged. "A little, I guess. My sleep's been erratic, to say the least."

Viper shifted in his seat.

Acid's cell rang and he reached into his leather cut. "Yeah? Sure, no problem. I'll take care of it." He hung up and stood. "Thanks for dinner. I gotta run." Acid slapped Savage on the back.

"Well, like hell I'm gonna sit here and be a fifth wheel," Savage said. "I'm out too."

The two of them left, and it was just the four of us.

The couples.

"Sutton needs clothes," Viper said, addressing Willa.

Willa frowned. "What kind of clothes?"

I answered, "Biker gal clothes. My mode of transportation for the foreseeable future is the back of Viper's bike."

"Ah." Willa smiled. "I'll take you to Leather and Ink. We'll get you outfitted properly. Let me know when you want to go."

"Tomorrow? Is that too soon?"

"Tomorrow's good," she said. "I can pick you up at the clubhouse if you want."

"Oh, that would be great. Thanks."

"No." Viper's voice reverberated through the air.

Willa looked at him. "It's no trouble, really. I don't mind."

"Babe," Duke said softly to her.

She glanced at her husband, who was shaking his head.

"What the hell is wrong with me taking Sutton to the boutique?" Willa demanded.

"I'll take her. She can meet you there," Viper explained.

Why was it when he was around other people he had such a hard time communicating normally, but with me, his words flowed like beer from a tap?

"I don't understand," Willa said, her gaze bouncing from me to Viper, demanding an explanation.

"Sutton staying at the clubhouse is club business. Viper's job right now is to stick close to Sutton," Duke clarified.

He looked at Viper, who nodded.

"Club business," Willa muttered. "If I never hear those two words ever again it will be too soon."

"You're an Old Lady," Duke said. "Club business is the only explanation you'll get."

She glared at him. He placed his hand on the back of her neck and drew her close for a kiss.

Willa wrenched her mouth away from him, flung off his palm, and stood up. She turned her attention to me. "I'll see you tomorrow, Sutton."

I nodded slightly. "Okay."

"Good night, everyone." She glowered at her husband and then marched into the house.

"What just happened?" I asked Duke. "And how do you seem to know about my situation?"

"All the brothers know," Viper said, answering in lieu of Duke. "They had to know. The Old Ladies, though. They aren't privy to what went down."

"What you got involved in is dangerous enough that they had to tell us," Duke said. "We can't have you around the brothers unless they're prepared to protect you no matter where you are, but we try to keep things from our women as much as possible. Willa knows that."

"Then why is she so mad?"

"She doesn't like being left out of the loop—especially when she *knows* there's something going on."

"So you don't let women in on club business, whatever that is?" I asked.

"Need to know basis," Duke said. "If there's shit that they need to know, we tell them. But we try to protect them —shield them—from it, as best we can. Doesn't always work, but that's the life."

"I'm sorry I upset her."

"You didn't. I did," Duke replied. "The three of us know what's going on. She doesn't. She doesn't like feeling left out."

"But she is left out," I said.

"Absolutely."

"Why don't you just tell her?" I asked.

"You need to trust us on this. You don't want people knowing your business, or why you had to come to the club," Duke said. "Aside from a legal standpoint, it's a shit idea, blabbing about stuff like that. Never ends well."

I sighed. "Yeah, okay, I get the point."

"She knows what she signed up for when she became my Old Lady. She might not like it all the time, but that's how we are. It's better this way. Trust me."

Chapter 22

Viper's phone chimed right as we got to his motorcycle. He pulled out his cell from his leather cut and glanced at the screen. "Duke texted me Willa's number to give to you."

"Thanks," I said. "Can I have that now?"

"Why can't you wait until we get back to the clubhouse to put it into your phone?"

"Why can't I have it now?"

Shrugging, he told me her number and I punched it into my cell. After I saved it, I called her.

"Hello?" she answered.

"Hi, it's Sutton."

Viper was staring at me, a frown on his face.

"Oh, hey."

"Sorry things got weird," I blurted out.

She paused a moment and then laughed. "No, *I'm* sorry things got weird. It was my fault."

"Why don't we just blame the men for making it weird?" I asked, flashing a grin at Viper, who was definitely not amused.

"That works for me. Are you already back at the clubhouse?"

"No. We haven't left yet," I said. "We're about to hop on Viper's bike."

Willa laughed. "Well, I appreciate the call. I'll see you tomorrow?"

"Sounds good." I hung up with Willa and stuck my phone back into my purse.

Viper handed me the helmet. He sighed and muttered something under his breath.

"What was that?" I demanded.

"Nothing. Let's get home."

Home. Funny word.

"You really view the clubhouse as home?" I asked, clipping the strap around my chin.

"It's as good as any, I guess."

I looked back at Willa and Duke's home. A house was just a house, but their home had a feeling.

I'd never lived in a place that felt like that. Warm, inviting.

Safe.

Viper cranked the engine, pulling me back to the present. I slid on behind him, wrapped my arms around his middle, and we drove off.

My head was full of thoughts and questions. About Viper's past. About why I wanted to know. And about why I was completely determined not to ask him about it.

Getting in deeper with Viper, exploring our past wounds, our canyon of traumas, was a sure-fire way to bond. And I didn't want to bond. Not any more than I already had.

Tonight had probably been a mistake to begin with. Not that I hadn't enjoyed dinner and the company, and the energy of teenagers, and a family that was close. But it was for that reason that it shouldn't be repeated.

Viper and I had a deal. And complicating a sexual relationship with food and dinners with his club brothers and their Old Ladies was something I should avoid in the future.

This would end. Our time together was finite. And that realization shot a pang of remorse through me.

We arrived back at the clubhouse. Smoke and Bones were sitting in the living room, having a couple of beers with two women I didn't recognize. I briefly wondered if they were from the party the other night, but I didn't really care.

I waved at them and then headed for the stairs. Viper was hot on my trail. When I made a move to go to my own room, he reached for my hand and dragged me to his.

I sighed but didn't bother fighting.

He opened the door to his room and flipped on the light. I walked inside and the moment I did, he shut the door and pushed me against it. Viper caged me in with his arms and bent his head down.

I looked up at him. His brown eyes swirled with emotion.

"You want to talk about it? Or you want to fuck it out?"

I let out a breath. "Fuck."

"Good answer."

He removed his hands from the door and shoved away from it. Viper grasped the hem of my tank and pulled it over my head. His thumbs grazed my nipples, making them pucker. He cupped my breasts, kneading them in his large hands.

I placed a palm on his muscled abdomen, stroking him

through his shirt before pushing him away. I bent over and unlaced my boots and kicked them off.

His fingers went to the button of my jeans.

I shoved them down my legs and stepped out of them. He slid his fingers into my panties.

He played with me with one hand while the other grasped the back of my neck and tilted my head up. His mouth covered mine. Viper's tongue thrust into my mouth as he robbed me of my thoughts.

I gripped the lapels of his leather cut and attempted to undress him. I wanted him naked, and fast.

"Easy," he whispered against my mouth.

"No." I tugged harder, and he chuckled.

He stopped kissing me and took a step back so he could remove his leather cut, which he hung up on the hook of his bedroom door. Next came his boots, followed by his jeans.

We were both completely naked and we stared at one another for a moment before I rushed to him.

He lifted me into his arms, and I wrapped my legs around him. Our mouths bonded together, and it wasn't until I was on my back that I realized he'd walked us to the bed and placed me in the center of it.

His mouth left mine to kiss my chin, my collarbone, my breasts. He slid a finger inside me, and my back bowed from the pleasure.

"Viper," I moaned.

He added another finger, working it into my body, pumping it in and out.

Goose bumps broke out along my skin and a kernel of desire bloomed low in my belly.

Viper angled my leg, opening me up so he could drive deeper.

I gasped as shockwaves crackled between my thighs. I was close, so close.

He stopped his ministrations and then slowly removed his fingers.

"No," I whined.

Viper smiled, bent down, and kissed the inside of my thigh. He released me and then patted my hip.

"Roll over, Sutton. Put your elbows on the bed, your feet on the floor, and your ass out."

I swallowed in trepidation.

His gaze softened. "Trust me?"

I nodded slowly.

He moved away from the bed to give me space. I flipped over and placed my elbows on the bed, my feet hitting the planks of the floor.

I heard him open the nightstand drawer and, a moment later, the tearing of a foil packet. Once he'd sheathed himself, he stood behind me. The heat radiating off him made me shudder.

"Spread your legs," he commanded.

I widened my stance and then jumped when I felt the crown of his shaft teasing my entrance.

He went slowly, and even though I was wet, he was huge. I hissed in pain.

Viper stopped immediately. "Sutton?"

"It's okay. Just…give me a minute to adjust."

He reached around, his fingers gliding through my folds. Pleasure suddenly came roaring back.

I spread my legs even wider and lowered myself onto the bed further, angling myself up to him.

Viper sank all the way inside me.

My fingers clawed at the comforter.

"All right?" he rasped.

"Yeah. More."

He began to thrust, gently at first, but when he realized I could take him, he was a little rougher.

His fingers still played with me while he drilled into my body.

I screamed into the comforter and came, writhing, my skin on fire.

Viper gripped my hips, pulled me against him and orgasmed with a guttural groan.

He pressed his face between my shoulder blades, his warm breath fanning my flesh. Viper released me and slowly pulled out.

I felt something dribble down the inside of my leg.

"Viper?"

"Yeah?"

"Did the—uh—I think the condom broke." I looked at him over my shoulder.

He'd removed the condom and tied it off, but he then lifted it in the air. "It didn't break."

I frowned and showed him the inside of my thigh. "Then what's this?"

Viper smiled slightly. "You."

"Me?" I paused and then heat rushed to my cheeks. "Oh…"

"Yeah, *oh*." His smile was a full-on grin.

"I'll just…yeah." I rushed past him to his bathroom and shut the door.

I quickly grabbed some toilet paper and cleaned myself up. I splashed some cool water onto my red cheeks and wiped them with a towel.

The main light was turned off when I went back into the bedroom, but the lamp on the nightstand illuminated him. He was sprawled out in the middle of the bed with the comforter up to his waist, leaving his naked chest on display.

"Plan on making any room for me?" I asked in amusement.

He lifted the covers but didn't move over.

I went to the bed and crawled on top of him. He tugged the comforter up until my shoulders were concealed. I curled against his warm body.

"Were you panicking?" he asked.

"Panicking?"

"When you thought the condom broke."

"Oh. Well, kinda…yeah. I'm not ready for a baby. My life is insane. I live in a clubhouse with a guy I just met, and my house burned down a few days ago. Doesn't scream financially or maternally stable, you know?" My eyes were drifting shut even though the lamp was still on. I was warm and sated. My thoughts were hazy clouds drifting across the sky.

"I'd take care of you. You and the baby."

Suddenly, I was very awake. I shot up, startling him.

"What?" Viper asked. "What's wrong?"

"You'd take care of me and *the baby*?" I asked.

"Well, yeah." He frowned.

"But there is no baby."

"But every time we fuck, there's the potential for that."

"Well, no shit, Sherlock. I know basic human biology. It's the frog reproduction cycle I had a problem with in class."

"Frogs?"

"Yeah. Tadpoles? Come on. They look like giant sperm."

"This conversation is getting out of control."

"You started it."

"How did *I* start it?" he demanded.

"By saying you'd take care of me and *the baby*."

"If," he stressed. "*If* it came to that."

"That's a rotten thing to say," I groused.

He blinked. "Are you—you're not serious?"

"Of course, I'm serious! You can't say something sweet like that to a woman you're expiration dating."

"I can't? I'm so damn confused."

I climbed off him, careful not to knee him in his delicate area. My feet hit the floor and I looked around for my underwear. I found them and hastily pulled them on.

"You're not leaving this room," he growled. "We're finishing this conversation."

"Nope. No way. I'm not staying trapped in here with you."

"Trapped in here with me? It's not like the door is barricaded."

"Tank," I muttered. "Where's my tank?"

"Sutton, stop." It was his turn to get up.

"No. Stay where you are." I put out a hand. "I can't think when you look like that."

"Look like what?"

"Naked and tattooed."

A low rumble escaped his mouth, and it took me a moment to realize he was laughing. Outright laughing.

"You think this is funny," I accused.

"Well, yeah. I do actually."

"It's not."

"Sorry, but you freaking out over something that hasn't even happened is kind of hilarious."

"I'm not freaking out because of that. I'm freaking out because of what you said."

"And what did I say?" With a sigh, Viper grasped my wrist and pulled me toward him. He opened his knees and wedged me between them. He then settled his hands on the curve of my ass, his thumbs playing with my thong. "Explain why me saying I'd take care of you and the baby freaked you out."

I nibbled my lip.

"You don't want to need anyone," he fished.

I shook my head. "Not that."

"Then what?"

"It wasn't what you said. It was how you said it."

"And how did I say it."

"Like it wasn't a big deal."

He frowned. "It's not a big deal."

"Being tied to a woman and baby for the rest of your life is *the biggest deal*. And you just…I don't know."

"What? You expected me to be the kind of guy who'd bail? It takes two people to create a kid, Sutton. Leaving you with something like that, all alone…that would be a real shit thing to do."

"Yeah." I nodded. "I know. I just wasn't ready for this conversation. I didn't really think we'd ever have to have it. You know?"

"Because there's a time limit on this thing."

"Yeah."

"Do babies scare the shit out of you?"

I shook my head. "No, not really. They're small and squishy. Should I be scared of them?"

He shrugged. "I just didn't want you to worry, okay? If something were to happen…"

"Okay." I swallowed. "I feel kind of stupid. For over-reacting."

He fell back onto the bed and took me with him. I straddled his body and ran my hands up and down his chest, over the tattoo that I'd noticed before. It looked familiar, but I still couldn't place it.

"While we're talking about this," he said, his hands

wandering down my hips toward my ass. "Are you on birth control?"

"I am. Yeah."

"Probably should've had that conversation before I slid between your thighs."

"Probably, yeah, but hormones."

"Hormones," he agreed.

"It's not fair, you know."

"What's not?"

"When you need to clear your head, you get to go for a ride. I can't go anywhere. I don't even have a car. I have no freedom."

"Just for now," he said quietly. "Just until we know you're safe and the dust has settled."

"Still. As fun as it is having sex with you all the time, I'm going to need to find other things to do between that and working."

"Speaking of sex." He suddenly rolled, plopping me onto the bed. "I'm done talking."

Chapter 23

I slept the night through, pinned beneath one of Viper's massive thighs. Somehow, neither of us hogged the bed or the covers. He didn't snore, and if I dreamed, I didn't remember it.

When I woke up, I expected to find him in bed next to me, but he was gone. His boots were missing and so was his leather cut, so I knew he wasn't in the shower.

I sat up and yawned. My phone was on the nightstand, and it was plugged into the charger. I didn't remember going to sleep with it that way, so I deduced Viper had done it for me before he'd left the room.

The knob turned and the door opened slowly. Viper loomed in the space. "You're awake," he said unnecessarily

"That I am."

He closed the door and came over and sat down on the edge of the bed. "I thought for sure you'd sleep a few more hours."

I yawned again, hastily covering my mouth.

Viper's lips twitched but he didn't smile. He just offered me his cup of coffee.

"It's missing all the cream and sugar," I said.

"It's mine. I would've made you a cup if I'd known you were awake."

"Hmm." I took a sip and grimaced. "Thanks for the offering, but I don't drink toxic waste."

He chuckled. "I'll get you a cup just the way you like it before I leave."

"You're leaving?"

Viper nodded. "I've got some club shit to handle."

"But you were supposed to take me to Leather and Ink," I said.

"Rain check."

"So wait, I'm just supposed to sit here until I go to work? Will you be back to take me to Shelly's?"

He nodded. "Yeah. In plenty of time."

"You've got it all figured it out, don't you?" I glared. "Leave me here to rot."

Viper gripped the back of my head and pulled me toward him. His mouth covered mine, his coffee breath strong. "If I didn't have somewhere to be, I'd fuck that attitude right out of you."

"If you didn't have somewhere to be, I wouldn't be stuck here," I said glumly.

"I'm sorry. Just the way it needs to be right now."

"Fine." I scooted out of bed, my tank riding up my legs to show off the curve of my ass.

Viper's eyes tracked me.

I threw on my pair of jeans and jammed my feet into my boots, not even bothering with socks. "If you'll excuse me," I said, yanking my phone from the charger. "I'll do my walk of shame now."

"You're cute when you're mad."

"You think that compliment will make me like you right now?" I demanded with my hip cocked.

"No. I think caffeine will restore your usual good mood. Have a cup. Or two." He stood up from the bed and walked over to me.

He leaned down to kiss me and because I was a damn sucker, I let him. There was no point in holding a useless grudge. This was my situation for the time being. I could take my chances without the protection of the club if I wanted…

Yeah, no thanks.

I went with him downstairs because now that I was awake, coffee was the most important thing on my agenda. The living room was empty, so at least there would be no one there to witness our goodbye.

"Actually, the more I think about it, the more I like it when you're angry," Viper said, wrapping an arm around my waist and hauling me close. "Because you bring that energy to my bed and I'm here for it."

I frowned. "Are you teasing me? Or flirting? Is this you flirting again?"

"Do you like it?"

"I don't know. It's disconcerting. It's keeping me on my toes, that's for sure."

He kissed me one last time and then released me. "See ya."

I rolled my eyes. "See ya."

The front door slammed shut. I went to the coffee maker and poured myself a mug, leaving a ton of room for cream and sugar.

I stood at the counter to enjoy my coffee and sent off an apology text to Willa, telling her that I'd have to bail because of Viper's last-minute *club shit*.

My phone buzzed with an incoming call. It wasn't a

number I recognized, but I answered it anyway. "Hello?"

"Hello, may I please speak to Sutton Woods?"

"Speaking."

"Sutton, it's Chief Daniels. I have news about what started the fire."

"Oh?"

"A hair straightener was left on."

"Oh," I said slowly. "I can't believe that's what happened."

"We've sent everything we have to the police department so you can make an insurance claim now. Put your insurance company in touch with the police department. They'll take it from there. I'm sorry about your home."

"Thank you, Chief Daniels. I appreciate your time."

I hung up the phone with him and took a sigh of relief. That was one thing I didn't need to worry about—there would be no fight with the insurance company. The plan had worked, and the club and I were off the hook. The cartel member had been disposed of, there was no longer any evidence of what I'd done, and the trailer had burned to the ground.

I was in the clear.

I felt relief, of course. But did that mean I would be moving out of the clubhouse sooner rather than later? Before that could happen, I needed the insurance money. The trailer hadn't been worth a lot, but it was enough to buy a used vehicle, and I wasn't going anywhere without wheels.

And with a car, I could drive out of town and never look back.

The front door opened and Savage and Acid came in.

"Hey," Savage said.

"Hi."

"Nice outfit," Acid teased.

"Shut up."

"Viper called me," Savage said. "Apparently, I'm supposed to keep an eye on you while he's gone."

"Lovely," I said bitterly. "What is there to do around here?"

Acid and Savage looked at each other. Acid shrugged. "You been down to the theater room yet?"

"No."

"You like video games?" Savage asked.

∽

"Die you evil motherfucker!" I yelled, pressing the button a bajillion times in a row.

"Fuck no!" Savage yelled.

The TV screen lit up with a blazing inferno and the game declared me the winner.

"Ha! In your face!"

"I never should've introduced you to this," Savage muttered. He tossed his controller to Acid. He had positioned himself on the floor while Savage and I battled it out on the couch.

Time had no meaning in a theater room with no windows.

The sound of heavy footsteps shuffling along the floor above momentarily distracted me from reveling in my win.

A door opened and suddenly I heard the chattering of several women in conversation.

Willa's blonde head appeared. "There you are," she said with a smile.

"Here I am. But what are you doing here?" I asked.

"Well, just because Viper is keeping you under lock and key, doesn't mean the rest of us can't come and go as we please," Willa said. "Come upstairs. I've got some stuff for you."

"Stuff for me?" I asked.

"Do you have anything for me?" Savage asked her.

"Not unless you can fit in size tiny-leather-pants with rhinestones on them," she said.

"Not really my style," Savage drawled.

"You brought me leather pants?" I gave my controller to Savage and then hopped up to follow Willa.

"Not just leather pants, but some other stuff too. Stuff boys shouldn't be privy to," she whispered.

"But why would you do that for me?" I asked in shock.

"Because I used to work at Leather and Ink," she explained. "And Laura still gives me the employee discount. But these clothes don't come without strings."

I followed her up the stairs. "There are strings?"

We made it into the living room of the clubhouse where a bunch of women were assembled.

"Strings." Willa gestured to the women. "The Old Ladies."

"You lured me here with the promise of hot leather pants just so the rest of the Old Ladies could grill me about Viper, didn't you?" I demanded, placing my hands on my hips.

"Mia helped," Willa said with a smile.

"Thanks for throwing me under the bus," Mia said with a laugh as she patted a baby resting against her shoulder.

Willa took my hand. "I'll introduce you to everyone."

"Should we get name tags? I feel like name tags are a good idea," I quipped.

"I like her already." A slender brunette who looked to be in her early forties with teased hair stood at the counter, sipping from her to-go soda cup. "I'm Darcy."

I waved.

There were three women on the couch, all of whom had babies or were pregnant.

"Jeez, what's with the biker sperm?" I blurted out. "Is it, like, more potent than average male sperm?"

The pregnant woman laughed. "*Absolutely*. Did you like the breakfast I brought yesterday?"

"Oh, that was you!" I said in realization. "The bakery owner."

"That's me. I'm Brooklyn."

"Yes, it was delicious. I'm so sorry I didn't get a chance to meet you yesterday."

"That's okay." Brooklyn's eyes twinkled. "You were…occupied."

Heat suffused my cheeks.

"I know that look," Joni said, looking down at her baby in his sling. "That's the look of a woman who's getting it good."

All attention turned to me.

"What, you think I kiss and tell?" I demanded.

"You don't have to tell nothin'," Mia said with a laugh. "It's plain as day."

"You're walking funny," a bottle-blonde joked with a wink. "I'm Allison."

"Save me," I said to Willa.

"Clothes," Willa said. "Let's give the girl a break."

"We should have a barbecue," Darcy announced. "So you can officially meet everyone. Doc and Rach aren't here."

"There are more of you?" I asked in surprise.

"Yep," Darcy said with a grin. "There needs to be more though. We have far too many single brothers who need good Old Ladies."

"Well, if that isn't beating me over the head with it," I muttered, which caused everyone to laugh.

I sat on the floor in front of the bags and riffled through them. The leather pants with rhinestones were absolutely adorable and I couldn't wait to try them on. Willa also got me a leather jacket with fringe and rivets. The boots though. They were to die for. Thick soled, leather, and laced up half my calf.

"Okay, I'm officially obsessed with everything you brought me," I said. "How much do I owe you?"

"You don't," Willa said, still standing by the couch.

"What are you talking about? Of course, I have to pay you," I protested.

"I won't take your money," Willa said.

I looked around the room at the other Old Ladies. "Help me out here."

Joni shook her head. "Nope. This is what we do."

"Oh, I see what this is," I said with amusement. "This is bribery, isn't it? This is, *please stick around and tame Viper*. For my trouble I get some cool leather pants?"

"For the record, you've already tamed Viper," Savage announced as he popped into the living room. Acid was behind him.

"That's my professional opinion on the subject, anyway," Savage continued.

"Hey, no boys allowed," Willa quipped.

Savage walked over to her and threw an arm around her shoulder. "We're on our way out. Don't worry, you can talk freely without any of us here." He looked at me. "Rematch."

I nodded. "You're on."

"You're a worthy contender. Acid is a shit player."

"Hey," Acid said. "I'm no slouch."

"Compared to Sutton you are," Savage said.

The two of them moved toward the front door. "Ladies," Savage said. "Always a pleasure."

Acid looked at Willa. "I'm meeting Sailor and Waverly at The Ring."

Willa nodded. "I'll meet up with you guys later."

"Cool." With a wave, Acid left.

"What's The Ring?" I asked.

"A boxing gym the club owns," Willa explained. "Acid is teaching my sister and Sailor self-defense."

"Oh. I see," I replied. "That's kind of cool actually."

"So let's get back to this barbecue. Does Sunday work?" Joni asked.

"Yeah, Sunday works for me. I'll make sure to bake enough for the party," Brooklyn said.

"What about Doc?" Allison asked. "Is she working?"

"She's always working," Darcy said, and then looked at me to clarify. "She runs the Waco Health & Wellness Clinic. Wait, that's not completely accurate. She owns the clinic. It's her seedling."

"Wow," I said. "No doubt the clinic keeps her busy."

"Swamped is more like it," Mia said. "But it's important for the community, and our club is part of that."

I frowned. "Not following."

"The clinic was Doc's idea," Joni jumped in to explain, "but the club helped. So, our name rings out when people think of it. It's still her baby, but the community knows."

I mulled over their words. "Is the club pretty active in the community?"

"We try to do our fair share," Mia said slowly. "But it never seems to be enough."

I nibbled my lip, feeling the desire to ask a blunt question, but not wanting to be rude to these women. The club was involved in some violent shit, I knew that much. Were they trying to balance that out by giving back to the city?

"As much as I want to stick around here all day, I've got to get back to the bakery. It's like everyone decided to get married this month." Brooklyn grinned. "Though I'm not complaining about the business."

"Wait," Darcy said. "Have we officially decided to have the barbecue?"

"Yeah, let's do it," Mia voiced. "Then we can *really* overwhelm Sutton when all of us are there."

"And the kids too," Darcy said with a laugh. She dumped out the ice of her to-go cup and filled it with tap water.

A barbecue with families was a very different thing than a party where all the single brothers were trying to get their stingrays wet.

"Welcome to the club, honey." Darcy walked over to me and gave me a hug.

"I'm not in the club," I protested.

She rolled her eyes. "If you say so."

"Do yourself a favor and admit it," Brooklyn said, struggling to rise. Willa quickly hopped off the arm of the couch and offered her a hand. "You can pretend all you want that you and Viper are not anything to write home about. But we've heard how he's been with you."

"I've seen it with my own two eyes," Mia interjected with a wink. "The man is smitten."

"You're crazy. Viper is not *smitten*."

"Hmm. I'm with Mia on this," Willa added. "He hardly speaks to anyone. But with you…everyone sees it."

"That's because I talk incessantly. He *has* to engage in conversation with me or it's weird," I quipped.

"You can protest all you want," Brooklyn said. "But we are all very aware of your influence on him."

"Influence," I repeated.

"The night you worked at Shelly's, he was clocking

you. Like he *lived* for the moments that you'd look at him and shoot him a glance or a smile," Mia said.

"Oh my God, you have to stop," Brooklyn said. "I'm going all gooey."

"Let's get out of here then, before you melt." Joni stood up.

"Viper and I are finite," I said. I didn't like the immediate remorse I felt when I said it, but it was the truth. "We're just having a fun time before we head our separate ways."

"Who's going to tell her?" Allison asked with amusement. Her son began to fuss, and she bounced him up and down in an attempt to soothe him.

"Tell me what?"

"Tell you that when one of our men decides he's found *the one*, it's full steam ahead," Joni said.

"You're wrong. We don't mean anything to one another."

"So you'd be okay if he started flirting with another woman at a clubhouse party?" Darcy asked. "And not the family barbecue. I mean the ones where the guys are single and looking to get rowdy."

"He won't flirt with anyone because we have a deal," I said.

"What deal is that?" Allison inquired.

"Neither of us will be with anyone else while we're together," I explained.

"That's called exclusivity," Darcy said.

"Yeah, I know that." I rolled my eyes.

"Was it his idea or yours?" Mia asked.

I frowned. "I don't remember."

"Honey," Darcy drawled. "Don't know how to break this to you, but I'm pretty sure Viper intends to keep you."

Chapter 24

Keep me?

I wasn't a dog. I couldn't be kept.

What did that even mean?

The Old Ladies, including Willa, left quickly after Darcy had made that pronouncement. It was like they wanted to give me time to myself to stew over her words.

I wasn't a stewer by nature. I didn't sit and think about things deeply or for a long period of time. In fact, I believed I was the opposite of a stewer…which I guess meant I was a *doer*. I leapt before I looked, sometimes landing in hot water, sometimes not.

It wasn't for lack of impulse control; I just didn't like to deliberate. When I knew something needed to be done, I acted. Maybe it was a form of resilience, of needing to be in control of my life. Even if I made a bad decision—a wrong decision—no one could ever accuse me of regret.

Regrets were a waste of time.

It was why I'd had no qualms about jumping into bed with Viper. Sure, from an outsider's perspective, it seemed like a foolish decision. I hadn't known him long.

But you could spend your entire life with someone and still not truly know them.

Viper had made me feel things I'd never felt before. Sexually, definitely, but it was more than that.

Maybe I belonged in the biker-club world. Maybe around these people I wouldn't be judged for what I'd done…

As I thought about the club, I wondered if I'd grown to accept a mundane life before meeting them. Living in a trailer, taking the bus to and from work. Spending my days running errands or doing laundry. Filling my time with monotonous, meaningless tasks. There was no one to blame for my life turning out the way it had. My childhood had been rough. So what? A lot of people had the same experience, or worse. I wasn't unique. I wasn't special. I was just another pleb the world had chewed up and spat out.

What would my life look like if I decided to stick around the club?

Is that really what Viper wants?

They were criminals. You didn't get involved in a cartel war unless you were a criminal yourself. But criminals came in all shapes and sizes.

Some wore leather.

Some wore suits.

The world was a cruel place, and I was starting to believe that if you wanted anything good in your life, you had to be the one to go after it. You had to take chances, live your life to the fullest and never stop until you took what was rightfully yours.

But I hadn't been doing that. I'd been living small. Small and scared. It was easier to live small and scared. But the truth of it was that if I wanted my dreams to come true, I had to make them happen.

But what *were* my dreams? Did I even have any? Sure, I was enjoying my time with Viper, but then what? What would a future look like with him? What would a future look like without him?

"Stop, stop, stop," I muttered, tapping my third eye.

The Old Ladies could believe whatever they wanted, but Viper and I were not going to go the distance.

"Ugh, stop being such a sappy girl."

I needed to get out of the clubhouse. More importantly, I needed to get away from my own thoughts.

There were two men at the gates who I still hadn't officially met, and since there was no one else around, I decided to befriend them.

I went to the fridge and pulled out two bottles of water before I headed outside. I approached them, waters held out in front of me in silent offering.

"Thanks," one of the guys said after he'd downed half a bottle.

"Yeah," the other added. "That was nice of you."

Both of them looked really young. Their faces weren't lined with age yet.

"I'm Sutton."

"Yeah, we know." One of the guys with dark hair and blue eyes smirked. "You're Viper's woman."

I rolled my eyes. "Not you too."

"Me too what?" he asked.

"Never mind," I muttered.

"I'm Crow," the guy introduced himself.

"I'm South Paw," the other dark-haired biker piped in.

Their leather cuts looked new, not at all weathered like Viper's.

"Have you been part of the club long?" I asked politely.

"Patched in just a few weeks ago," South Paw said. "But we were prospects for a while before that."

"What are prospects?" I asked.

"Club bitches," Crow said with humor. "We do grunt work."

"Like guard duty," South Paw muttered. "The bane of my existence."

"But if you're patched in, why are you still doing guard duty?" I asked in confusion.

"We're on rotation," Crow explained. "But we get stuck doing more shifts because we haven't found new blood yet."

"New blood?"

"New prospects," South Paw expounded. "The club is…going through some changes."

"Club puberty?"

The guys let out booming laughter.

"Ah, I see why Viper likes you. I mean, from what we can tell he doesn't usually like anybody," South Paw said.

"Yeah, I've gathered as much." I kicked at the gravel. "Sorry to bother you guys. I'm just going crazy in there with nothing to do until I go to work later."

"You could play video games," Crow suggested.

"Already done it," I said. "I kicked Savage's ass."

"I'm liking you more and more," South Paw said.

I heard the faint rumblings of a motorcycle, and the both of them snapped to attention.

"You should head back inside," South Paw said. "I'm sure it's one of our guys but don't know for sure."

"Are you expecting trouble?" I asked.

"Plan for the worst, hope for the best," Crow said.

I couldn't really argue with that, so I walked toward the clubhouse. I watched from the porch as the guys opened the gate and a few motorcycles drove through. They parked on the gravel lot and cut the engines. I recognized Viper immediately, but not the other two.

Viper came up the porch, his steps heavy, his boots clomping across the planks of the wooden deck. He was wearing aviators so I couldn't see his eyes. But when he lifted his hand to remove them, my gaze immediately tracked his raw, split knuckles.

Without thought, I reached out and grabbed his hand to stare at it.

He didn't say anything, merely waited for me to come to my own conclusion.

"Club business?"

He nodded slowly.

Viper had said he was muscle for the club. After seeing his knuckles, it became real for me. He lived violence. He sought it out.

"You good, man?" one of the bikers asked as he came up the porch steps.

Viper nodded.

"Your woman gonna take care of you?" the blond biker asked.

I bit my tongue to stop from replying.

"Yeah, she'll take care of me." Viper's tone sounded far too suggestive.

The other men smiled.

"Brooklyn doesn't like it when I come home to her without a shower," the silver fox said. He had salt and pepper hair and several days of dark scruff. "Don't want her blood pressure to skyrocket. She is pregnant, after all."

The blond looked at me. "Hey. I'm Boxer."

"Slash," the silver fox introduced.

"Nice to meet you," I murmured.

"I'll be taking Sutton to work, and then I'll hang around for her shift," Viper said.

"I'll see if I can convince Doc to stop off for a beer," Boxer said.

"Count me out," Slash said.

"Ah, domestic bliss," Boxer joked.

"Why would I want to be out with you assholes when I could be in bed with my woman?" Slash asked. "On that note, I'm showering and heading home."

"She's not at home," I said. "She came to the clubhouse to hang out for a bit, but then she said she had to get back to the bakery. Something about this being wedding season."

"Motherfucker," Slash growled right before he turned and strode to his bike.

"What did I say?" I asked in confusion.

"Slash is overprotective and wants Brooklyn off her feet," Boxer explained.

"Okay." I frowned.

"He thought she was at home. That's where she told him she'd be," Boxer added.

"Ah." I winced. "Did I just start a fight?"

"Yup." Boxer grinned. "Don't worry. It'll end well for both of them. I'm gonna crash for a bit. I was up at the ass-crack of dawn. Later, guys."

Boxer went into the clubhouse and left me alone with Viper.

I gently took his hand again and examined it. Then I took the other and did the same. "We should ice them."

He paused for a moment and then said, "Good idea."

We walked into the clubhouse, and I moved around the kitchen, finding plastic bags and dumping ice into them.

"Your room? Or the couch?" I asked.

"My room."

I headed up the stairs, holding the bags of ice. When we got inside, Viper flipped on the light and then took a seat on the bed. I closed the door behind me and joined him.

"Is that okay?" I asked, placing the ice bags on his knuckles. "Want me to get a towel so it doesn't hurt your skin too bad?"

"It's fine."

I knelt down and reached for his boot.

"What are you doing?" he asked.

I looked up at him in confusion. "Taking care of you. I was going to take off your boots so you could get comfortable."

"I'm a biker. Comfort is the least of my concerns."

I raised my brows. "I'd love nothing more than *to take care of you*, but logistically, how would we make that happen?"

"Unzip and suck."

"Wow," I muttered. "Fucking *wow*."

"You asked."

"Well, you're an asshole." I glared at him. "Sex isn't the only way I can take care of you."

"I don't need you to take care me any other way."

My mouth thinned. "So, unless I use one of my holes, you're not interested in any kind of comfort?"

"I don't need comfort. I need sex."

"Well, I'm not in the fucking mood, asshole. Whose face did you use to bust your knuckles, anyway?"

"None of your business."

"I see." I nodded. "Got it. I'm just a piece of ass with a mouth—and said mouth is only good for one thing—sucking your dick."

I took off his ice packs and flung them across the room. I was suddenly so angry my vision went hazy and red. I didn't know why I was so pissed.

Viper was a biker.

His job was violence.

His relief was sex.

The Old Ladies were wrong. Viper didn't want to keep me. I was nothing more than a convenient fuck toy for whenever he needed to get off.

"Am I a whore?" I asked quietly. "Do you think I'm just some whore who will get on her knees because you told her to? If you think that, then maybe you should be fucking one of those girls who comes to one of your parties looking for a good time."

"You can't be pissed at me for this," he growled. "We're just sex, Sutton. We both agreed to that. Why should it matter if I come to you wanting sex after a fight versus wanting sex just because? I never called you a whore. You called yourself that."

I blinked. He was right. I was angry because I'd wanted to comfort him with soothing touches and gentle, caring actions. Not just sex.

But Viper wanted sex and nothing else.

He hadn't lied. He hadn't promised me something just to get into my pants and then redacted. No. He'd been honest from the start.

Then why does this feel so bad?

"You almost punched one of your brothers because he called me tail. And yet, you're treating me like I'm nothing more than that," I said. "I don't get it."

"It's about respect. Smoke doesn't get to talk about you that way. I wanted everyone to know that."

"Why do I feel like I'm playing a game I don't know the rules to?" I asked.

"Rules? You don't even know what the game *is*," he said. "You're too young to—"

"Not my age again, please, I beg you."

"No. Listen. You're young, and you're inexperienced.

You said you understood what we were doing. You said you got that this was just sex. That we were going to let this run its course. But we're not in a relationship."

Everything he said was true, but the real danger was that my heart was cracking open for a man who neither wanted me long term, nor could promise me that. I talked a big game. I was all bravado. But if you hit my armor just right, you'd get to the sensitive part of me.

I raised my brows. "I may be young, but I'm not stupid. This *is* a relationship, Viper. Whether you want it to be or not. We're exclusive. We might be causal, and our time together might be finite, but you're the one who said you'd take care of me and the baby if I got pregnant."

"Because I'm not a shitbag."

There was no way I was going to admit that I was hurt —and I wasn't sure I even had the right to be. He'd never promised me anything, and yet the more time we spent together, the more I liked him. Really liked him.

I had to take control back. I had to show him that I wasn't in danger of falling for him. I had to show him that when we ended this, I wasn't going to be a broken shell of a woman who fell apart when another man disappointed her.

"You want comfort the way you want it?" I dropped to my knees and reached for his fly. "I can do that."

Chapter 25

I wrote a fake number down on a coaster and slid it to the tipsy guy across the bar. "There you go, sugar. Text me."

He beamed. "I will."

I winked at him and then watched him saunter away to the table with all his friends. He waved the coaster around like a war trophy.

"That makes what?" Mia asked. "Five guys you've slipped a fake number to tonight?"

"Six," I said absently.

"Impressive." She rinsed a few pint glasses in the sink and set them to dry. "Viper looks more and more pissed every time you do it."

"Does he? I hadn't noticed," I lied.

Oh, I'd noticed. I'd noticed every time his jaw clenched when a customer asked to buy me a shot. I noticed when he flexed his sore knuckles like he wanted to punch out every man who spoke to me.

So, I'd made it my mission to flirt harder, smile brighter, and be as effortlessly charming as my personality would allow.

It paid off.

Not only was the tip jar already full and it wasn't even nine, but I'd succeeded in making Viper violently jealous.

"Careful," I said to him as I refilled his water.

"Careful what?" he rumbled.

"Careful or your face might freeze that way," I said cheekily. "At least your bad mood hasn't affected my tips. Let me know if you need anything." I turned on my heel and put a little sway in my hips.

"Margarita on the rocks with salt, please," a college girl ordered.

"Margaritas have a shitload of sugar," I said. "Unless you're ready for a wicked hangover, how about a shot of tequila instead?"

The woman smiled. "Done and done. Better make it two shots, then."

"My gal," I teased. I poured her two shots, set limes and a saltshaker down in front of her and watched her throw them back.

"Fuck yes," she said. "That was perfect. Now I have enough courage to ask that hot guy in the corner to play pool."

I glanced over her shoulder at said guy in question. He was already watching her.

"You're good as gold," I assured her. "He's looking at your ass as we speak."

"God, I love this place." She smiled. "You're awesome." She strode off with confidence and headed for the guy.

"You're a natural matchmaker," Mia said.

"Booze helps people get laid. I'm like the fairy godmother of tequila and hookups."

"Whatever you're doing, keep doing it. Everyone's happy. The tip jar is full, and I can't remember the last time I enjoyed bartending so much. Normally I don't do this. But a few of my bartenders quit a few weeks ago. My best ran off and got married to an oil field worker and moved to Oklahoma, so I've had to fill the gaps."

"Your bad fortune is my good luck."

The hours flew by. Customers were wonderful and I didn't have to use the water gun once. Aside from Viper's brooding silence, I was happy. It felt great to be busy. My days in the clubhouse without work felt so long with nothing to do.

"Do you need me to cover more shifts?" I asked Mia.

She looked at me as she unscrewed a fresh bottle of well tequila. "I've got you scheduled for three late nights already."

"Yeah?" I asked. I wiped up a puddle of beer with a damp bar rag and then chucked it into the bin in the corner.

"How do you feel about that? Do the late nights fuck up your daytime schedule?"

"I'm not really doing much with my days," I said slowly. I lowered my voice. "Except Viper."

Mia blinked and then cracked a grin. "And that doesn't keep you busy?"

"It keeps me plenty busy," I assured her. "But today he had to run out to do some stuff. Club stuff."

Mia glanced from me to Viper and then back to me. "I see."

"If it hadn't been for you guys stopping by, I would've been bored out of my skull."

"I don't usually like to schedule my bartenders more than three bar shifts," she said. "The hours are late and the customers are nonstop…you need that break to recharge."

Disappointment curled through me. I was going to get

stuck during the days hanging out at the clubhouse with nothing to do.

"Do you have any experience with ordering and inventory?" Mia asked.

"Nah. At Spurs I just waited tables, tallied my receipts, turned in the cash and left. Very in and out. Not a lot of responsibility."

"Would you be interested in learning that kind of thing?" Mia asked. "I'm asking because I'm looking for a new bar manager. Someone to do the schedule and keep up with inventory, and maybe get behind the bar and sling drinks if it gets crazy."

"That sounds kind of like a permanent position," I said.

She shrugged. "If you like it, it can be permanent. I've had to be at the bar more than I want lately, and I don't really like the time away from my family to be honest. Colt would be thrilled if I was home more. But he gets that this bar is kind of my baby."

"Your bar baby is contending with your real baby, huh?" I asked.

"And my teenage son," she said. "We have a thirteen-year-old boy."

"You have a *teenager*?" I asked in shock.

"Adopted," she explained with a grin. "Silas. You'll meet him Sunday at the barbecue."

"The barbecue, right," I said. "Why am I getting the feeling that the barbecue is more than just a barbecue?"

"Whatever do you mean?" Mia drawled.

"I mean, you say it's so I can meet everyone, but is it that? Or is it so everyone can scrutinize me and Viper?"

"Yes. That." Mia laughed. "My word of advice for all of this? Just roll with it."

"Easy for you to say. No doubt you had your own scrutinizing when you got together with Colt."

"Boy, did I," she said. "But that's another story for another day. Now, let me teach you how to make flaming shots. It drives the college crowd wild."

※

Viper somehow managed to hold his tongue. After my shift, without a word, I hopped on the back of his bike, and he drove us to the clubhouse.

It was familiar and comfortable, and I had to be careful. This wasn't my home.

There were several bikes parked on the gravel lot, and when Viper cut the engine, I immediately heard laughter and conversation in the air. A party was clearly underway in the backyard.

Viper grabbed my hand and led the way into the clubhouse. I took two steps for his every one, nearly jogging to keep up with him. He led me past the kitchen with liquor bottles and red cups. Acid sat on the couch with a woman straddling him. She ran her fingers through his hair and bent down to kiss him.

Raze was in the recliner, getting similar ministrations.

Booze and sex were rampant this night.

I kept my eyes on Viper's back as he led me deeper into the clubhouse and up the stairs. He guided me to his room and shut the door.

Energy crackled between us.

I turned to face him, prepared to give him sass, but his expression said he wasn't in the mood.

"You were a flirty brat tonight," he rumbled.

"Was I?" I crossed my arms over my chest and cocked

a hip. My stance was pugnacious, and Viper's eyes suddenly gleamed.

"You know you were."

I shrugged. "Tips were good tonight. So, I won't make any apologies."

"You did it on purpose. To piss me off. You gave out your number seven times."

"Six," I corrected.

"Seven. There was that guy who cornered you when you came back from the bathroom."

"Oh right. I'd forgotten about him."

He strode toward me, his steps controlled.

My heart beat in trepidation, but not outright fear. I didn't fear Viper. Even when he was in a shit mood.

He reached out and gently grasped my neck in his massive hand. His thumb brushed the spot below my ear. Viper gave the column of my throat a gentle squeeze.

"You punished me tonight," he growled softly. "For the shit that happened earlier."

"Earlier?"

"When you were on your knees, pretending you were fine with it all."

"I am fine with it."

"Liar," he whispered. He leaned down and took my lips with his before I could respond. His mouth covered mine and he consumed me. When I didn't open to him immediately, he squeezed my neck again.

I gasped and his tongue swept inside my mouth.

His other arm came around to hold me in place. He kissed me until my knees were weak and then he let me go.

"You going to be honest with me now?" he asked quietly.

My lids fluttered opened, and I stared up at him. "Honest. Okay."

"Admit it. You were pissed about how I wanted you this afternoon."

I shook my head. "If I'd been pissed, do you think I would've gotten on my knees for you?"

He arched a brow as he slowly stripped out of his leather cut. Viper hung it up on the hook behind the door, then he removed his pistol and holster and set it on the nightstand. "Take off your clothes, Sutton." He sat on the edge of the bed and began unlacing his boots.

I nibbled my lip as I watched him.

He stopped his movements when he saw I wasn't getting naked. And waited.

Swallowing, I bent over and kicked off my shoes. Next came the tank which I tossed aside, followed by my jeans. For some reason, I balked at removing my thong.

Viper didn't say anything as he finally began to strip down again. He leaned back and clutched his erection, giving it a few long strokes.

"Come here," he said, his voice low.

I stalked toward him and stopped when I was at the edge of the bed. He let go of himself and reached out to drag my thong down my legs. I stepped out of it, now completely naked.

"Bed," he ordered as he rose. "Lie on your back."

We switched places. I settled onto the mattress and peered at him. He stood by the bed, my thong still in his hand. He wrapped it around his shaft.

I frowned in confusion.

"Spread your legs for me."

I did.

"Now touch yourself while I watch."

I blinked. "What?"

He repeated himself.

"I don't—I don't understand. You're not going to fuck me?"

"No," he said, continuing to clench my thong around his shaft.

"I've never done this."

"First time for everything," he said.

"So you want me to touch myself while you touch yourself and we're not touching each other?"

"That's right."

"I don't get it."

"I want to watch you get yourself off. What's hard to understand about that?"

This was intimate in a way I hadn't expected. This was more than just fucking. He wanted me to be vulnerable in front of him, and he was going to be vulnerable in front of me, too.

My eyes dipped to his erect shaft. I loved having him inside me, but this was exciting and I was tantalized.

"Can we turn off the main light and switch on the lamp?" I asked.

"No. I want to see every inch of you. Don't try and hide from me."

I swallowed and then I slowly trailed a hand over my breast. I swirled a nipple until it pebbled. I pinched it between my thumb and forefinger and then cradled my breast.

I slid my flattened palm over my belly down to my mound. My legs were spread, and I slipped my fingers between my folds. It was quiet in the room, except for Viper's breathing.

My lids lowered as I watched him continue to stroke himself, using my thong to aid him.

"Eyes on me, Sutton," he commanded. "I need to see your eyes."

Our gazes locked as I continued to touch myself. I felt lost, out of control. I enjoyed touching myself, but I was too in my head about it.

"I need help," I whispered. "I won't get there on my own."

"You will. Put your fingers deep inside yourself, Sutton. Do it for me."

Viper's order had the desired effect I'd hoped for. I shivered from the command in his tone, and I glided my fingers into my wet, welcoming body.

I moaned.

"Yeah, baby," he growled. "Just like that. Deeper. Use your thumb to brush your clit. Imagine it's my mouth between your thighs. You'd like that, wouldn't you? Imagine me licking you until you come."

"Yes," I breathed.

Sparks ignited between my legs.

"You know what I want to do?" he asked, his strokes changing rhythm. He slowed it down, drawing out his pleasure while he waited for me to catch up.

"What?" I asked.

"I want to make you come with my tongue," he said. "Just my mouth. No fingers. And when you're still shaking from your orgasm, I want to slide into you. Make you come hard on my dick."

Nodding, I pumped my finger faster. But it wasn't thick enough. It wasn't Viper. So I added another finger.

"But that wouldn't be the end, Sutton."

"No?"

He shook his head and took a step toward the bed, close enough to touch me if he wanted, but he didn't.

"I'd flip you over and I'd take your ass. I'd work in nice and slow. I'd play with your pretty little clit, making sure you were nice and wet. I'd work all the way in, seated inside you, but I wouldn't move until you were writhing and begging me to. Only then, Sutton. Only then would I fuck your ass and come in it."

His filthy words painted a picture I desperately wanted to become a reality. His voice, his entrancing eyes, him fisting his cock finally had me convulsing around my fingers.

I came with a cry.

Viper's strokes were almost violent as he thrust his hips forward until he finally came. His essence hit my chest and belly. It was warm on my skin, and it fueled a second orgasm.

As I lay on the bed, covered in his seed, I couldn't stop the smile that spread across my face.

"If that was punishment, I think I'll be bad more often."

Chapter 26

"Sutton," Viper growled. "Sutton, wake up."

I was jarred from unconsciousness, my foggy brain confused and addled.

"Wha—what is it?" I asked.

"You were having a nightmare."

I felt like I was burning up from the inside out. I flung the covers off me and took a deep breath. My heart was racing inside my chest.

"I'm hot," I gasped.

Panic and anxiety gripped my throat. I scrambled from the bed like a rabid animal.

"Sutton—"

"I can't breathe," I panted.

The lamp on the nightstand came on and Viper climbed from the bed.

I scurried away from him until my back hit the wall.

"Hey," Viper said as he strode toward me. He wore boxers, but his chest was bare.

I held out a hand to stop him. "Just…give me a moment."

He nodded.

I sank down to the floor and curled my knees to my chest. I closed my eyes and took slow, even breaths. The floor was cold, and I shivered as my body cooled. After a while, my T-shirt no longer felt like it was going to strangle me. When I finally got myself under control, I looked up at him.

He scrutinized me, his expression dark.

"I'm okay," I assured him.

I wasn't sure I believed the words coming out of my mouth, but at least it no longer felt like my heart was being squeezed by a fist. My breaths became regular, and my pulse began to slow.

"Sorry I woke you."

He sat down in front of me, his body mirroring mine. He placed his large hands on my knees. "What were you dreaming about?"

"No idea," I said truthfully. "You woke me up and I was just…panicked."

"You were thrashing around and whimpering, but you weren't coherent."

I bit my lip, hard.

"You really don't have any idea what you were dreaming about?" he asked slowly.

"Do *you* have an idea what I was dreaming about?" I asked.

He paused a moment before he said, "I have a pretty good idea, yeah."

"Enlighten me."

"Come on, Sutton."

"Come on, what?" I demanded.

"You're not stupid. You were having a nightmare about killing someone. You've been burying it. But when you sleep, you can't control what you dream about. Am I right?"

I rubbed the back of my neck. My muscles were tight. "I don't want to talk about it."

"We're talking about it."

"Talking about it won't change what happened," I said.

"Burying it won't make it go away."

"Oh, you're an expert, huh?" I pushed a strand of hair behind my ear. "What am I supposed to do? Talk about all my trauma, get into the nitty gritty about what a shitty human I am?"

"Sutton, it was self-defense—"

"I know that."

"But a man died," he said, his voice suddenly quiet. "Self-defense or not, that's still going to fuck with you."

"Why, though?" I asked, my voice cracking. I cleared my throat. "He was evil. I shouldn't feel bad about what I've done."

"How *do* you feel about it?"

"I don't know," I admitted. "I refuse to let myself think about it."

"If you don't deal with this, the nightmares are gonna get worse."

"Yeah, but there's no guarantee the nightmares will go away, even if I confront this."

Viper stood. "Get up."

"Why?"

"Just, get up." He reached a hand down for me to take.

I seized it and he hauled me to my feet.

"What are you doing?" I asked.

He didn't reply as he marched me into the bathroom. He flipped on the light.

"Viper—"

He gripped my hips and turned me around so that I

faced the mirror. My eyes were wide in my pale face and my hair was a tangled mess. He loomed behind me.

"It wasn't your fault," he said.

My gaze met his in the glass. "I know that."

"Then say it. Look yourself in the eye and say it."

I took a deep breath. "It wasn't my fault."

"You did nothing wrong."

My mouth clamped shut.

"Say it," he commanded.

With a sigh, I said, "I did nothing wrong."

"You defended yourself."

"I defended myself."

"You were not a victim."

"I was not a victim."

"You are strong."

A bubble of emotion surged up my throat. "I am strong," I croaked.

"This will not define you."

"This will not define me."

"Bad shit happens all the time."

"Bad shit happens all the time."

He placed his hands on my shoulders. "You are not alone."

"I am not alone," I whispered.

"Louder."

"I am not alone."

"Again."

"I am not alone."

Something about saying it for the third time broke the dam holding back all the emotion walled within me, and it came flooding out.

I clutched the counter and let the tears stream down my cheeks. When I realized Viper was witnessing my meltdown, I tried to turn away.

"No," he said gruffly. "Let it out. I'm here for you. You're not alone."

I cried harder.

He pulled me to his chest and held me. He stroked my hair and cradled me in his arms.

"Guess I'm not such a badass now," I muttered. "Am I?"

"You're still a badass. And in the long run you'll be better for all this. Trust me."

I nodded and a hiccough escaped me lips. I wiped my cheeks and took a few minutes to let my breaths even out.

"Come on. Let's get back to bed."

Once we were settled and the lamp was off, I said, "Viper?"

"Yeah?"

"Thanks for that."

"You're welcome."

We were both silent for a few minutes when I asked, "Viper?"

"Yeah?"

"Can we act like my nightmare never happened?"

He paused. "It wasn't the first nightmare you've had, Sutton."

"No?"

"No."

I swallowed, hating that Viper had seen me vulnerable and I hadn't even known about it.

"I won't mention it again," he said.

"Thank you," I whispered.

It took me a while, but eventually I fell back asleep.

My phone rang early the next morning. With a groan, I launched myself over Viper to grab it. It slipped through my fingers and clattered to the floor. Unfortunately, that didn't stop the ringing.

"Fuck, careful," Viper growled as I almost kneed him between the legs.

I hit the floor and picked up my screaming phone, quickly silencing it.

"Who the hell is calling this early?" he demanded.

"Spam," I lied. I climbed off the floor and padded into the bathroom. I quickly turned my phone off and then did my business. Just as I was about to hop into the shower, Viper came into the bathroom and shut the door.

His boxers were tented and his morning wood was raging.

I stepped into the steam and slid the curtain shut. I closed my eyes and turned my face up to the shower spray.

"You've been getting a lot of spam calls." The sound of the curtain gliding along the metal rod was loud in my ears. I opened my eyes and rotated slowly so I didn't slip and then gave him the water.

"Yeah, I guess so."

"Why are you lying to me?"

I wrapped my arms around my body, as if concealing my nudity also concealed my vulnerability. After him comforting me through my nightmare, I was feeling exposed and raw. "I'm not lying. It really was a spam caller."

"Do you think I'm stupid, or just not observant? The way you leapt from the bed and reached for your phone…"

"It's early in the morning," I said. "I wasn't expecting it to ring."

"Why wasn't it on silent?" he asked, leaning forward and pressing his forearm to the wall.

He towered over me. He was so big that even when he was doing nothing more than standing there, he was intimidating. He didn't have to try, he just was.

"Sutton? Why wasn't your phone on silent even though you just worked a night shift at the bar?"

"I forgot," I defended. "And your phone is never on silent."

"Mine can't be." His gaze narrowed. "But yours can. So that leads me to the conclusion that you were expecting a call that you didn't want to miss."

"Wow, your detective skills are next level." I pressed a hand to his chest, covering the familiar tattoo, and gently pushed.

Viper took the hint and eased back. I inhaled a deep sigh of relief, glad that I no longer felt trapped, but I kept my hand on his chest.

I traced his ink with my finger, wondering why I couldn't place the design. I knew I'd seen it before.

"You're keeping something from me," he said.

"About who's calling?" I rolled my eyes. "Please. You're overreaching here."

"I'm not going to let this go. I trust my gut. And you're hiding something from me. Ex-boyfriend?"

"No."

"Loan shark?"

I burst out laughing. "Seriously?" I reached for the soap and made a lather.

"Okay, let's see. In debt with the mob?"

"Keep going. Your imagination is hilarious."

"You're secretly still married and the guy's stalking you?"

"Careful, Viper, you sound downright playful."

Instead of using the lather to wash myself, I covered Viper in bubbles. I washed his arms, his chest…lower.

I got my hands slippery and soapy and then gently grasped his erect shaft. He clenched his jaw and closed his eyes.

I breathed an internal sigh of relief when Viper gave himself over to the moment instead of continuing to interrogate me. I coaxed an orgasm from him, extracting every bit of pleasure from his body. His seed spurted in long thin ropes between us.

Viper's eyes were slits, and his breathing was heavy as he peered at me. I continued to massage him, even after his release.

My hand went to his hip, and I used him as an anchor to move out from underneath the shower spray and give it to him. I washed quickly and then got out.

"We're not done with this conversation," Viper growled, poking his head from behind the shower curtain.

"Sure we are," I chirped, wrapping the towel around me. I shot him a cheeky grin and then escaped to the bedroom. I quickly threw on my jeans and tank and left my soiled thong that Viper had used to get himself off. I left Viper's room before he was even out of the shower.

I made it back to my room without encountering anyone. The guys who lived in the clubhouse were late sleepers since they were up at odd hours of the night.

I quickly changed out of my dirty clothes and tossed them in the corner. The laundry was already in a pile, and I needed to do a load.

But first, coffee.

The living room and kitchen area were devoid of people, and I plopped down on the couch.

Viper's scrutiny had been intense. He was observant and curious. I wondered how long I'd be able to fend him off before having to come clean.

The coffee maker beeped, and I got off the couch to pour myself a cup. Viper strode into the room, fully dressed.

"Do you have more club business you have to deal with today?" I asked.

He poured himself a cup of coffee and then lifted the mug from the counter, but he didn't move toward the living room. "I always have club business to deal with."

I rolled my eyes. "Yeah, okay, but what I meant was, are you leaving me here to my own devices while you go off and do biker things until it's time to take me to work?"

"Biker things? What are biker things?"

"I dunno." I absently rubbed my knuckles. "Roughing some people up. Breaking some kneecaps with a bat. Tinkering with motorcycle engines? That kind of stuff."

"I don't break kneecaps with bats," Viper stated.

"I know. I was joking…"

"I shoot them in the knees instead. Sends a clearer message." He took a sip of coffee and watched me intently.

I blinked a few times. "You're kidding, right?"

He didn't say a word, but instead just flexed his hand that was resting on the counter, emphasizing the raw, broken skin on his knuckles. Viper wasn't joking. If he said he shot people, I'd be wise to believe him.

The clomping of heavy boots interrupted our conversation and South Paw appeared in the kitchen.

I wasn't sure how I felt about what Viper had said. And if I had a problem with it, would that make me a hypocrite? My actions a week earlier had been in self-defense, but if Viper killed or injured anyone for the sake of the club, it was different.

Wasn't it? Or was I being delusional about the level of violence the club was involved in?

"Morning, kids," South Paw greeted.

"Morning," I muttered.

"Rough night at the bar?" he asked with a sympathetic tone.

"Not really, just busy. I'm tired, that's all." The lies were spilling out of me this morning.

South Paw opened the fridge and pulled out a carton of creamer. He poured the remainder of it into his cup before chucking it into the garbage.

Viper took two large swallows of his coffee before putting his cup in the sink. "I'm out. I'll see you later."

He stalked toward me and right in front of South Paw, grasped my waist with one hand, cradled my head with the other and then plundered my mouth.

I vaguely heard South Paw chuckle, but I didn't care because Viper was kissing me with possession and purpose. When he released me, his stare was heated and penetrating. Without another word, he stalked from the clubhouse.

South Paw looked at me. "That dude is intense as fuck."

"Right?" I asked with a slow smile.

"I'll be damned," he said with a chuckle. "You actually like him."

"Why does everyone keep saying that?" I asked in exasperation. "Is he so unlikable?"

"Not at all. He's a good guy. A loyal brother."

"I know he's prickly," I said slowly. "But I think he's got a soft heart."

"The best heart. What he did for that girl…it's an honor to call him family."

I frowned. "What girl? What did he do?"

South Paw stilled. "Oh, uh, never mind." He clenched his cup tighter. "Gotta go. See you later."

"Okay, I'm not gonna lie," Annabella said. "I didn't think you were going to be able to hold your own with this crowd and the rush, but I stand corrected."

I grinned. "Judged me before you met me, huh?"

The other bartender had the grace to look sheepish. "Well, when Mia said she hired a new girl who'd waited tables but never bartended, I thought for sure I was going to have to carry you. But nope. You hold your own. Plus, you're cool."

"How long have you been bartending?"

"Better part of ten years," she said wryly.

"Ah, a seasoned warrior, got it. I'm glad I measure up."

The door to the bar opened and in strolled three gorgeous, tatted men who looked neither like bikers nor the preppy crowd. But they all had swagger and big-dick energy as they sauntered up to the bar.

"I was wondering if I was going to see you tonight," Annabella said to the dark-haired man.

"Hey, gorgeous." He leaned his tall body over the counter and brushed his lips along her cheek. His gaze slid to me, looking at me with interested blue eyes. "I haven't met you before."

"Lay off the charm, Virgil," Annabella said with a laugh. "Her very scary biker boyfriend is sitting in the corner, and it looks like he's already locked onto you with his eyes."

Virgil looked at Viper, who was doing exactly as Annabella said.

"You're dating Viper?" Virgil asked, a slow smile appearing on his lips.

"Don't tell me—you're surprised…"

"*Very* surprised," Virgil said.

The blond giant standing behind Virgil was scowling at everyone. "Pilsner."

"Say please, Homer," Annabella demanded.

Homer clenched his jaw and then gritted out, "Please."

The third man whipped out his wallet and placed his credit card on the counter. "We'll keep a tab."

I scooped up his card while Annabella got to pouring Homer his beer. I glanced at the name on the plastic. *Three Kings, Roman Jackson.*

"What's Three Kings?" I inquired.

"She's never heard of us, Roman," Virgil said, slapping the tall man on his back.

"Should I have heard of you?" I asked.

"Based on who you're dating? Yeah," Virgil said.

"Your arrogance is stifling," Annabella quipped.

"Don't mind my brother. He's got the energy of a Jack Russell," Roman said.

"But the heart of a Golden Retriever," Virgil jested.

"Oh, you're brothers," I said, finally understanding. "Got it."

"We own the Three Kings tattoo parlor," Roman announced. "We ink the Tarnished Angels and all their Old Ladies. Guess I'll have you in the chair soon…"

"Wait, I'm not an Old Lady," I said. "We're just dating. Nothing serious."

"Hmm. Right." Roman raised his brows.

Why does no one seem to believe me?

Annabella handed over the beers and the Jackson brothers headed to a vacant booth.

I glanced at Viper and gave him a little finger wave.

My conversation with South Paw had been brewing in the back of my mind for hours. It wasn't the first time someone had said something about Viper's past. They all knew the truth, and here I was, sleeping with the man who hadn't told me a thing.

Who was the girl, and what had Viper done for her?

Chapter 27

"I NEED to use the restroom real fast," I said.

"Go," Annabella urged. "Before the next rush."

"I didn't think we were going to get a lull tonight," I said with a laugh.

"Just long enough to play catch-up and restock." She winked.

I went to the end of the bar and told Viper I was going to the restroom and to please not follow me. He reluctantly nodded. I'd hoped by wearing jeans and my cowboy boots and a gray V-neck tee instead of daisy dukes, he wouldn't feel inclined to push me against the wall and distract me as he'd done in the past. No doubt it would be enjoyable if he did, but I didn't want to leave Annabella on the floor by herself, and I especially didn't want it getting back to Mia that I couldn't be professional. She'd given me a chance because Colt had asked her to, but I refused to be a disappointment or a drain on her.

As I was coming out of the bathroom, Roman was strolling down the hallway toward the men's room.

"Hey," he greeted. "I didn't get your name while we were ordering, and I feel like a dick."

"Sutton."

"Sutton, nice to meet you." He inclined his head and was just about to move along when I placed my hand on his arm to stop him.

"Sorry to bother you," I said, "but I have a really random question for you."

"Shoot."

I dropped my hand. "You said you ink the club."

"Yeah."

"So you're familiar with their artwork," I pressed.

"Well, some of them, yeah. I haven't inked any of the new guys."

"New guys. You mean like Viper?"

"Yeah."

"Right." I nodded. "I know this is a long shot, but if I show you a tattoo, would you be able to tell me its meaning?"

"Depends on what it is. But yeah, maybe."

I peered down the hallway. The bar was still quiet. "Let's go to the office real fast."

I unlocked the door and pushed it open. I flipped on the light and then immediately went to the desk. I grabbed a piece of paper and a pen and drew the design I'd seen on Viper's chest.

"I'm not an artist," I said, "but this is the idea." I turned the page around to show Roman.

He stared down at it for a long moment and then he said, "I recognize it."

"You do?" I asked, my heart beating in excitement.

"Yeah. Where'd you see it?"

"On a customer," I lied.

He looked at me and I held his gaze, hoping he'd

bought my story. Finally, he said, "It's a prison tattoo. For someone who's done real time."

"Oh," I said quietly.

Now I remember.

"Thanks," I said, plastering a fake smile on my face.

He examined me and looked like he was going to say something else, but at the last minute, all he did was nod. "Glad I could help."

"I better get back out there," I said. "Before the next rush."

Roman went out of the office first and I locked up behind him. I needed a minute to get my head around what he'd said, so I went to the storeroom to grab a few bottles of liquor I knew we'd need later on.

I made it back onto the floor just as the trickle of customers turned into a flood.

"Thought you got lost," Annabella said.

"Nah. I just realized we'd probably need a resupply for what's coming." I set the bottles down, out of the way of foot traffic behind the bar.

"Good thinking," she said.

I glanced at Viper as he sat in the corner and when he saw me, I forced a smile. The rush came shortly after, obliterating all my questions about Viper and his past.

～

I straddled Viper and ran my fingers across his tattoo. His arms were folded beneath his head as he peered at me, his eyes heavy. His cheeks were still flushed with color, but his heartbeat was already back to normal.

"I think I want one of these," I murmured.

"Yeah?"

I nodded.

"Any idea what you want?"

"Something that has some meaning," I said. "Maybe a butterfly on my hip."

He cracked a grin. "Your hip, huh? Sure you don't want a tramp stamp?"

"Evil." I tickled his ribs to see if it made him squirm. He didn't budge. "Not ticklish?"

"Not my ribs."

I raised my brows. "But somewhere else?"

"If I tell you, you have to promise never to use it against me."

"I promise."

"Back of my knees."

"No kidding."

"I swear."

"How random." I continued tracing his ink. "Do your tattoos have meaning?"

"Yes."

"All of them?" I pressed.

"All of them."

"This one I get," I said, stroking his tattoo of the club logo. "It's pretty self-explanatory. But what does this one mean?"

I was asking about his prison tattoo, and I wanted to know if he'd tell me the truth.

"It's a reminder of how to live my life," he said.

"What does that mean? How do you live your life?"

"Brotherhood. Family. Protect the innocent."

I nibbled my lip, still debating if I wanted to open up this can of worms. And even though Viper and I didn't have a future, I still wanted to know whose bed I was sleeping in.

"I know you were in prison," I said quietly.

His expression didn't change. "Who told you?"

"No one. Well, the Old Ladies alluded to you having a past, and that it was dark. But it wasn't them. I saw your tattoo and I asked Roman about it—to see if he recognized it."

"Why did you ask Roman? Why didn't you ask me?"

I suddenly realized the danger in asking about something so particular—I hadn't thought through what would happen if he connected the dots as to why I was so curious about it.

"Would you have told me?" I asked, panic rising in my belly.

"Not the point of the question, is it?" He removed his hands from beneath his head and sat up, catching me in his arms so I couldn't escape. "What aren't *you* telling me, Sutton?"

My eyes widened. "What? What do you mean?"

"Do you think I'm stupid? Or do you think I'll let the matter drop? This has something to do with the phone calls, doesn't it? Who called you the other morning? It has something to do with all of this, doesn't it?"

I swallowed but didn't reply.

"I think it's time we had some real honesty between us."

"You know what? Never mind. I don't need to know why you were in prison. None of my business."

"You could be sleeping with a convicted murderer."

"Am I?" I asked.

"Would it change what we're doing if I said yes?"

"I know you're involved in…stuff. Your club wouldn't have been able to help me without being on the other side of the law. Would it stop me from sleeping with you? I don't know. I guess I'd have to know why you were in prison."

We stared at each other, and then he said, "Is this one

of those leap-of-faith moments? Where I tell you the truth and then you finally tell me what's going on with you?"

"This goes beyond just sleeping together," I said. "This is like...actually getting to deeply know each other."

"Why do you think I don't do shit like this?" he demanded. "I'm not the guy to promise women anything, and if I don't promise, then I don't have to explain myself or worry about their fucking feelings."

"You worry about my feelings?"

"I'm starting to, which bugs the fuck out of me."

"I knew there was a soft underbelly to your beastly exterior."

His hands skimmed up my bare back. "Let's get dressed."

"I don't want to go anywhere," I grumbled.

"Just outside. I want to have this conversation under the open sky with a bottle of bourbon."

It was three in the morning and the clubhouse was quiet. No wild party this evening.

We stopped by the kitchen and Viper pulled a full bottle of bourbon from the top of the fridge. He didn't even bother with glasses.

The night air wasn't as muggy as I'd expected, and Viper lit a few torches to keep the bugs away. I sat in a camp chair and lifted my knees to my chest and hugged them. He sat in another chair and faced me.

Viper unscrewed the bottle and handed it to me.

"You first." I took a long draught and then handed it back to him. He took three drinks to my one.

"I've got a younger sister," he began. His tone was dark, as though he was reliving something he could barely stand to discuss. "Her taste in men is worse than my mom's —which says a lot. I went over to her house one day while she wasn't home to grab something I'd left over there. I've done that a dozen times before and never thought anything of it. But that time I walked in on my sister's boyfriend raping my thirteen-year-old niece, Chloe."

My breath hitched. "Oh God, no."

He nodded. "I went into a rage like I'd never been in before. I beat that motherfucker so bad it looked like a war zone in the room. I bashed his face and skull in with my bare hands until he was unrecognizable, and then I left him for dead. I thought he was a goner, and I was glad. Fuck the consequences. I wasn't me in that moment. It wasn't about *me*. It was about Chloe…she…that *motherfucker*. But somehow, the bastard lived. They rushed him to the hospital, and he fucking lived. He was in a coma for three months before he woke up. I did five years for it."

"That's *bullshit*," I blurted out. "You did time? Because you were protecting your niece?"

"I did time because my sister convinced my niece not to testify on my behalf. My sister is a lost cause. She's mental. She was still in love and in total denial. She convinced Chloe that it would be better if she didn't relive what happened, and before Child Protective Services got to her, she clam-shelled, and that was that. I could have gotten fifteen years, but the club got me a good attorney and he was able to get the sentence down to five."

"Your sister stayed with the boyfriend, didn't she?" I asked quietly.

"She tried. Went to visit that piece of shit in the hospital while he was healing. But when he came out of the coma, he bounced as soon as he could. I hadn't been convicted yet, and he was worried if I got out, I was going to come back and finish the job. And I fucking would, in a heartbeat. My mom was furious with my sister over it. Never forgave her. Mom died while I was in prison."

Emotion lodged in my throat. So many lives had been ruined because a piece of shit preyed on a young girl. Viper spending time in prison. His mom dying without getting to see her son free again. A family torn apart.

Without a word, Viper handed me the bottle of bourbon. I downed a good amount, my nose singeing.

"What happened to Chloe?" I asked.

"She ran away from home at fifteen. I have no idea where she is or what she's doing."

"Are you—I mean, do you want to try and find her?"

"I wouldn't even know where to look. I just hope she knows that if she needed me, she could call and I'd be there for her."

My heart split open as I looked at this brutal, giant of a man. A man who groused and scowled, who barely tolerated other people.

"I knew it," I murmured.

"Knew what? That I was a bad guy?"

"No. I knew you try to keep yourself shut away because it's too hard caring about others. And you're not a bad guy. What you did was…God, Viper…"

"I only wish I'd killed him. Rid the world of one more shitbag who steals the light of innocents."

"You were afraid to tell me. Why?" I asked. "What you did was heroic."

"I'm not a hero," he protested. "And I'm not a good guy. I've done shit for my club that in no way makes me a hero."

"But I'm not talking about that. I'm talking about what you did for Chloe."

"I just don't want you looking at me with rose-colored glasses. I do bad shit. The club does bad shit, too. But I protect those I care about."

"The club knows you did time. Right?"

"Yeah."

"And the Old Ladies? Do they know?"

"They know."

"So, everyone knows. And now I know," I said.

"I'm losing the point of this conversation."

"I guess the point I'm trying to make is, should I run off? Should I back away because of what you've done? Fuck, Viper, what kind of person would I be to judge you for what you've done when I've killed in self-defense. Are we any different? You and I?"

We shared the bottle for a few quiet moments and then he said, "Now you."

Nodding, I realized I couldn't hide the truth from him any longer. Not after what he'd shared with me. When he'd been prepared to see me walk away and end all of this for the truth. We both refused to admit that this was more than just sleeping together.

But it was.

"My dad is in prison," I said as I met his gaze. "For something far less noble than what you did."

"What'd he do?" Viper asked.

"Tried to rob a bank and failed. He went in when I was nineteen. He's serving a twenty-year sentence. He's the one who's been calling me." I gripped the neck of the bottle.

"You take his calls?" Viper asked.

"Usually. It's been kind of hard…what with where I'm currently living. I haven't had a lot of privacy."

"You mean you were trying to hide it."

"Like you were hiding that you went to prison?"

"I wasn't hiding that."

"Maybe not, but you weren't forthcoming about it either."

"So, was it the tattoo that finally made you ask?"

"Yeah, but honestly that was just the culmination of

things, I guess." I didn't want to throw South Paw under the bus. I doubted Viper would've appreciated South Paw's slip up.

"Why do you take the calls from your dad?" Viper asked.

"Because he's my *dad*," I explained. "He did a bad thing. I get that. But he's still my dad and he's all I have left."

He didn't say anything for a moment as he scratched his jaw. "You visit him?"

I nodded. "It's been hard, without a car. But there's a bus route that gets me within walking distance of the prison."

I'd sold the car I had for the down payment on the trailer. I'd worked like a dog the last few years. The trailer had just been paid off. And now I'd cash in on the insurance money and move on with my life.

"Where's your mom?" he asked.

"Died when I was a baby. Despite my dad being a criminal, he was a pretty good dad growing up. We bounced around a lot, but it is what it is."

We sipped on the bourbon in pensive silence and then I asked, "Are we going to continue lying about this?"

"Lying about what?"

"About what we're doing. We just shared some really personal shit, Viper. Granted, I don't have a lot of experience with relationships, but even I know this isn't just sleeping together."

"You want it to be something more?"

I looked him in the eyes. "Do you?"

"I asked you first."

"Right," I muttered. "I'm supposed to tell you how I feel about all this, hanging out on a limb all by myself. And then you'll saw off the damn tree branch and I'll fall to the ground."

"You can still get out," he said quietly. "The cartel war that's coming…it's gonna be bad, Sutton. People are gonna fucking die. That's what happens in war. Good men, bad men, innocent people who have nothing to do with any of it…no one is safe. You can get out of all this. As soon as you're in the clear, you can take your insurance check and get out of town. Hell, it's probably smarter for you to do that."

"You want me to stay," I said softly. "Don't you?"

"Don't expect a declaration from me. I'm not the kind of man who will pour it on thick. Women have come and gone in my life, and I've never wanted anything more from any of them. But you…"

"Me?" I prodded.

He sighed. "You're different. And I can't bullshit anymore. I like you. In and out of bed."

"*Like* isn't enough to stick around for the long haul," I said. "Especially when shit is gonna go hot. *Like* is not enough to build a life on. And what am I even talking about? Building a life. I've known you the better part of a week. You can't catch feelings that fast."

"Yeah, you can." He leaned forward and wrapped his large hand around my ankle.

"I have no real experience with this stuff," I muttered. "I have one ex-boyfriend. *One.* I fell into bed with you because I wanted to, but sex is not love."

"No shit, sex isn't love," he agreed.

"I don't know what I'm doing."

"Makes two of us."

"We barely know each other," I protested.

"You know more about me than some people I've known for a decade."

My lips softened ever so slightly and then I snapped my spine straight. "Do not woo me with your words."

"I don't woo." He cocked his head. "Admit it, Sutton. You're afraid to get close to anyone."

"So are you," I lashed out.

"Afraid is the wrong word," he said. "I choose not to. It's easier."

"Lonely," I murmured. "It's so lonely living that way, Viper."

"So, don't live that way anymore."

"What are you saying?"

He let go of my ankle, but only so he could grasp the camp chair and haul it toward him. "What if we do this?"

"We *are* doing this."

"No end date," he said quietly. "What if we really try this?"

"My, how quickly the tables have turned." I grinned, but it quickly slipped. "You're serious?"

"Yes."

"Why?" I demanded. "Why now? Why try a real relationship with me when you've never wanted one before?"

My heart lifted in my chest as I waited for his answer.

"You've never been afraid of me and you don't take my shit. I was hoping you wouldn't freak the fuck out when you found out the truth about my past. Takes a strong woman to stand by the side of a biker."

It wasn't a flowery proclamation. It wasn't majestic prose full of bullshit words. It was real and honest.

Viper wanted me. And not just for now. Maybe he wanted me forever.

Only time would tell.

Something unlocked inside me.

There had been very few moments in my life when I'd felt completely right in time and space. But here, under the stars with Viper, sharing our pasts over a bottle of bourbon, I knew I was meant to be here.

With him.

I leaned forward and brushed my lips softly against his. "Let's go to bed."

Chapter 28

I came awake slowly. I stretched underneath the covers, my body deliciously sore.

It had been a late, intense night—one I wouldn't trade for the world.

I cracked an eyelid open and let out a startled yelp. There was a little girl standing next to the bed. Her blonde hair was a pile of ringlets, and she was wearing a pink tutu.

"Uh, who are you?" I asked, bringing the covers closer to my body even though I'd thrown on Viper's undershirt to sleep in.

"I'm Lily. Who are you?"

"I'm Sutton." I frowned. "Are you supposed to be in here?"

"No." She raised a brow. "But I don't think you're supposed to be in Uncle Viper's room, either. Why are you sleeping in his bed?"

"Oh, um…" I was definitely not going to answer that question, but the scrutinizing gaze I was getting made me want to fold. "How old are you?"

"Six."

The door opened and Darcy appeared. "There you are! I thought I made it very clear you were not supposed to go into any of these rooms. These are private, Lily, you know that."

"Sorry," she said, not at all sounding contrite.

"Out," Darcy commanded, pointing to the door. "And you're in trouble. No cookies today."

Lily's lip began to wobble.

"No crocodile tears," Darcy said.

Lily shuffled out of the room past Darcy and disappeared into the hallway.

"I'm so sorry," Darcy apologized.

"Oh, it's fine," I said, sitting up. "I was just startled. What time is it?"

"A little after two."

I blinked sluggishly.

"In the afternoon," Darcy clarified with a smile.

"I slept late," I murmured.

"Well, take a little time to get yourself sorted. Most of us are already here."

"Most of us…right, the barbecue." I ran a hand down my face. "I'll be out there in a bit."

Darcy smiled and then sailed out of the room, closing the door behind her.

I got out of bed and quickly threw on my pants. I grabbed my boots and phone and padded barefoot back to my room.

Five minutes later, I was in the shower, dowsing my head under the spray. The bathroom door opened, followed by the sound of heavy boots.

"Heard you had a wandering visitor," Viper said.

"Yeah, that's not how I expected to wake up this morning. Except it's not morning, it's early afternoon and you let me sleep. Now everyone is already here and I'm the girl who can't get her ass out of bed."

"Everyone knows you worked at Shelly's last night."

"How?"

"Mia told them. And I told them. They get why you slept late."

"That's not the real reason I slept late," I teased. "And you know it."

After Viper and I'd had our discussion, we'd crawled back into bed and crashed. But a few hours later, I'd woken up with Viper's head between my legs and he hadn't let me go back to sleep before wringing three orgasms from me.

"You're not complaining."

"What's there to complain about?" I shut off the water and stuck my hand out through the shower curtain slit to grab a towel. I hastily dried off and wrapped it around me before drawing the entire curtain back.

"You feeling okay this morning?" he asked.

"Yeah." I frowned. "Why wouldn't I be?"

"So, you're not regretting our conversation last night?"

"Are you?"

"I asked you first."

"No. I don't have any regrets."

"Good."

"And you?" I prodded.

"I'm glad you know." He reached for me, cupped the back of my head, and gave me a thorough kiss. "Hurry up and get dressed. Food's going on the grill."

"I'll be there as soon as I can," I promised.

He kissed me one final time and then left me alone to get ready. I quickly threw on a pair of jeans with ripped knees and a black tank top. I didn't want to waste the time drying my hair, so I pulled it into a messy bun and slid into a pair of flip-flops.

There was no one in the living room or the kitchen of

the clubhouse. I followed the sound of voices out into the backyard. Several folding tables covered in side dishes and cutlery had already been set up. A cluster of men congregated around the grill.

"Sutton!" Mia called out, waving me toward the group of women who sat in camp chairs.

I quickly made my way over to them. "Hi, sorry I slept in."

"Don't apologize," Mia said. "We all get the late nights. Biker chicks, remember?"

"So true," a blonde with a pixie cut said. "We haven't met yet. I'm Linden. Everyone calls me Doc."

"Oh, *you're* Doc. Nice to meet you." I smiled.

"My reputation precedes me?" she asked with a grin.

"Yeah, your workaholic reputation precedes you," Darcy teased. "When we bombarded Sutton at the clubhouse the other day, we said she'd meet you and Rach later."

"I'm Rach," a pretty brunette greeted.

"Aren't a few of you missing babies?" I inquired.

Allison giggled. "They're down for their naps."

"Thank God, too," Joni said. "Everett had a night. Meaning Zip and I had a night."

"I'm just glad Cash is with my mom," Rach said. "So I can enjoy myself without having to worry about him."

"Hmm, something to look forward to," Brooklyn said, rubbing her baby bump. "Right, Willa?"

"Right," Willa agreed.

Two gangly boys on the verge of teenager-hood were kicking a soccer ball back and forth, and the little girl—Lily—was sitting under the shade of a tree with Waverly and Sailor. Waverly saw me and waved. I waved back.

"I want an update on the Sutton-Viper situation," Joni said.

"It's been like two days since I've seen you. How much do you think has changed?" I asked in amusement.

"With these men?" Joni said. "A lot."

Mia nodded in agreement. "Viper keeps glancing at you, and I swear he looks ten percent less scowly."

"A marginal improvement. Give me a few more days, I'm sure I can bring that number up," I said with a laugh. "You guys have no filter; you get that, right?"

"That's this crowd," Doc said. "I felt the same way when they brought me into the fold. You get used to their straight-shooting ways."

"I'll be better for it, I'm sure," I said. "I'm gonna go grab a soda. Anyone want anything?"

They all shook their heads, and I left them to talk. I went to one of the coolers and pulled it open. Beer.

"The one by the table," the guy at the grill called out. He was shorter than most of the bikers, had a gray ponytail and had definitely settled into middle age.

I went to the cooler he mentioned and pulled out a soda. "Thanks," I said, walking to him. "I would've been looking for days. I haven't met you yet. I'm Sutton."

"Gray," he said. "Darcy's my Old Lady."

"Ah, Lily is your little tutu-wearing hellion." I grinned. "Nice to meet you."

"You too. How do you like your burgers cooked?"

"Medium-rare," I said.

"I'll make sure not to overcook yours." He winked and immediately got back to manning the grill.

I cracked open the soda and took a long drink. I wandered toward Viper, who was standing with Savage, Duke, Smoke and Bones. I gently stole a hand across his back as I passed the men but didn't stop to engage in conversation with them.

I continued my trek across the lawn toward a shady tree with the girls sitting underneath it.

"Mind if I join you guys?" I asked.

"Sit," Waverly said.

I plopped down next to her. "No boyfriend today?"

"He left for Sicily a few days ago with his uncle," she said with a frown. "He'll be gone six weeks."

"The time will fly," Sailor said. "The furniture business is on fire, so we have that to occupy us."

"And if you're not with Dylan, that means you get to babysit me!" Lily said.

Waverly tugged on one of Lily's ringlets. "That's true."

One of the boys kicked the ball in our direction and it flew by our heads. "Cam!" Lily screamed. "That wasn't nice!"

She jumped up off the ground and ran to the boy who'd kicked the ball at us. Lily tackled him with all her force, and he went down. She was on top of him, open-handedly smacking him as he laughed.

"Lily, cut it out," Cam begged.

"Just because you're my brother, doesn't mean you have to be mean," she yelled, continuing her assault.

Bikers ran over to the kids, and Boxer easily lifted Lily off Cam. "Come on, Lily Burger. Let's get you something to eat. I think your blood sugar's low."

"You," Gray stated, pointing the tongs at his son. "Get over here, now."

"Told you not to do it," the other boy said, jogging toward the errant ball.

"Shut up, Silas," Cam growled.

When Cam was within arm's distance of his father, Gray grabbed his son's T-shirt collar and hauled him off.

"Dude, you can't leave the burgers!" Savage called as he ran after Gray and took the tongs from him.

I got up off the ground and went to Viper. "Are all your parties like this? Full of drama and action?"

"Pretty much." His mouth flickered with humor. "I had five bucks on Lily."

"You would've won, too, if I hadn't pulled her off Cam," Boxer said with Lily on his back. He looked over his shoulder at her and said, "What's gotten into you lately?"

"I dunno," she said. "I'm feisty."

"And going into rooms you haven't been given permission to go into," Viper said to her. His tone was lighter than I'd ever heard it, and I wondered if he realized he was trying not to frighten the little girl.

"Not okay, Lily Burger," Boxer chastised. "You know you're my favorite person, but you gotta respect boundaries."

Darcy approached us and said, "Boxer, can you put my daughter down, please?"

"Uh-oh," Lily muttered. "I'm in trouble."

"Probably." Boxer set her on the ground.

Darcy took her daughter by the hand and marched toward the clubhouse.

"Watching kids fight gives me an appetite," I joked. "Savage? Are those ready yet?"

"How about you bring me a few plates before I torch them accidentally?" he called back.

"We can't have scorched burgers," I said to Viper. "I'll go help him."

He hooked a finger through my belt loop and tugged me toward him. Viper tilted my head back and kissed my lips. "I'd like two cheeseburgers with the works."

"You think I'm your servant?" I demanded.

His mouth fluttered like he wanted to smile. "Please?"

"Okay. But you owe me."

"I'll pay in full."

"You guys aren't as clever as you think you are," Boxer drawled. "I know what you're talking about."

"I'd love it if I could flirt with Viper without comments from the peanut gallery."

"Darlin', the entire peanut gallery is watching the two of you." Boxer grinned. "It's just how it goes. The minute Savage or Bones or any of the other single brothers start sniffing around a woman, the peanut gallery will move on. But for now, you're it."

"You're done now," Viper said to Boxer.

Boxer just grinned at him and slapped him on the back.

I went to the table to grab a plate before bringing it over to the grill. Savage was sliding burger patties onto a tray when I approached.

"Are you still sniffing around Carla?" I asked.

He raised his brows at the question. "You haven't talked to her lately, have you?"

"No," I admitted. "I've been a little busy."

"We've gone our separate ways," he said.

"You don't sound upset about it."

"I'm not."

"Did she end it, or did you?" I asked. "Three cheeseburgers please, medium-rare."

Savage scooped up three patties with slices of white cheddar, set them on buns, and then put them on my plate. "Eh, it was mutual. Neither of us planned on it lasting. And when we were done, we both knew we were done."

I looked at Viper, who was standing with Boxer several feet from me, smiling at something Boxer had said.

"How did you know it wasn't going to last?" I asked quietly.

"Neither one of us wanted it to."

"It was that simple?"

"Yeah." He glanced at me. "You gotta want to make it last for it to last, and even then, that's no guarantee. To be honest, I haven't met anyone I'd consider something lasting with. Carla's a good woman. I liked spending time with her. She's smart and takes no bullshit. But she didn't see me as her next ex-husband."

I glared at him.

"Relax. Those were her words, not mine." He chuckled. "She can laugh at herself. She knows her own flaws. Can't fault the woman for not seeing a future with me. I never see a future with any of the women I date."

"Date is a term he uses loosely," Willa said as she approached.

"Well, you went and married my best friend, leaving me no choice but to find comfort in the arms of other women," Savage said with a wry grin.

Willa rolled her eyes and shoved against his arm. To me, she said, "Don't let his words fool you. He never felt that way about me."

"That's true," he agreed. "Completely platonic from the time we met. You want a burger, Willa?"

"Hmm. No. I'm only supposed to eat meat well-done now that I'm pregnant, but the idea of overcooked meat makes me sad. I'll take a chicken bratwurst though."

I fixed our cheeseburgers and loaded them up with fixings. I grabbed another plate and added a sampling of all the side dishes, including a pile of potato chips.

Viper sidled up next to me. "What do you want to drink?"

"Another soda is good."

"I'll meet you at the picnic table."

"Will you grab some napkins and forks for us?"

"Yep."

I sat down at the picnic table, but didn't wait for Viper

to dig in. I was in the middle of chewing a huge bite when he slid onto the bench across from me.

"How is it?" he asked, a smile flickering at the corners of his mouth. He handed me a napkin which I used to clean my fingers of meat juice.

"Perfection," I said when I'd swallowed. "How long do these things last?"

"Several hours. There's usually a bonfire for a few hours before the married guys get their kids home. Then the single women show up and the party rages."

"Hmm. Yeah, I recall that party."

I grabbed a chip and took a bite.

"We had our own party." He cracked a smile. "And you enjoyed it."

We ate in silence for a few minutes and then I said, "We gotta talk about something."

"More talking? Already?"

I shot him a glare and he grinned.

"What do you wanna talk about?"

"I can't hang around here during the day while you're off doing your thing."

"You get to go to work a few nights a week."

"Get to?" I raised my brows.

"You know what I mean."

"No, I don't. Explain."

"You get out of the clubhouse. That's all I meant."

"Not for enjoyment. Not for the purpose of recharging my batteries."

"What are you asking for?"

"Freedom to come and go as I please."

"It's not safe yet. We still don't know if you were a specific target, or if what happened was random. So, it's work and clubhouse for the foreseeable future."

"Work and sex with you is not enough to keep me entertained," I muttered.

"Right now, that has to be enough." He shrugged. "Besides, it's not like you have a car to get you from point A to B."

"Not yet, I don't have a car. But I'm gonna buy one with the insurance money I get from the trailer. The loan on the thing was already paid off. So I can do what I want with the cash I get."

"We're not going to agree on this. So you've got to hang in there for a little while longer." He finished off the last of the potato salad after making that oh-so-very-helpful announcement.

"But I don't want a cheeseburger!" Lily screamed.

The noise pulled my attention, and I watched the little girl have a meltdown and stomp her feet.

Darcy looked like she was at the end of her rope. "You're on thin ice, kid."

"I got you," Boxer said. "Lily Burger, let's figure out what you want to eat."

"No," Darcy snapped. "Do *not* coddle her. She needs to learn to eat what's offered to her."

Doc hopped up from her seat and quickly came to Darcy's side. She touched her arm and whispered something in her ear. Darcy nodded and let Doc lead her away.

Boxer got the little girl some food and she looked happy. Everyone else was finally moving toward the table to get plates.

"Seconds?" Viper asked as he polished off the last of the coleslaw.

I nodded and moved to stand up. Viper beat me to it and waved me down. I sipped on my soda, enjoying the early afternoon warmth.

"Can we join you?" Mia asked. Colt stood by her side holding a mountain of food.

"Of course. You don't have to ask," I said with a welcoming smile.

She grinned. "You guys looked pretty cute and cozy. Didn't want to interrupt."

"Please interrupt."

I moved Viper's beer to the spot next to me so Mia and Colt could sit down on the same side of the picnic table.

"I have about ten minutes to shove food into my mouth before Scarlett wakes up from her nap," Mia said as she picked up her burger. She glanced over my shoulder and hollered, "Silas! Leave the ball and eat some food. And wait fifteen minutes before you start running around again!"

A few moments later, Colt boomed, "Silas! Listen to Mia!"

Mia rolled her eyes. "Is there something in the water? None of the children are listening. It's like they're going through a collective rebellion."

"Maybe they all got together and had a discussion about how to drive adults crazy," I stated.

"I wouldn't put it past any of them," Mia said.

Viper returned to the table, and I scooted over so he could have the end. He folded his large body and slid next to me, swallowing space. He set his hand on my thigh and gave it a squeeze.

Mia's phone buzzed and she sighed, "I didn't even get ten minutes."

"Sit," Colt said. "I'll go."

"She's going to want to be fed," Mia said. "You don't have the body parts." She kissed her husband's cheek and then stood up. "I shall return." Mia squeezed Colt's shoulder.

He lifted his hand to touch hers before letting go, and she headed for the clubhouse.

"How are you doing, Sutton?" Colt asked, his gaze darting from me to Viper and then back to me.

"I'm okay," I said. "Getting a little stir crazy on days I don't work, but aside from that, I'm fine."

"You'll be out of here before you know it," Colt said.

Viper tightened his grip on my leg. I covered his hand with mine, wanting to tacitly reassure him that even when I moved out, it wasn't the end for us.

I didn't want it to be the end for us.

Chapter 29

Evening set in and we lit insect torches. But it was too hot for a bonfire.

Babies were asleep against their mothers and everyone else was full of food and drink. The older kids, including Waverly and Sailor, were inside watching a movie in the theater room.

"Construction starts next week on the expansion," Colt said as we sat in a small group with Mia, Joni, and Zip.

"Permits finally came through?" the VP of the club asked. "It took long enough."

"What was the problem?" Joni queried her husband.

Zip rubbed his jaw and looked at Colt.

"Other players in town. More competition now than ever before," Colt explained.

"Competition?" I asked. "I don't get it."

"We have ways of communicating with people," Zip said baldly. "So we can get what we want done sooner rather than later."

"Oh. I see," I said with a nod. "You bribe people or give them offers they can't refuse."

Joni displayed a slow smile. "And how do you feel about that? If that were true?"

I frowned. "Should I be taken aback by the fact that a bunch of bikers do illicit things? We're good."

"Love your sass, doll," Mia quipped.

"Reminds me of someone else," Colt said, setting his hand on his wife's thigh.

I looked at Viper. "You biker men like your women sassy, don't you?"

"I could live without the sass," Viper taunted. His tone was gruff, but his eyes were lit with humor.

"Hmm. Seems like I'm the only one who puts up with your grumpy attitude around here. You need me."

"Do I?" He yanked my chair closer and lifted my legs and placed them on his lap. He wrapped his hand around my ankle and began to stroke the side of my foot.

Viper and I were staring at one another, lost in the moment.

Someone sighed, reminding me that we had an audience.

"I wish you still looked at me the way Viper looks at Sutton," Joni said to her husband.

"I looked at you that way last night right before I bent you—"

"Dude," Colt growled. "That's my sister."

Joni grinned and patted her brother's cheek. "Be happy that I'm happy."

"I am happy that you're happy. Otherwise Zip's jaw would be on the other side of his head," Colt growled. "I just don't need to hear about shit I have no business knowing about."

Joni stole a hand across her sleeping infant's back. "How do you think we got one of these?"

"Immaculate conception," Colt said. "Stork. Left on your doorstep. Anything but the real way."

"Mia told me you lifted her legs up in the air and held her there for ten minutes hoping your seed would take," Joni stated. "Turnabout is fair play."

Colt looked at his wife. "You *told* her?"

"She's a nurse," Mia defended. "I wanted to make sure you'd done it right."

"My daughter is asleep in your arms. I did it right," Colt muttered.

"Hee-haw, both of you pound on your chests and then have a pissing contest," I said.

"Not going to happen," Zip said. "Besides, I'd win."

"You wanna bet?" Colt asked.

Zip rose. "Let's go, Prez."

"You're on." Colt stood up. "Viper? You in?"

"You really expect me to whip my dick out and have a pissing contest when I'd rather take my woman back to my room and throw her legs over my shoulders?"

I hastily covered his mouth with my hand, even though it was clearly too late.

Mia and Joni cackled in amusement.

Viper's warm tongue snaked out to graze my palm. I yanked my hand away.

"Behave," I commanded.

"No," he said easily.

"I think Viper's got a better plan than a pissing contest." Colt reached a hand down to help his wife out of the chair. "You ready to go, sweetheart?"

"Hell yeah." Mia looked at me and winked. "Thanks, doll."

I saluted.

"Why are you thanking her? I'm the one who gave your husband the idea," Viper stated.

"Thanks, Viper," she said. "You both have good ideas. Happy?"

Viper shrugged.

"Babe?" Zip asked.

"Yeah, let's get out of here. If we're lucky, Everett will sleep the entire car ride home."

As the group began saying goodbye, other couples began to stand and do the same.

"Seems like you had a very good idea," I said.

Viper's hand inched up my jeans to massage my calf. "I have them on occasion."

Rach stayed behind, talking to Smoke and Savage. She was the only woman to remain at the party, but I didn't understand why.

"Who's Rach's man?" I asked Viper.

"Her man died," Viper said. "Cartel war."

"Oh." My heart suddenly felt like lead. "She has a son."

"Yeah."

"Sad."

"Yeah. But at least she has the club. She's not alone. She'll never be alone."

I watched Rach saying goodbye to the Old Ladies, hugging them and smiling. How could she smile after what she'd been through? Losing a husband, having to raise a son alone…

"Hey," Viper said, grasping my chin and turning my face to his. "She'll be okay. She's strong."

"How do they do it?" I asked softly. "How do they live knowing that at any moment one of their men could just die? Joni could lose Zip. Or her brother. Or—"

"That's the club life, Sutton. If you choose it, at some point you'll lose someone you love. It's just part of how we live."

"I guess, yeah. You're right. I know you're right."

My dad had gone to prison. He wasn't dead, but he wasn't really alive, either. And I'd lost my mom when I was too young to miss her.

Still, life went on. The world turned. And you found a way.

"None of us know how long we have on this planet," Viper said quietly. "You just live life as best you can, knowing it could all end tomorrow."

"How do you live with that kind of conviction?" I asked.

He paused in thought. "Have you ever almost died?"

I shook my head.

"Then you don't know."

"Know what?"

"There's this clarity," he said. "It washes over you. All of a sudden, the trivial, meaningless bullshit part of life just falls away and you're left with this fearlessness… You're left with this bravery, and you hold on to that feeling and you live your life every day from that newfound place. And suddenly you're not so scared of it all ending tomorrow, because you live for today."

It felt like I'd lived my entire life up until this point, waiting for these words.

"I'd like to try to live like that," I said quietly.

"I'll help you."

I slowly sat up so I could reach his face. I gently ran a finger down the side of his cheek, to brush behind his ear.

"Thank you."

"For what?"

"For letting me in."

He smiled slightly. "I didn't let you in. You took a battering ram and got in yourself."

"Crossed the moat, scaled the walls, crashed through the drawbridge?"

"Something like that."

"If it makes you feel any better, you did the same to me, Viper. You did the same to me."

Chapter 30

"That's why you sleep with a knife," I murmured, my cheek pressed to Viper's bare chest. "Isn't it? Because you were in prison?"

Viper tightened his arm around me, and his palm settled on the curve of my back. "Old habits."

I turned my head and brushed my lips against his skin. "I'm sorry."

"For what?"

"That you had to be there at all. That you sleep with a knife because of it."

"I didn't tell you partly because I didn't want pity."

"I don't pity you."

"No?" He got up and I was forced to move. A moment later, the nightstand lamp came on. The corners of his eyes were lined with tiredness. But it seemed like more than just a night's exhaustion.

"Five years of your life were taken from you," I said, sitting up and facing him.

His eyes dipped to my bare breasts. I knew where his thoughts were leading. Viper would much rather put his mouth to a different use than talking. Normally, I was amenable to it. But I didn't want to get dragged into a bout of desire and lose this thread of conversation.

It was too important.

I grasped the sheet and pulled it up to my chest. He gently tugged at the corner of it, but I batted his hand away.

"I want to talk about this," I said.

"I don't."

"What else is new?" I grumbled.

With a sigh, he settled back down and put his arm beneath his head. He looked at me with dark, hooded eyes. "I'll listen, if you want to say something."

I opened my mouth and then hastily closed it. I hadn't expected him to give in so quickly.

"When did you get out?" I asked.

He paused. "About a month ago."

"*What!*" When I realized I'd yelled, I immediately shut my mouth. "Viper, are you serious?"

"Yep."

"No wonder you want to have sex all the time," I quipped. "Making up for lost time, huh?"

"Fuck yeah, I am. Bones, Kelp, Smoke and Raze were already down here, getting the lay of the land, settling in for what's coming. I joined them as soon as I got out." His fingers brushed against the upper meaty part of my arm. "Wasn't expecting a little spitfire like you to get in the way."

"I got in the way?" I asked, my brow furrowed.

"Got in the way of trying to remain detached."

"Oh." I bent my legs and wrapped my arms around them and rested my chin on my knees when I looked at him. "Spitfire, huh?"

"Firecracker? Pistol? Take your pick."

"We're at the nicknames phase, are we?" I smirked. "This is all happening so fast, Viper. You sure you're ready for that?"

"Stop being a brat."

"Too late," I quipped. "Hit the light, will you?"

He turned off the lamp. I waited for him to get comfortable before I sidled up next to him, nuzzling into his nook.

"I never thought a guy like you would like snuggling."

"I don't snuggle," he protested.

"No? What do you call what we're doing right now?"

"Post-coital cuddling."

I scooted down the bed and found the back of his knee and ran my finger in his ticklish spot.

"Hey, cut that out. You're not supposed to use my weakness against me."

"But it's so fun watching a big guy like you squirm," I teased. "I'll try to control myself."

"Glad to hear it." He pulled me into his arms again.

I was dreamily floating to sleep when he murmured, "Don't feel sorry for me, Sutton. I don't regret what I did. Five years in prison was worth it. For Chloe. The only thing I regret was that he didn't die. Besides, I'm free now, living the life I want to live. How many people can say that?"

"Not enough," I replied.

"Are you living the life you want to live?"

"I'm twenty two. My life is just getting started."

"You didn't answer the question."

With a sigh, I was wide awake again. I sat. "Light."

The sheets rustled with his movement and the lamp flicked on.

I rubbed my tired eyes as I thought about my answer.

"I'm not sure I spend a lot of time thinking about it, to be honest."

"You have to think about it. Otherwise, you'll wake up on the other side of thirty, wondering what the hell happened to your life."

I raised a brow. "You speaking from experience?"

"I just said I don't have any regrets. I live how I want. Not the last five years, I get that. But before I went in and now that I'm out, I live the way I want to. By my own rules. With my club. On the back of my bike. How do *you* want to live?"

"Not the way I grew up, that's for sure." I frowned. "Dad and I bounced around a lot. We were never in one place for long. I hated that, so I settled for the trailer. It wasn't what I wanted, but it was better than moving all the time and not having a home. Every day in that trailer I felt like I was crawling out of my skin to go do anything else but what I was doing."

"Why'd you stay?"

"Because I thought that's what adults did, you know? Have an address, go to a job, get a boring boyfriend."

"And how did any of that work out for you?"

"Trailer's gone, I quit my job to work at a biker bar, and you're anything but boring. The guy before you though… Yeah, he was boring."

"Does boring boyfriend have a name?" Viper asked, his voice suddenly low and raspy.

"Of course, he has a name."

"Tell me."

"Why?"

"So I can murder him for being the guy who took your virginity."

I rolled my eyes. "Hold on, Neanderthal. That wasn't the point of this conversation."

He sighed. "Continue."

"My life has been a big pile of nothing. And I told myself it was better that way, you know? Boring meant stable. I'd never had stable before. But I'm not sure I'm cut out for stable. Can you have an exciting life without being a complete nomad?"

"Your life can look however you want it to look. You just gotta make the choice that it's important to you. What is it you really want out of life?"

"Do I have to decide now?" I asked. "Right here, at two in the morning?"

"Why not? Deciding to live with purpose stops you from just floating through life, hoping shit just works out."

"What's your purpose?"

"Brotherhood, protect the innocent, live free."

"But you weren't free."

"For a while I wasn't. But I knew I'd get out. Get back to where I needed to be. There was a reason I was in prison, you know. It wasn't an accident."

"Yeah, but that's a shit outcome for protecting a young woman," I said bitterly.

He tucked a strand of hair behind my ear. "I appreciate the sentiment. I do. But it's no use being pissed about it. I've had five years to think about it and I can promise you it won't change anything." His thumb grazed my chin. "You have the tiniest cleft. You were born a fighter, Sutton. I like that about you. A lot."

His words caused shivers to erupt all along my skin. "Look at you, complimenting me." I leaned over and traced his prison tattoo with my fingers. "I wish I knew my purpose."

"You'll figure it out."

"What if I don't?" I rolled back and propped my elbow underneath my head and peered at him. "What if

I don't ever figure it out? Am I just supposed to be a bartender for the rest of my life? I look at the Old Ladies, and they all have this…*drive*. I'm not sure I have that."

"Career and purpose aren't the same."

"I don't think I want a career. Does that make me horrible?" I asked. "I didn't go to college. Never even wanted to go to college. I don't like being stuck inside learning. I like being in the real world, talking to people. I like getting to know them and hearing their stories. I like listening to them talk about their problems—not because they have problems, but sometimes, being an objective listener is all someone needs, you know?"

He smiled slightly.

"What?" I demanded.

"What do you think a bartender does?"

"They serve drinks and they…holy shit. No way." I let out a laugh.

"You don't have to take life seriously just because the world tells you to."

"But is what I do *enough*?" I asked.

"What's enough? What does that even mean?"

"So, you'd be okay if I just wanted to be a bartender for the rest of my life?"

"That's what I'm trying to tell you, Sutton. It's not about me. It's about you and what *you* want. If you wake up every day and you get to do the thing that you love to do, that fills you with purpose, fuck what anybody else has to say about it. If that's bartending, fine. If it's something else, that's fine too. And I don't mean to keep bringing this up, but you're twenty-two. You have time. You can change your entire life at any moment."

"I don't want to work my life away," I said slowly. "I want to travel and explore. I want to adventure."

"Sounds like you've got more of life figured out than you think you do."

"Yeah, I guess." I frowned. "Can I ask you something?"

"Sure."

"Do you—I mean—that night when I thought the condom broke but it didn't…"

"Hmm? What about it?"

"The kid thing. If I remember correctly, you didn't seem terrified by the idea."

"I wasn't."

"So, kids…"

"What about them?"

"Do you like them?" I blurted out.

"Haven't spent that much time around them, to be honest."

"Yeah, okay, but do *you* want kids?"

He paused before replying, "Haven't thought much about it."

"Oh." I nibbled my lip.

"You?"

I shook my head. "I don't know how I feel about them."

"You don't have to know how you feel about any of this right now. Like I said, you're young."

"You're not," I blurted out.

He raised his brows. "Did you just fucking call me old?"

"*No*," I immediately backtracked. "I just meant, old for being a parent."

"Slash is older than me, and he's about to be a father."

"Valid. I just, ah fuck. Never mind."

"Not never mind. Spit it out."

"I don't want to talk about the future because…do we even have a future? There's a cartel war coming and who the fuck knows what life will look like when it's over. Besides, I'm not even sure I want to stay in Waco, and we can't do this indefinitely and sleeping together can have consequences and—"

Viper gently placed his hand over my mouth to get me to stop talking. "My turn."

"But—"

He shook his head. "My turn. Will you be good and keep quiet?"

I glared at him, but reluctantly nodded.

Viper dropped his hand. "You're worried about the future."

"No, I'm simply—"

"*My turn*," he interrupted.

I sighed and nodded again.

He waited to see if I was really going to keep my mouth shut. When he was satisfied, he said, "You're worried about the future. You know what worrying does most of the time? It ruins the present. I was in prison for five years, and do you know how I got through it? One step at a time. One day at a time. I lived in the moment. And then one day I was free. Live for the present with me, Sutton. The future will sort itself out."

Chapter 31

Three days later, I was smiling from ear to ear and nothing could bring me down. Not cheesy eighties music playing on the jukebox, and not the kid who left me change after I made him a fancy drink he claimed was for his girlfriend.

"Okay, seriously," Mia said as she threw a wet bar rag into the orange bucket in the corner near the cash register. "You're like, *beaming*. You get that, right?"

"I'm trying not to, but I feel like I slept with a coat hanger in my mouth." I touched my cheeks.

Mia chuckled. "Things are good with Viper?"

I glanced at the man who was sitting at his usual stool. His gaze was intense as it raked over me.

"Forget I asked," she said. "Of course, they are. You've entered *the phase.*"

I somehow forced myself to look away from him to peer back at Mia, but I swore I could feel Viper's eyes on my ass, burning a hole through my jeans. "What phase?"

"The phase where you're suddenly in sync. In between the hot sex, there's the talking, and then more hot sex. You know each other's bodies and it's like a bubble forms around you."

"God, that's *exactly* how it feels," I admitted. Each conversation in private with Viper felt richer, deeper. More meaningful somehow.

"Hmm. It's a great phase," Mia said with a knowing smile.

"You don't think this is happening a little fast?" I asked with concern. "Like, am I being a total idiot?"

"I'm the wrong girl to ask. Colt and I were, like, instantly together. And it was perfect. Everyone's different. Don't judge what feels right by what you think society is screaming at you to do. A lot of people will tell you to take it slow, get to know each other. That kind of thing. Do what's right for you."

"Good advice," I admitted, looking at Viper again. "Very good advice."

"Can't claim it as my own. Joni gave me the same pep talk when I was terrified I was falling in love with Colt." She grinned.

A few more customers came up to the bar and sat at the end near the restrooms, and Mia and I poured them pints before they headed off to the pool tables.

"Do you think I'm too young for him?" I asked.

"Do *you* think you're too young?"

I crossed my arms over my chest.

"It's called the Socratic method. Answer a question with a question to get you to dig a little deeper," she said.

"Socratic method, huh?"

"Just one of the few things I learned in college."

"You went to college?" I asked.

"Yup. Thought I was going to be an accountant."

"I can't picture you as an accountant."

"I'm much more cut out for owning a bar. Oh, which

reminds me—are you good to start some extra day shifts this week? Get the lay of the land so far as being a manager goes?"

"Oh, let me check my wide-open schedule. Sorry, I'm busy playing a video game tournament and can't make it," I teased. "The more you want me here, the better. I'm going nuts in the clubhouse."

"Not very conducive for a private sex nest, huh?"

A startled laugh escaped me. "That sounds raunchy."

"If the boat's a rockin'," she quipped.

"Right?"

The door opened and South Paw sauntered inside. He walked to the end of the bar on the far side, away from the bathrooms, and sat next to Viper.

I traipsed over to him and tossed a coaster down in front of him.

"What are you doing here?" I asked with a smile. "Aren't you glued to the gates at the clubhouse?"

"Say that five times fast," South Paw joked. "I got a reprieve. New prospects."

"Hallelujah," Mia said as she approached. "First round is on me. What'll it be?"

"Whatever pilsner you've got on tap."

I poured him a pint. "Enjoy your freedom."

"I will, thanks." South Paw placed a twenty on the bar. "I know Mia said it's on her, but this is for you."

"That's too much," I protested.

"Nah."

"You sure?"

"Yep."

"I'll give it a nice home, I promise." I picked up the twenty and placed it in the tip jar.

Working with Mia was the best, and not just because it felt like working with an old friend. Because she owned the bar, she didn't take a cut of the tips, and I was already pocketing so much cash it put my job at Spurs to shame.

I'd have more than enough to rent a tiny apartment when the time came. But I was also trying to take Viper's advice, so I put the thought out of my mind and focused on the present.

South Paw and Viper began to chat. It was odd, seeing Viper actually speaking in full sentences to someone who wasn't me.

"Well, that's new," Mia quipped, gesturing with her chin to the two of them.

"I feel like a regular Professor Higgins. That's my handiwork, right there."

Viper rose from his stool and then headed past Mia and I toward the hallway where the restrooms were.

The front door opened, and a man came in. I grabbed a piece of scrap paper and a pen and walked to the mini fridge at the end of the counter to take stock.

Mia stood at the register, her back to the bar and the rest of the room. "Be right with you," she called out over her shoulder.

I rose, my eyes raking over the customer as he took a seat in front of Mia.

Mia finished at the register and then turned to the man and asked, "What can I get you?"

"Shot of tequila—Añejo," he replied.

"Sure thing." Mia smiled and then turned around again to grab a bottle of top-shelf tequila.

The customer angled his head slightly and looked at me, and I smiled at him.

He didn't smile back.

The hair on the back of my neck stood up.

Something's wrong...

"You paying cash, or do you want to start a tab?" Mia asked.

"Cash," he said as he slid his hand into the inner part of his jacket.

Jacket.

Why was he wearing a jacket? It was summertime in Texas. And that's when I noticed the sweat on his brow and—

"Gun!" I cried out as he pulled a pistol from his pocket and swung it toward South Paw. I lunged for Mia to try and protect her, knocking her to the ground in the process. South Paw leapt from his stool and reached into his leather cut for his weapon.

But it was too late. The gunman already had a draw on him, and with a single shot a small hole appeared on South Paw's forehead, and the back of his head exploded.

His body slumped to the floor.

Customers screamed, drowning out Louis Armstrong's warbling voice on the jukebox.

Pandemonium ensued.

We were sitting ducks with no weapon to wield.

The gunman pivoted to face us.

He pointed his gun directly at Mia and then—

Bang!

Half of the gunman's skull blew apart as he was shot from behind.

His lifeless corpse collapsed against the bar and then he slid down and fell to the floor.

Viper lowered his pistol but didn't put it away.

I whirled to look at Mia. Her arm was bloody, and a broken bottle lay next to her on the ground.

"You're okay," I said to her. "Viper got him."

Nodding, she scrambled up from her spot. "South Paw," she murmured.

I grabbed a clean rag and handed it to her so she could put it on her arm and then I ran around the bar to South Paw, but it was already over. He was lying on his back, his glazed eyes open with a small hole in his forehead and a pool of blood on the ground beneath his skull.

"No…" I whispered as I kneeled next to him. I touched his shoulder and gave him a futile shake, but South Paw didn't stir.

"Sutton, are you okay?" Viper asked. When I didn't reply, he snapped, "Answer me!"

I couldn't find the words, so I shook my head.

"Mia?"

"I'm okay. A bottle broke when I fell. My arm is cut," she said as she came to crouch next to me. Mia reached out and covered South Paw's eyes. When she withdrew her hand, his eyes were closed. Almost like he was sleeping.

Only he wasn't sleeping.

He'd never wake again.

Not an hour earlier, he'd been standing upright, cracking jokes, enjoying a night off with his whole life ahead of him.

Now he was dead.

Mia grasped my hand in hers, linking her fingers through mine in a silent show of solidarity and comfort.

"What a Wonderful World" came to an end on the jukebox, and it fell silent.

I couldn't stop staring at South Paw.

Not even when I saw Viper make a phone call. Not even as we tried to get Mia's arm to stop bleeding. Not even minutes later when I heard the sirens.

Several police cars and two ambulances arrived. Two brawny men placed white sheets over South Paw and the gunman's corpses. Cops moved around the bar like a

Venom & Vengeance

swarm of angry wasps, taping off the carnage and clearing a way for the detectives to photograph the scene.

Vance Raider, the club's attorney, was a well-built, attractive man in his late thirties. He strode with confidence, his perfectly tailored black suit screaming authority. He had his cell phone in hand.

"Vance," Mia greeted, her tone relieved.

"Mia." He wrapped an arm around her shoulder. "Colt is five minutes behind me, and he's not happy."

"I'm sure that's the understatement of the century," she said with a wobbly smile as she continued to press the rag to her arm.

"Mr. Maxwell," a detective said, addressing Viper. "Are you ready to give your statement?"

"My attorney just arrived," Viper said. "I'll give you my statement so long as he's present."

Vance dropped his arm from around Mia's shoulder, and the detective, Viper, and Vance headed to one of the booths. Vance whispered something in Viper's ear and then the conversation commenced.

Nerves I hadn't allowed myself to feel finally jumped from my stomach into my throat.

"Don't worry about Viper," Mia said, patting my arm. "Vance is a seasoned warrior at what he does. And we've got cameras in the bar. It'll show what happened."

I let out a breath. "Was I that obvious?"

"Yes."

The front doors to the bar burst open. Colt Weston looked like a man hell-bent on violence. His eyes searched the room, landed on his wife, and he immediately stalked toward her.

"I'm okay," she said before he could say anything.

"I'll be the judge of that," he growled. He grasped her

face in his hands, his gaze taking in every part of her. He looked at her arm.

"It's just a cut. Bleeding has stopped. It looks worse than it is."

He lowered his lips to hers. When he was done kissing her, his eyes were somber. "Just one more rotten thing we've got to deal with. *Motherfucker*."

"Hey." She swallowed and reached a hand up to touch his cheek. "We'll get through this like we've gotten through everything else before."

He nodded. "Sutton? You injured?"

I shook my head and bit my tongue, not wanting to speak of things around a bunch of cops. I wanted to tell him the gunman had shot South Paw, but then turned his gun on Mia and me. I wanted to divulge I thought Mia was the target all along, and that South Paw had just gotten in the way. I wanted to say so many things.

"Good," he said with a sigh.

Viper, the detective, and Vance all got up from the table and came back to us.

"Mrs. Weston," the detective said. "I'll take your statement now. And I'll need the security footage to corroborate Mr. Maxwell's statement."

"Of course," Mia said. "Whatever I can do to help."

Vance, the detective, and Mia moved to the table this time, and I was left with Colt and Viper.

"Prez," Viper greeted.

"Viper." Colt reached out and placed a hand on his shoulder. "Thank you."

Viper nodded and then glanced at me. "This is just a formality with the cops. Nothing's gonna come of this. You know that, right?"

"I *don't* know that," I said quietly. "But Mia said I didn't need to worry."

Viper threw an arm around my shoulder and tugged me into his side. "The law in Texas allows us to defend ourselves, and this was a clear case of self-defense. Even Vance said I didn't need to hold back when talking to the cops. Between a few witnesses and the cameras, this thing is cut and dry."

It was clear we couldn't speak about anything club-related until we were in private, but I felt better hearing what he'd said. My mind was still reeling from the commotion and the sudden loss of South Paw.

Mia's statement didn't take long, and before I knew it, I was sitting next to Vance and communicating to the detective myself. Vance had told me to tell the police exactly what happened, and not to hold anything back except *why* I thought any of it had happened. He said to keep it simple.

"You didn't recognize him?" the detective asked.

I shook my head.

"And you have no idea why someone would target either of you?"

In fact, I had a very good idea about why someone would target us, but I'd have that conversation with the club later.

Again, I shook my head.

The detective scribbled a few notes on his notepad before sticking it in his pocket. "Okay, thank you. You're free to go. I'll be in touch with your attorney if we have any more questions."

Vance scooted out of the booth so I could climb out behind him.

"Let's take a look at the security feed," the detective said.

Vance accompanied the detective and they went to

Mia, who sat in a chair at one of the tables in the center of the room. Colt's hand was on her shoulder.

As the detective spoke to them, Viper slipped away and came to meet me. I leaned against the table in the booth, my eyes wandering back to the spot on the floor where the body of South Paw used to be, and then back to the bar where he'd been shot right in front of me.

"Shouldn't be too much longer," Viper said.

"It's okay," I said quietly.

He didn't respond. He just moved to stand next to me. Our arms brushed and I derived a strange sort of comfort from Viper not being overly soft with me. In that moment, I was still functioning. I was still keeping it together. Who knew what would happen if he offered me some measure of comfort…

Or maybe he was waiting until we were alone to say what he really wanted to say.

And then our eyes met, and he said more in that look than he could ever say with words.

Chapter 32

THERE WERE NO CHARGES, and we were free to leave. The cops said they'd look into the gunman's identity and that if anything came of it, they'd get back to us. For now, we'd just have to wait and see. But his true identity didn't matter. This had the cartel written all over it.

Why else would someone come into Mia's bar, where bikers were known to hang out, and try and gun down the president's wife?

Someone was proving a point.

The parking lot was swarming with bikers. They sat on their motorcycles, and with hooded eyes, watched as the four of us crossed the parking lot.

"I have to go to the hospital," Mia said to her husband. "The bleeding has stopped, but the EMTs are insisting I need stitches."

"Doc," Colt said. "Doc can take care of you at the clubhouse."

"I'll get her," Boxer said, his voice tight. "What happened to Mia?"

"Bottle broke when I fell. Glass cut my arm." She lifted

her arm to show the boys. "And really, I don't mind going to the hospital. I don't want to bother Doc—"

"You're kidding, right?" Boxer asked. "You're family."

Mia sighed. "Okay."

"Ride for the clubhouse," Colt said. "We'll follow in the truck."

Viper led me to his bike. What I wouldn't give to be in a real car where I didn't have to hold on to Viper. I wanted the protection of a metal vehicle, not the open skies and asphalt.

But I wanted to be with Viper more than I wanted to beg to sit in the back of Mia and Colt's truck. Plus, they needed time together.

I snapped the helmet buckle, made sure it was tight enough, and then climbed onto the back of Viper's motorcycle.

He revved the engine and then tore out of the parking lot. My arms were around him as we zoomed toward the clubhouse.

How fast life changed. I'd been happy that afternoon. Smiling, laughing, joking with Mia. And it had ended with death and carnage, and a sick feeling lodged in the pit of my stomach about what the future held.

The gates of the clubhouse were being guarded by two men I didn't know—prospects, I assumed. It only reminded me that I'd never see South Paw standing at the gates again.

The thought made me indescribably sad. I hadn't known South Paw very long or very well, but every interaction I'd had with him had been pleasant, jovial. I was slowly becoming accustomed to the club. Maybe I was never meant to know South Paw. Now I never would.

Viper parked in the gravel lot near the clubhouse,

quickly followed by several other brothers who'd trailed us home from the bar.

He cut the engine and I climbed off. I slowly removed the helmet and handed it to him. His eyes met mine. They looked dark and glassy in the lighting in front of the clubhouse.

Colt's truck came through the gates, and he parked far enough away not to interfere with any of the motorcycles. He got out of the driver's side, and then the passenger side door opened.

"Woman, wait," Colt growled.

"I'm fine, Colt," Mia insisted. "Don't treat me like an invalid. I've got it."

"I'll treat you any damn way I please. You're injured. Let me take care of you, for Christ's sake."

"You text Waverly?" she asked.

"Kids are fine," he muttered. "Sailor's helping out and Acid hasn't moved from his spot outside the house. Let's worry about you."

"Bourbon," Mia said. "I don't want Doc stitching me up without a drink first."

"You sure that's a good idea?" he asked.

"I pumped for the baby before I went to work. Scarlett has plenty of food stockpiled," she said.

"*And* they're talking about breast milk," Savage said as he came up the walkway. "I need a drink."

"Breast milk and bourbon? That's a new one," I quipped.

Mia laughed. "I thought nothing fazed you, Savage."

"Nothing fazes me. It was meant to be two separate thoughts that got crammed together," he said, his mouth pinching. "The drink is to toast South Paw."

Any levity that had been brewing suddenly drained out of the group. I noticed that a few of the married brothers weren't present. They must've been home with their wives and children. But the South Dakota boys, along with Crow, had been in the bar parking lot and were now at the clubhouse. The mood was angry and somber.

"How you doing, doll?" Mia asked as she came to stand by me.

"I'm okay," I said quietly. "Sad though. Real fucking sad." I glanced at Crow, whose features were tight with controlled pain. He'd just patched in with South Paw, and it was clear they had been good friends. I couldn't imagine how he was taking the news.

"It's tragic," Mia agreed. "He tried to protect us. Went for his gun and then…"

"He died with honor," Colt said grimly. "Went out trying to protect the club. That's all any of us could ever hope for. A good death."

Mia looked at Viper. "Did I get a chance to thank you?"

Viper shook his head. "You don't have to thank me. I did what I had to do."

"Thank you, all the same." Mia grabbed Viper's hand and gave it a squeeze.

He looked momentarily shocked that she'd touched him of her own volition.

Everyone headed inside while Viper and I brought up the rear. The guys had already popped open bottles of beer and liquor. Mia lowered herself onto the couch. Colt moved around the kitchen, filling a cup with bourbon before bringing it to his wife.

She took a sip and breathed deeply. "Bless you." Mia then handed me the cup.

Viper took a seat in one of the recliners and patted his leg. I settled on his lap, curling into him. His hand wormed its way underneath my tank and rested on my lower back. His palm was warm and comforting.

"What happens now?" I asked.

"We wait for Boxer and Doc," Colt said. "Then we have church."

"I'll call the rest of the boys," Smoke offered.

Colt nodded. "Get the women and children here, too. And nobody drink too much. It's gonna be a long night."

Chapter 33

"Colt, you're in my light," Doc said.

Boxer slapped Colt on the shoulder and said, "Come on. Mia's in good hands. Let Doc work without hovering."

Colt looked at his wife.

"Go," Mia urged. "I'm fine. Sutton'll keep me company. Won't you, Sutton?"

"Yep." I hiccoughed. "I'm not drunk, I swear."

"Doc, don't let them drink anymore," Colt commanded.

"I won't," Doc said, head bent as she extracted a piece of glass from deep within Mia's arm and dumped it into a tin bowl. "Remember what you promised me?"

"I remember," Colt said. He glanced at Boxer. "Porch?"

"Porch," Boxer agreed.

Viper had fallen silent the moment we'd gotten to the clubhouse, but we were quickly learning how to speak without words. He looked at me, cupped my face and raised my chin up so I could meet his gaze.

I grasped his wrist and gave it a squeeze before

releasing him.

He let go of my chin and brushed a strand of hair behind my ear before following Colt and Boxer, closing the office door behind him.

"What did Colt promise you?" I asked Doc.

"I said I didn't want to do any more surgeries at the clubhouse without a proper space and equipment. He promised me a surgery room with the expansion of the clubhouse. Disguised as a daycare for sick kids, of course."

"Any *more* surgeries?" I queried. "So there have been a lot then?"

"Surgeries is misleading. But I have patched up a few of the guys," Doc said. She looked at Mia. "I didn't think Colt was going to leave you. Even to let me work."

"I needed a reprieve," Mia admitted. "The truck ride back here was intense."

"I bet," Doc murmured.

"He's in that mood of his," Mia said.

"Ah." Doc nodded. "Got it."

"Mood? What mood?" I asked.

"He's put a lid on his emotions for the time being. Shut them down enough to power through the night and have church. But I know Colt, and when his emotions blow, it's going to be *bad*."

"Oh," I said, clasping my hands together and resting them in my lap.

"Any leads yet? On who this guy was?" Doc asked as she dropped another sliver of glass into the bowl. "Little numbing agent and then I'll get to stitching."

"Not officially," Mia said.

"I see." Doc picked up a vial of clear liquid and a needle.

"Are we just going to talk around what we're all thinking?" I demanded.

"And what are we thinking?" Mia asked, her glassy eyes focusing on me.

"Little pinch," Doc said to Mia as she numbed the area she was about to stitch.

"It was the cartel," I said. "You know it was the cartel. And you know it was a hit on you."

"Well, you get ten points for bluntness," Mia said. "Wait, you know about the cartel?"

"I know the club is at war with the cartel," I said.

Mia shook her head and even Doc paused her ministrations to look at me.

"There's something you're not saying," Mia said. "You jumped immediately to the cartel. Not some random guy with a gun. Why? What do you know that you're not telling us?"

I nibbled my lip, realizing there was no way I could get around what I knew.

What I wasn't supposed to talk about.

"I can't say," I said. "I swore to Colt I wouldn't tell anyone."

"Well, too late," Mia said. "You know about the club's beef with the cartel, which can only mean…you had your own run in with cartel. It's why you're staying here."

I looked down at my lap and didn't reply.

Mia rubbed her eye. "Doc, are you almost done? I'm losing steam here."

"Almost," Doc promised. "A few stitches and you're done."

"This is a fucking mess," Mia said. "My bar is trashed. A gunman tried to…and South Paw…"

"He didn't even think. He just went for his gun to try and protect us," I said quietly.

Sadness swelled in my chest, permeating every spot between my ribs.

"Does he have any family?" I asked.

"Us," Doc said. "We're his family."

"Funeral," Mia murmured. "We have to plan a funeral. We have to do this right."

"Let Joni and Brooklyn handle the details," Doc suggested.

"Good idea," Mia said. "Everyone will be here in the morning, anyway. It'll be a madhouse. I miss my kids."

Mia bowed her head and a moment later she sniffed.

"This isn't my first rodeo. This is the life. South Paw patched in. He knew the world he was getting into. But goddamn, how many more people will I have to bury?" She shoved away from Doc's touch and stood up from her chair.

"I haven't bandaged you yet," Doc said.

"I'll do it in Colt's room. We've got a first aid kit." She dashed from the office, the door slamming hard behind her.

We both stared after her. Finally, Doc sighed and then stripped off her gloves and tossed them into the metal bowl resting on the desk.

"Is she…gonna be okay?" I queried.

"Are any of us going to be okay?" Doc asked with a shrug. "The losses hit hard and deep, every time. Sometimes, it's hard to get back up again. But you do. And you find a way to live with the consequences of being part of this club, a part of this life, or you don't."

"It's that simple?"

"Not simple, but it is that cut and dry," she said. "You've got your entire life ahead of you. You don't have to stay and be a part of this. You can leave."

"Why didn't you leave?" I asked.

"It's complicated."

"Life usually is."

She cracked a smile. "Word of advice?"

"Yeah?"

"Nothing is black and white."

"I know," I said.

"Nothing is black and white," Doc repeated. "And there are several shades of gray. Don't bother trying to figure out how others reconcile the club life. Your job is to figure out if *you* can. Then you'll know."

"Then I'll know what?"

"Know if you have what it takes to live this kind of life with Viper."

My eyes widened.

"Because that's what this is really about, isn't it? You want a life with Viper."

"I do?" I asked.

She smiled. "I'm thinking you do."

I snorted. "For a while I actually pretended that I could just sleep with him and not want more. Stupid, right?"

Doc raised her hand that was riddled with gruesome pink scars. "Hi, I'm Linden and I'm a Boxer-a-holic."

"What happened to your hand?" I blurted.

"Club business," she drawled.

"I see," I murmured. "And you didn't walk away?"

"Some things you just can't walk away from."

"Some things, or some people?"

She shrugged. "It wasn't just Boxer for me. It was all of them. They became my family. It wasn't what I expected or planned on. But I decided to take the good with the bad. Losing South Paw—that's the bad. But we have each other to lean on to get through it. That's the good. See? Not all black and white."

"And different shades of gray," I said. "Yeah."

"You get it."

I sighed. "Starting to. I'm starting to."

Chapter 34

Viper's bedroom was empty. I placed my phone on the nightstand and then sat down on the bed to remove my shoes. I was in the middle of stripping off my jeans when the door opened and Viper strode inside.

Without a word, he lifted me into his arms and set me on the top of the dresser. He moved between my legs, the rough denim of his jeans grazing the inside of my thighs.

I shivered from the intensity of his gaze.

He cupped the back of my head and took my lips in a brutal kiss. His tongue entered my mouth as he pillaged.

My back bowed and my legs opened even more.

Viper inched closer, his erection pressing through his fly into my cleft.

"I won't be gentle," he growled against my lips.

"I don't want gentle."

He lightly slapped the side of my ass, silently commanding me to lift up. He glided my panties down my legs and tossed them aside. Vipers mouth was on mine again while his fingers slipped inside me, causing me to shudder. I tore my lips from his and threw my head back as I trembled in rapture.

He pumped his fingers in and out of me, relentless, determined. And when his thumb grazed my clit, I came.

I was still shaking when he removed his fingers from my body and painted my thighs with my own release.

I unbuttoned his jeans, unzipped his fly, and took out his erection. I slid my thumb over his crown. My mouth instantly watered and I had the desire to taste him.

But Viper was in control and he wouldn't let me. He batted my hands away. Then he gripped my lower back and urged me to scoot toward the end of the dresser.

"Spread your legs for me," he rasped, taking his shaft in hand.

I spread my thighs, opening myself to him.

He lined himself at my entrance and slammed into me.

I gasped from his invasion and my back arched. He placed his hands underneath my ass and lifted me up, drilling into me over and over again.

Our moans echoed off the walls and I didn't care if I was being loud.

"Viper," I begged.

"I know, baby. I know," he panted.

His lips took mine in a ravenous kiss. I gripped the lapels of his leather cut, trying to move our bodies even closer. I wanted no space between us.

He picked up his pace. Relentless, ruthless.

My legs locked around his hips and my eyes closed while his pelvis ground against me, hitting the spot that was sure to make me combust.

"I'm close again," I whispered against his mouth.

"I'm close too."

I pulled my lips from his and opened my eyes. Viper's gaze met mine as he continued to thrust. We didn't take our eyes off one another, not even when a soft cry escaped me as I came.

And while I was feeling tremors deep within me, Viper thrust hard one last time, clenching my ass in a bruising clutch as he spilled his release.

My fingers loosened on his lapels, and I leaned my forearms back onto the dresser as my heart drummed mercilessly in my chest.

Viper slid out and then scooped me off the dresser, carting me into the bathroom. He set me down and I stood on wobbly legs.

The insides of my thighs were wet and that's when I realized that Viper had come inside of me without protection.

My breath hitched.

"Did I hurt you?" he asked, his hands tugging on the tank top that I hadn't shucked. He didn't wait for an answer as he turned my body for his examination. He palmed the curve of my ass cheek.

"You might be bruised tomorrow." He gently stroked my skin, silently apologizing for the roughness we'd both wanted.

"That's not my concern," I said quietly. I slid my fingers between my legs and held the evidence of his release up to him.

He looked at it and then at me. "No condom."

"No condom." I swallowed. "I'm on birth control, but…"

"But I lost my cool." He sighed. "Fuck, Sutton. I didn't even think about it, and then I was inside you raw, and it was the best thing I've ever felt."

"Yeah." I lowered my hand and curled my fingers into a fist. "It was pretty amazing for me too."

I suddenly collapsed onto the closed toilet seat.

Viper tucked himself back into his jeans and then crouched down in front of me. He placed his hands on my thighs and gripped them.

"Look at me," he commanded.

I lifted my gaze to his.

"I'm sorry," he said. "If I'd been thinking—"

"If *I'd* been thinking," I interrupted. "It takes two, yeah?"

"It's my responsibility to protect you," he said gruffly. "In all ways."

My insides melted. "Still," I began.

"No, let me get this out. Okay?"

I nodded.

"I haven't…been with anyone. Since before I went to prison."

I frowned. "Well, what about when you got out?"

"You."

"Me?"

"I've only been with you, Sutton."

"But you were in prison five years!"

The corner of his mouth flickered. "Which was why it was so hard not to maul you."

I reached out and cradled his cheek. "That didn't work out too well for you. Thank God for that. You're dynamite in the sack."

He finally cracked a smile, but it dimmed almost immediately. "I just wanted you to know that I don't usually lose my head like this. That I've always taken precaution…until now. I'm clean, Sutton."

"I'm relieved to hear it," I admitted. "But what about the other thing?"

"What other thing?"

"Birth control isn't foolproof, you know."

"Thought we already talked about that," he said quietly.

"We talked about you taking care of me and any potential offspring. But, Viper, I'm not ready for all that. And I'm definitely not ready for all that with the violence that's going on." I reached out and grasped his lapels. "What am I supposed to do? What if I got pregnant and you died? I'd be on my own."

"You'd have the club," he said reflexively.

"But I'm not your Old Lady," I said. "They'd have no obligation to help me."

"They don't have an obligation to help you now," he pointed out. "Two weeks ago, you were a stranger. Your friend was sleeping with Savage and that's the only reason any of us got involved."

I nodded. "You're right. The club doesn't have an obligation to help me. I'll grab my shit and leave."

I attempted to get up, but Viper blocked me.

"Hold on a second," he said, placing his hand on my knee. "First of all, like hell I'm going to let you leave. And second, where would you even go?"

"A motel," I said. "Or Carla's."

"How long could you stay at a motel before your money runs out? Shelly's is closed for the foreseeable future. And you don't have a car."

"You make me sound like a loser."

"No. You're not a loser. You've had a rough go of it recently, that's all."

"I don't want to be a burden or an obligation."

"Mia gave you a job."

"Because Colt asked her to."

He rubbed the back of his neck in frustration. "For fuck's sake, will you stop twisting everything around? How did our conversation even get here?"

"I'm not sure," I said. "Oh, wait, I remember. You came inside me without a condom."

"Right. Okay, then let's focus on one thing at a time."

"Fine."

We stared at each other and neither of us said anything.

Finally, I said, "You got a solution?"

"To what? There's no problem."

"Not right now there's not. What if we keep sleeping together and—"

"Not *if*. We *are* going to keep sleeping together."

I snorted. "Noted. Okay, we're going to keep sleeping together. Condom or no condom?"

"How scared are you of actually getting pregnant?" Viper asked. "On a scale of one to ten."

I hadn't been prepared for his question. "About a seven."

"Then we use condoms."

"Do you know how much better sex without a condom is?" I demanded.

"Yeah. I was there, like, three minutes ago. It's light-years better."

"Well, now I know what I've been missing too," I said. "You expect me to go back to sex with a condom when I've just had the real deal?"

His lips twitched.

I rolled my eyes and pressed my finger to the corner of his mouth. "Smile. It's okay. I know you want to."

Viper cracked a grin.

"Better," I whispered. "You're handsome when you smile."

"So then, if you want to have sex without condoms, then this isn't about you getting pregnant, is it? This is about something else," Viper said.

I sighed. "No, it's not really about the baby thing. Though make no mistake, I'm not ready for that. I wouldn't be ready for that even if there wasn't a looming cartel war. Okay?"

"Okay. Then what's this about?"

"I'm not ready to lose you," I admitted. "How's that for honesty?"

"You want to talk honestly? Christ, I just admitted I hadn't fucked a woman in over five years."

"Seriously?"

"Seriously."

"But—*why*? I would have thought most men who just got out of prison would've been fucking anything that walked."

"I could've done that. But I didn't."

"Why were you honest about that with me?" I asked softly. "You could've kept that to yourself."

"For the same reason you just told me you're not ready to lose me. That's what you're really scared of, isn't it? You're terrified I'm going to die in this cartel war."

"It's so horrible I can't even think about it. My life wasn't much before I met you, but it was simple and not…violent."

"Fuck, Sutton. I don't want to die either. But this is the life I chose."

"I know," I murmured.

"I thought you and I were just going to roll in the hay a few times and then be done. You'd go back to your life, and I'd go back to mine. That's not looking like much of an option now though, is it?"

I shook my head. "It definitely isn't."

"So, you gotta decide what you want. A life with me and all the shit that could mean. Or you can walk away.

You cash your insurance check, buy that car, and hightail it out of here."

"And do what?" I asked. "Go to another city? Get another waitressing job? Get *over* you? Damn it, Viper. Don't you get it? I don't want to leave you."

"Then be my Old Lady," he said. "For real. Until one of us takes our last breath. However long that is. Three days, three years, or thirty…who the hell knows. None of us know how long we have. I'm asking you to live whatever time we've got left as my Old Lady."

I swallowed. "Isn't it too soon?"

"Too soon? Baby, from the minute we're born, we're dying. Fuck time. Fuck it all. Let's just be together."

Tears I never allowed myself to shed suddenly came bubbling to the surface.

Here was a man willing to stand by my side through anything.

Willing to protect me.

Shelter me.

Love me.

"Are you sure, Viper?" I asked, giving him a watery smile. "If you ask me to be your Old Lady, you're *never* getting rid of me. I'm gonna stick to you like glue."

He leaned forward and brushed his lips tenderly against mine. "That's the hope, Sutton. That's the motherfucking hope."

Chapter 35

"So, what happens now?" I asked sleepily, curled up in Viper's arms after our shower.

"What do you mean?"

"Now that I'm your Old Lady and you're my Old Man."

"Old?"

"What? You can call me an Old Lady, but I can't call you an Old Man?"

"Nope."

"How about hot, virile, silver fox?"

"That works." His hand slid down my back to grab the meaty curve of my ass. "Nothing changes. We still sleep together. I still protect you. You still give me your sass day in and day out, and then I punish you by getting you on your knees."

"Not much of a punishment."

He chuckled.

"What about tattoos and stuff?" I asked.

"What about them?"

"Do we get them?"

"Eventually."

"Marriage?"

He paused. "Eventually."

I snuggled closer. "I'm not rushing anything—I just wanted to know."

"Marriage and permanent tattoos don't freak you out, but a baby does?"

"I didn't say a baby freaked me out. I said I'm not ready for that."

"But you *are* ready for marriage and tattoos?"

"Viper," I snapped. "Stop twisting my words."

"Sorry, spitfire. Just figured I'd give you a taste of your own medicine. You like giving me shit, so I returned the favor."

I was slightly mollified by his endearment—and by his fingers drawing lazy circles on my skin.

"You ever been married?" I asked.

"No."

"Had an Old Lady before me?"

"Splitting hairs, isn't it?"

"You could've had an Old Lady but never married her," I pointed out.

"No. No Old Lady."

"Kids?"

He chuckled. "No."

"Why are you laughing? That's a valid question. I know you've fucked a lot of women before you went to prison. It's a possibility."

"I've always been careful. Besides, don't you think I would've told you if I had a kid? I wouldn't have hidden that from you."

"Well, when you put it that way." I sifted my fingers through his chest hair. "Viper?"

"Hmm?"

"I know you said you'd take care of me and a baby if there was one, but…"

"But?"

"But do you actually want kids?"

"I thought we already discussed this."

"No. We kind of danced around it when you told me to live in the present and not think so much about the future. That didn't last long, by the way."

"I was trying to get you not to panic."

"Panic? Who's panicked?"

"You're twenty-two."

"Back to that, are you?"

"I just really wanted to make sure you were ready for all this shit."

"All this shit. You mean life?"

"Yeah."

"Won't know until I try, right?" I swung my leg over his body and slid on top of him. "You didn't answer my question."

"What was your question?"

"Kids, Viper. Do you want kids?"

"Yeah. With the right woman."

I poked him in his ribs. "Am *I* the right woman?"

His hands slid down my back, over my butt, to spread my thighs. "Wouldn't have asked you to be my Old Lady if I didn't know you were the right woman."

"Viper," I whispered, my mouth searching for his.

I found him in the dark, our tongues meeting. I ground against him, wanting him inside me with nothing between us.

I pulled away but only so I could lift myself up and guide him into my welcoming body.

"You sure you want to risk it?" he asked.

I moved ever so slightly, loving the hard feel of him inside me with nothing between us. "I'll risk it. If you will."

He cupped the back of my neck and dragged me down for another kiss. I rode him slowly, taking him deep.

And when I came, it was soft, like an afternoon nap in a patch of warm sun. It was no less meaningful, but it was so different compared to the volatility of earlier.

I collapsed on top of him in a sweaty heap, my breath covering his skin.

"Whenever you're ready," he murmured, his fingers plowing through my hair.

"Oh, should I get off you?"

I made a move, but his arms tightened around me, keeping me tethered to him.

"No. I meant, whenever you're ready to have kids. It's all up to you, Sutton."

"What if it's five years from now?"

"Then it's five years from now."

"What if it's ten? You'll be forty-six."

"The kids'll keep me young."

I bit my lip and then asked the question I'd been dreading the answer to. "What if I'm never ready?"

"Then it'll just be you and me, and that'll be more than enough."

∼

Shouting woke me from a dead sleep. I rolled over and placed my hand on Viper's side of the bed and cracked an eye open.

He was standing up, already pulling on a pair of jeans.

"What's going on?" I asked sluggishly.

"No idea. Going to find out." He grabbed a clean T-shirt from his drawer.

"I'm coming, too," I said.

My legs were tangled up in the covers and I nearly fell to the floor. Viper tossed me my tank top and I quickly put on my jeans and padded behind him, barefoot.

"Zip, get the fuck out of my way!" The burly biker president tried to move past his VP, but Zip blocked his path. Boxer and Gray stood behind Colt.

It was like they were flanking a feral animal.

"No," Zip said. "You're drunk and you're liable to get yourself killed."

"Fuck you!" He swung out, missing Zip by a good foot.

"Prez," Gray said softly. "Easy, man. Now is not the time for this."

"They put a hit out on my woman," Colt snapped. "I'll kill 'em all."

"You go charging into cartel territory without a plan and you're gonna make Mia a widow." Boxer placed his hand on Colt's shoulder. "You guys have kids. Come on, man. Let's get you some coffee. Take a breather."

Joni, Doc, and Darcy were in the kitchen, watching everything unfold. Joni went to the cabinet and pulled out a mug. She quickly filled it with coffee and handed it to Boxer.

"Thanks," he said.

She nodded, looking somber.

Boxer led the way, followed by Colt and Gray. Zip brought up the rear. Viper glanced at me, grasped the back of my neck and quickly brushed his mouth against mine before following his brothers out of the clubhouse.

"He woke you guys," Joni said.

"It's okay." I nodded and then looked at Doc. "Did Colt sleep at all last night?"

Doc shook her head. "As far as I know, he holed up in the shed where they have church and began drinking."

"And Mia?" I asked.

"Still asleep," Doc said. "I gave her something to help."

"Let me get you a cup of coffee," Darcy offered.

"Thanks," I murmured.

Darcy poured me a cup and I added cream and sugar from the containers on the counter.

"You guys heard, then? About South Paw?" I asked, raising the mug to my lips and looking at Joni and then Darcy.

"Tragedy." Darcy sipped her coffee.

"Funeral's tomorrow," Joni said. "I've got the details planned. And Brooklyn is taking care of the food."

I lifted the coffee to my mouth. "What happens after?"

"After?" Darcy asked. "After the funeral, you mean? We'll come back here, have a wake of sorts."

I shook my head. "I mean with the cartel. Where do we go from here?"

"Not sure yet," Joni said slowly. "The guys will have church, they'll talk, they'll vote and we'll take it one day at a time."

"It's escalated though, right?" I asked. "I mean, they put a hit out on Mia. The guys won't just stand for that, will they?"

"No, they won't," Mia said as she came into the kitchen. Her forearm was bandaged, and she had bags under her eyes. Her brown hair was disheveled.

Without a word, Darcy poured her a cup of coffee.

"Has anyone seen my husband?" Mia asked.

"Your husband is currently drunk as a skunk. Zip is trying to talk him out of attacking the cartel," Joni said.

"Oh." Mia looked at me. "You doin' okay?"

"Me?" I asked. "Yeah. But I'm not the one who's injured."

"I've had worse." She shrugged. Mia's shoulder's

sagged and she took Darcy's offered hand. "I'm trying really hard not to cry, but I might fail."

"Cry," Doc said. "Let it all out."

"I've been on the verge of crying all morning," Joni said. "I'm just afraid if I start, I won't be able to stop."

"God, this is all so horrible," Mia wailed and promptly burst into tears.

The Old Ladies swarmed her and enveloped her in a hug. I stood at the sidelines, feeling uncomfortable but wanting to lend support.

Darcy looked up from the group hug and said, "What are you doing? Get in here."

I wrapped my arms around Doc and Darcy and the five of us stood as one until Mia's tears subsided.

"Thanks," Mia mumbled as she wiped her cheeks.

Several cell phones vibrated, and they all took a moment to check them.

"Old Ladies group text," Doc explained.

I nodded.

"Willa and Duke are on their way," Darcy said, putting her phone back in her pocket.

"Can I talk to you a second," Mia asked, directing her question at me.

"Sure," I said.

"Porch," she suggested.

I nodded.

"Oh, the funeral arrangements," Mia said.

"Brooklyn and I are taking care of it." Joni squeezed her hand.

Mia and I took our coffees to the front porch. I breathed in the humid air, wondering how I could feel such duality inside me. Elated one moment because of Viper. Despondent because of South Paw the next.

"I'm sorry," Mia blurted out. "I kinda blew out of the office before I fell apart."

"Oh, it wasn't even a thing," I insisted. "You have nothing to be sorry about."

She sighed. "How are you doing. Really?"

"Still trying to make sense of everything…"

"How's that coming for you?"

"I'm worse off this morning," I said with a tremulous smile.

She nodded. "That's usually how it goes."

"Viper…he asked me to be his Old Lady last night. For real, I mean. Not for a finite period of time. But for as long as he's…"

"Alive?"

"Yeah."

"And what did you say?"

"I said yes."

"You sure that's the right thing for you? I mean, with what just happened…"

"Trying to talk me out of it already, huh?"

She shook her head. "No. I wouldn't do that. Only you and Viper can decide what's right for you both. I just—you're young, you know?"

"*You're* young," I pointed out. "And what does age have to do with it?"

"This is a hard life. That's all I meant. You won't get the white-picket-fence, the stability, the routine. Nothing about this life is normal."

"And walking away is the answer to that? I thought you liked Viper. I thought you wanted him to have someone."

"I do. But, Sutton, this is a big deal. Just make sure you're in it for the long haul."

"What about you?" I asked.

"What about me?"

"What was it like when you met Colt?"

She smiled and peered out over the porch. "Immediate combustion. I tried to resist. But I'm a sucker for a grump with a heart of gold. Don't tell him I told you that."

"His secret is safe with me," I assured her. "He's losing his shit, you know."

She sighed. "Yeah. I know."

"Zip and the others took him outside to try and calm him down. Or at least sober him up. Apparently, he was drinking all night…"

"I wouldn't know. I was zonked out." She absently touched her bandaged arm. "He's usually very level-headed. There isn't much that riles him up."

"I guess where you're concerned, it's personal," I said.

"Yeah. When it comes to me and the kids, he loses all rational thought." She smiled slightly. "I love him so much."

"He loves you, clearly," I said.

"He could die," she said quietly. "During this war."

"He could. Or he could get hit by a bus. You don't know how it all turns out. And as you said, you chose this life, right? You chose him and everything that comes with it."

We stood there for a moment in silence.

The front door to the clubhouse opened and Boxer came out. He wrapped an arm around Mia's shoulder and gave her an affectionate hug.

"Your husband has been corralled. He could use your attention, though," he said.

"Thanks." She kissed his cheek. "I'll go to him now. Sailor's bringing the kids soon. Keep an eye out?"

"Will do." He gave her one last hug and then released her.

Chapter 36

Boxer and Mia went inside, leaving me alone with my cup of coffee. I hadn't spoken to Carla in a few days, so I pulled out my phone and called her.

She answered, but before she said anything, I heard static on the other end of the line. "Hey, it's Sutton. Are you in your car?"

"Hey. And yes, I'm in my car. I'm on my way to Lincoln."

"Nebraska?"

"Yep."

"Why?" I asked in confusion.

"Because I've decided to move there," she said.

"Wait, what?" I asked.

"Savage and I ended things, and I made the split decision to get out of Waco. Don't want to be around when shit goes down, you know?"

"So you know…what's coming?" I asked.

"Yep. Savage gave me a heads up. I had no reason to stay, so I sold the trailer, packed up my car, and I'm out."

"You didn't tell me. I didn't get to say goodbye."

"Oh, sugar, you know I'm not one for goodbyes."

"Were you ever going to tell me?" I asked.

"Eventually," she said. "But your life is there, and my life is taking me somewhere else."

"How do you know my life is here?" I demanded.

"Honey, I saw what was brewing the minute you and Viper met. You want to tell me that hasn't turned into something more?"

"How the hell did you know?"

"Just had a feeling about it. I'm right, right?"

"You're right." I sighed. "I've officially become his Old Lady."

"Sounds permanent."

"It is."

"Well, you're in for it now, hun."

The front door opened, and I turned to see who was coming out. It was Viper.

"Call me once in a while?"

"I'll try."

"Carla?"

"Yeah, sugar?"

"Thanks," I said. "For that night."

She paused. "Glad it turned out all right in the end."

"Yeah." I glanced at Viper. "It did. Take care of yourself, Carla."

"You too."

I hung up with her and placed my cell in my back pocket. Viper sauntered up next to me and rested his forearms on the railing.

"Carla," I said.

"Ah."

"She left town. Sold her trailer and just packed up and left. She didn't even tell me she was leaving."

"You don't sound upset about it."

I shrugged. "Just kinda strange, you know? She can't say goodbye like a normal person?"

"Would you have wanted that? A teary goodbye with hugs and promises to keep in touch?"

I glared at him. "Let me guess, you don't do goodbyes. You just get on your bike and ride off into the sunset."

He peered at me for a long moment and then said, "I'm not going anywhere."

"I know that," I replied automatically.

"What's this really about?"

I tightened my grip on the railing and my knuckles turned white. "How'd you know it was about something deeper?"

"It's always about something deeper. It's never about what you think it is."

"I'm a shit friend," I said quietly. "I feel bad that I don't feel bad that she's left town."

"Makes sense, based on what you've told me of your relationship. Not all people are meant to be in your life forever."

"No one's been in my life forever," I murmured. "They all go away. At some point. I don't stay in touch with work friends. My dad is…my dad. I lost my mom. Maybe I'm defective. Maybe I don't know how to hold on to people."

"Or maybe you haven't found your tribe." He looked over his shoulder at the clubhouse. "Until now."

I thought about Willa, Savage, Mia. They already felt familiar. Like we had history.

"I'm glad she's getting out of town. She'll be safe. And who knows, maybe she'll find a good man and be happy."

I also knew she'd never call me again. Our paths had diverged. Maybe Viper was right. People didn't always stay in your life for a long time, but that didn't mean their presence wasn't necessary. That they didn't teach you something vitally important.

"Don't hurt your brain trying to think your way out of this," he teased.

I bumped my hip against him. "I guess I have to decide if I'm completely full of shit or not. I don't really have the right to be upset that she up and left without so much as a goodbye when really, I never made a true overture to become close with her. It was easier not to."

"You're not going to be able to remain detached now," Viper said. "Not with the club and definitely not with the Old Ladies."

My phone lit up with an incoming text, quickly followed by a few more. I unlocked my cell and read the text thread, a smile blooming across my face.

"What?" Viper demanded.

"Mia added me to the Old Lady group text."

"It's official then." He smiled. "Full stamp of approval. Hell, I don't even need to bring it up at church."

"Bring what up at church?" I asked in confusion.

"That I'm making you my Old Lady."

"You have to talk about it at church? What, like you need the club's permission?"

"Not like that," he said. "It's consideration. Letting the brothers know I'm making the step. Making it official. It's a declaration."

"Oh." I bit my lip. "So is this a formal thing?"

"Is what a formal thing? Making you my Old Lady?"

I nodded. "Like, do we get a party or something? Like, congrats you guys are shackled to each other now."

"There's usually a celebration. I guess normal people would call it an engagement party."

"That sounds fun."

"Might have to be put on hold though. All things considered."

I sighed. "Yeah. I'd feel like an utter shit celebrating on the heels of a wake."

The rumble of motorcycles preceded the arrival of several bikers. It was a caravan of sorts, and SUVs were behind them. Prospects at the gates let them in and they parked in the gravel lot.

"Cue pandemonium," I said as everyone began making their way toward the porch.

Slash and Brooklyn were holding hands, and he helped her up the stairs. "Watch your footing," he said.

"Thanks." She grasped the handrail.

"Hey, guys," I said quietly.

Brooklyn looked at me. "Hi." She dropped Slash's hand and then moved toward me.

I instinctively took a step back.

She frowned. "What are you doing?"

"Moving away in case you were going to slug me."

"Slug you? Why would I slug you?" she asked in confusion.

Slash interjected, "Because she was the one who told me you were at the bakery when you promised you were at home resting."

"Yeah, that," I said with a nod.

Brooklyn shook her head. "I was going to give you a hug."

"Why?"

She raised her brows. "Because of what you went through last night."

"Oh, uh—"

Brooklyn embraced me and whispered in my ear, "Are you doing okay?"

"I'm fine," I said, even though tears pricked my eyes.

She pulled back to look at me. "Not sure I believe you."

"I'm okay," I insisted. "But all the hugging has me freaked out."

Brooklyn smiled. "Emotion averse?"

"Something like that."

Slash and Viper had moved away from us, as if to give us a measure of privacy.

I pitched my voice lower when I said, "I didn't mean to get you into trouble."

"You didn't," she assured me. "Slash is overprotective, and I love him for it." She looked at her husband, her face softening.

I wondered if I had the same gooey expression when I stared at Viper.

God, I hope not.

Another motorcycle engine rumbled in the distance and the prospects opened the gates again.

"Who's here?" I inquired.

"That's the rest of the crew," Brooklyn said. "Everyone except Duke and Willa."

"As soon as Duke gets here, we can have church," Viper said.

"Is Prez in the headspace for that?" Slash asked.

"Guess we better go find out," Viper replied.

We moved inside and the men went to the shed out back.

As the Old Ladies settled into the living room and kitchen, the front door opened, and Willa and Duke came inside. Duke leaned close and whispered something in Willa's ear before pulling away.

"They're all in the shed," Mia said to Duke.

"Thanks," Duke said, touching her shoulder as he passed by the couch.

Willa came into the kitchen and gave me a side hug. She released me and then took a stool at the counter since all the seats in the living room were taken.

I went and sat on the floor next to Mia's feet. I looked up at her and asked, "How's Colt?"

"Sobering up. Still angry as fuck," she said, her mouth strained.

"What did you tell Silas?" Brooklyn asked her.

"The truth," Mia said grimly.

I looked at her in shock. "Seriously?"

She nodded. "He's thirteen. And this is not his first experience with the darker side of club life. Unfortunately."

I wanted to delve deeper, but it didn't seem appropriate. And even I knew when to bite my tongue.

"It was so much easier when the kids were babies and I didn't have to explain anything," Darcy said. "But now… with South Paw gone…"

"Are they—going to the funeral?" I asked.

Darcy shook her head. "Waverly and Sailor will stay with them. Here."

Joni rubbed her sleeping son's back, a pensive frown crossing her face.

That was something I hadn't considered. What did you tell children who grew up in this life? Would they grow up knowing violence? Expecting it?

Questions I hadn't even pondered suddenly blasted through my head and a sick feeling swirled in my belly.

"I need some air," I said, hopping up. As I headed for the front door, I heard Mia say, "Should I—"

"No," Willa interrupted. "Let me."

I went out onto the porch and took a seat on the steps. The air was muggy.

"Mind if I sit?" Willa asked, shutting the door behind her.

"Go ahead," I said.

She plopped down next to me. "I saw it all across your face."

"What?"

"The freak-out you just had the moment you realized what you've actually gotten yourself into." She smiled softly and bumped her knee against mine.

"I was happy for like five minutes," I said quietly. "Viper asked me to be his Old Lady—and I thought I knew what that really meant. But hearing Mia talk about her son knowing what went down…" I shook my head.

"You thought it was going to be all sunshine and roses?"

"No. Of course not. But you can kind of compartmentalize things that haven't happened yet, you know?"

"You must think we're all crazy to marry bikers and have babies with them."

"I don't think you're crazy. That would make me crazy, but…fuck, it's just a lot. And it happened fast."

"Life's a rollercoaster," she said. "My suggestion is to hold on for dear life and scream your fright out."

"What, like right now?" I asked in amusement.

"No. You scream like a banshee and all the men will come running."

"I'll just tell them I saw a giant cockroach."

She chuckled. "Does this change things for you? Mia put you on the group text, you know. She didn't do that lightly."

"No, it doesn't change things for me," I said in realization. "We live by different rules, don't we?"

"We, huh?"

"Yeah, we. I'm one of you now. And I'm no Victorian

maiden. I won't faint or need smelling salts, but Mia being honest with her son really threw me. I didn't know that was allowed."

"I think we're all kind of figuring it out as we go. Sailor and Waverly know what's going on with the club. Why do you think Savage and Acid are training them in self-defense?"

"Oh. I see."

She nodded. "Maybe you were thrown because Silas is only thirteen."

"Yeah, maybe."

"He's an old thirteen, though. Seen a lot. Lived a lot in his short life. He can handle it. It's why they don't treat him with kid gloves."

Darcy opened the front door. "Church is over. Colt wants everyone in the backyard for a meeting."

Chapter 37

We gathered out back. Viper was sitting on a log in front of the fire pit. I immediately went to him and sat next to him. He scooted over to give me more room, but I didn't need much.

"The kids?" Colt asked.

"Waverly and Sailor are keeping them occupied in the theatre room," Mia assured him.

The club president stood in front of the group, looking no worse for wear despite his night of drinking.

Zip was posed next to Colt in a silent show of support.

"We all know why we're here," Colt began. "The funeral for South Paw is tomorrow. We'll have a wake after that, and then we're going into immediate lockdown. Everyone is staying at the clubhouse. No work, no play."

"For how long?" Darcy inquired.

"I don't know yet," Colt stated. "What I need from you all right now is patience while I sort this out. We always knew it was going to get ugly, and now it's clear the cartel has escalated things. What they did to Mia was a declaration of war."

"Should we go to the cabins?" Allison asked.

Colt shook his head. "Can't spare the men to guard you. Everyone stays here. The permits are finally in the system. We'll start construction on the clubhouse expansion immediately. It's going to be tight. It's going to be uncomfortable, but this is the way it has to be. We're going to rotate you each home in small groups. You'll pack what you need for your families and then return immediately. I don't want you on the streets alone. I don't want you sitting ducks."

"What about me?" Rach asked as she moved her son to her other shoulder. "Me and Cash, I mean."

"You're family," Colt said immediately. "You'll stay here."

Rach nodded.

"It's going to take a lot of cooperation, a lot of moving parts. We've added several brothers to the club. And a new Old Lady, too." Colt looked directly at me and inclined his head.

"Sutton will move into my room," Viper announced. "That frees up a spare room."

"Good. Rach and Cash will take Sutton's room," Colt said. "The rest of you, figure it out. Order beds if you have to or throw mattresses on the ground, I don't care. Just make your plans and make them fast."

Everyone began to dissipate. Couples spoke to each other in low tones as they headed for the clubhouse. Viper and I followed.

It was mayhem as everyone began preparing for the impending lockdown.

I headed up the stairs to my room and quickly shoved my dirty clothes into my duffel. I cleaned out the bathroom and stripped the bed. And then I grabbed my pistol from the nightstand.

"I need to do laundry," I said.

"You should do it before everyone else gets the same idea."

We headed to Viper's bedroom. I dropped my toiletries in his bathroom, setting my toothbrush next to his. I put my shampoo and soap in the shower.

We were co-mingling hard and fast.

I went back into his room and found him sorting through his clothes.

"I don't want you to freak out," I said. "But our toothbrushes are looking very cozy next to each other."

"That's not all that's getting cozy." He tossed a pair of underwear into a laundry bag. "Let's do a load."

"Big step, Viper," I teased. "Our intimates are getting intimate."

"Speaking of intimate. You're going to hear people having sex in the clubhouse."

"Noted. We're all going to be stepping on each other's toes." I sighed. "This is going to be intense, isn't it?"

"Yeah. It will be."

I dumped my dirty clothes into the laundry bag and was about to pick it up when Viper said, "Let me get that for you."

We traipsed down into the theater room. The kids were sitting on the couch, watching a movie. I wondered how they'd handle staying at the clubhouse. I doubted it was their first time.

The black and white mutt jumped off Silas's lap and came to investigate. I crouched down to give him a hearty scratch and he flopped onto his back and showed me his belly.

"Good boy," I whispered.

Viper was at the washing machine, dumping all our laundry into the drum.

"Uh, no," I said, going to him and pushing against his hip to move him out of the way.

"What?" Viper demanded. "I've done laundry before."

I yanked out several lace thongs. "These get their own cycle."

His eyes heated.

"Don't look at me that way," I muttered. "There are children present."

"How do you think they came into creation?"

I sighed. "Start the cycle, Viper."

∼

The rest of the afternoon passed in a state of frenetic energy. Families came and went, rooms were rearranged, and bunk beds were set up.

We placed long folding tables outside to prepare to feed the masses. Food, it seemed, would be a communal event. At least for tonight. Who knew how that would unfold over time. It might turn into an *every man for himself* situation.

Darcy and Mia were in the kitchen, slapping hamburger patties together and setting them on trays. I took one of the trays out to Gray, who was at the grill.

"Your favorite spot," I teased.

"I'm the unofficial grill master," he stated.

"Can I get you anything?"

He lifted his empty beer bottle. "Another one of these would be good."

"Sure thing." I grabbed two beers from the cooler and popped the tops off before handing him one.

"How are you doing with all this, Sutton?" he asked, taking a sip. He set his beer aside and then began laying hamburger patties onto the grill.

"I don't know," I admitted. "Time seems to be moving

really fast. I can't believe the funeral is tomorrow. Feels like he died weeks ago. I can't believe it was yesterday."

Crow sat alone at the picnic table and was drinking right from a liquor bottle.

"Crow's not doing great, is he?" I asked softly.

Gray shook his head. "No. He and South Paw were close. Buddies, you know? Young brothers with their entire lives ahead of them."

"No doubt Crow is thinking about his own mortality."

"We all are, Sutton. We all are."

Chapter 38

"You awake?" I whispered.

"Of course I'm awake," Viper muttered into his pillow. "Another baby cried. I swear they've got surround-sound lungs."

"That's what babies do. They cry."

"I know they cry. I just didn't know that if one cried, it would set off all the others like car alarms."

I grinned even though he couldn't see me.

"Is that why you're awake?" he asked.

"No."

He reached for me and pulled me on top of him. "Was *this* the reason you're awake?"

"Not that either."

"Then what?"

"I've just been thinking," I said quietly. "About all this. The club. What you're involved in."

"Ah."

"I have been thinking about kids."

"Our future ones?"

"The ones that currently exist."

"Spell this out for me. I'm tired and my ears are ringing."

"You know if we have a baby, it'll cry and you won't be able to get your beauty sleep. You know that, right?"

"What's on your mind, Sutton?" he asked with a sigh.

"How does the club make its money?"

"I knew this was coming…"

"The man that came after Mia…that wasn't about what happened to me. So, what was it? Did I just find myself in the middle of a drug war between a biker club and a cartel?"

"I can't get into details, but I can say with confidence, no. That's not what this is about. Colt told you about the skin trade going on in Waco. Our club has put a stop to a number of the cartel's shipments. We've rescued women and children, and been a general pain in their ass. We've cut into their profit and they don't like that. That's what this is all about."

"So you're not in the drug business?"

"I didn't say that."

"Oh." I sighed. "Okay."

"Like I said, I can't get into the details. But how we earn our living isn't on the up and up. Got it?"

"Yeah." I fell silent.

"You're upset about that, aren't you?"

"No. I don't think I am. I know that you and the club protect women and children. Right now, that's all I need to know."

"Fuck, fuck, fuck," I said as I dug through my newly cleaned clothes.

"What?" Viper asked as he laced up his boots.

"I don't have an appropriate dress for the funeral." I looked at him from the spot on the floor. "I can't wear jeans."

"Well, I don't have anything you can wear."

I rolled my eyes. "Hand me my phone, please."

He grabbed it from the nightstand and tossed it to me. I caught it, opened it, and immediately opened the Old Lady text thread.

ME

> SOS. I don't have a dress or shoes for the funeral.

JONI

I don't have anything that'll fit you.

ALLISON

My stuff has spit up on it.

RACH

Same.

DOC

I have a black cardigan you can borrow.

MIA

What size shoe do you wear?

ME

> Five.

WILLA

You're the same size as Waverly. Let me see if she has anything that could work.

DARCY

If they don't have anything, I'm sure Lily's clothes would fit you. :P

Waverly came through. She had a strapless black lace dress with several skirt layers which I paired with Doc's black cardigan and Mia's heels.

I smoothed my hand over the skirt one last time before turning toward Viper. He sat on the edge of the bed, his elbows resting on his knees, his dark eyes intense.

He rose and held out his hand. I set my palm in his. He brought my hand to his lips, and he kissed the back of it.

"Honored to have you stand by my side today," he said gruffly.

We went to the cemetery with Brooklyn and Slash in the back of Brooklyn's red Ford. Slash reached over and placed his hand on her thigh, and she covered his hand with hers.

All the single bikers rode their bikes, and they pulled up and parked behind the brigade of SUVs and trucks.

The kids had stayed at the clubhouse, supervised by Waverly and Sailor. Prospects were on guard duty. It was a sad day and security measures were in place.

The sky was clear and there was a slight breeze in the muggy air. Slash helped Brooklyn out of the passenger side and slammed the door shut.

We all walked with quiet intensity to the plot of land where we'd lay South Paw to rest. The earth was newly dug, green and brown, a symbol of life in a place where the dead rested.

I shuddered from the thought.

Viper wrapped an arm around my shoulder and pulled me into his side. The minister began to speak, but I tuned him out. Instead, I stared at the faces of those around me. Men draped arms around their Old Ladies, while they held their sleeping babies in their arms. Rach stood with her son, and it was so obvious she was lonely. Crow's eyes were bloodshot, and I wondered if he'd even slept last night.

Brooklyn's shoulders shook as she cried, and she dug through her clutch for a tissue. Joni's tears streamed down her cheeks, but she made no move to wipe them away.

Aside from those two, everyone else was tearless.

I met Savage's gaze. His expression was a mask of commiseration.

The minister fell silent. Zip, Colt, Boxer, and Gray took the shovels and threw dirt onto the lowered coffin.

We all wind up here.

Either in the ground, or ashes on someone's mantle.

It was a depressing thought.

And in that moment, I finally understood why Viper and his brothers lived the way they did. If we all wound up in the same place, then there was no time to waste.

But for me, living every day like it could be my last didn't come naturally.

I stayed small. Safe.

But by choosing to become Viper's Old Lady, I wouldn't be able to do that anymore.

I reached out and grasped his hand, linking his fingers with mine.

He squeezed gently and pulled me closer.

Life was for the living. And I was going to live it boldly.

With Viper.

Chapter 39

As I was climbing into the back of Brooklyn's car, I stopped to watch Mia. She turned from South Paw's grave and walked a few steps to the headstone next to it. Mia pressed her fingers to her lips and then placed them on the tombstone. She moved to the next grave site and repeated the gesture.

Colt stood a few feet behind her, holding their baby daughter. When she was finished, she walked to her husband and leaned her head against his arm.

I suddenly got in the car, feeling like I'd watched something personal that hadn't been meant for my eyes.

"Nice service," I muttered.

"It was," Brooklyn agreed, glancing at her husband, who didn't reply. Her mascara hadn't smudged despite her tears.

Her phone vibrated and she glanced down at the screen. "Jazz and Brielle just finished setting up." She turned around to look at me. "My business partners."

"Oh," I said.

"You'll meet them soon. You'll like them," she said before turning back around.

The rest of the car ride was silent. No one was in the mood to talk, and I felt the heavy weight of loss on my heart.

I wondered if this was the start in a long line of funerals. I glanced at Viper, who was staring out the window, clearly lost in his own thoughts.

Would I have to stand by his grave and watch his coffin being lowered into the ground?

He looked at me, as if he had eyes in the back of his head and could tell I was thinking about him.

His mouth softened as he reached for my hand.

We linked our fingers. He was warm.

He was alive.

"You're going the speed limit," Brooklyn said.

"Yep," Slash said. "You're in the car. I'm not going faster."

"Five over," she pleaded.

"Jazz and Brielle handled everything. It'll be fine. You've got to learn to relinquish control."

"Because I'm so good at that," she drawled, looking over her shoulder at me and winking.

I smiled, enjoying their banter. It made everything feel lighter after the oppressive somberness of the funeral.

We arrived back at the clubhouse, and we were one of the last cars to get there. I thought it was adorable how protective Slash was of his pregnant wife. He was attentive to her needs, and he never lost his patience with her.

"I have to change," I said as the four of us went up the porch steps.

"Same," Brooklyn said. "The elastic on this dress is itching."

Folding tables had been set up in the living room and

kitchen area. The furniture had been pushed against the wall to accommodate them. It was congested and noisy, and I immediately threaded my way through the throng to the stairs. I was already pulling off the cardigan before I even made it to Viper's room.

Our room.

It would take some adjusting, just like sleeping in the same bed with a huge man who took up all the space was an adjustment.

I closed the door and sat down on the bed to remove the heels. A few seconds later, Viper strode inside.

"What are you doing?" I asked.

He closed the door. "Just wanted to make sure you were okay."

"Oh." I frowned. "I'm fine. I told you I was changing."

"Yeah." He leaned against the wall.

"How are *you* doing?"

"Fine."

I raised a brow. "Is this one of those moments where you're burying your true thoughts deep?"

"This is the life."

"So you've said."

"I've known Raze, Bones, Smoke, and Kelp for years. Their deaths…"

"Would've hit you harder."

"Yeah."

I set the heels aside and then folded the cardigan. "I feel the opposite."

"Do you?"

I nodded. "I didn't know South Paw well. But I liked him and felt like he was someone I would've been friends with down the road."

Viper pushed away from the door and sat on the bed

next to me. He took my hand in his but didn't say anything.

"How do you do it?" I asked quietly. "How do you love people, connect with people, knowing all the while they might die on you?"

"I don't know," he admitted.

"I guess this is just a risk you have to take, huh?"

"Yeah."

I leaned my head against his shoulder. "It would be so much easier if I was a cyborg. No feelings. No hurt."

"You wouldn't feel the good things either."

"True." I sighed and lifted my head. "Let me change real quick and then we'll go have a drink in South Paw's honor."

We walked down into the living room and kitchen area. Kids took their plates of food, and I watched Lily sneak a piece of cheese to the yellow lab that was thumping his tail hard enough to leave bruises.

Darcy said something to Joni and the two women embraced. Brooklyn was already seated with her feet up while she conversed with Allison who bounced her son on her knee. Torque brought his wife a plate of food but saw that her hands were full and fed her a bite.

Colt tapped his beer bottle with a spoon to gather everyone's attention. The crowd fell silent and looked at the biker president.

He raised his beer. "To South Paw. Tonight we honor a fallen brother. We remember his bravery."

"To South Paw," Zip said, raising his drink.

"To South Paw," we echoed.

∽

"I think I'm drunk," I announced.

Allison giggled. "I don't know if that's true."

"Can you still feel your face?" Mia inquired. "That's always my test."

I touched my cheeks. "Yeah, I can still feel them. Am I slurring my words?"

"No." Doc snorted. "I warned you Boxer's moonshine was strong."

"I'm a bartender!" I said, affronted. "I thought my body was one giant liver."

It was early evening, and I was sitting with the Old Ladies. The kids and dogs were hanging out underneath a shady tree, and the bikers sat on logs and camp chairs.

"Does anyone else feel like we're perpetually at a seventh-grade dance?" Joni asked. She'd put Everett to bed an hour ago, but she checked her phone every few minutes to make sure he was still asleep.

"The boys over there, the girls over here?" Doc said. "Yeah, I feel that way."

"I like it, though," Rach said. "There are things you don't mind saying in front of your girlfriends that you'd never want the men to hear."

"Like what?" I asked. "I'm pretty loose-lipped around Viper."

"But would you be loose-lipped around all of them?" Darcy inquired.

I paused to think. "What would I not want to say around them?"

"I don't know. You wouldn't talk penis size with that group. They'd turn it into a contest," Mia said.

Brooklyn rubbed the side of her head and adjusted her body in the chair.

"Go lie down," Allison said to her.

"I'm fine," Brooklyn assured.

"You're not fine. You have a headache," Doc said.

"And as your doctor, I recommend rest. Especially knowing the babies will wake at all hours tonight and you won't sleep soundly."

"I can sleep through anything," Brooklyn said. "I didn't hear them last night."

"Sleep," Doc commanded.

"You're just as bad as Slash." Brooklyn sighed and then stood up. "Good night, everyone."

"Night," I said.

"Food was excellent," Mia said, taking Brooklyn's hand and giving it a squeeze.

"Thanks." Brooklyn headed toward the group of bikers. Slash saw her coming and got up to greet her. They exchanged a few words and Slash gently touched her head. She nodded and the two of them headed into the clubhouse together.

"Sex gets rid of a headache like no one's business," Darcy said.

"They're not going to have sex," Doc said.

"No? How can you be sure?" Joni asked.

"Because Slash is Slash. He's going to rub her head until she falls asleep," Doc said.

"That's your professional assessment?" I asked.

"Yep." Doc smiled. "I'm pretty good at these sorts of things."

I looked at the crowd of men. "What do you think they're talking about?"

"They're telling their favorite South Paw moments," Mia said.

"And talking about the war," Doc said quietly, tapping her fingers against the top of her thigh.

"Have you ever…" I trailed off.

"What?" Mia prodded.

"Has the club ever been on lockdown for an extended period of time?"

Mia looked at Darcy. "You've been around the longest."

"This isn't the first time, obviously, but this is the most, ah, intense, I'd say," Darcy said. "Usually the women and children go to the cabins. You know about the cabins, right? Viper told you?"

I shook my head.

"We have some off-grid cabins in the Kisatchie National Forest in Louisiana. About six hours from here. We take the kids there when things could go hot. But this time we can't," Darcy said.

"Why not? It would be safer for you—and the kids, right?" I asked.

"The cartel put a hit on Mia," Darcy explained. "That means they're watching."

"We drive to our cabins, there's a good chance they follow," Joni said. "Putting us in worse danger."

"And there's not enough men to go with us and still take care of things here," Rach said. "So we're all one big happy, criminal family, living together in a teeny tiny clubhouse for the time being."

"This is what happens when the family grows," Darcy said, holding out her arms for the baby in Rach's embrace. "I'll give you a break for a bit if you want."

"Thanks," Rach said, handing her son over to her friend. "Maybe he'll conk out in your arms, and you can put him to bed for me."

"I miss this," Darcy said as she cradled a sleepy Cash. "Lily barely lets me hold her anymore. And Cam doesn't want to be seen with me in public."

"Sounds about right," Mia drawled. "Every time I try

to tame Silas's hair, he fluffs it right up and says the girls like it."

"Something to look forward to with Tank," Allison said, but she smiled when she said it.

"Where does the time go?" Rach asked, her gaze softening as she looked at her son.

"No idea," Mia replied. "Colt's already hinting at another."

"Another what?" I asked.

"Baby." Mia wrinkled her nose. "I think the man is certifiable, but there you have it."

"My brother hinting?" Joni shook her head. "I don't buy it."

"I was being diplomatic. He wants another baby and he's starting to get very vocal about it."

"Scarlett's not even a year old," Darcy said.

"Yeah." Mia scratched the side of her head. "But I must be crazy, because I'm actually considering it."

"Seriously?" Rach asked.

"Seriously," she said. "I know it's nuts. But I'm already fucking exhausted. I might as well have another and then I can be done. Three kids is a good number."

"What do you think, Doc?" Darcy asked.

"I think Mia didn't ask for my opinion," Doc said with a smile. "And it's a decision between her and Colt."

"I don't think you're crazy," Joni said. "I've been thinking the same thing."

"Yeah, but you're baby-crazy," Allison said with a wink.

Joni grinned. "Have you *seen* my husband? I can barely keep my hands to myself."

I stood up and hastily covered my mouth but didn't stifle my yawn. "Anyone need anything?"

They shook their heads.

"I'll be back. I need to use the restroom."

I headed into the clubhouse and heard someone moving around in the kitchen. Frowning in confusion, I went to investigate.

It was Crow. He was standing at a cutting board, wielding a knife. He looked over his shoulder at me.

"Hey," I said.

"Hey." He turned his attention back to the cutting board.

I bit my lip, wondering if I should stay or go.

"Are you cooking?" I asked.

"Yeah."

"But there's food already."

"Cooking is something I can do without thinking. And I need to be occupied, you know?"

"I know. You want me to leave?"

"You don't have to."

"Is that biker talk for *you can stay*?"

He cracked a smile.

I pulled out a stool from underneath the counter and sat down. "What are you making?"

"Fried green tomatoes."

"No kidding? Where'd you learn how to cook?"

"My mother owns a restaurant in New Orleans."

"Handy skill to have. Cooking."

"You cook?"

"Not well," I admitted. "I'm good at ordering takeout."

He chuckled.

"So, working in the family business didn't appeal to you, huh?" I queried.

"I was a sous chef for a few summers," he said. "Learned what I needed to know. But I'm restless. I wanted something different."

"So you joined a motorcycle club?"

"What can I say, I'm an adrenaline junkie." He set the knife aside. "You want to help?"

"Sure," I said, hopping up from the stool. I washed my hands at the sink and then dried them with a clean dishrag.

Crow showed me the steps for dunking the green tomato slices before setting them into a sizzling hot pan. "I usually do these in bacon grease, but it wasn't on hand. Oil works," he explained. "Flip them. Ah, see, nice and golden brown. You're a natural."

I heard the back door open and then close and the heavy clomp of boots across the wooden floor.

"What's going on in here?" Viper asked.

"Crow's teaching me how to make fried green tomatoes," I said, shooting him a smile over my shoulder.

"Smells good," Viper said.

"Tomorrow I'll teach you how to make pulled pork so tender you can pick it apart with a fork. If you want, I mean." He glanced at Viper and then at me.

"Someone's gotta teach me how to cook," I quipped.

Crow and Viper stared at each other for a moment and then Viper nodded. "Sounds like a good way to pass the time while we're stuck here, yeah?"

"Yeah," Crow said. "Make a list, Sutton."

"Huh?"

"Make a list of dishes you want to learn how to cook. We'll learn one a day until you have enough in your arsenal."

"Thanks," I said. "I appreciate it."

I left the kitchen with Viper, who followed me up the stairs.

"Keeping tabs on me?" I asked.

"Yep."

"No hesitation, no shame, huh?"

We got to his room, and I pushed open the door. "I was on my way to the bathroom when I got waylaid."

"I had no idea he was in the kitchen," Viper said.

"He kind of slipped away, I think. When everyone went outside."

"You guys talk?" Viper asked.

I shrugged. "Not really. Not about anything important. He asked if I wanted to help him cook, and I said yes."

"Why? You really care about learning to cook?"

I shook my head. "No. I cared about being a friend. If he needed one."

Viper didn't say anything. After a moment, he walked to me, put a hand on my shoulder and pulled me into his arms.

I buried my face in his chest and hugged him, wondering if we'd make it out of this without any more losses.

Chapter 40

"I stepped in dog shit!" Lily wailed, completely ignoring the soccer ball that Silas had kicked to her.

Willa glared at Waverly.

Waverly held up her hand. "Don't look at me. I try not to swear around her."

Darcy sighed. "It was inevitable."

It had only been a week, and everyone was already annoyed. Not only were the babies up at different hours of the night, but the brothers were on guard duty rotation every four hours. The dogs thought the entire backyard was their bathroom, and trying to play soccer when there were poop landmines everywhere put a damper on things. Plus, it was full-blown summer now, and the heat and humidity were oppressive. So there were only a few hours in the morning and the evening that weren't completely miserable. Most of us were stuck inside, either in our tiny clubhouse rooms or in the common areas that didn't have enough seats.

Expansion on the clubhouse had begun. Construction workers showed up early in the morning, interrupting sleep with their power tools. But it was necessary because we needed more space. The club would only continue to grow.

"Let's clean your shoe," Darcy said, holding out her hand to Lily.

Lily bounded toward her mother. Darcy placed a hand on Lily's cheek and then moved it to her forehead. "You feeling okay?"

"Yeah," Lily said. "Why?"

"Your cheeks are red."

"It's hot," Lily explained.

"I'm aware," Darcy drawled. "Let's get you inside into the air."

"Can I have some lemonade?"

"Yes." Darcy looked at her son. "You too."

"Me too what?" Cam demanded.

"Out of the sun," Darcy said.

"Mom," Cam whined.

"That's a good idea," Mia said, rising from her chair. "Silas!"

Silas jogged after the soccer ball, grabbed it, and walked to Mia. She slung her arm around her son and said, "I just put Scarlett down for a nap. I challenge you to a *Call of Duty* tournament."

"Oh, you sure you want to do that?" Silas asked. "You know, because you're gonna lose."

"Make you a deal," Mia said. "Loser has to pick up all the dog bombs in the backyard."

"You're on," Silas said.

"You know, even if you win, you're going to be the one picking up dog poop."

Silas laughed. "Yeah, I know. Captain!"

The black and white mutt pranced after the boy.

"Where's Monk?" I asked, curious about Doc and Boxer's yellow lab.

"Taking a nap with Boxer," Doc said with a grin. "Ten buck says he's spooning the dog."

"I'll pay you five dollars to get a picture of that," Mia quipped. "And then I'll never let him live it down."

The clubhouse AC was cranked, and the air was cool and dry. I trekked up the stairs and quietly traipsed into our room. Viper was spread out on the bed at a full diagonal. The covers concealed his lower half, but his back was bare.

Except for the ink.

I kicked off my shoes and crawled into bed next to him, scooting my body close to his. I ran my fingers up and down his spine.

He'd stopped sleeping with a knife under his pillow, so I had no concern of going through that again.

Viper stirred.

"Psst," I whispered. "You awake?"

When Viper didn't reply, I brushed my lips along his shoulder blade and then lower. I tugged down the covers to reveal the curve of his naked ass. I gave it a squeeze.

"Nice way to wake up," he growled. "Wish it had been your mouth on my cock, though."

"If you slept on your back, I could've made the dream a reality. Unfortunately, I don't have enough strength to roll you over."

Viper flipped onto his back and angled an arm behind his head, cracking his sleepy eyes to peer at me.

"What about now?" he rasped.

There wasn't much to do to occupy our time indoors, so it was no surprise that we spent a lot of time in our room.

I slid the covers off him and grasped his erection. I glided my hand up slowly, my thumb teasing the crown of his shaft. I bent down and licked his slit. He was salty and warm, and I wanted more of him.

His hand went to my head, and he fisted my hair but didn't command my actions. He let me set the pace.

I took him deep into my mouth, twirling my tongue up the length of him. One hand held his shaft, but the other cupped his testicles. I gently massaged them while changing my sucking rhythm.

Viper groaned.

I smiled around his erection.

"Get naked," he commanded. "I want to see you."

He popped from my mouth, and I moved back. I stripped out of my tank and shimmied off my shorts and thong.

"Flip around."

I frowned in confusion. "I don't understand."

"I want this," he sat up and slid his hand between my legs, "near my face. And your mouth on my dick."

"That would mean…"

"Sixty-nining, babe. You'll like it."

"I don't doubt it," I said, suddenly breathless.

I'd loved everything I'd done with Viper thus far. It was all new territory, and I was up for any adventure.

He lay back down. I turned around and straddled him, scooting until I was close to his face.

Apparently, it wasn't enough because Viper grasped my hips and hauled me closer. And then he tasted me.

"Mmm. Fuck, that's good."

My hands curled into fists, and I closed my eyes at the pleasure I was feeling from this position.

He spread my folds and delved deeper.

"God, Viper," I moaned.

"Dick, babe. Suck my dick."

I took him into my mouth again. Our rhythm was off, but after a few licks, we figured it out.

Viper wasn't shy, nor would he ever let me be. When he did something I liked, I was vocal about it. And handsomely rewarded.

I leaned back, wanting more of his tongue.

"Viper," I moaned around his cock.

"That's it—just enjoy it," he growled.

We pleasured each other, taking, giving. I came on his tongue with violent tremors and while I was in the throes of my release, Viper came in my mouth.

Warm. Musky. Salty.

And I swallowed every drop of him.

I lifted my leg and flopped down onto the bed next to him, my feet near his head.

"That was nice," I said with a sigh.

He snorted. "Nice."

"Different."

"Already bored with our sex life, huh?"

I rolled my eyes. "No, idiot. I just meant this is a new frontier. I liked it. That's all I'm saying."

He ran a hand up my calf. "I've got some other frontiers I'd like to explore."

"I'm aware," I teased.

"You up for it?"

"Now?" I asked. "I need some recovery time."

"Not now," he said. "And not while we're in the clubhouse."

"Why don't you want to do it in the clubhouse?" I asked.

"Everyone'll hear."

"But no one heard what we just did? I'm confused."

"Some things I want private between us."

"Well, as long as we're here, there is no real privacy."

"We'd have some privacy if we lived together."

"We do live together," I pointed out.

"I mean, you and me, in an apartment or a little house. Something with a bit more space. Something for just the two of us."

My gaze narrowed. "Are you talking about making a plan to officially live together?"

"Yeah. When all this shit is done, we're going to need a place. Right?"

"Well—"

"Your trailer burned to the ground. So you need a place."

"So this is about me needing a home?" I frowned. "What about you?"

"We can't live here indefinitely," he said. "You see how strapped everyone is for space."

"They're expanding the clubhouse."

"There's no privacy."

"The new build will offer more privacy."

"For fucks's sake, Sutton. I want to fuck your ass and I'd like to do it where my brothers can't hear."

"Then maybe you shouldn't bellow your words," I snapped. "The walls are thin."

"Yeah, they are!" Raze called from the other side of the wall.

I sat up and grabbed a pillow and smacked Viper in the face with it. "Great, now everyone's going to know about our sex life."

"You're an Old Lady. Don't you women talk about this stuff?"

"Yes," I said. "They have talked about some stuff, but I never say anything about you."

"So they don't know how big my dick is? Or that I made you come four times yesterday?"

"Seriously, guys, lower your voices," Raze called. "Some of us aren't getting any and I don't need a live-action porn event in the next room."

"Shut up, Raze!" I yelled. I glared at Viper. "You happy?"

"Not really, no. So, we living together or what?"

The idea did hold a sort of appeal. More privacy, more space, more time to figure out a rhythm with Viper. Unlimited hot water.

With everyone staying at the clubhouse, we had to shower on rotation.

"Fine. We'll live together," I said. "Just one little problem."

"What?"

"I had a job where I was earning good money. Now I have no job. And I wanted to use my insurance money to buy a car."

"Yeah? So?"

"So." I rolled my eyes. "I don't know if I can swing my share of the rent."

"Is that all that's stopping you from living with me?"

"Money?" I snorted. "Kind of a big deal. Especially when you don't have it."

"I have it."

"I didn't mean you, I meant me."

"I know what you meant. And I'm telling you I have enough money for you not to worry about it."

"You say that like it's not a big deal."

"It's not. You want to live me or not? Forget the money. Money's not an issue. I'll take care of it. I'll take care of you."

"I don't want to be taken care of," I protested.

"Okay. Then what do you want?"

"I want… I want… I don't think I know what I want."

"Why does the idea of letting me pay for the apartment freak you out?"

"I've been paying my own way for a long time. It just feels…imbalanced."

"Sounds like a you problem," Viper said.

"That's insensitive."

"I'm not really known for my sensitivity. Asshole persona. For sure. Big dick. Definitely."

I rolled my eyes and flung off his hand and climbed out of bed.

"It's not a big deal, Sutton. I have money. It'll get us a nice place. You'll go back to work. You'll contribute. You'll be okay."

"I want to work at Mia's bar," I said. "But I don't think that will be happening any time soon."

"There might not be a bar to go back to," he said. "Customers don't really want to go to bars where they could get shot."

"Point taken."

"There will be other jobs at other bars."

"But I want to work at Shelly's," I insisted. "It was more than a bar. It was—never mind."

"Not never mind. Tell me."

I sighed. "It's gonna sound stupid."

"Say it anyway."

"It felt like home," I admitted. "A job I could stay at for years and not feel restless to move on to something else."

Viper got up and padded naked toward me. He reached out and dragged me against him. "Home is important."

"Yeah."

"You've never had it."

"No."

"I haven't had it in a very long time," he said quietly. "So move in with me. We'll have a home together."

Wrapped in his warm embrace, the smell of his skin in my nose, the promise of something so normal after years of the complete opposite had me nodding.

"Say it."

"I'll move in with you."

"And?"

"And I won't worry about the money."

"Good." He brushed his lips across the top of my head. "I'd never hold it over you. You get that, right?"

"I get that."

"Then you were just putting up a fight because?"

"I'm sass and ass, remember? It's what I do."

He lightly smacked the curve of my butt. "And you do it so well."

Chapter 41

"Can I hold that?" I asked.

Allison frowned. "Hold what?"

"That." I pointed at her baby.

She raised her brows. "My son? You want to hold my son?"

"Yeah."

"Okay. It's a *him*, not a *that*," she said with a laugh as she handed him over. "Why do you want to hold him?"

I took Tank and put him to my hip. "Trying it out. See how it feels. Whew. Is he a baby or an anvil?"

"He's a healthy eater," Allison said.

I looked at Tank and he gave me a gummy grin. I smiled back. He fisted a handful of my hair in his chubby little fingers.

"Jeez, I think that's the fastest I've seen a woman succumb to baby fever," Darcy remarked.

Brooklyn had her feet propped up on the coffee table and a bowl of ice cream resting on her belly. "There's something about these men...are you seriously already thinking about kids with Viper?"

The other Old Ladies turned their attention to me. We'd congregated in the living room while everyone else was outside watching a movie on a projector screen.

"He asked me to move in with him," I admitted.

"When?" Willa demanded.

"This afternoon," I said with a grimace. "Tank, I don't think I can rock the bald look." I gently removed his hand from my hair. He curled his little fingers around mine and my heart melted.

Wait, no. That wasn't my heart melting. That was one of my ovaries getting ready to drop an egg for Viper to fertilize.

"And you said yes, didn't you?" Rach asked. She was sitting in the recliner with Cash asleep on her lap, resting in the cradle of her thighs.

"Yeah, I said yes."

"That'll be good for you guys," Joni said. "Some privacy. Some space."

Mia nodded. "Definitely."

"Wait, you don't think I'm crazy?" I asked in shock.

"That's kind of a different question, isn't it?" Willa teased.

"This world moves pretty fast," Mia said. "If you want to be part of it, you kinda have to buckle up and go along for the ride."

"I think it's sweet," Allison said. "That you guys are making plans."

She didn't say what we were all thinking. We were making plans, but what happened if they changed…

I shoved thoughts of Viper dying in a bloody battle with the cartel out of my brain. It was too awful to contemplate, so I simply refused to do it.

Tank let go of my hand and then patted my breast.

"Sorry, kid, I don't have what you're looking for," I said. "Here, Mama, your son is hungry."

"When is he not?" Allison asked as she scooped her son into her arms. "I think I'll say good night, then. I need to bathe him before he nurses and then I can put him to bed."

"Night," I called.

"She has a good idea," Rach said. "Babies are cute but they're hell on your sleep."

"So much truth to that," Joni said.

Doc rose from her seat. "I think I'll go snuggle up next to Boxer and Monk and finish the movie."

Rach lifted her son in her arms and headed out of the living room, Doc behind her.

"I'm standing, right?" Joni asked.

"Just like I'm standing," Mia remarked with a smile.

"On the count of three?"

"One, two, three," Mia said.

Neither of them moved.

I walked over to Mia and held out my hands. She grasped them and stood up. "Thank you. I'd never have made it otherwise."

"Do me," Joni said.

I helped her rise.

"Uh-oh," I murmured.

"What?" Joni asked.

I chin-gestured to Brooklyn, who'd fallen asleep.

"Let her be," Darcy said, removing the empty ice cream bowl from her belly and taking it to the sink.

"See you guys in the morning. You cooking tomorrow?" Joni asked. "Those biscuits and gravy you made today were diabolical."

I grinned, feeling proud of myself. "I owe it all to

Crow. But no, I won't be cooking tomorrow. Crow is on guard duty, so I won't have a cooking buddy."

"I'll help," Brooklyn murmured, finally opening her eyes.

"Hey, Sleeping Beauty," I teased.

"How long was I out?" she asked.

"Just a few minutes," I assured her.

"What time is it?" she asked.

"A little after eight," Darcy said with a smile.

"Oh, I became that person, didn't I?" Brooklyn joked, holding out her hand. Mia was closest to her and helped her stand.

"I'll become that person in a few months," Willa said. "Don't feel bad."

"And here I am, asleep where I'm standing. Night all," Joni said.

"Hmm. Bed," Mia moaned.

They left the living room and a few moments later I heard several doors shutting.

"And then there were three," Darcy said. She poured herself a glass of white wine and moved to the couch.

"This does feel a bit lopsided," I announced.

"You're not actually feeling the pressure, are you?" Willa asked.

"Pressure?"

"Baby pressure," she clarified.

"Nah, not really. Tank's cute. They're all cute. But no, I'm not actively thinking about a baby."

"Hard not to think about it, though." Willa looked at Darcy and then back to me. "I thought I was going to wait."

"Why didn't you?" I asked.

She shrugged. "I felt safe and comfortable in my relationship and then I realized it was something I really wanted."

"Duke was baby-crazy," Darcy said with a laugh. "I swear, all these men are. That's how they're wired."

"Did Gray want babies before you?" I asked.

Darcy nodded. "He's older than me. But we were together awhile before we had kids. That was right for us."

"I miss my house," Willa announced. "I want to go home."

"Girl, same," Darcy said.

"Any word about how much longer we have to be here?"

Willa shook her head. "No news yet."

"Trust me. When shit goes hot, you'll be wishing for moments like this. All of us stepping on each other's toes, too many bodies crammed into one space, having to cook for large groups. All of it." Darcy took a sip of her wine and settled back in her seat.

"What kind of place are you looking for?" Willa asked, clearly wanting to change the subject.

"Don't know. We haven't really discussed it," I said. "I mean, not specifics, anyway. Space, though. Space sounds nice. And anything that's not a trailer."

"Makes sense," Darcy said.

"I like your house," I said to Willa. "But Viper and I don't need that much space."

"Yet," she teased.

"Yet," I agreed with a smile.

The back door opened, and soft footsteps trekked across the floor before Lily appeared.

"Hey, Lily Burger," Darcy said.

Lily wedged herself between Willa and Darcy on the couch and put her head in Darcy's lap.

"What's wrong?" Darcy asked as she ran her fingers through Lily's curls.

"I don't feel well," Lily muttered.

"Sit up for me," Darcy said.

Lily sat up and Darcy pressed her lips to her daughter's forehead. "You're warm."

"I don't…" Lily paused and then vomited all over Darcy's lap.

"Wow, that's a lot of puke." I hopped off the recliner and ran to the kitchen for paper towels.

"Oh, God, the smell," Willa said, pinching her nose. She shot up from the couch, a hand pressed to her mouth. Willa ran outside and I heard the unmistakable sounds of retching.

"Leave it," Darcy said as she stood, picking up Lily and putting her to her shoulder. "I'll clean it up after I clean her up."

"I got it," I assured her. "Feel better, Lily Burger."

Lily buried her face in her mother's neck and Darcy carted her out of the room.

Willa came back into the clubhouse, looking a little bit green.

"So, babies, huh?" I asked, ripping a paper towel from the roll. "Think I'll be holding off for a while."

Chapter 42

A wave of flu hit the clubhouse. By that evening, not only did Lily have a temperature over one hundred, but several other people did too.

It started with the kids—Silas and Cam got sick almost immediately. But then Waverly and Sailor came down with it.

By day three, half the bikers were laid up in bed. The healthy ones had to do double guard time.

"This is one nasty bug," Doc said as she washed her hands in the kitchen sink. "How are you feeling?"

"I'm fine," I assured her as I stirred another batch of chicken soup.

"Good." Doc dried her hands on a paper towel.

Laundry was constant—the hot water barely had time to refill before it was used again by someone needing to shower off their fever.

Day four of the flu wave, Viper came down with it.

"I'm not sick," he protested.

"Sit," I commanded, pushing him toward the bed.

I pressed a hand to his forehead and gently placed a

thermometer in his ear. He glared at me. A few seconds later, I pulled it out and read it.

"Uh-huh. Just as I thought. Ninety-nine point eight."

"That's not a fever," he protested.

"I'm not doing this with you," I said, setting the thermometer on the nightstand. "You're going to get in bed and let me take care of you."

"Woman, I do not need—" His eyes widened. He hastily covered his mouth and made a run for the bathroom.

I went to his dresser and pulled out a pair of sweats and a T-shirt. The toilet flushed and then the sink turned on.

A moment later, Viper appeared.

"I think I'm sick," he said.

I nodded. "Yep. Change, get comfortable, and climb into bed. I'll go tell Colt you've got the flu."

Viper sat down on the edge of the bed and slowly began to remove his boots. "Fuck, I never get sick."

"First time for everything," I said.

I closed the door behind me and went downstairs in search of Colt. Brooklyn stood at the stove, ladling out a bowl of chicken soup.

"Have you seen Colt?" I asked.

She shook her head. "You okay?"

"Viper's got it now."

Brooklyn's mouth quirked up. "And I'm sure he's going to be just as fun to take care of as Slash."

"Is Slash feeling better?"

"He says he is, but every time he gets out of bed, he gets dizzy." She rolled her eyes. "Why do they insist on pushing it?"

"Got me. When I get sick, I lay there like a lump in the dark and theatrically moan like a Victorian woman."

"Well, let's hope you don't come down with it."

"You feeling okay?"

She nodded. "Yeah. Thank goodness."

"Thank goodness, indeed."

I left the kitchen and headed down the hallway. I peeked into the office, but it was empty. I went out back. Colt was pacing by the fence, his face painted with anger. He was yelling at someone on the phone, his knuckles clenched with rage.

I was about to leave him to it when he called out, "Sutton!"

"Sorry," I said, turning around to face him. "I didn't mean to disturb you."

"It's fine," he gritted out. "What can I do for you?"

"Oh. I just wanted to tell you that Viper's got the flu."

Colt's jaw tightened. "Wonderful. Just fucking wonderful."

"I'm sorry," I said. "I really—"

"It's not your fault." He sighed and rubbed the back of his neck. "I never really got a chance to say congratulations, or welcome to the family."

"It's been busy."

"We'll celebrate. After."

After.

"I'd like that."

I headed back into the clubhouse and traipsed up the stairs. I was quiet when I walked into the bedroom. Viper was already asleep. I quickly tidied up the room and then pulled the covers up past his shoulders.

How could such a big, tatted man look so vulnerable? His mouth was soft in sleep and all I wanted to do was take care of him.

I leaned over and brushed my lips across his warm forehead.

Viper didn't even stir.

I ran into Rach as I was coming down the stairs. "Oh, no, are you sick too?" I asked her.

Her brown hair was lank and greasy, and she had bags under her eyes. "No. Cash is sick. And every time I put him down in his crib, he cries. The only way to keep him quiet is to hold him, so he's been sleeping on my chest for the better part of the day. Doc's with him now, giving me a reprieve."

"Thank God for the village, right?" I asked.

She nodded. "Yeah. The village. I kind of wish I'd stayed with my mom."

"Does she know what's going on?"

"Kind of. I mean, club stuff, yeah. She wasn't that supportive when I said I was going to stay here for the duration."

"She's just worried about you," I said as we moved into the kitchen. "You hungry?"

Rach nodded as she took a seat on the stool. "I need food and a hot shower, and then hopefully Cash will let me sleep."

"Soup okay?"

"Soup sounds great."

While I was heating up soup for Rach, Darcy wandered in.

"Soup?" I asked.

Without a word, she went to the cabinet, pulled out a bottle of Kahlúa and poured a splash into a cup.

"That was going to be my next offering," I joked.

"How are the kids?" Rach asked.

"On the mend. Taking care of sick kids in your own home with your own kitchen is hard enough. But in a clubhouse where you can't escape?"

"Pass me that Kahlúa," I stated. "Viper's sick now

too."

Darcy poured a bit into a coffee mug and held up the bottle in Rach's direction. She shook her head and dug into her soup.

Mia ascended the stairs from the theater room, carting a laundry basket. "I'm finally caught up."

"My turn," Darcy said with a sigh. "But I'm taking the Kahlúa with me."

"I think the washer is on its last leg," Mia said. "It's gotten more of a workout in the last two weeks than in the last year."

"What, bikers don't do their own laundry?" I asked in amusement.

"Not usually. There's a clubhouse cleaning crew. We've gotten spoiled."

"We pay them well enough that we don't have to do much other than cook and a few dishes. It's totally worth it," Rach said. She got up off her stool and went to load the dishwasher, but it was already full of clean dishes.

"Damn it," she muttered.

"Go," I stated. "I'll take care of it."

"You don't mind?" Rach asked.

I shook my head. "Viper is still asleep. I got this."

"You're a godsend. I'd hug you, but I'm disgusting," Rach said.

"Enjoy that shower. I think you've earned it." I winked.

She left the living room and headed for the stairs. Mia put down the laundry basket.

"I'll help you clean up," she said.

"Thanks. So, what are you going to do with the bar?"

"What do you mean?" Mia unloaded the silverware.

"I mean, are you going to reopen it? Close it? What?"

"We'll probably reopen."

"Are you worried about the reputation being

damaged?"

"A little. But frankly there's nothing I can do about it. I guess we'll see how it turns out."

My phone buzzed in my back pocket, and I reached in to read the text.

> VIPER
>
> Mind bringing me some ginger ale?

"Hey, do you mind finishing up?" I asked her. "Viper's awake."

"Go," she said. "There's not much more to do."

I grabbed a bottle of ginger ale from the fridge. I went to our room and quietly entered.

He wasn't in bed.

A moment later, I heard the toilet flush and then the bathroom door open. He was pale and looked like he was in danger of falling over.

I set the ginger ale on the nightstand and then lifted the covers.

He walked over and then slid into bed.

I unscrewed the bottle and held the ginger ale out to him.

It seemed to take all his effort to take a drink. When he was finished, he fell back against the pillows and closed his eyes.

"Do you need anything? Tea? A cool washcloth?"

"No. I just need more sleep. Thanks for taking care of me."

I gently ran my hand through his hair, made sure he was tucked in, and then headed for the door.

"Love you," he murmured.

I stopped, my hand on the knob. I turned to look at him, but he was already asleep.

I tiptoed from the room, a huge smile on my face.

Chapter 43

A WEEK LATER, the flu had run its course. Everyone was either already healthy again or getting back to normal—and incredibly irritable.

Kids were antsy, Waverly and Sailor were bored, and there was still no sign of the lockdown ending.

"Something's got to change," Willa said as the Old Ladies sat together outside in the backyard.

Heat be damned, we were tired of being cooped up.

"I know," Joni said. "We can't live like this much longer. If I have to target practice one more time, I'll lose my shit."

"You're just annoyed I beat you," I teased.

The club had a shooting range at the other end of the property. We'd all been spending time at target practice. Just in case.

"Nothing's happening," Brooklyn said.

"But you know how this goes, don't you?" Mia asked. "If Colt ends the lockdown, and we all go home, you know that's when something's gonna happen."

"I feel like I've been put in a pressure cooker," Rach said. "I'm ready to blow."

Though I understood how they all felt—and I, too, was getting ornery from cabin fever—I was preoccupied with Viper's pronouncement.

Though he'd said it while he was sick and feverish, I didn't doubt the sincerity of it. Unfortunately, he hadn't said it since, leading me to believe he didn't even remember he'd said it at all. I was doing everything in my power to coerce it out of him again. Difference was, I wanted him alert and coherent this time.

"What do you think?" Darcy asked me.

"About what?"

"About getting to the end of our rope," she said. "With this lockdown."

"I'm with you. I'm ready for it to end. But if it wasn't for the lockdown, I never would've learned how to cook. Thanks, Brooklyn."

She grinned. "I think Crow deserves more credit than me."

"Look at you, nesting and stuff," Joni teased.

"I've never had a chance to nest," I said. "Feels good."

The back door opened, and Allison stormed out with Tank on her hip. Torque was behind her, his face an angry scowl.

He called her name, forcing her to stop. She turned and spoke to him, her voice too low for me to hear what she was saying. She adjusted Tank to her other hip and shook her head.

Torque gently grasped the back of her neck and pulled her close, putting his forehead to hers.

I looked away from the private moment, staring at my hands in my lap. The Old Ladies had fallen silent.

Torque marched to the shed. Allison straightened her shoulders and came toward us.

"Hey," Mia said. "Are you okay?"

Allison shook her head and shrugged.

"What was that about?" Brooklyn asked.

"He was telling me what to do in case he died," she said bluntly.

Rach flinched. "Oh…"

"Yeah." Allison sighed. "If something happens to him, he wants me to leave Waco and be close to my sister. I didn't want to talk about it, but he insisted. And now we're fighting."

Several bikers came outside, immediately heading for the shed.

"What's going on?" I asked.

"It's looking like church," Mia murmured, her face pale. "I think something's up."

We all fell silent again as we watched men file out of the clubhouse. Viper walked with Raze and Bones, but his eyes found mine.

I swallowed at the look in his gaze.

We were going to war.

I could feel it.

Conversation was stilted as we waited for the men to finish church. It didn't take long, and when they came out, I knew.

They walked to us, bikers moving to stand near their women. Viper came to my side and set his hands on my shoulders while we waited for Colt to speak.

"We ride tonight," he said.

Doc stood up from her chair and without a word strode into the clubhouse.

"What's she doing?" I asked.

"Making sure she has enough supplies. In case..." Boxer sighed and went after her.

Viper squeezed my shoulders.

"Take a few hours," Colt said. "Spend time with your families."

Couples began to break off, either going inside or walking to the edges of the backyard.

I looked up at Viper, who was peering down at me with glittering brown eyes. I got up and he took my hand, leading me to the picnic table.

"Sit," he said, helping me up onto the tabletop. He remained standing and put his large hands on the bare skin of my thighs.

"Viper, I—"

"Me first," he growled.

I nodded and fell silent.

"There's a chance I won't come back to you."

"Viper—"

"Sutton," he said quietly. "Let me get this out."

"Okay," I whispered.

"There's a chance I won't come back to you," he repeated. "But there's one thing you have to know. These last few weeks with you have been the happiest of my life."

I quickly covered my ears. "No. Don't say what you're about to say."

"What am I about to say?" He grasped my hands and lowered them from my head.

"You're about to say you love me. And if you're going to say it now, then it's like you're saying goodbye. Well, I don't accept that. So you hold that shit in and you say it when you come back to me."

We stared at each other. I tried to memorize his face. I tried to burn him into my brain.

I didn't even have a photo of us together.

If he died…I'd have nothing to remind me that we'd once loved each other. So I tried as hard as I could to immortalize him now in my memory.

"If you won't let me say it," he said, moving closer. "Will you let me show it?"

I reached out and grasped his shirt, pulling him toward me. "Show me."

He scooped me off the picnic table into his arms and carried me into the clubhouse, into his bedroom.

Viper set me down on the bed and then worshipped every inch of my skin.

And when he slid inside me, I prayed it wouldn't be the last time.

∽

Viper's phone vibrated on the nightstand. I stirred against his chest.

"It's time," he said.

"I know," I whispered. I brushed a kiss against his heart and then rolled out of his embrace.

I sat on the edge of the bed and watched him get dressed. It felt like watching an ancient warrior don his armor for battle.

He laced up his boots.

He threw on his leather cut, the club logo a proud emblem across his back.

He clipped a holster with his pistol and several magazines of extra ammunition onto his belt behind his cut.

I climbed out of bed and got dressed with him. When I was clothed, I followed Viper out of the bedroom.

Everyone except for the children had gathered in the living room. Colt and Zip were handing out shotguns to the Old Ladies.

"What's this?" I asked.

"Every brother rides tonight. The prospects will guard the gates. Anyone that isn't us who tries to get inside, you blow them away," Colt said.

Zip handed me a shotgun, his mouth quirking into a little smile. "I've seen you at target practice. I know you can handle yourself."

I grasped the shotgun and said, "We'll hold down the fort."

I looked at Viper, who was peering at me with pride in his eyes. He grasped the back of my neck and leaned in to kiss me. I kissed him back with all the love I hadn't verbally expressed, wanting him to know exactly how I felt.

When I pulled away, Raze was smiling at me. No doubt he'd heard us earlier.

"When's your birthday?" I demanded.

"Mine?" Raze asked.

"Yeah. Yours."

"Later this month, why?"

"I'm buying you a pair of noise-cancelling headphones," I said.

Brooklyn threw herself into Slash's arms. He whispered something against her hair, and she nodded. She kissed him and then pulled back, straightening her resolve. Slash lovingly stole a hand across her belly before heading outside.

Willa, Savage and Duke were in a three-way hug, but Savage stepped back after a moment, giving the couple time to themselves.

Sailor looked forlornly at Acid but made no move to go to him. He glanced at her and clenched his jaw before turning around and heading outside, Savage behind him.

Zip leaned down and brushed his lips across his son's head before staring deep into Joni's eyes. She grazed her hand along his cheek and kissed his mouth. She then turned to her brother.

Colt seemed reluctant to let go of Mia, but he finally dropped his arm from around his wife to embrace his sister and nephew.

Gray had Darcy pinned against the counter and his hand was gripping the back of her neck. They'd been married the longest, had two children together, and still they only had eyes for one another.

Darcy said something softly that caused Gray to bend his head back, laughter escaping his mouth.

The sound momentarily eased the tension in the room, and I took a deep breath.

I faced Viper. There was nothing to say to him, nothing I could say that would make this any easier.

His mind needed to be clear. He had to ride with his brothers without thoughts of me clogging his brain.

So I stood on my toes and tilted my head back.

Viper devoured my mouth, kissing me like it was his absolution.

Without a word, he strode from the clubhouse and went to join his brothers.

Finally, it was just the women and children.

"Why do I feel like Penelope waiting for Odysseus to come home?" Brooklyn asked.

No one replied.

We listened to the rumble of motorcycles as they faded into the distance.

"I guess we should get back down to the theater room," Waverly said.

Waverly and Sailor were going to keep the kids entertained and watch over the babies, even though most of them were already asleep.

Joni set her son into his carrier and handed him off to Waverly. "You sure you guys can handle all the infants?"

"They're sharing cribs and all the breast milk in the fridge is labeled," Sailor said. "We've got this. Don't worry about a thing."

"Lock the door behind you," Willa said.

The door to the theater room closed, followed by the sounds of the girls' footsteps.

"Get comfortable, kids," Mia said. "It's gonna be a while."

Chapter 44

We sat in relative silence for hours, armed to the teeth. Brooklyn squirmed with discomfort and finally excused herself to go to the bathroom.

Doc paced back and forth down the hallway, every now and again going into the office, no doubt to check her supplies, even though she'd already checked her stash several times.

"So," Mia said, forcing a smile. "Sutton. Is being an Old Lady everything you thought it would be?"

I stroked the shotgun strewn across my lap. "Everything and more. I never thought they'd ask us to defend the castle, though."

"Is it too late to put in for a moat?" Willa joked with a strained smile.

"We need a dragon," Allison said. "Perhaps some trebuchets."

"What about Viper?" I suggested. "He's got a fierce scowl."

"He's not so scowly now," Joni commented. "You did a number on him."

"I hope—"

"Wait," Mia said. "Quiet a second."

I clamped my mouth shut.

"You hear that?" Mia asked.

"Motorcycles," Darcy said, standing up from her chair and heading to the front door.

"Don't open it," Joni commanded.

"I wasn't. Damn, I wish I could see out there, but it's too dark."

We fell silent again and listened. There were no sounds of struggle at the gates, no scuffles or gunshots.

Everyone stood up as we waited for the men to come through the front door. It was as if we all were collectively holding our breaths.

The growl of engines ceased and then I heard heavy boots clomping up the porch steps.

"It's us," Colt stated. "Let us in."

Darcy unlocked the door and opened it before moving out of the way as a flood of bikers poured into the living room.

Viper's head appeared through the doorway and my grip tightened on the shotgun. My muscles trembled as we rushed toward each other.

He had a gash along his forehead and the corner of his mouth was bleeding, but he wasn't riddled with bullet holes or stab wounds. I leaned the shotgun against a wall and then dashed to him, colliding into his body.

Viper grunted.

"Oh shit. Did I hurt you?" I asked, immediately pulling back.

He yanked me forward. "My ribs are a little sore. Don't let that stop you."

I wrapped my arms around him but was mindful not to squeeze him.

"Where's Duke?" Willa yelled. "And Savage! Where are they, Colt!"

Colt was holding Mia's face in his hands and staring at her, but he managed to pull his attention away from his wife to answer. "Acid and Duke took Savage to the hospital. Savage took a bullet meant for Duke and he's in critical condition."

Willa reached out and placed a hand on the counter. Doc left Boxer's arms and went to Willa's side. "Breathe," she said, placing her hand on Willa's back. "Breathe for me. That's it."

When Willa was under control, she stood up. "I have to go to the hospital. Right now."

"You're not driving yourself," Colt commanded. "You're in no shape to."

"*I have to go!*" Willa screamed, tears gathering in her eyes.

"I'll drive you," Raze said. His lip was split and his jaw was bruised, but he seemed intact overall.

"Let's go," Willa commanded. "Fuck, where's my purse?"

"Right here," Brooklyn said, grabbing it from next to the couch and handing it to her.

"Thanks." She ran out the open front door, Raze following behind her. She exchanged a few words with Darcy, and then Darcy appeared in the doorway.

A frown of confusion marred her face. "I just saw Willa, and she told me about Savage." She looked at Colt. "Is Gray with them, too?"

Colt released Mia and turned to face Darcy.

He slowly walked toward her.

Darcy's eyes widened and she shook her head. "No."

"Darcy," Colt said, his voice soft. "I'm sorry, Darcy. He didn't make it."

"What do you mean *he didn't make it?*" she shrieked.

"He was covering our exit after we went in, making sure no one snuck up behind us. He was ambushed. After he…we had to fight our way out. We barely made it. He killed two of them before they—"

Rach pushed her way through the crowd and went to Darcy. She pulled her friend into her arms.

"Mama?"

My heart leapt into my throat when I saw Lily, her blonde ringlets askew, her eyes soft with sleep, clutching a blanket to her chest.

"Hey, baby," Darcy said with a shaky voice, somehow pulling herself together. "Did we wake you up?"

She nodded. "Is Daddy back yet?"

"Daddy's running a few errands," she lied, clearly holding back tears. "Let's get you tucked back into bed."

"I don't want to sleep downstairs. Cam snores."

"I'll take you to my room, okay?" She stepped away from Rach toward her daughter and guided Lily from the room.

"Who else died?" Doc asked quietly.

"No one," he said, expression grim. Mia snuggled up close to him and closed her eyes.

"Who's injured the worst?" Doc asked.

"Zip," Joni gasped. "Your leg."

"Just a gash," Zip said. "I cut my leg on some industrial metal when we were trying to get out of there."

Joni swiped a hand at her husband's thigh. Her palm came away bloody.

"You first," Doc commanded. "Office, now."

"Usually, I only take orders from my wife." Zip grimaced. "But you've got the painkillers."

From what I could see, most of the injuries were superficial.

"I need to sit," Viper murmured.

He eased into a recliner and released a breath.

"What can I get for you?" I asked him quietly.

"Bourbon and a bag of ice."

"Got it." I brushed my lips across his forehead.

I went to the kitchen and smiled at Allison, who was running her hands all over Torque's body, checking for wounds. Rach was attending to Bones, Smoke, and Kelp, but all they wanted was liquor.

Brooklyn and Slash had disappeared, no doubt looking for a more private place.

"Sit," Mia commanded her husband.

"If I sit, I won't get back up again," he said, his voice filled with exhaustion.

Waverly appeared in the living room, her red hair thrown into a messy bun. "I heard voices," she explained. "And Lily is missing."

"Lily's with Darcy," Mia said.

"Is Willa with Duke?"

Mia stepped away from tending to her husband to grasp Waverly's hand. "Willa went to the hospital. Savage was shot. He's in critical condition."

Waverly blinked blue eyes—the message slow to register. When it finally hit home, she nodded and swallowed.

"We lost Gray tonight," Mia said quietly. "The kids don't know yet."

Waverly closed her eyes and nodded again. Her phone buzzed in her hand. She opened her eyes and looked down at the screen.

"It's Willa," she said. She pressed a button and put the phone to her ear. "Hey. No. You didn't wake me."

Waverly headed to the door, obviously craving some privacy. "Yeah, I just heard…"

She shut the front door, and I could no longer hear her voice.

A door opened and a moment later, Doc appeared in the living room. "Who's next?"

"Viper," I volunteered.

"Sutton," he growled.

"Don't *Sutton* me. Let her examine your ribs."

He rose from his spot and grimaced, but he dutifully followed Doc down the hallway to the office. Zip was coming out, leaning against Joni.

"Can you make it up the stairs?" Doc asked him.

"Yes," Zip said.

"Don't tear your stitches," Doc warned.

"Yes, Doc," Zip drawled dutifully.

They moved out of the way and Doc went into the office first, followed by Viper. I marched in behind them and closed the door.

"Let's get your cut off," Doc said.

Viper made a move and released a groan. I jumped into action to help him.

"Easy," I whispered.

"There's no way in hell I'm going to be able to remove my T-shirt," Viper muttered.

Doc pulled out a blade. "No worries. I'll cut it off you."

She slashed at his shirt, revealing his bare chest. His arms were covered in scrapes and bruises, but they were superficial. His ribs though…bruised and blue as hell.

"What happened?" she asked.

"I took a baseball bat to the ribs," he said.

My breath hitched.

"Yeah, you definitely need to go to the hospital. You need an X-ray. You might have internal bleeding."

A hiss of air left his mouth as she palpated his ribs and his lower back and stomach.

"Ribs are probably broken."

"Hospital," I commanded. "Right now."

"Sutton—"

"No arguments," I stated. "You called the shots when it was me needing protection. I'm calling the shots now. Get your ass up. We're going to the hospital."

A slight smile lifted Doc's lips as she looked at Viper. "Your woman is feisty. I'd listen to her if I were you."

Viper grumbled, but he reluctantly got up off the desk and stood.

"You can't even move without wincing."

"I just wanted bourbon and ice," he growled.

"You'll get it later once you're in the clear," I commanded. "You're a man, not a god."

"Debatable," Viper muttered. "Let's get this shit over with."

Doc opened the door for us and then followed us out.

"Wait for me on the porch," I said. "I need to grab my purse and phone and find us a car to borrow."

"Fine," he stated.

I took the stairs two at a time and returned to the living room a few moments later.

Doc was leading Bones to the office to examine him.

"Let me know what's going on with Viper as soon as you can, okay?" Doc said to me.

"I will."

Mia was brushing Colt's hair off his forehead and pressing sweet kisses to his hairline.

"Lockdown is over," Colt said to me. "Everyone is safe."

I frowned. "What? But how? You just attacked the cartel."

"Don't worry about the logistics of it. You're safe. The club is safe. And that's all you need to know."

"So, what does that mean?" I asked.

"It means you're no longer a prisoner in the clubhouse," he said.

"I thought I wasn't a prisoner?" I taunted.

He smiled slightly.

I asked Mia if I could borrow her car and then went out to the front porch to meet Viper. What I found had me hiding my smile.

Viper was patting Waverly's shoulder with a heavy hand, while she blubbered.

When she saw me, she hastily pulled back and wiped her cheeks. She looked up at Viper. "Thank you."

Viper took the porch stairs slowly. I hit the clicker to Mia's car, and it beeped and flashed its lights. I ran to the passenger side door and opened it for Viper. He ambled his way to the car and bent his large body into the seat. I shut the door and went to the driver's side.

Mia and I were nearly the same size, so I didn't have to adjust her seat too much. The prospects opened the gates and we drove through.

"So Waverly was crying," I said quietly. "About Savage?"

"Some of it was worry for Savage. But it was mostly about Gray," he said, his voice low. "She babysits his kids, you know?"

"Yeah." Emotion I hadn't let myself feel at the news of Gray's death finally crawled up my throat to clobber me.

"It was a fucking shit show," Viper confessed.

I swallowed.

He looked out the window. "Sometimes, I wonder what the entire fucking point of all of this is. We're trying to do some good for a change, but everywhere we go, death follows. For what? What's the goddamned point?"

I didn't have an answer for him.

Chapter 45

"Any word about Savage?" I asked.

"Still in surgery," Willa said. Her eyes were wide in her pale face and her lips trembled from an attempt not to cry.

Duke reached over and took her hand in his, but he stared down at the floor, not saying a word.

Acid stood by the window, staring off into the lit parking lot.

Raze had gone to get some coffee and hadn't yet returned.

I folded my fingers together.

Viper had been taken away for an X-ray and I was waiting for the results.

I still couldn't believe Gray was dead and that Savage was fighting for his life.

Willa dropped Duke's hand and stood up. She pressed a hand to her mouth and looked around, her eyes crazed.

"Trash can in the corner," I said softly.

She dashed for it, leaned over, and upchucked into it just in the nick of time.

The waiting room was empty except for us, so thankfully we weren't disturbing anyone.

Willa rose and hastily wiped her lips. Duke stood and ate up the space between them. He placed his hand on her back and rubbed it.

She nodded and the two of them left the waiting room.

I didn't feel like talking and neither did Acid.

Eventually, I got up and began to pace.

I wondered how Darcy was doing. Had she told her children yet, or had she put Lily back to bed? Was she going to wait until morning to tell them? Would one more good night's sleep really matter when they found out their father was dead?

South Paw.

Gray.

Savage fighting for his life.

The losses were stacking up and people I knew were dying…had died. How many more would I grow to care for only to have them ripped away?

Willa and Duke returned to the waiting room. Willa had a bottle of ginger ale, and she twisted the cap but didn't remove it.

"Feeling any better?" I asked lamely.

She shrugged. "I'm going out of my ever-loving mind waiting on news about Savage."

"This is just like him," Duke said, forcing a smile. "Always so dramatic. Has to do everything with flare."

Acid asked, "Has anything been decided about Gray's funeral?"

"Not that I know of," I said, my throat tight. "When we left the clubhouse, Doc was examining the brothers one by one."

"This is all so fucked," he said with a sigh. "I'm going to go have a smoke."

He left, passing Raze on his way out. Raze came into

the waiting room and sat down next to me.

He took a sip of his coffee and winced.

"Hot?" I asked.

"Nah, just tastes like shit."

I took the cup from him and sipped. "What are you talking about? It's perfect."

"Then you can have it. I don't think I'll be able to suck it down," Raze said. He paused for a moment and then asked, "You talk to Rach before you left?"

I shook my head. "She was with Darcy. Why?"

"No reason." He leaned forward and set his elbows on his knees.

"No reason," I repeated. "Then why did you ask?"

"She doesn't have anyone."

"She has the club," I pointed out.

Willa and Duke were watching us, but not saying anything.

"It's not the same, and you know it," Raze said.

I peered at him. "You like her. Don't you?"

"Sure I like her. What's not to like? She's strong. Smart. Gorgeous. Understands the life. And that kid of hers is adorable."

"Her kid is cute," I agreed. "Does that mean…wait… are you considering making her your Old Lady?"

"Fuck no," he said quietly. "Nothing's going on between us. And she's not the kind of woman you fuck around with casually. But we're friends."

"Friends…"

"Why are you repeating everything I say?" he demanded.

"Just trying to wrap my brain around what's going on there."

"Nothing's going on," he insisted. "But I like her, all right? And I just want to make sure she's okay."

I pulled out my phone and searched through my contacts for Rach's number. I showed him my cell.

"Ask her yourself," I said.

He looked at me for a second and then nodded before plugging her number into his cell. He dialed and put the phone to his ear and then got up and strode to the other end of waiting room.

"Playing cupid?" Duke asked.

"Nothing so blatant," I said. "But pushing them toward one another and letting them figure out? That, I'll do."

"You're meddling where you shouldn't meddle," Willa said. "Rach isn't ready for another relationship."

"Did she tell you that?" I asked.

"Well, no."

"Then how do you know?"

"Point taken," she drawled.

While Raze was still on the phone, the doctor came into the waiting room. Willa immediately lifted her head off Duke's shoulder and stood. Duke rose too.

Raze said something into his phone and then hung up and came to join us.

"Ms. Woods?" the doctor asked, looking at Willa mistakenly.

"That's me," I said.

"Follow me, please. Viper asked for you."

"Oh, sure," I said, shooting Willa a look of commiseration.

She collapsed back into the chair and threaded her fingers through her hair.

"Fuck this," Duke growled. "I'll go talk to the nurse again."

"Be nice," Willa called.

"I'm always nice."

The doctor glanced at me in confusion, so I explained.

"We're waiting on news of another friend who's in surgery. They thought you were coming to talk to them."

"I see," the doctor said.

We headed down the hallway to an exam room. The doctor opened the door and held it for me.

Viper was sitting on an exam table, wearing a hospital gown over his jeans. I immediately went to his side.

The doctor pulled out a tablet from his coat pocket and tapped the screen.

"You have a few broken ribs," he said. "They're bad enough I'm sure you're in pain, but no surgery is required. And, there's no internal bleeding. That's the important part. Your ribs will heal in about six to eight weeks, and depending on your pain threshold, I can prescribe you medication if aspirin and ibuprofen don't cut it. You'll want to minimize movement as much as possible. If you need, you can wrap your ribs with a medical bandage, but frankly it's going to hurt every time you breathe for a while. The real goal is to take it easy on yourself."

"What about sex?" Viper asked.

"Viper," I muttered with a roll of my eyes.

The doctor smiled. "If you can handle the pain, go for it. But you might have to experiment with certain positions to find what works for you."

"I have no problem experimenting," Viper said as he lowered himself off the exam table.

"*Shut up*," I growled. "I'd elbow you, but your ribs…"

The doctor chuckled. "Just remember, resting is the goal for a while. No strenuous activity for at least a week." He walked with us into the hallway, but then left us at the nurse's station.

Viper signed his discharge papers and then we headed back toward the waiting room. There was still no news about Savage.

We offered to stay with them, but Duke told us to go home. Said he'd call when there was an update.

By the time I got Viper back to the clubhouse, the sun was coming up. Everything was quiet and no one was awake in the living room.

We went up to our room and Viper all but collapsed onto the bed. His face was etched with pain, but he didn't make a sound.

I knelt on the floor and began unlacing his boots.

"I can do that."

"Let me take care of you," I said, continuing my ministrations.

"Are you going to take care of me in another way?"

I set one of his boots aside. "Maybe after I've had a few hours of sleep. You need some rest too."

His other boot joined its mate and then I went for the button on his jeans, and then his fly. I eased his pants off him and then helped him remove the hospital gown.

"You can't do this for me for the next few weeks," Viper said.

"I know you won't let me, but for now, I'm helping. Just until you no longer grimace every time you move."

Viper's phone vibrated and I grabbed it for him off the nightstand.

He looked at the screen and then let out a sigh of relief. "Savage made it out of surgery. He's alive."

"Oh." Air left my lungs. "Good. That's good, right?"

"That's good. Now we wait and see. He's a fighter. He'll pull through." He set his phone aside. "I need a shower before I crash."

"Want some company?" I asked.

"Fuck yeah."

I quickly stripped out of my clothes, and then helped

Viper remove his boxers. We padded naked to the bathroom where I started the shower.

"How hot do you want it?" I asked.

"Hot."

I nodded and pulled the shower curtain back. Viper stepped into the tub, and I climbed in behind him. After he doused himself, I grabbed the soap and made a lather. I washed his skin, my touch tender as I tried not to hurt him.

"I lied," he said as he stepped back under the spray.

"About what?"

"I could get used to you taking care of me." He cradled my cheek in his hand and forced me to look into his eyes.

They were warm with emotion, dark with longing.

"You said not to say it until I came back," he said.

"I remember."

"I'm going to say it now."

"Okay." I nodded.

He paused for a moment and then lowered his lips to mine. His kiss was tender, passionate, and it made me ache. "I love you, Sutton."

I let out a breathy sigh. "I know."

He reached around to pinch my ass.

I grinned. "I warned you, didn't I?"

"About what?"

"That you were going to fall in love with me."

"You did." He smiled slightly.

I sniggered and grabbed the shampoo bottle and squirted it into the palm of my hand. I ran my fingers through his hair and massaged his scalp.

"Viper?"

His eyes were closed when he mumbled, "Yeah?"

I smiled even though he couldn't see me. "I love you, too."

Chapter 46

Voices in the hallway infiltrated my cocoon of sleep and I opened my eyes. Viper was on his back, staring at the ceiling. He made no move to get up.

"How long have you been awake?" I asked, covering my mouth to stifle a yawn.

"Twenty minutes, maybe. I gotta piss, but my ribs hurt and I don't want to get up."

"What's going on down there?"

"No idea." With a sigh and a grimace, he finally forced himself to sit up. While he was in the bathroom, I climbed out of bed and put on some real clothes and then I fished around in Viper's dresser.

"What are you looking for?" Viper asked as he came into the bedroom.

"A button up shirt for you. It'll be easier to get on than a T-shirt. You can roll up the sleeves to stay cool."

"Don't own a button up shirt."

"Okay, first order of business is to change that. I'll buy you some. Ah, that reminds me. We need a car now more than ever since you can't ride your motorcycle."

"I can ride my motorcycle."

I rolled my eyes. "Even if I thought that was a good idea—which I don't—I can't ride on the back of it with you. My arms wrap around your ribs, and I'll hurt you."

"So, we'll get you a car."

"Okay. Something big enough that you can fit in comfortably."

"Not a Honda Civic, then."

"That car would look like a wind-up toy next to you."

He grimaced his way into a T-shirt and a pair of jeans, but he didn't bother with his leather cut. Viper suddenly looked very dressed down.

"Might want to do something with your hair," I said, fighting a smile.

"What's wrong with my hair?"

"You went to sleep with it wet and it's sticking up. It makes you look a lot less fierce and a lot more boyish."

"Can't have that," he said as he once again strode into the bathroom.

We finally left the bedroom and headed downstairs. Mia and Brooklyn were in the kitchen, holding mugs of coffee and chatting in low voices.

"You're awake," Brooklyn said, her gaze bouncing between me and Viper.

"Heard people talking," I explained.

"Coffee?" Brooklyn asked.

"Please," Viper said.

"Colt, Zip and Boxer are outside," Mia said to Viper.

"Thanks," Viper said to Brooklyn as she handed him a mug full of coffee. "I'll join them."

Viper trekked out of the kitchen, heading to the backyard.

"Did Colt sleep at all?" I asked Mia. I took the carton of cream and poured it into my coffee.

"A few hours," she said. "Tossed and turned a lot."

"How's Darcy?" I asked. "Stupid question, I guess. Considering…"

"Holding it together," Brooklyn said. "She left with the kids about thirty minutes ago. She wanted to tell them at home."

"What about the funeral?" I asked.

Mia sighed. "Tomorrow. God, I'm sick to fucking death of funerals." When she realized what she'd said, her face flushed with color. "I'm horrible."

"You're not," Brooklyn said.

"Any word on Savage?" I inquired.

"Yeah. He's awake. Willa won't leave his room and Duke refuses to leave Willa, so they're at the hospital for the time being."

"We were discussing Waverly and Sailor," Brooklyn added. "Willa doesn't want them home alone, even though we've gotten the news that it's clear. Usually, they stay with Darcy and Gray, but…"

"But that's not an option now." I nodded. "I'd offer to house them for a bit, but I don't have a house."

"Speaking of that," Mia began. "You and Viper are looking for a place together, right?"

"Right." I sighed. "God, I hate the idea of apartment hunting."

"You don't have to hunt," Mia said. "I've got a rental."

"You do?" I asked.

"I do," Mia insisted. "Cute little two bedroom, one bath. Recently renovated.

"It's a rite of passage," Brooklyn said with a laugh. "Almost all of us have stayed at The Love Shack at one point or another."

"It's unfurnished," Mia said as her laughter died down. "But it's currently vacant. It's yours if you want it."

"First you give me a job. Then you give me a house to live in? Are you, like, my tattooed, badass fairy godmother?"

"Something like that," Mia said with a chuckle. "But only if I get to wear leather instead of a cloak."

"Absolutely," I said with a sigh of relief. "I need to buy a car. Something reliable but cheap. Something Viper can sit in comfortably. We can't ride his motorcycle because of his ribs."

"I might be able to help," Brooklyn said.

"What, you know a guy?" I teased.

"Well, yeah, actually. Horace Jackson owns an auto garage. He cut me a deal on my catering van."

"Horace Jackson. Jackson," I repeated. "Why does that name sound familiar?"

"His sons own Three Kings tattoo parlor," Brooklyn said. "You've heard of Three Kings, right?"

I smacked my forehead. "Ah, I knew I'd heard that name before. Yeah, they came into the bar one night when I was working with Annabella."

"My business partner—Brielle—she's their younger sister," Brooklyn explained.

"So, they're all intertwined with the club, huh?" I asked.

"Kinda," Mia said. "They're on the fringes—just enough not to experience any blowback meant for the club."

"Speaking of blowback," I began. "How can we all just leave the clubhouse now? How are we all safe?"

"Colt didn't tell me details—he rarely does," Mia said. "But he assured me we're all safe, the club is safe, and we can move about our lives. We're not going to get more of an explanation than that."

"It just doesn't make sense," I muttered.

"Colt wouldn't say it's safe unless it was," Mia said. "You just have to trust him."

"Oh, I trust him," I assured her. "I just wish I knew *why*. You know?"

Mia nodded. "I know."

"Sailor and Waverly will stay with us," Brooklyn said, getting back to the matter at hand. "We have more than enough room. They can help me batch cook."

"Batch cook?" I asked.

"Darcy's going to need some meals for the next few weeks," Brooklyn said sadly. "I don't want her to have to worry about food while she's in the thick of it, you know?"

"Oh." I sighed. "Yeah."

"And Willa's going to have her hands full when Savage gets out of the hospital. So I'd like to cook for her too," Brooklyn added.

"Call me when you do that," I said. "I'd love to help."

Brooklyn nodded. "I'll text you Horace's number. When you call, tell him you're my friend. That'll sweeten the deal."

"I will, thanks," I said, gratitude permeating every part of me.

"Let me get you the key to your new place," Mia said as she grabbed her purse sitting on the counter. She riffled through it for her key chain. She quickly removed the key and handed it to me. "I'll text the address to you. You can move in whenever. Today, if you want."

"When should we sign the lease and pay rent?" I asked.

She waved her hand. "No lease. Rent we can handle later."

"This is about as formal as my job interview," I said with a laugh.

"You don't need formality with family." Mia took a sip of her coffee.

Emotion built in my throat, and I cleared it.

"Here, take my key to the green truck," Mia said, reaching for her key ring again.

"Why do you have a key to the green truck?" I demanded.

She grinned. "Because that used to be mine, too. Colt didn't want me driving it anymore, and Sailor and Waverly needed a vehicle. I sold it to Duke for a steal."

"You're like a mafia queen who has a finger in every pie," I joked.

Mia laughed. "I'll tell Sailor and Waverly that you borrowed their truck."

"Borrowed implies asking," I said. "Teenagers who don't have a set of wheels? They'll make your lives hell."

"Won't be for long," Brooklyn said. "And they like you, so it'll be fine."

"Thanks." I hugged them both. "I'm going to see if Viper is ready to get out of here."

I went to the backyard. Colt, Zip, Boxer and Viper were sitting in a cluster of camp chairs. They all looked exhausted.

"How are you doing?" I asked Zip.

"No pain," he assured me with a smile.

I looked at Viper. "You ready to go?"

"Go where?" he asked.

"I scored some wheels," I said. "Let's go for a drive."

Viper rose, and to his credit, didn't grimace.

My phone buzzed in my back pocket. It was the address for the rental. And then Brooklyn's text came through with Horace's contact number.

Mia and Brooklyn weren't in the living room as we passed through to the front porch.

"Whose wheels are we taking?" Viper asked.

"We're borrowing Sailor and Waverly's truck until I buy a car," I said.

He opened the driver's side door for me. "So where are we going?"

I grinned. "Our new rental."

Chapter 47

I UNLOCKED the front door of Mia's rental and pushed the door open. "Oh, this is perfect," I said.

Viper came in behind me.

I looked up at him. "Could you live here?"

"Sure."

I raised my brows. "Sure? That's all you've got to say?"

"You'll be living here with me, right?"

"Right."

"Then I don't care where we live. As long as you're there."

My gaze softened. "This doesn't seem fair."

"What?"

"Darcy just lost her husband. Lily and Cam lost their father. The club lost a brother—a good man." I shook my head. "And I'm—"

"Happy."

I swallowed and nodded. "Yeah, happy." I walked farther into the house, opening the cabinets in the kitchen and exploring the bathroom and the two bedrooms.

"You're allowed to be happy."

"Even when everything goes to shit?" I asked softly.

"Especially then."

"Didn't take you for an optimist."

"I'm not. I'm not even a little bit of an optimist. But what if the shoe was on the other foot, huh? What if I'd been the one who died?"

My breath hitched.

"Darcy would have been relieved to have Gray come home to her. She'd lie in bed next to him, thanking her lucky stars that she didn't have to bury him."

"Lucky," I repeated. "Right."

"It's the luck of the draw. And she and Gray got the fucking short end of the stick. But his death wasn't in vain. He died because the club made a tough call. Gray died a hero."

"Lily and Cam," I murmured. "Losing their father so young…"

"Was it any easier at nineteen when your dad went to prison?"

"My dad didn't die."

"Didn't he? In all the ways that matter?"

I sighed. "I guess. Yeah."

"It's our job to be there for them," Viper said, walking to me and pulling me into his embrace.

I wrapped my arms around him and squeezed.

He grunted.

"Shit!" I let go. "Sorry. I forgot."

"It's okay. Come back here. Let me hold you a minute."

I let him take me into his arms and I pressed my cheek to his chest. "I think this is my favorite spot in the world. This, right here."

"Not my bed?"

"Mmm…tied for first." I sighed. "I like hearing your heartbeat."

"You can hear that better when you're on top of me—naked."

"Get no ideas. I'm not putting out. You're injured."

"I'll be injured for a few weeks. Are you going to hold out on me for that long?"

I grinned. "Doubtful. I'm not a saint. I just think a week of rest would be good for you."

"Blow jobs. I can still get blow jobs. I don't have to do anything except lay back and enjoy."

I grinned. "Have it all worked out, huh?"

"I'll rest for a week," he said.

"Yeah?"

"On one condition…"

"Uh-oh. You and your conditions," I teased.

"You give me dirty peep shows."

"Need stuff for your spank bank, huh? Or will you not be spanking the bank?"

"I'll spank the bank while I watch you."

I reached out and stroked his cheek, smiling up at him. "You're fun."

∽

We buried Gray next to South Paw. The earth hadn't even had time to recover since we'd put him in the ground.

Now there were two.

Two brothers set to spend eternity with each other.

Two brothers waiting for others to join.

I stood underneath an umbrella with Viper next to me. It was raining and the sky was murky as we lowered Gray into his final resting place.

Darcy shielded herself and her children with an

umbrella. Lily clung to her leg and Cam stared down at the coffin with swollen, somber eyes.

The Old Ladies were in different stages of grief. Several of them were shedding tears. But Darcy remained stoic. I wondered if she'd cried at all, or if she was in complete shock over the loss of her love.

Despite being able to move in the world again after being set free from the chains of lockdown, I didn't breathe deeply. It still felt like there was something waiting in the shadows for me.

After the funeral, we congregated at Darcy's. Jazz and Brielle—Brooklyn's business partners—had set up for the wake. There were tasteful white flowers, platters of food, and the entire kitchen was full of liquor and drinks.

It was all so familiar, because we'd just gone through the same thing not even a month prior. Even though I'd only been with the club for a little while, I could already see that each loss took the club down another notch.

Raze stood with Rach in the living room. Both of them were sipping drinks, and it seemed to me that something was brewing between them. I kept the smile to myself.

Willa was coming out of the bathroom as Viper and I made our way to the kitchen.

"Hey," she said, leaning over and giving me a hug.

"Hey. How's Savage?"

"Already ornery," she said with a slight smile. "Ready to get out of the hospital."

"When's he going to be discharged?" I asked.

Viper placed his hand on my shoulder and moved toward me so Kelp and Bones could move past him.

"Probably in a week," she said.

"Did Brooklyn tell you what we're doing?" I asked.

"No."

"We're going to cook for you guys—and for Darcy. Make it easy for you to eat well over the next few weeks."

"Oh, that's too sweet," Willa said, tears glistening in her eyes. She hastily brushed them aside.

I squeezed her hand and then looked at Viper. "Food?"

He nodded. Viper placed his hand on Willa's shoulder to comfort her. Surprise flitted across her face.

"I see you," I said to Viper as we headed to the dining room. I handed him a small plastic plate.

"See me what?"

"I see you softening," I said. "Getting comfortable around people."

He didn't say anything as he spooned egg salad onto his plate.

"I promise not to tease you about it."

"Yeah, right," he muttered.

I chucked him under the chin. "Could it be that you actually *like* my teasing?"

"I've learned to live with it." He shot me a wink.

We took our plates of food and wandered outside. The rain had stopped, and the Old Ladies sat together at the glass patio table. The brothers gave them space and gathered on the other side of the backyard.

I looked at Viper and he nodded. He went to join his brothers and I headed to the table and took an empty chair.

Darcy was staring into her glass.

"Need a refill?" I asked her.

She shook her head. "No. I'm fine."

I met Mia's gaze across the table. Her mouth turned up at the corner and then she shrugged.

There was no murmur of conversation, and I ate in silence.

"Someone say something," Darcy finally said. "I can't stand the quiet."

"Where are the kids?" Brooklyn asked. "I baked Lily's favorite cookies."

"She ran upstairs after we got back. Boxer went up to sit with her."

"Two peas in a pod," Doc said.

Darcy nodded. "Cam and Silas are playing video games." She looked at Mia. "Thank God for your son."

Mia reached out and took Darcy's hand and gave it a squeeze.

"The three of us dogpiled in the bed last night," she said quietly. "What am I supposed to do without him?"

Her eyes met Rach's and the two of them shared something that the rest of us couldn't understand. How could you go on after the love of your life died? The father of your children. The man who swore to love and protect you until death do you part.

"You put one foot in front of the other," Rach said. "And you lean on us."

"Whatever you need," Allison said. "Any hour of the day or night, you call."

"And we'll answer," Doc whispered.

"Because that's what we do," Brooklyn chimed in.

"And if you need us to drive over in the middle of the night, we'll do that too," Willa added.

There we all sat—mothers, wives, friends. We'd be there for each other through it all. Births, deaths, and everything in between.

Because that was life.

Chapter 48

Two days later, I was the proud new owner of a silver Toyota Tacoma. Well, new to me. It was a used truck, but it was all mine.

"You look good in my truck," I said to Viper as he climbed into the passenger seat. "You especially look good as my passenger prince."

"That's another sass added to the tally," he stated, buckling himself in.

"How many does that make?" I asked.

"Three...hundred thousand."

"So basically, what you're saying is, I'll never stop being sassy and you'll never stop wanting to spank my ass."

"Pretty much, yeah." He leaned over, grasped my chin, and kissed my lips.

When he pulled back, I was an emotionally drippy mess. "Are you sure you don't mind hanging out with Slash while Brooklyn and I cook?"

"Nah. It's fine. Slash is a good guy. You're finding your way, aren't you?"

I nodded and turned the key in the ignition. "I wish

there was something more I could do for Darcy. But I guess food is the language of grief."

"Hmm."

"How are your ribs?" I asked.

"You asked me that an hour ago."

"Well, I'm asking you again."

"They're fine."

"Take your meds?"

"No."

I sighed. "Viper."

"Sutton. I don't need them."

"Is this you being a big, strong man?"

"I *am* a big, strong man and you know it. But this is me not wanting to rely on addictive painkillers for something that's just inconvenient."

"Okay," I said.

"No argument?"

"You're a grown man. You've been taking care of yourself for a long time. Far be it from me to tell you what you need."

"This is reverse psychology, isn't it?"

"No psychology. You let me take care of you when you had the flu. For now, that's enough."

He reached over and set his hand on my leg. "It's hard for me. Letting you take care of me doesn't come easy."

"Well, we're supposed to take care of each other, right?"

"That's the word on the street."

We finally pulled up to Brooklyn and Slash's house. It was a beautiful home on the outskirts of the city, giving them more space than they'd have in town.

I'd only just rang the bell when the door opened.

"Hey," Waverly greeted as she bit into an apple.

"Hi," I said with a smile.

"Brooklyn's already dicing and chopping and doing things to vegetables that *so* didn't deserve it."

"You're in good spirits," I said to her.

She nodded. "I'm better." She shot Viper a look. "Sorry I cried. I'm not usually a crier."

"That's okay," he said.

"Well, come on in." She stepped back to let us through.

"Are you going to hang around? You and Sailor?" I asked.

She shook her head. "No. We're going to go visit Savage and try and get Willa to leave the hospital. She needs food that's not cafeteria crap."

"Sounds like you're going to drag her away whether or not she wants to go," I said with a grin.

"She can't say no to me." She sighed. "Duke enlisted my help. Between the two of us, hopefully we can get her out of there. And maybe, just maybe, she'll want to sleep in her own bed tonight, which means Sailor and I can finally go home. Brooklyn and Slash are great, but they're kind of all over each other."

"Aren't Willa and Duke all over each other?" I asked with a laugh.

"Yes, but at least Sailor and I have our own living space. We don't have to see it all the time."

"Then why couldn't you guys just stay at your place?" I asked.

"Willa wanted us with family." She shrugged. "I didn't fight her on it."

We followed Waverly through the hallway into the kitchen. Sure enough, Brooklyn was dicing veggies, but she put down the knife to greet us.

"Can I get you all something to drink?" she asked.

"Water for me, please," I said.

"Same," Viper added.

"Slash is in the den," Brooklyn said as she filled a glass with ice.

"Kicking me out already?" he asked lightly.

Brooklyn blinked and then smiled. "I can put you to work if you'd prefer."

"Oh no. Unless you want me to start a fire, you better kick me out," Viper said.

"How were you ever going to take care of yourself if I didn't come along and learn how to cook for both of us?" I teased.

"Luckily I don't have to think about that anymore." He grasped the back of my neck and leaned down to kiss me. "If you have a jar that needs opening or the trash needs taking out or something, give a shout."

Brooklyn handed him a full glass of water. I grinned at his retreating back and then turned my attention to Brooklyn who had an amused smile on her face. "You guys are adorable."

"Don't tell him that. He thinks he's still terrifying," I joked.

"He's a big teddy bear," Waverly said. "They all are."

These big, tough bikers who'd just gone to war with the cartel also comforted teenagers when they cried and sat with little girls who'd just lost their father.

They were a dichotomy, for sure, but no matter how sweet and tender Viper was with me, I'd never forget that he'd slept with a knife, that he'd been to prison, and that he had killed men in cold blood for his club.

"Speaking of teddy bears," Brooklyn said. "Have you talked to Dylan?"

Waverly nodded. "I didn't tell him about the lockdown, though."

"Why not?" I asked.

"He'd lose his shit if I told him. He's really protective of me." She beamed.

"I guess you're not upset about that," I said in amusement.

"Not at all. I just think it's better if I tell him when he gets home from Sicily. I didn't want to fight over the phone." Waverly walked over to trash and threw away her apple core. "I'm gonna grab Sailor and then we're going to take off."

"Keep me posted," Brooklyn said.

"Will do."

"Where is Sailor?" I asked.

Waverly's lips twitched. "Upstairs. She's primping."

Sailor appeared in the kitchen a moment later, her cheeks rosy, her eyes lacquered with mascara, and gloss on her lips. "I'm ready to go."

Waverly looked at her. "Finally."

Sailor rolled her eyes. "Hi, Sutton. Bye, Sutton."

I waved.

"You guys think you'll be back for dinner?" Brooklyn asked.

"Not sure," Waverly said. "Depends on Willa."

Brooklyn nodded.

"Bye," Waverly said, pushing against Sailor's hip to get her moving toward the door.

The two of them gabbed all the way to the front hall. Eventually, the door opened and then closed, and I couldn't hear them anymore.

"Primping because of Acid?" I asked Brooklyn.

"You know it," Brooklyn said. "He may or may not be at the hospital when she gets there. Poor girl can't hide her crush even a little bit."

"Being a teenager is the worst," I said. "You're trying

to be an adult but you're not yet and no one takes you seriously."

"The in-between."

I went to the sink and washed my hands. "Okay, put me to work. Let's make some food."

～

"Did you see Raze and Rach at the funeral?" I asked as I finished off the last of my tea.

Brooklyn lifted her leg and rested it on a spare chair in the kitchen.

We'd been cooking for hours and were enjoying a much-needed break.

"I saw them talking," Brooklyn said. "You think something's there?"

"I think something *could* be there," I said. "Another cup of tea?"

"Yeah, that would be great," she said, moving to get up.

"Stay," I commanded. "I'll get it."

I filled the kettle with more water and turned on the stove.

"Something smells good," Slash said as he and Viper came into the kitchen.

"That would be the chicken and dumplings," Brooklyn said, tilting her face up to receive Slash's kiss.

"Do I get any of that, or is that for Willa and Darcy?" Slash asked. He crouched down next to Brooklyn's chair and placed his hand on her swollen belly.

"Both," Brooklyn said. "We made extra. You hungry now?"

"No. Just coming in to get something to drink before I head back out to the garage."

"How's the motorcycle?" she asked.

"Giving me grief." He kissed her again and stood up but didn't move away from her.

Viper came over to me and placed his hand on my hip. "You good?"

"I'm good." I leaned against him. I loved that he touched me in public. I looked at Brooklyn. "We need to get going. We have a hot date at a furniture store. Viper told me I can buy anything I want."

"You might come to regret that, my man," Slash joked.

Brooklyn grasped the back of his thigh. "Do *you* regret spoiling me?"

"Nope," he said.

"Come on," I said to Viper. "They've got that look."

"What look is that?" Brooklyn asked.

"The look that says Slash'll be eating you for dinner in place of the chicken and dumplings."

"Sutton!" Her cheeks flushed.

"The woman isn't wrong," Slash said as he looked down at his wife with hunger in his gaze.

"I'd tell you to use protection, but you've already got a bun in the oven. So I'll just say, have fun and don't hurt your back," I said.

"That was directed at you," Brooklyn said to Slash.

"Yeah, I got that," he drawled. "She has no filter."

"None," Viper agreed. "But I'm learning to live with it."

"It's nice to have things you can count on," I said.

Slash shook his head. "See you guys later."

Viper and I left their house and climbed into the truck.

I sighed as I buckled myself in.

"What?" Viper asked as he settled into his seat.

"I'm so jealous of them right now."

"Why? Because they're about to have sex in the kitchen?" he asked.

"Sex in the kitchen, but also just sex. I miss it."

"It's only been a day."

"I know, but you jump-started my libido just by existing. I might be humping your leg by the end of the week."

"I'm willing to have sex with you before the week is out. Damn my injured ribs."

"Willing?" I asked as I put the truck in gear. "Don't do me any favors."

He flashed a grin. "I'll do you so many favors."

"Fuck furniture shopping," I quipped. "I'd rather fuck you."

"And you say I have a way with words."

Chapter 49

"That doesn't go there," I said.

Viper held the glass in his hand. "Where does it go?"

"In the cabinet near the sink," I explained. "Coffee mugs go in the cabinet near the coffee maker, and the silverware goes in the drawer near the dishwasher. Makes it easy when you have to unload it."

"I never thought you were going to be this particular," he said as he placed the glass in the correct cabinet.

"Rethinking this cohabitation thing already?" I asked lightly.

"Nah. You walk around in a tank and your thong a lot. I'm a fan of the view."

"I aim to please," I said with a grin.

"Which you did this morning. Thanks for the wake-up blow job."

"Living together is super fun."

As much as I'd wanted to move into the rental immediately, I'd realized how much we needed for it to be comfortable. We'd bought a king-sized bed because Viper needed the space, but no other piece of furniture had been delivered.

The house felt empty and echoey.

"How do you feel about me putting on real pants and we can go grocery shopping?" I asked. "I want to cook you dinner."

"You don't have to do that, you know," he said.

"Do what? Do nice things for you?"

"Nice things are good. I like nice things. No, I just mean, you don't need to feel obligated to cook if you don't want to. I know you only helped Crow and Brooklyn at the clubhouse to keep yourself busy."

"At first that's why I did it," I admitted. "But I actually really like cooking."

"You sure?"

"I'm sure. It's fun."

"Cooking is fun for you?"

I nodded. "I like it. Look, I didn't have a mom growing up and my dad and I lived off takeout and frozen things from cardboard boxes. This is a nice change. I want…"

"What?"

"The hearth makes a home." I shrugged. "I like the idea of you walking in and smelling something homemade."

He stalked toward me and grasped the back of my neck in his big hand. Viper bent his head and took my lips with his.

When he pulled away, I was breathless.

"Yeah," I sighed. "I'm definitely a fan of living together."

Viper took his free hand and slid it into my panties. "Mmm. I like that I can do this anytime I want to."

"Me too," I whispered.

"You know what we haven't done since moving in?" he

asked, nipping my ear as he slipped his finger between my thighs.

"What?"

"I haven't fucked you in the kitchen yet."

"No, you haven't," I agreed.

He removed his hand from my panties and stepped back.

I hopped up onto the counter and wiggled my underwear down my legs.

Viper unfastened his jeans and undid the fly before lowering his pants and boxers in one fell swoop.

"Spread your legs, baby," he growled. "And show me how wet you are."

I did as he said and he dragged a finger through my wetness. He pumped his hard shaft at the sight of it.

I scooted closer, wanting him inside me.

He grasped my hip and pressed the head of his crown to my entrance. Viper slid in slowly, and I groaned in pleasure.

I left my legs open, not wanting to wrap them around him for fear I might hurt his ribs.

He moved his hand from my hip to the small of my back and I tilted my pelvis to take him deeper.

"Oh fuck," he muttered, thrusting harder.

I grasped the hair at his nape and tugged him closer, wanting his mouth on mine.

His kiss was violent, and I couldn't get enough.

He fucked me hard and deep on top of the kitchen counter. I fisted his hair as I clenched around him, my orgasm shooting through me as though I'd left the stratosphere.

"Yes," Viper rasped. "Just like that. I'm coming."

He rammed into me and then stilled.

I gently released his hair and placed my hands on the counter to steady myself. "Oh, yeah, I'm all about this."

Viper chuckled. "Living together might be the best idea I've ever had."

～

"Your ass looks amazing in those jeans," Viper said, moving closer to me as we headed up the steps of Willa's porch.

"Sir, your words!" I gasped.

"You have no idea what you do to me, do you?" he demanded.

"They're jeans, Viper. It's not my fault they hug the curves of my ass."

"The curves of your ass are begging for my hands…"

The front door opened, and Willa appeared, a smile on her face. "Hey, guys! Come on in."

We stepped into the foyer, and Willa closed the door.

"Don't be offended that I didn't get up," Savage called out from his spot on the couch. "Willa refuses to let me move. Even though the doctor told her I need to be up and moving."

"Hush, you," Willa said to him. She gestured with her chin at the platter in my hand. "What'd you make?"

"Cookies," I said with a grin.

"Cookies?" Savage asked. "What kind?"

"Chocolate chip, sprinkled with sea salt."

Willa took the platter from me. "Oh, these look amazing. Duke will be back in a bit. The grill was out of propane, so he went to get it filled. Come on in. Let's get you a drink."

"I could use a drink," Savage said.

"You already have a drink," Willa replied as she headed into the living room. Viper and I followed.

"I have water," Savage said. "I'd kill for a beer though."

"You don't need a beer. You're recovering from surgery." Willa rolled her eyes.

"Viper, do a brother a solid and get me a beer," Savage pleaded.

Viper shook his head. "I'm not getting in the middle of this."

"Where's your loyalty?" Savage demanded.

Viper draped an arm around my shoulder and pulled me into his side. "Right here."

"Whipped already," Savage said, and then grinned.

"Come talk with me," Willa said to me.

I left Viper to entertain Savage and went to the kitchen with Willa.

"Quiet house," I said.

"Dylan got back into town, so Waverly is with him."

"And Sailor?"

"Hanging out in the guesthouse." She frowned. "I'm kind of worried about her."

"Why?" I asked.

Willa set the cookies down onto the counter and then went to the fridge. "This crush on Acid is starting to affect her mood. She's super mercurial lately. One minute, she's fine, the next her world is ending."

"She's a teenager," I said. "Big emotions."

"Right. Have I already forgotten what it was like at her age?"

"I don't know, have you?" I teased.

She opened the fridge. "Beer?"

"Sounds good."

She pulled out two bottles and then opened a drawer and found a bottle opener.

"What about Waverly and Dylan? Their relationship seems intense for their age."

Willa nodded and handed me a bottle. "It is intense. They're in love. First love."

"First heartbreak?" I inquired.

She shook her head. "On the contrary, I think this one might be the real deal. But they're *so* young. I don't have room to talk, though. Duke and I were childhood best friends and look how that turned out."

"Pretty well, I'd say. How's the morning sickness by the way?"

"Sometimes it comes in the afternoons, but I'm okay. How about you? How's living with Viper?"

I grinned and took a sip of my beer. "Fun."

"Yeah?"

I nodded.

"You guys settled?"

"Well, the rest of our furniture arrived a few days ago, so that's good. Still trying to remember where I put things. It's an adjustment, but it's kind of amazing. A real house."

She nodded. "I get it. I so get it. This is the first nice home I've ever lived in. It makes all the difference, doesn't it?"

"Yeah, it does." I grabbed the second bottle of beer. "Let me give this to Viper and then I'll come back and help you."

I dropped off the beer to Viper, who was sitting in a chair, smiling—actually smiling—while Savage talked.

When I returned to the kitchen, Willa had a glass casserole dish on the counter.

"I already peeled the potatoes, but will you slice them for me?"

"Sure. What are we having?"

"Grilled salmon and potatoes au gratin. When Waverly was a kid, she called them lava potatoes." She grinned and shook her head. "Even though she's not eating here tonight, I'm still making enough for her to have leftovers."

"Sweet," I said.

Willa handed me a knife and a cutting board and then set the bowl of peeled potatoes in front of me.

Duke returned just as we put the casserole dish into the oven. He kissed his wife, grabbed a beer, and then went out back to hook up the propane.

"Have you been by Darcy's this week?" I asked.

Willa shook her head. "No. But I've called. You?"

"Not yet. I thought about dropping by, but I don't want to intrude, you know?"

The truth was, I didn't know what to say to her. I didn't want to ask her how she was doing because it was such a bullshit question.

Hey, how are you doing after your husband just died and left you a widow with two small children who are both emotionally crushed by the loss of their loving father?

I was also having trouble hiding how happy I was about the changes in my life. It felt wrong to be around Darcy and shove that in her face, and I knew it was best if I stayed away.

We ate dinner in the living room, so Savage didn't have to get off the couch. Conversation was easy and light. While we were in the middle of dessert, the front door blew open and Waverly stormed inside.

"Hey," Willa called to her sister. "You're home earlier than I thought you'd be."

Waverly stopped, her angry expression clearing. "Oh. Hey. Sorry, I won't interrupt. I'll just head out to the guesthouse."

"You okay?" Willa asked with a frown.

"*I'm fine*," she clipped and then marched through the house. The back door slammed shut.

Silence permeated the living room.

"She doesn't seem fine," Savage said. "What happened?"

"My guess?" Willa asked. "A fight between her and Dylan."

"About what?" Duke asked. "He's been gone for weeks. I didn't expect her home until well after her curfew."

"I'll see if I can pry it out of her tomorrow," Willa said as she got up from her chair. "Anyone need anything? Coffee? I have decaf."

"I'm good," I said.

"Same," Viper proclaimed.

"I'll load the dishwasher," Duke said, placing his hand on Willa's arm. "Sit."

She peered at him. "You're not taking a play from Slash's playbook, are you?"

Duke grinned. "Maybe. Relax. I've got this."

"I'd offer to help too," Savage said. "But I just had my spleen out."

Willa went over to him and flicked his ear.

"Stop doing that." Savage batted her hand away.

"You like the torture—admit it," Willa said.

"I'll put up with it since you take good care of me," he joked.

She leaned down and hugged him. "You need anything?"

"Maybe a dose of my pain meds."

"You got it." She headed into the kitchen, leaving the three of us alone.

"You guys might want to get out of here. Once those things hit my system, I crash."

"I'm glad to see you're in good spirits," I said to him. "You had us all pretty worried."

"Better you were worried about me than Duke. I'd rather be the one laid up."

"I'd rather have neither of you laid up," Willa said as she came back into the living room with a glass of water and two of his pills.

"I told you I'd do anything to make sure Duke got home safe." Savage took the pills and the glass of water from her.

"You more than delivered," she said quietly.

He threw back the painkillers and drank half the glass of water. He leaned over and set it on the coffee table, wincing as he did.

Savage looked up at Willa and his expression softened. "You don't have to cry over me."

"I'm not." She hastily wiped her eyes and took a shaky breath.

"No?" He raised his brows. "So, I took a bullet for your husband. Does that mean you'll finally name your kid after me?"

Chapter 50

"You're quiet," Viper said on the drive home. He reached over from the passenger side and set his hand on my leg.

"I feel like a shit," I admitted.

"About what?"

"I haven't called Darcy or stopped by her house."

"Why not?" he asked.

"I don't want to bother her."

"Try again."

I glared at him. "I don't know what to say to her…"

"You don't have to say anything to her. You can just sit with her."

"Wouldn't that be weird?"

"Might be weird, but it's better than trying to ignore her loss altogether."

"I'm not ignoring it."

"Maybe not, but you haven't gone over there because you're thinking about how all this affects *you*. But it's not about you—it's about *her*."

"Ouch."

"I'm right, aren't I? You don't want to see her because you're worried about what you'll say, not how she'll feel."

"Well, it's official I feel even worse now. Thanks."

"But you'll go over to her house tomorrow, won't you?"

"Yeah, I will."

By nine the next morning, I was standing on Darcy's porch steps. I paused for a moment and then took a deep breath before knocking on the door.

When no one answered, I rang the bell.

It took a few minutes before the door opened. Darcy was in a pair of sweats and an old T-shirt and had answered the door without a stitch of makeup on.

She blinked exhausted eyes. "Hey."

"Hi. Sorry to show up unannounced."

"Oh. That's okay." She stepped back. "Come on in."

The house was somber and quiet. "Where are the kids?"

"Day camp," she explained.

We stared at each other and then I said, "I'm sorry I haven't called."

"It's fine. You helped Brooklyn with the food. Thanks for that, by the way."

"Doesn't feel like enough," I murmured.

She rubbed her eyes. "There's nothing you can do. There's nothing anyone can do. It is what it is. The only one who gets it is Rach, and frankly, she's the only one I can tolerate being around right now. The rest of you guys are so damn happy it makes me homicidal."

I swallowed.

She cracked a smile. "It was a joke."

"It was funny," I said with a straight face.

"You know what I need?" she asked.

"What?"

"For people to stop looking at me with pity. For people

to stop tiptoeing around what happened. My husband died. I'm a widow. I'm now a single mom living in the house I shared with him. It sucks, and nothing will make it better. Not even time. I'll just have to learn to live with it."

"What are you doing during the day while the kids are gone?"

"I sit at home and stare at nothing until Rach comes over for an hour or so in the afternoon. Then I pick the kids up at five. This is me, living."

It was as bad as I thought it would be.

No, it was worse.

She was acerbic and sharp-tongued. Honest with a layer of dark humor that I didn't find amusing at all.

But this wasn't about me. Darcy was grieving, and no one could tell her how she was supposed to do it.

"If you need anything…" I trailed off.

"I don't."

"Okay, I guess I'll go then," I said, backtracking toward the exit.

"You think you have an idea of what you've signed up for. You don't." She marched toward the door and opened it for me.

I stepped outside and then turned to say goodbye, but before I could speak she said, "It's not too late, you know."

"Too late for what?" I asked.

"To leave him."

I flinched. "You think I should leave Viper?"

"I think you haven't been inked with his name yet. I think you're a fool if you think this ends any way but you being alone. Just like me."

She said it close enough to me that I felt her breath on my face. I straightened my spine and stood taller.

"You've been drinking," I said.

"Damn right I have been. And so what?" Her mouth

pinched. "My kids aren't here. I'm not going anywhere. And my life is a pile of *shit*. If I want to have a fucking bourbon with my coffee I can. I'm a fucking grown up."

I took a deep breath, my concern for her growing.

Before I could say anything else, she slammed the door in my face.

I stood for a moment in silence and then walked to my truck.

I didn't know what to do. Grief affected everyone differently, but this wasn't the Darcy I'd come to know in our brief time together.

She'd been fun-loving, smiling, teasing.

Now she was drinking early in the morning, and her words about leaving Viper…

When I got home, Viper's motorcycle was gone.

I didn't want to tell anyone Darcy's business, but I felt like I couldn't really stay silent about it either.

So, I called the only person who'd understand what Darcy was living through.

"Hey, Sutton," Rach said when she answered my call.

"Hey."

"You okay?"

I paused. "No. No, I'm not okay."

"Where are you?"

"I'm at home."

"I'll be right over."

∽

"I love what you've done with the place," Rach said as she sipped her tea. She'd left Cash with her mother, and it was just the two of us. It was nice having a private conversation with her, with no other distractions.

"Thanks," I said. "It's weird, living with a dude."

"Never done it before?"

"No."

"I miss it," she admitted.

"Can I ask you something? Something really personal?"

Her brow furrowed and she nodded.

"Do you regret it?" I blurted out. "Getting involved with the club? Becoming an Old Lady? Knowing what you know now? That you're going to raise Cash without a father…"

"Ah," she said with a slight smile. "I see."

I nodded.

"You're questioning the whole thing, aren't you?"

"No. Actually, I'm not." I bit my lip. "But I stopped off at Darcy's this morning. Just to see how she was. And it wasn't good."

She sighed. "Yeah. I know. I've been by several times this week in the afternoon."

"She was drinking," I said. "Heavily. I smelled bourbon on her breath. I was there at nine…"

"Damn."

"Yeah. I was trying not to think too much about it, you know? I mean, fuck, we just buried her husband…but it's more than just that. She told me I was a fool for sticking around—and that because I haven't gotten tattooed yet, that I should just walk away from Viper. From all this."

"She said that? Really?" Rach asked.

"Really. She was mean, Rach. She didn't sound like herself. I'm a big girl. I can handle mean. But I'm worried about her."

"That's the grief talking—I'm sure of it. I went through a similar phase. But I came out of it. She will too."

"I hope so. The drinking though…"

"Yeah, that's not good. Did you tell anyone?"

"Just you. I thought, maybe because…"

"I've already gone through what she went through that I'd get it?"

I nodded.

She sighed. "Yeah, I mean, I was pregnant. So I couldn't drink, but I definitely wanted to. I'll keep an eye on her."

"Thanks. It feels like tattling, but she's not in a good place and I haven't known her long enough to know if it's a real problem or not, you know?"

"I know. Are you worried about what she said? About leaving Viper?"

The key turned in the lock, followed by Viper coming inside.

"Rachel," he greeted. "Hello."

"Hi, Viper." Rach finished off her last sip of tea. "I better get going. No doubt Cash is destroying my mother's sanity."

"Thanks for coming over," I said.

"Any time." She hugged me and then waved to Viper as she left.

The door closed behind her.

"Sorry, babe, I didn't mean to interrupt your girl time."

"It's okay," I murmured.

"You alright? You look funny."

"I look *funny*?" I asked, raising my brows.

"Well, not funny. Just not like yourself. Something weighing you down?"

I couldn't tell him what Darcy had said. They were just words from a grieving woman. I wouldn't let them infect what I had with Viper. I wouldn't let her pain and anger dictate whether or not I walked away. It was a choice I had to make on my own.

"Just thinking about you," I said quietly. "And how much I…"

"Love me? Adore me? Can't get enough of me?"

"Arrogant much?" I asked with a smile.

"I know what you're really thinking. You can't wait to have my huge dick inside you."

"Definitely arrogant." I laughed. "And I'm totally here for it."

Chapter 51

ANOTHER WEEK PASSED in a blissful haze of cohabitation. The sex I was having with Viper was unbelievable, but the little moments of sharing space with him was a new sort of intimacy, exciting in its own way.

Every now and again Darcy's words would attempt to pop my bubble of happiness, but I was determined not to let them.

One morning, Viper sat in a kitchen chair and I was straddling his lap. I wore one of his shirts, which was bunched around my waist and his hands were settled on the curves of my ass.

"You're spoiling me," he said.

"Trying to. Open your mouth."

He opened his mouth, and I fed him a piece of bacon. After he chewed and swallowed, he said, "We've got a good thing going, don't we?"

I covered his lips with mine. "Mmm, greasy. Yes, we've got a good thing going."

"I woke up next to you this morning, and I—"

"I know what you did. I was there," I said, cheeks flushing.

He grinned, grabbed my ass, and scooted me even closer so I was pressed against his fly. I ground against him for good measure.

"And then I got to watch you walking around the kitchen in my shirt and your thong while you made biscuits and gravy from scratch."

"You can thank Crow for that recipe," I said.

"The food was good, but I was happier about the view."

"Yeah, I bet you were."

"There was just one thing I didn't like," he said.

I frowned. "What? Was the gravy too spicy? Next time, I'll—"

"Not about the food."

"Then what?"

"I didn't see my name inked on you anywhere."

"Oh," I said quietly. "You want your name inked on me?"

"Very much."

My fingers curled into the hair at his nape. "I'd like that too."

"Yeah?"

I nodded. "I might've been thinking about a tattoo. I sort of have an idea."

"You gonna tell me about it?"

"No. I want it to be a surprise."

"I can be surprised," he said with a slight smile.

"Yeah?" I asked. I leaned back far enough so that I could pull my shirt off and toss it aside.

He slid his hands underneath my ass even more so that he hoisted me up, putting my nipples within reach of his lips. He sucked one into his mouth and my head bent back with pleasure.

"God," I moaned.

"Call me Viper."

My hands slid into the hair as I let him bathe my nipple with his lips.

He removed one of his hands from underneath me so that he could slip it into my panties. His finger stroked me.

My nipple popped from his mouth. "So fucking wet. How are you always so wet?"

"It's your fault." I gasped as he glided his finger deeper, but not deep enough.

I climbed off his lap and slithered my panties down and kicked them off. "I need your dick. Like right fucking now."

He chuckled and went for his belt buckle.

Viper wasn't moving fast enough, so my fingers went to his button and fly.

"Easy," he said with a laugh. He pulled his pants down, including his boxers. I straddled him again, grasping his erection in my hand and guided him into my body.

I sank down on top of him, groaning in pleasure from the sensation of him filling me completely.

"God, I love this," I moaned.

He grasped my hips and urged me to ride him. My skin flushed with heat and our eyes were locked on one another.

I was never going to get enough of him.

"Kiss me," he commanded.

I leaned forward and covered his mouth with mine. Our tongues met and danced, desire shooting through me.

Sex with Viper was sweaty, needy, necessary. It grounded me, made me feel connected to my body and his. To the moment.

Nothing else mattered—the world fell away.

The smell of his skin, the rough pads of his fingers on my body, the intoxicating delirium that came from feeling completely safe and secure.

Viper allowed me to be vulnerable, to demand what I wanted.

And right now, it was in his power to give it to me.

So I took my pleasure, wringing every drop of it from his lips and body.

I collapsed against him, pressing my forehead to his shoulder while I gulped air into my lungs.

"It can't be this easy, can it?" I asked, lifting my head to stare into his dark brown eyes.

"What can't be this easy? Sex?"

"Living together," I said with a wry smile. "I've hardly wanted to murder you at all."

He grinned. "Glad to hear it."

"And?"

"And what?"

"And you like living with me too."

"I already told you that, didn't I?"

"Tell me again."

"I don't like living with you."

"But you just said—"

"I *love* living with you."

"It's because I parade around in my underwear and cook you bacon and then have sex with you before you've even finished your coffee, isn't it?"

"Yeah, those are all really good things, but there's more to it than that."

"What else, then?"

He thought for a moment, his brow furrowed. "You make a house a home."

My smile softened. "Oh."

"It doesn't sound romantic, I get that—"

I quickly covered his mouth with my hand. "It's perfect." I removed my palm and kissed his lips. "Let's go to Three Kings and get it done."

⁓

"You sure your ribs are up for it?" I asked, taking the helmet from Viper's hand.

"Pain is temporary. I'll be fine."

"Don't say I didn't warn you," I said as I snapped the buckle on my helmet and climbed on the back of his bike.

I gingerly wrapped my arms around him.

"You're gonna fly off. Tighter, babe. You won't break me."

I was giddy with excitement as we zoomed down the road. I didn't have any tattoos—I hadn't really thought of getting one until Viper. Now, I couldn't wait for some ink.

Hello, bad-girl phase.

Viper pulled into the Three Kings parking lot and cut the engine. He kicked the stand out, and I got off before he leaned the bike over and then got off as well. I removed the helmet and shook out my hair.

"You're gonna look so sexy with my name on you," he said as we stood next to his motorcycle. He cradled my face in his hands and bent down to kiss me.

His lips brushed mine.

I was closing my eyes to sink into his kiss when I heard the shot.

Viper jerked away from me, and his face contorted in pain.

"*Viper!*" I cried. I dropped the helmet on the ground and looked over my left shoulder in the direction of the sound, attempting to find the source of the threat.

A man across the street had his pistol aimed at Viper.

I jumped in front of Viper in an attempt to shield him.

Another shot rang out and the skin on my left arm burned. I cried out in pain.

Viper wrapped his gigantic arms around me and pulled us to the ground and then rolled on top of me, his body covering mine. We were concealed behind the motorcycle when I heard the front door to Three Kings burst open. Roman appeared in the doorway with a pistol in hand.

Viper pointed in the direction of the shots and yelled, "There!"

Roman raised his weapon and fired in the direction of the gunman. "Fuck, he's gone!"

He lowered his arm and jogged toward us. He looked down at us as he approached. "You two okay?"

"Sutton's been shot. Call an ambulance!"

Chapter 52

"Oh my God," I growled. "I'm fine. It was superficial. The bullet went in and out. I'm doped up on painkillers and they plied me full of antibiotics. *I'm fine.*"

Viper glared at me from his spot in the chair next to the hospital bed. He had a bandage around his midsection. He'd been shot along his side—but it was nothing more than a graze. I'd been hit in the left arm near my tricep. We'd both gotten extremely lucky, with no serious debilitating injuries.

Vance Raider, the club attorney, had met us at the hospital. All police questions had been answered to their satisfaction. We were free to leave the hospital as soon as Viper let me off the bed.

"You're fine?" he repeated.

"Yes. I'm fine, and also very pissed off. I wanted to get a tattoo today."

He glared at me. "We need to have a few words…"

"You're not seriously about to lecture me for trying to protect you, are you?"

"Damn fucking right I am," he snapped. "Both of those bullets were meant for me!"

"How do you know?" I yelled back.

He paused, and then said, "Because I recognized the shooter."

His admission had me clamping my mouth shut for a moment. "So...who was he?"

Viper rubbed the back of his neck. "I told you about my time in prison..."

I nodded.

"What I didn't tell you is that on my first day in, someone tried to put me in my place by attacking me in the cafeteria. He didn't realize I could handle myself, and when he started losing the fight, he pulled a shank. I beat the living shit out of him. Put him in the infirmary for three weeks. And because he attacked me with a weapon, he did time in solitary and they added to his sentence." He swallowed. "They moved him out of C block to an isolation unit to keep us separated, but I kept my head on a swivel for the rest of my time in there. I knew it wasn't over, but I couldn't do anything. What was I supposed to do? Anything I did on the inside was going to extend my sentence, or worse, get me life in the can. He isn't supposed to be out, especially after getting his sentence extended. How the fuck does a guy like that get parole?"

He leaned forward and placed his elbows on his knees. "You were shot because of me, Sutton. I could have lost you. You could have—"

"Viper, hey, it's okay," I whispered, holding out my hand toward him.

He rose from the chair and came to me.

Viper grasped the back of my neck. "You didn't even hesitate. You dove in front of me."

"You didn't hesitate either. You pulled me to the ground and protected me, even after you'd been shot."

"Sutton, you don't take a bullet for—"

"*Viper*—"

"Sutton, no. Let me get this out. You don't take a bullet for me. I take one for *you*. That's how this works."

"No, that's not how this works." I wrenched away from his grip and peered up at him. "My life isn't more important than yours."

"Don't you get it? If you die, I've got nothing. If you die, everything won't just go back to the way it was before you—it'll be worse. My entire life will change. You opened all this shit up inside me and I can't fucking lose you."

Tears gathered in my eyes. "And I'm supposed to lose you? Why is this an either-or situation?"

"Because when bullets start flying, that's just how it is."

"We're not going to agree on this. I love you as much as you love me, and if I want to use my body to shield you from bullets, I will."

"What if you're pregnant?"

I blinked. "But I'm not pregnant."

"Okay, but one day you will be."

"But I'm not."

"*Sutton*," he growled.

"*Viper*," I growled back.

We glared at each other.

"One day you're gonna be pregnant," he tried again.

"But—"

"You're not now, yeah, I know. But when you are, you can't throw yourself in front of me if there's danger. I have to protect you—protect you both when the time comes."

"But that's in the future. Way, way in the future."

"Promise me."

"Promise you what?"

"That when you're pregnant, you won't do anything stupid like trying to be my body armor."

"I won't," I said quietly. "Until that time comes, though…"

He tilted my head back and kissed me.

"You're wrong, though."

"About what?" I asked breathlessly.

"It's not possible for you to love me more than I love you."

My hand moved up his chest to settle on his heart. "Tell you what. Why don't we spend the rest of our lives trying to prove who loves the other more?"

He smiled slightly. "I can live with that."

"Can I get out of here now, or what?"

∼

After I'd signed a few forms, Viper and I headed toward the elevators.

"Wait," I said.

"What? You leave something in the room?"

"No. How are we getting home? You rode in the ambulance with me—and I couldn't ride your motorcycle even if it was here."

"I've got it handled," he said.

I frowned at him in confusion, but he ignored me and pushed the elevator button.

When we got down to the lobby and went outside, it was obvious what he meant.

Duke and Willa were sitting in her car, waiting for us.

"Oh my God," Willa said as she jumped out of the vehicle.

"I'm fine," I assured her.

Duke climbed out of the driver's side and came over to us.

"Thanks for coming," Viper said as he shook Duke's hand.

"Of course. We dropped Crow off at Three Kings to get your bike."

Viper nodded and opened the back door and gestured for me to get in. He closed the door and then went around to the other side.

The drive was silent, but every now and again Willa turned around to look at me.

I glanced out the window, my painkiller-addled brain trying to process what had happened.

It seemed like every time I finally felt comfortable taking a deep breath, life tackled me, knocking the wind from my lungs.

I frowned in confusion when I saw we were driving the opposite direction of our house.

"Where are you going?" I asked Duke. "Home is the other way."

Duke looked in the rearview mirror, meeting my gaze, but then Viper's.

It was Viper who answered. "We're staying at the clubhouse."

"Damn it, Viper. I just got sprung from the clubhouse. I don't want to live in the dude fortress again."

Willa snorted out a laugh.

"Don't have a choice," Viper said. "Not until all this shit is sorted."

"Any idea when that might be?" I demanded.

"No."

With a sigh of frustration, I leaned my head back and closed my eyes.

"What happened?" Willa ventured to ask.

"Willa," Duke warned.

"We were both shot," Viper said.

"Yeah, I got that much. You're not going to tell me, are you?" Willa asked.

Viper didn't reply for a moment and then he said, "I made an enemy in prison. He got out, and it looks like he's got his heart set on vengeance."

"Oh." Willa turned back around.

"Fucker shot my woman," Viper stated. "He's a dead man."

I reached over and grabbed Viper's hand, linking my fingers with his.

He glanced at me, and I gave him a cheeky grin.

"What?" he asked, pitching his voice softer.

"I kind of like the violent side of you. Your protective streak is making me all gooey inside."

Viper's crack of laughter echoed in the car. "You are batshit crazy, woman."

"I'm *perfect* for you."

"Guys," Duke said. "You know we're still here, right?"

"Be quiet," Willa said to him. "They were just getting to the good stuff."

Chapter 53

"Well, if you aren't the most badass woman I've ever met," Smoke said the moment I stepped into the clubhouse.

I blinked, not having expected to see the South Dakota boys. Crow and Acid were standing in the kitchen drinking beer.

"Want one?" Acid asked Viper.

Viper nodded.

"Can I get one, too?" I asked.

"None for you," Viper said.

I raised my brows. "Excuse me? I took a bullet for you and you're denying me a beer?"

The South Dakota boys burst into laughter, but Viper's jaw clenched.

"Too soon to joke about this?" I asked cheekily.

"Uh-oh. Viper's gonna blow a gasket," Raze said.

"It's not like this is the first time you've been shot," Smoke said to Viper.

"It's not?" I demanded. "I'd like the story, please."

"You're on painkillers and I actually give a damn about your liver. So, no beer for you."

"It's beer. It's basically water," I said. "And why are you allowed to drink?"

"Because I'm not on any painkillers," he explained.

"You're on antibiotics. You're not supposed to drink on those either. Besides, you and I have a rule, remember?" I asked.

"Rule? What rule?" Acid queried as he took a sip of his beer.

My cheeks flamed when I suddenly remembered that we weren't alone. "If I can't, he can't."

Viper handed the bottle of beer back to Crow.

"Aww, aren't you guys sweet," Bones quipped.

"Why are you all here?" I demanded.

"We live here," Smoke pointed out.

"Yeah, I get that," I said. "But I meant *here*, in the living room, having a beer. Almost like you were waiting for us."

"We *were* waiting for you," Raze said.

"Sit down, Sutton," Viper commanded.

"Will you stop ordering me around?" I snapped.

"Sit down before you fall over—you're swaying," he said.

With a disgruntled look, I finally plopped my ass in a recliner.

"Are you thrown by this at all? You've been through a lot the last few weeks…" Smoke inquired, studying me like I was an animal in a zoo.

"Not yet," I said. "I'm wondering if I'll feel it later. You know, like jet lag."

Smoke grinned. "I like you."

"I know." I smiled back. "Shit-fuck of a day though. I

was supposed to get a tattoo. And that was shot to shit. Pun intended."

"Sutton," Viper snapped.

"I have to crack jokes, so I don't crack up, okay?" I said to him.

"Come on, brother. Let's go out back," Raze said to Viper.

"You can punch a tree or something. You know, to make yourself feel better," Bones added.

The three of them, along with Kelp and Acid, headed outside. Crow moved to the spot on the couch next to Smoke and kicked a foot up.

"So, what happens now? God, I'd kill for a drink," I muttered.

"What happens now?" Smoke repeated, stroking his chin. "Damn fine question. He called Prez already."

"Oh?" I asked.

Smoke nodded. "Yeah. Had to let him know about the situation. Viper will get this shit sorted."

"But where is the guy? It's not like there's a trail that'll lead right to him," I pointed out.

"Let Viper handle that. Don't worry about a thing," Smoke said.

"Worried? Who's worried?" I asked.

"You look a little worried," Crow said.

"I'm worried that Viper is going to do something insane."

"So, what if he does?" Smoke asked. "This can't go on. He's got to end it."

I swallowed. "So, you know then…about who shot us?"

They both nodded.

I rubbed my third eye. "I think I need to lie down," I said, but I made no move to get up. "The stairs seem so far away."

Crow grabbed the blanket on the back of the couch, got up, and draped it over me. "How about some tea?"

"You'd make me tea?" I asked in surprise.

"That's what friends do, right?" he asked with a smile.

"Right." I paused. "So, you guys know what happened…and Colt knows what happened. And we told Willa and Duke what happened because they picked us up from the hospital. But does that mean everyone else knows?"

"Definitely," Smoke said.

"That includes the Old Ladies, I'm guessing."

"Yep." Smoke nodded.

"Great," I muttered.

I didn't want them descending upon me, checking in on me like we were doing with Darcy. I didn't want to talk about it or explain anything. I just wanted to sit in silence with what happened and try and move past it. Not everything had to be dissected or torn apart.

"You know what?" I asked, flinging the blanket off me. "Don't worry about the tea. I'm going upstairs. Thanks for the offer, Crow."

I was suddenly so tired I didn't think I'd have the energy to climb the stairs, but somehow, I made it. I closed the door behind me and immediately dropped my purse on the floor and sat on the edge of the bed to unlace my boots.

Next came the jeans, and then I crawled beneath the covers.

It was easy to banter and joke in front of everyone, but now, in the quiet of the room, I finally let my guard down.

I was coming to terms with what could've happened.

Viper could've died.

I could've died.

But I didn't have any regrets about my actions. To protect Viper, I'd do it again.

I drifted off to sleep in a haze of painkillers and acceptance. I'd done the right thing.

I'd taken a bullet for the man I loved.

∽

"Sutton," Viper whispered.

"Hmm."

"Sutton, move over. You're in the middle of the bed."

"Get your own bed," I slurred.

"This *is* my bed."

With a bitter curse, I scooted over and tried to get comfortable again. "What time is it?"

"A little after one."

"In the morning?" I asked.

"Yeah."

"I took an eight-hour nap. Damn it. Now I'm awake and my arm hurts."

"Need some painkillers?"

"Yeah. We didn't get our prescriptions though," I said. "We were supposed to do that."

"I had a prospect grab them. Hold on, lamp is coming on."

I shielded my eyes but could still see the golden light spreading through my fingers. I slowly lowered my hand to allow my eyes to adjust to the light. Viper was still fully dressed, and he stood next to the bed. He riffled through a white prescription bag. "Nope, that's mine." He dug around in the other. "This is yours."

"We have matching antibiotics and painkillers. How cute are we?" I quipped.

He didn't smile at my jest.

The couple that gets shot together stays together.

I swallowed that joke, knowing he wouldn't find it funny.

Viper didn't seem to have a sense of humor about me getting shot.

He grabbed a water bottle from the side table and handed me a couple of pills. I downed the painkillers, hoping they worked their magic quickly.

"So, what did I miss?" I asked.

"A lot," he said. He pulled his holster and pistol from his waistband and then set them on the nightstand, and then sat on the edge of the bed. "I talked with the South Dakota boys for a long time. We came up with a plan."

"A plan? Am I allowed to know this plan? Or are you going to have sex with me to distract me from asking questions?

"Can you for just one second be serious?" he demanded as he set his boot aside.

"Can I be serious? Fuck no, I can't be serious. We almost died today. Fuck being serious. It's called gallows humor. You've heard of it? It's my coping mechanism. Did you punch a tree like Raze suggested?"

"Do you actually want to know the plan, or are you going to continue with the snark?"

"Can't I do both?"

Viper's mouth flickered.

"Ah-ha! That's your tell," I said, leaning over and pressing the corner of his mouth with a finger. "Come on pookie, give me a lip curl."

He turned his head and kissed my finger.

I sighed. "Damn, don't be sweet to me. I might finally break down in tears if you're sweet to me."

"Well, we wouldn't want that now, would we?"

"You couldn't handle my tears."

"Try me," he said.

"No thanks. Continue, please."

"I reached out to a guy I met in prison. He's going to ask around about Lenny and see if we can get a lock on his location."

"Lenny?"

"Lenny the Mooch. He has a bad habit of borrowing money from new inmates who don't know him. Later, when they ask for it back, he shanks them."

"Sounds like a nice guy…"

"You saw what he tried. Look, we obviously know his plan. He wants to take me out. He won't leave town until it's done. I just have to make sure I get to him before he gets to me."

I sighed and leaned my woozy head against his shoulder. "And to think my biggest concern was the cartel war…"

"I won't be hunting him alone, Sutton. My boys will go with me."

"So, you'll have them watch your back?"

"Yeah."

I nodded. "Okay. I can deal with that."

"You can?" he asked, quirking an eyebrow.

"I can. The sooner you take care of this, the sooner we can get back to living happily ever after."

"We're living happily ever after?"

"Yeah, we are." I grasped his shirt and tugged him toward me. "I'm basically Cinderella. Only instead of a tux, my Prince Charming wears leather and kills people."

He threaded a hand through my hair and tugged my head back. "You want charming? I can be charming."

I slid my hand across his fly. "I'll be the judge of that."

Chapter 54

I woke up alone.

Viper's side of the bed was cold, and I knew that meant he'd been gone for a while. This was nothing new. Even living together for just a few weeks, I'd grown accustomed to his random hours of sleeping. He'd wake up in the middle of the night and not come to bed until dawn.

My body was sore and achy, my wound nothing more than a dull annoyance. As far as gunshots went, I'd been lucky.

I went into the bathroom and splashed some water on my face and did my business. By the time I threw on yoga pants and flip-flops, I felt semi-awake.

I pulled my hair into a messy bun and headed down the stairs.

All the Old Ladies were hanging out in the kitchen and living room—even Darcy. She'd styled her hair and put on makeup, but more than that, I was surprised to find that she was even here.

"Hey, doll," Mia greeted.

"What time is it?" I asked. My mouth was dry, and I was in desperate need of water.

"A little after eleven," Willa said.

"How long have you all been here?" I inquired.

"Few hours," Brooklyn admitted.

"Oh." I ran a hand across my face.

"I have to get to the clinic soon," Doc announced, "but I wanted to wait until you were awake."

"I'm guessing you all know then?" I looked at Willa in accusation.

She held her hands up in supplication. "It wasn't me. I swear."

"I heard from Colt," Mia said.

Joni grinned. "I heard from Zip."

"Rach texted me," Darcy admitted.

"Allison told me," Rach said.

Allison nodded. "Torque told me."

I looked at Brooklyn and then Doc. "Boxer and Slash told you?"

They both nodded.

"Sit," Rach said.

"I need water…and coffee."

"I'll get it," Rach said.

"Where are the kids?" I asked. "It's entirely too quiet in here."

"It's why you slept late," Rach said with a smile. "Kids are all over the place, but none of them are here."

Rach brought me a glass of water and a cup of coffee that had been heavily creamed and sugared.

"Thanks," I said, taking them both from her. "Has anyone seen Viper?"

"He left about an hour ago with Raze and Smoke," Mia said.

"Hmm." I took a few gulps of water.

"How's the arm feeling?" Doc asked.

"Okay, actually. It's a discomfort more than an actual pain."

"That's good," Doc said. "Let me know if you need me to take a look at it, okay?"

"I will."

"Well, I need to get out of here. Glad you're okay, Sutton." Doc grabbed her purse and left the clubhouse.

"You hungry?" Brooklyn asked. "I made muffins."

"What kind?"

"Blueberry, lemon poppyseed, and cranberry." She beamed.

"And I'm guessing they're not from a mix, right? You made them from scratch?"

"Yep. And they were made in the middle of the night, much to Slash's consternation." She chuckled. "So how about it?"

I nodded. "Lemon poppyseed, please. I need to run upstairs and grab my antibiotics."

"Where are they?" Rach asked. "I'll get them for you, so you don't have to get up."

"Angel," I murmured. "Nightstand. Viper has a bottle too, so make sure you read the label, please."

"Got it," she said and headed for the stairs.

Darcy was looking into her cup of coffee. I wondered if she was even listening to our conversation.

"Darcy?" I asked.

She lifted her head. Her eyes were dull, but she met my gaze.

"Thanks for coming," I said.

"Why wouldn't I come?" she asked.

I shrugged, and then winced when it tugged on my skin as my arm moved. "I just figured…with all your stuff going on…"

And the words we'd exchanged…

"This is how we pull through," she said. "By being there for each other."

I heard what she said, but it didn't ring sincere. She was trying, though.

Rach returned with my antibiotics, and Brooklyn handed me a warm muffin.

"I have news," Mia announced.

"You're pregnant again?" Allison asked.

Mia shook her head. "Nope. That's on hold. I came to my senses for now."

"Then what's the news?" Rach asked.

"I'm selling Shelly's."

Silence descended upon the room.

"But, why?" I finally asked. I opened the bottle of antibiotics and fished around for a pill.

"I decided I wanted a fresh start. So, I'm selling the building and opening a new bar."

Brooklyn suddenly burst into tears.

"What's wrong?" Willa asked.

"Everything's changing," Brooklyn said, swiping at her eyes. "And I don't want it to."

"It's just a bar," Mia said with a smile as she went to sit by Brooklyn. "It's going to be okay."

"But I never got to really enjoy it because I'm pregnant!" Brooklyn wailed. "And now you're selling it!"

I couldn't help it. A giggle started up my throat and escaped my mouth. Suddenly, I was laughing so hard I was bent over in half.

Brooklyn looked at me in horror and then suddenly started to laugh with me. Soon, the room was filled with laughter.

"Oh, man." I wiped the tears away from my face. "I needed that so much."

"Me too," Darcy admitted with a soft smile.

"You'll be able to drink at the new bar," Mia said.

"What kind of bar will it be?" Joni asked. "Something similar to Shelly's?"

"I don't know," Mia admitted.

"Well, it's official. I'll have to find a new job. Damn," I muttered. "I really liked working for you."

"Then work for me in the new place," Mia said with a smile. "I still think you'd make a great bar manager."

"Done and done," I said eagerly.

"See? Not all change is bad," Mia said.

A cell phone rang. It was Darcy's.

She put the phone to her ear. "Hello? Yes." She paused. "He did *what*? Yeah, okay. I'll be right there." Darcy hung up her phone and shoved it back into her purse. She grabbed it and then hopped off the stool. "Sorry, I can't stay. That was the soccer camp. Cam just got into a fight. I have to pick him up."

"Oh damn," Mia said softy.

Darcy nodded as she clenched her jaw. "See you guys later."

Once she was gone, I looked at Rach. "How's she doing? Really?"

Rach shrugged. "Hanging in there. One day at a time, I guess."

I waited for her to say more, but I quickly realized she wouldn't. She was keeping my confidence. I didn't know if that was good or bad.

"So, Rach," Joni said.

"So, Joni," Rach parroted.

"What's going on with you and Raze?" Joni asked.

Rach's eyes widened. "What? Nothing's going on."

"No?" Mia teased. "I noticed you guys are getting friendly."

"Because we're friends. Nothing more," Rach said.

"I'm not sure I believe you," Allison teased.

"Believe what you want," Rach said, her cheeks suddenly pink.

I smiled to myself.

Oh, yeah. There's definitely something there.

∽

Three days later, Viper brushed his lips across my bare shoulder, causing me to stir.

"Sutton," he whispered.

"Hmm?"

"I've got to go."

"Go? Go where?"

"I think you know…"

I was suddenly wide awake. My eyes flipped open, but I couldn't see anything.

"Cover your eyes," he said right before he flipped on the lamp.

I squinted. He was already dressed.

"You'll be careful, right?" I asked quietly.

"Yeah."

He leaned down to kiss me. But when he tried to move away, I grabbed his lapels and deepened the moment. He grasped the back of my head and angled his mouth over mine, thrusting his tongue between my lips.

"I can't get caught up in you," he growled. "Even though I want to."

"I'll be here when you get back," I whispered, pecking his lips one final time.

He let me go, and I sank back down onto the bed.

Viper stroked a hand down my bare spine before standing up and heading for the door.

"Love you, Sutton," he said gruffly.

"I love you too."

The door closed with a quiet snick. It wasn't until I heard the motorcycle engines die off that I decided I wouldn't be going back to bed. I'd wait up until dawn for him to come home if I had to.

With a sigh, I heaved myself out of bed. I threw on a pair of leggings and one of Viper's T-shirts. I brought it to my nose and inhaled, wishing he was still with me.

The clubhouse was silent. There hadn't been a party in several weeks, and I wondered when things would get back to normal. It seemed like everyone was laying low, staying close to home even though there had been no rumblings from the cartel.

Why? Why haven't there been any rumblings? How are we all just free to live our lives without concern about payback?

I went out into the backyard to get some fresh air and saw the shed door open where the brothers held church.

It was the middle of the night and I doubted they were holding church now, so what were they doing?

The door was propped open, and I saw Crow, Acid, Kelp, and Smoke sitting around the table with bottles of liquor and a pack of cards.

"Sutton," Crow said when he saw me standing in the doorway.

"Sorry. Viper just—"

"We know," Kelp said.

"I get the feeling I'm not supposed to know where he went, or with who," I said.

"You're not," Smoke said. "You can't get tripped up answering questions if you don't know what's going on."

I nodded. "Makes sense."

"You know how to play poker?" Acid asked.

"No."

"Want to learn?" Acid took a bottle of liquor and drank from it.

"Depends," I said, stepping into the shed. "You sharing that moonshine?"

Acid handed me the bottle and I took a swig.

"Viper's not going to flatten me, is he? For giving you booze?" Acid asked.

"I haven't had painkillers in the last day or so," I assured him. "My liver is safe."

"Then sit down," Kelp said. "And we'll teach you how to play poker."

There was an empty chair next to Crow.

Smoke gathered the cards and began to shuffle.

"You want to talk about anything?" Crow asked.

I shook my head. "I want to learn how to play poker. And drink."

Acid smiled and slid the bottle closer to me. "We can make that happen."

I glanced at Kelp. "What's with your name?"

"Excuse me?" Kelp asked.

"Your road name. Crow, Acid, Smoke…pretty self-explanatory. But Kelp? You're named *seaweed*."

"Yeah," Kelp drawled. "Seaweed."

"What is that? You love sushi?"

I saw Crow out of the corner of my eye shake his head and gesture to his throat in the classic sign of *shut up*.

Kelp leaned back in his chair and pinned me with a look. "You really want to know how I got my name?"

Smoke dealt the cards.

"I really do," I said.

"Okay, I'll tell you, but only if you can keep a secret," Kelp said.

"I can keep a secret. I'm listening."

"A long time ago someone tried to hurt my family. I

took him out to the beach and drowned him in the shallow water. When they found his body a few days later, it was covered in kelp, and the nickname stuck."

I blinked. And then I glanced at Crow. He shrugged.

"Right." I cleared my throat and reached for my cards. "Are we playing poker, or what?"

Chapter 55

"Good thing we're not playing for real money," Smoke said. "You slaughtered us."

"Beginner's luck," I assured him. "But I definitely want a rematch. Where we play for real money."

"Name the time and place," Acid said.

"My house, next week," I said. "I'll provide the snacks. You guys bring your wallets and the liquor."

"You may be an Old Lady," Crow said. "But in a way you're also one of the guys."

"Anybody got the time?" I asked.

Kelp pulled out his cell phone. "A little after five."

Adrenaline and the liquor were keeping me going. I wouldn't sleep until I knew Viper was back safe.

"Thanks for letting me crash your poker game." I stood up.

"You going to try and get some sleep?" Crow asked.

I shook my head. "I'll be wandering around the clubhouse like a ghost. See you guys later."

Cool air hit me in the face the moment I stepped into

the clubhouse. I grabbed a glass of water and then took it out onto the front porch. The prospects waved to me in greeting, and I waved back as I sat on the steps.

The early morning air was muggy and thick. I swatted at my ear to dispel a hungry mosquito.

I was just finishing my glass of water when I heard the rumble of motorcycle engines. I hastily set my glass aside and stood up, waiting for the prospects to open the gates.

Viper drove through first, followed by Bones and Raze.

I was off the porch before Viper had even cut the engine. I ran to him. He swung a leg over his bike, barely having time to get his bearings before I launched myself at him.

He caught me, holding my butt with his large hands as I wrapped my legs around him.

"You're back," I whispered.

"Yeah."

"In one piece." I peppered his face with kisses and then finally planted my lips on his.

"Told you I'd come back," he said gruffly when I pulled away.

"You told me nothing," I protested.

"For your own safety."

"Right." I cradled his face in my hands and skimmed my thumbs along the apples of his cheeks. "So?"

"It's done. We're safe. No more looking behind us."

"We're safe." I let out a sigh.

He walked with me still in his arms toward the clubhouse. I had no idea where Raze or Bones went, and at the moment I didn't care.

All my focus was on Viper.

His warm skin.

His smile.

His promise.

"Take me home, Viper."

He captured my lips in a ravenous kiss. "I'm taking you to bed first."

Epilogue

A week later

VIPER

"It's official. I finally heard from Sanchez, and he's aware that working with him is out of the question from this point forward," Colt said.

Zip chimed in, "So we're good then? I mean, all this shit is settled?"

"Pretty much. After the raid, I told the Feds it wasn't going to go over very well with Sanchez, but they were pretty fucking clear that we could no longer do business with an Argentinian drug lord. Told me I'd hear from Sanchez just to button things up, but that we're done being mules for him."

"So, we're out of the drug game?" Raze asked.

Colt nodded. "Let's go over this again so everyone is on

the same page. It's critical you guys know where we stand. We got a pass from the Feds for the raid on the cartel safe house, but they're done cleaning up our shit. They're taking credit for the raid, so the cartel doesn't know it was us. That will prevent any blowback onto the club. The Feds also made it clear they've been watching us since we rescued the girls from the furniture truck, and that the only reason we aren't already in prison is they know who it was we killed. Every single thing we've done since then—all of it—is on file. If we get in hot with the cartel from here on out, it's for defensive purposes only. Anything on the offense, or to make money, and we all go to prison for the rest of our lives."

"Fuck that," Zip said.

"Agreed," Boxer added. "We've lost too many brothers already. Don't need any more of us taken out—and I'd rather die a free man than locked up behind bars. They really have all of it?"

"Everything. How do you think they got to the cartel safe house right after we did? I don't know about you, but I almost shit my pants when I heard *FBI*," Colt said.

Everyone in the room laughed, but the mood was tense.

"Yeah, that sucked," Boxer said. "I could barely believe it when it happened. Okay, so how do we know they're going to keep all this under wraps? We can't have other clubs thinking we struck a deal with the Feds. We're fucking outlaws. If anyone thinks we're working with the Feds, we're fucked."

Colt paused and said, "But we didn't make a deal, and we're not working with the Feds. They told us how it was going down and we didn't provide anything in return. It's different. Even if word got out, what would people say? We killed a bunch of human traffickers and rescued women and children, and then attacked the cartel directly? We didn't snitch. We didn't give them shit. They were watching us, and when shit hit the fan they gave us a pass, that's all. And at this point, we don't have much of a choice but to do what they say. The Feds made it clear they have bigger fish to fry, and so long as we stay out of cartel business, we are no longer big fish. At least not to them."

The room went quiet.

"What about Viper's thing?" Raze asked.

"Like I said, we stopped being big fish after we raided the cartel safe house and they put us on notice. When Viper and Sutton got shot, I knew they weren't keeping tabs on us anymore. It was radio silence. They didn't even reach out to question the club about it. Fact is, the shit is hitting the fan with the cartel in this country, and the Feds don't have the resources to stop petty beef between former inmates, even if that beef ends in murder. So, Viper is good. That thing is over, and not to be discussed again. So far as working with Sanchez, we'll vote, just to make it official," Colt said. "All those in favor of getting out of the drug business, say aye."

It was unanimous.

"It's settled then. We're no longer drug mules for Mateo Sanchez," Colt said.

We all smacked the table to signal our support.

"So, what are we doing from here on out?" Bones asked.

"That's my next order of business," Colt said. "We've made a shitload of money over the years from our enterprises. We have options now, and I've spoken with Vance. It's time to go legit."

"Legit? How?" Acid asked.

"Clubs, bars, real estate. We'll diversify. Look, Waco's a fucking mess. It's time for the club to own that we're part of that. But it ends here and now." Colt's brow furrowed. "Moving forward, we're going to have clean books and make sure our women and children are safe. No more looking over our shoulder for danger. The surprise we had with the Feds was the way out we didn't know we needed. It's going to be much better for everyone if the club is legit."

"Works for me," I said.

"Yeah, same," Zip said.

"All those in favor of going legit, say aye," Colt said.

The vote was unanimous once again.

It felt good belonging to a brotherhood—a real brotherhood. Kelp, Bones, Smoke, Raze and I had once had a club. But it hadn't been anything like this.

Colt ran his club with transparency, and in a short period of time I had come to respect him.

It was an honor to call these men my brothers.

Colt banged the gavel. "We're done. Now let's get out there and celebrate Viper making Sutton his Old Lady."

Hoots and hollers erupted, and they smacked the table in a round of support.

We all stood and made our way out of the shed. The sun was shining high in the sky, the air was blistering hot, but I barely noticed.

All I saw was the gorgeous, sassy brunette wearing a pink sundress and holding out her left forearm to show off her new tattoo to Willa.

She'd gotten the club's logo with a snake coming out of the skull's mouth with my name below it. It was bold. And big. No one could ever miss it.

As if Sutton knew I was thinking about her, she looked at me. Her eyes met mine and she winked before turning her attention back to Willa.

"You look happy, brother," Raze said, coming up next to me and sipping on his beer.

"I am," I admitted.

"Feel weird?"

"A little bit."

He chuckled and then slapped my shoulder. "Glad you're happy, man. The last few years were rough on you. She's a good woman. I approve."

"And if you didn't?" I glanced at him.

He shrugged. "Wouldn't matter. Your choice. But I like her—we all like her—and we're happy for you both."

I didn't have to say it but Raze knew what I was thinking. We were brothers. They hadn't abandoned me, even when I was behind bars. They'd visited. They'd checked in and provided me funds so I could stay comfortable. Then they had made a place for me here when I got out.

"What about you?" I asked.

"What about me?" he inquired.

"You and Rach. What's happening there?"

His gaze trekked across the backyard to stare at the brunette. "We're friends. She doesn't want more."

"You asked her yet?"

Raze paused and took another sip of his beer. "Yeah. I asked. Gotta respect her wishes, you know?"

"Yeah, I know." It was my turn to pause before I said, "She's got a kid."

"Yeah."

"Didn't take you for wanting to play the role of dad."

"Kids are okay." Raze quirked a brow. "What about you?"

"What about me?"

"You want kids?"

"The idea is growing on me," I admitted.

"You're thinking about knocking Sutton up, aren't you?"

"No," I lied.

I didn't tell him that we'd had a close call already. That Sutton had taken a pregnancy test, but it had come back negative. And I definitely didn't tell him that ever since I'd seen that negative test, it was all I thought about. All I wanted to do was fill her every damn day and night until she was round with my baby.

I hadn't told that to Sutton, either.

"I don't believe you."

"She's twenty-two."

"So what?" Raze asked.

"I want us to have a few more adventures together before we start a family."

"No bigger adventure than kids," Raze said.

"Like you know."

"Come on. I've been around enough kids in the club to know it would be an adventure. You need a beer—and you need to stop eye-fucking your woman," Raze said.

"I'll do no such thing," I said with a wry grin.

There was nothing like sliding into your woman raw, with nothing between you, and then finishing and getting to hold her while you both fell asleep after.

I left Raze and headed toward Sutton. She drew me to her like a magnet. I couldn't help myself, even if it made me look like a whipped asshole.

Then again, all the brothers who had Old Ladies acted the same, so I was in good company.

I slung an arm around Sutton's shoulder and yanked her into my side. "Hey, Willa," I greeted.

"Viper," she said with a large smirk. She turned to Sutton. "Let me know."

"Oh, I'm in. I'll definitely help," she said with a grin.

"Catch you guys later," Willa said as she went to go join Duke and Savage by the grill.

"What are you helping with?" I asked.

"Brooklyn's surprise baby shower," she said, her voice low. "You can't tell anyone."

"My lips are sealed," I promised.

She peered up at me, her eyes shining with happiness. "Know what else is a surprise?"

"What?" I asked.

"I'm not wearing any underwear."

I stilled. "Are you fucking kidding me?"

She shook her head. "Why do you think I wanted to take the truck and not your bike?"

"I thought it was because you wanted to wear a dress."

"Two birds, one stone."

"Not sure I believe you," I murmured. "About no underwear."

"Why don't you cop a feel and find out for yourself?"

She was still pulled against me, my arm flung around her shoulder, but I turned her toward me and slid my hands down her back until they grabbed a handful of her ass.

"Hmm. You're right. No panty lines."

Sutton batted her eyelashes at me. "I wanted to torment you the rest of the night."

I leaned down and gently bit her ear and whispered, "I'll be spanking that ass before I take it."

When I pulled back, her eyes were wide, her cheeks heated.

"Ah, have I finally rendered you speechless?"

She cleared her throat. "Nope."

"Guess I'll have to find another way to keep that mouth occupied."

"You, sir, know just what to say to a girl to get her out of her panties."

"You're not wearing your panties."

Sutton grinned wickedly. "Exactly."

"Let's get out of here."

She shook her head. "Nope. This party is for us. I plan to eat, drink, and be merry."

"And give me the biggest case of blue balls in the history of the world," I groaned.

"You can wait a few hours. It won't kill you."

"Don't be so sure," I muttered.

The next few hours were torture. It was bad enough that I knew Sutton wasn't wearing underwear, but the woman had clearly made it her mission to bring me to my knees.

I was talking with Zip and Boxer, listening with only half an ear, my eyes fixated on her. She was sitting in a chair, nodding at something Mia was saying, but then she looked right at me and rubbed her thighs together and pressed a finger to her mouth.

"Am I right?" Zip asked.

"Sure," I said.

"Dude, you're not even listening to us," Boxer said.

"Can't really blame him," Zip said.

"Hey, Viper, you want another beer?" Boxer asked.

"Sure, yeah, whatever," I said as I left them both standing exactly where they were and marched toward Sutton.

Their booming laughter echoed behind me.

The Old Ladies stopped mid-conversation when I arrived, peering up at me in surprise.

"Can I help you with something, Viper?" Sutton taunted.

Yeah, my hard dick.

"We're leaving," I said.

She raised her brows. "But I'm having fun."

"You'll have more fun with me. Let's go. Unless you want me to carry you over my shoulder."

"Aww, a throwback to when we met?" she teased.

"Is it hot out here?" Joni asked, fanning her face.

"Yes," Rach said, a twinkle in her eye. "But I don't think you can blame it on the weather."

Sutton slowly rose from her seat. "Love you, ladies, but I'm being summoned."

"Yeah, we know what you're being summoned for." Brooklyn snorted. "Enjoy yourselves."

"Oh, we will," Sutton said with a beaming grin.

Whistles and applause followed us as we headed for the clubhouse.

Sutton turned and gave a bow.

"Come on, big boy." She pushed against my lower back. "I've tortured you long enough."

It wasn't until we were in the hallway of the clubhouse that I said, "Your punishment is going to be long, thorough, and it's going to last all night."

"Promises, promises…"

∼

The moment we got home, I turned Sutton so her chest was flush with the closed door.

I dragged a finger slowly down her spine, causing her to shiver.

My hands gathered her dress and bunched it up around her waist, exposing her beautiful, glorious, bare ass.

Smack!

Her soft, tight skin bloomed red from my touch.

She shuddered against the door but didn't make a sound.

So, I smacked the other cheek, making it rosy to match.

My dick was hard as a rock, but I wasn't ready to give in yet.

"Spread your legs," I commanded.

She immediately did as I demanded.

"Ass out."

She popped her ass toward me, giving me a perfect view of her.

I dipped my finger between her wet folds but didn't enter her completely.

Sutton pushed back, trying to take more of me.

I withdrew my finger immediately. "You will do what I say, when I say it. You won't move until I tell you to. Understand?"

She nodded.

"Words, Sutton. Give me the words."

"I understand."

"Keep your ass out, just like that. Hold onto your skirt."

Her hands gripped the fabric, keeping her bared to me.

I lowered myself to my knees, spread her cheeks, and tongued her from behind.

"*Oh, God.*"

"That's right, baby. Just enjoy it."

I feasted on her until she was trembling and my lips and chin were covered with her desire. And still I ate like a man who'd been starved.

I couldn't get enough of her taste, her smell. I wanted to wrap myself in her and never leave.

Only when she began to quiver with her impending release did I stop.

I rose and grasped her arms, spinning her around. Her

cheeks were flushed, and her lower lip was rosy, no doubt from biting it.

"Go to the bedroom," I commanded. "Get naked. Get on the bed, on your stomach. Then wait for me."

She hesitated ever so slightly, searching my face.

I waited.

She took a deep breath and walked to the bedroom.

I gave her a few minutes—and also gave myself some time to pull it together. She was so responsive to my touch, up for anything, anytime, anywhere. The fact was it was hard to control myself around her.

All I wanted to do was fuck her, all the time.

And she never said no. Better, she initiated as much as I did.

How'd I get so fucking lucky?

When I'd relaxed enough and finally felt like I wasn't going to come in my pants, I headed to the bedroom.

Sutton could follow orders when she wanted to.

It was a glorious sight—all that smooth, pale flesh, waiting for my hands and tongue, her long brown hair spilling down her back in a perfect display of sensuality.

She turned her head and watched me.

I undressed slowly, drawing it out for her pleasure, and mine. I was a fan of a quickie as much as the next guy, but there was nothing like watching your woman's eyes dilate with hunger and need.

When I was completely naked, I fisted my cock, my tip glistening with precum. I walked over to the bed.

"Open."

She opened her mouth, and I slid my dick between her lips. She sucked me deep and hard, just the way I liked it. By the time she was making noises, I fucked her mouth for a few more minutes, getting it nice and wet before pulling out.

Sutton made a sound of protest.

"You like sucking my cock, don't you?" I rumbled, intentionally going to that deep register I knew she loved to hear.

She nodded.

"If you're good, I'll let you suck me off later and I'll come in your mouth. And you'll swallow every drop of me, won't you?"

She nodded again.

Over the last few weeks, living together and finally having true privacy, Sutton's inhibitions had lowered, and we'd discovered some things in the bedroom that we both enjoyed.

She loved dirty talk. It was exciting for her, and she loved it when I explained in detail what I was going to do to her. And she liked it when I was rough.

I grabbed a pillow and placed it underneath her, so her ass was angled in the air. Then I went to the nightstand and pulled out a bottle of lube.

She jumped when I touched the spot between her ass cheeks, my finger covered in slick fluid.

"Easy," I whispered. "I'll go slow."

She nodded and then I felt her relax. I played with the tight little hole, letting her get comfortable with me in a place I'd never been.

I slowly worked my finger in up to the first knuckle.

"Okay?" I asked.

"Yes," she whispered.

I pushed in a little deeper and felt her tense.

"You okay?"

"Yeah. Just…takes some getting used to."

She was too in her head, which meant I had to distract her. I gently removed my finger.

"All fours."

When she was in position, I took the pillow and threw it onto the floor.

"Touch yourself," I stated. "I want to hear you moan."

Her fingers slipped between her legs, and she began to stroke herself.

My hand skimmed over her spine, to her hip, and then to her backside. I grabbed the bottle of lube and dribbled it near her tailbone, beneath the small of her back, and then worked it between her ass cheeks. I spread her wide and touched the crown of my shaft to her hole.

She tensed for a moment and then she sank into my touch as she continued to pleasure herself.

Her body took the head of me easily. I worked in slowly, not even an inch at a time. I gritted my teeth at the pleasure I felt. She was so tight, and every time I pressed a little more I felt her relax and ease me into her body.

She was perfect.

"Viper," she moaned as she touched herself.

"That's it, baby. Play with yourself."

She was so wet that I could hear the noises her body was making as she stroked herself faster and faster.

I was halfway in when she gasped, "Viper, I'm coming."

She tensed around me, clenching tight as her release washed over her. She cried out in rapture, and while she was in the middle of her orgasm I couldn't control myself.

"Oh, God," she moaned.

I fucked her ass gently, not wanting to hurt her. It was her first time, and I wanted her pleasure to be the only thing she remembered.

My free hand slipped around her body, and I sifted through her folds to find the swollen flesh still primed for another orgasm.

"Viper, I can't," she gasped.

Venom & Vengeance

"You can."

"I'm too… I feel you everywhere."

"Good. You're stuffed full of me, aren't you, baby."

I pressed her clit, and she bucked her hips. I surged forward, thrusting in her tight body. It felt like it was made for me.

"I need you to come again, Sutton," I growled.

"I don't think I can!"

"You can. I'm not coming until you do."

Her hands clenched as I continued to swirl my fingers around her clit.

"You think you're full now?" I rasped. I slipped two fingers inside her. I thrust in and out of her pussy as I ground into her ass.

"Oh, fuck yes!" she moaned. "Fuck, fuck, fuck yes!"

She clenched around my fingers and writhed against me as she came again.

I couldn't hold back any longer, and I orgasmed with a roar. My fingers slid out of her wet body. I'd pumped so hard my balls were aching. We both collapsed onto the bed, breathing hard.

I was still inside her, my erection raging, refusing to go down.

"Sutton?" I asked.

"Yeah?"

"Are you okay? Was that too much?"

"You're asking me that while you're still inside me?"

I smiled against her back and then gently eased out of her.

A hiss of air escaped her lips.

"Fuck, I hurt you."

"No," she insisted. "Just…tender."

I kissed her shoulder and rolled out of bed. "Stay there."

She nodded and closed her eyes.

I went into the bathroom and cleaned myself up and then I drew her a bath. I lit the candles that she'd bought a few weeks ago. She always used them when she soaked in the tub.

When I went back into the bedroom, she was still in the position I'd left her.

"Sutton?"

"Hmm?"

"You didn't fall asleep—good."

"No." She yawned and hastily covered her mouth. "Almost though."

I took her hand and tugged her off the bed.

"Well, that's new," she said.

"What is?"

"I'm leaking you from a different orifice."

I barked out a laugh and led her into the bathroom.

"What did you do?" she asked with a smile.

"I thought you'd hear it from the bedroom. Bath time." I helped her into the tub so she wouldn't slip.

"Are you joining me?" she asked. She twirled her hair up to the top of her head.

"Try and stop me."

She scooted toward the faucet to give me more room. I climbed in behind her and then gently eased her back, so she rested against my chest.

When the tub was full enough, she leaned forward and turned off the water before settling back against me. "This is nice." She sighed.

"Very."

My hand snaked down her body to rest on her belly.

"Viper? Can I ask you something?"

"Yeah."

She paused before she asked, "Were you upset the pregnancy test was negative?"

"Truth?"

"Yes. The truth."

I took my other hand out of the water and gently rubbed her neck. "I wasn't upset. Disappointed is a better word. And to be honest, I didn't think I'd feel that way."

"Oh."

"It wasn't the same for you, was it?"

"No. I was relieved. But it did…make me wonder, you know?"

"Sure."

She covered my hand with hers. "I must be crazy. We, like, *just* got together. And all I'm thinking about is a little grumpy, handsome baby with your eyes and frown lines."

I chuckled. "Or we could have a bratty baby whose first word is fuck."

"That's a possibility too," she said.

"I told you I'd wait until you were ready. If you need more time, I'll give you that. I'll never say no to you."

"What if I get ready? I'm due for another birth control shot in a few months. What if…"

"What if?"

"What if I don't get it?" She lifted herself up off me and turned her body halfway around so she could look me in the eyes.

"You sure this is what you want?"

She nodded and smiled, her lips trembling with emotion.

I grasped the back of her neck and pulled her lips toward mine. I covered her mouth and kissed her breathless.

"Was that a yes?" she gasped when I released her.

"That wasn't a yes. That was a *fuck yes*."

"You want a baby with me?" Sutton raised her hand and cradled my cheek.

"Yeah, babe. I want a baby with you."

She stood up, water sluicing down her body, and then she turned all the way around before lowering herself on top of me.

Her fingers traced the ink that I'd asked Roman to manipulate. It was no longer a prison tattoo, but a heart lock with a key sticking out of it. Sutton's name was written on the side of the key.

"Give me a baby, Viper."

"Babe," I whispered.

"Let's make something that's a little bit of both of us. Let's love the shit out of our lives. We only get one, you know?"

"I'll give you a baby," I said. "But you gotta give me something in return."

She arched a brow. "A negotiation? I thought we both wanted a baby."

My expression sobered. "Take my last name. Let's make it legal."

"Why, Viper, I had no idea you were so incredibly old fashioned."

I cradled her head and pulled her toward me. "I want to protect you in all the ways I can. I want to love you forever. By giving you my last name, I can do that."

Her gaze softened. "Always a protector, aren't you?"

"I'll never stop," I promised. "I'll never stop protecting you."

"As far as I'm concerned, you just spoke your wedding vows." She grinned. "Okay, I'll make *you* a deal…"

"More negotiations?" I teased.

"The moment we find out I'm pregnant, I'll marry you."

My hand slipped between our bodies, and I stroked her. Sutton's eye lids fluttered in pleasure.

"Guess I'd better get busy then."

She leaned over and pressed her lips to mine and sighed. "Yeah, you'd better."

Additional Works

The Tarnished Angels Motorcycle Club Series:

Wreck & Ruin (Tarnished Angels Book 1)
Crash & Carnage (Tarnished Angels Book 2)
Madness & Mayhem (Tarnished Angels Book 3)
Thrust & Throttle (Tarnished Angels Book 4)
Venom & Vengeance (Tarnished Angels Book 5)
Fire & Frenzy (Tarnished Angels Book 6 - Pre-Order)

SINS Series:

Sins of a King (Book 1)
Birth of a Queen (Book 2)
Rise of a Dynasty (Book 3)
Dawn of an Empire (Book 4)
Ember (Book 5)
Burn (Book 6)
Ashes (Book 7)
Fall of a Kingdom (Book 8)

Additional Works

Others:

Peasants and Kings

About the Author

Wall Street Journal & USA Today bestselling author Emma Slate writes romance with heart and heat.

Called "the dialogue queen" by her college playwriting professor, Emma writes love stories that range from romance-for-your-pants to action-flicks-for-chicks.

When she isn't writing, she's usually curled up under a heating blanket with a steamy romance novel and her two beagles—unless her outdoorsy husband can convince her to go on a hike.

Made in United States
Troutdale, OR
11/26/2023

14955408R00278